C000193667

Agony

A Romantic Comedy
By
Julie Butterfield

For team Butterfield

Other Books

By Julie Butterfield

Did I Mention I Won The Lottery?

Google Your Husband Back

Did I Mention I Was Getting Married?

Lucy Mathers Goes Back To Work

Eve's Christmas

Contents

FROM: Ellie Henshaw   <Elliebellshenshaw@livewell.co.uk>
To: Fliss Carmichael   <agonyauntfliss@digitalrecorder.com>
Date: 11/03/2020

Dear Fliss

My name is Ellie, I'm 23, single and I have a problem. Well, it's not a real problem, or at least I don't think it is. You see, I'm in love and it's actually a wonderful feeling! I imagine that you've been in love and I'm sorry if that sounds presumptuous or even rude. As an agony aunt, I'm sure you get all sorts of emails from people who are being abused, in awful debt or being treated terribly by someone and I don't suppose you've had all of those things happen to you personally. But being in love is something that touches most people at some point so I feel certain that you will know how I feel and will probably agree that it is the most glorious experience.

The problem isn't being in love, it's the man I'm in love with. Well, not him exactly. He's gorgeous, tall and dark and heavenly to look at. He's called Logan. Don't you think that's a lovely name? Logan. He sounds like a tribal leader, strong and forceful although from what I've seen he is also kind and thoughtful and sensitive. And I just know that he would be the most amazing husband and an absolutely wonderful father. He's a Management Information Analyst so he must be very clever. I'm not exactly sure what the job entails but I know there's lots of figures and graphs involved because I've seen him wandering around the building with charts and they look extremely complicated.

Being in love has made me incredibly happy. I wake up in the morning and I'm sure the birds are singing that little bit louder and the sky is most definitely a shade bluer. I jump out of bed because I can't wait to see what the day might bring. I sing in the shower, which is annoying the people in the flat below, or so they said in the note they pushed through the door yesterday. And I can't stop smiling at everyone on the bus, which is worrying them because it's not the sort of bus route where people normally smile. In fact, we have a kind of unspoken agreement that there is no meeting of eyes and we certainly never speak so no-one wants to sit next to me. But I'm just so happy! Sometimes Logan walks past my office and I catch a glimpse of the back of his head and the feeling is sheer ecstasy. There are butterflies having a rave in my stomach and I feel sort of glowy. His face is the last thing I see in my head before I drift off to sleep and it's the first thing I think about in the morning when I wake up. Just hearing his name mentioned sends a shiver down my back and when I get close to him, and sometimes he's literally only feet away from me, my heart beats so fast that it hurts and my legs go wobbly. I love him, it's a wonderful feeling and I'm very happy.

The problem is that Logan doesn't know how I feel. Not only does he have no idea that I'm in love with him, he doesn't even know I exist. Well, I suppose he's aware of me because we work at the same place and we do occasionally bump into each other and on one occasion we were even in the same meeting. But if you asked him what my name was, I don't think he would have a clue and he's never looked me in the eye or said 'Good Morning' so I suppose on that level I'm invisible to him.

And that's the problem. My friend says that it's not normal and I either have to do something about it or forget him so I'm writing for advice, although I have to admit that forgetting all about him isn't an option so I suppose what I'm really asking is, what can I do to make him notice me? I lose the power of speech when he's nearby, I started dribbling when I sat opposite him in our meeting so communication in general is not easy. But Laura, that's my friend at work, says that I need to speak to him. She thinks I should just walk up to him, say hello and start chatting. Do you think that's a good idea? And what on earth do I say? Please don't tell me that it's just a crush. It's love. I've felt love before, at least, I thought I'd felt love but now I realise it was nothing but a pale imitation. I'm in love, truly in love, I'm just not sure what to do about it.

Looking forward to your advice

Ellie From Leeds

Chapter 1

Felicity Carmichael, Agony Aunt for the Digital Recorder, finished reading the email she had plucked from her inbox and couldn't help the smile that spread across her face. How wonderful to read about someone who was happy, well, almost happy. And to be asked for advice about love, straight forward love and the passion it aroused was a particularly pleasing start to her day!

Ellie was right, Fliss did read all manner of emails in the course of her job. So far this week she had advised a young man to take his festering, pus-filled toe to the doctor and stop trying to cure it through meditation; she'd read a harrowing email from a young woman who Fliss had implored to seek help before her abusive husband broke more than just her heart, and she'd sent a very firm response to a middle-aged woman who had been playing footsie under the table with her daughter's new boyfriend and was now considering offering the young man a crash course in the joy of older women.

Fliss had no personal experience with any of these situations, it was all very much a matter of common sense. She had never held any aspirations to be an agony aunt before the job was dropped in her lap by a frantic editor one chaotic Monday morning, but her innate kindness and empathy had kept her in the position for many years. Over time she had built up a large repertoire of sensible answers for the most outrageous of situations, always taking a moment to stare out of the window, tapping her chin with her pencil as she tried to imagine exactly what she would do in such a situation.

But love was different, love she did understand. And not just love, but the overwhelming feeling of love for a work colleague. Reading the email, Fliss had been immediately whisked back to the halcyon days of 20 years previously, when she had also caught a glimpse of the back of a young man's head and immediately lost the power of speech. Her heart had fluttered so wildly in her chest that she'd been unable to breathe and she'd slipped her hands, clammy and shaking, under the desk to hide the effect the tall, wickedly handsome young journalist was having on her trembling young body. She remembered all too well the butterflies that would career around her stomach, crashing into each other in sheer delight whenever he walked towards her, the shiver that would run down her spine if ever he turned in her direction. And should he send a smile winging across the room, one of those slow intimate smiles that told her exactly what he was thinking, she would almost pass out with ecstasy.

Smiling happily, Fliss got to work. This response wouldn't need much thinking about. She would be able to give Ellie from Leeds some excellent advice although she may keep this one private, not everything belonged on the pages of the Digital Recorder and running a hand through her short, red hair, she spread out her immaculately manicured fingers and began typing, allowing her thoughts to drift back to the early days of her relationship with Jasper Carmichael, when even hearing his name mentioned would bring a flush to her cheeks.

The birds had most definitely sung far louder after she had met Jasper, the sky had turned a delightful shade of blue and Fliss had walked on air. A colleague at the time had shrugged and labelled it a workplace crush but Fliss had been certain it was love. She had known they were meant to be together and had refused to listen to anyone who suggested otherwise.

And she had been right. Her feelings were very definitely reciprocated and as the weeks passed, despite agreeing that it was foolish to tie themselves into a relationship when they were both on the cusp of bright new careers, Fliss and Jasper had become a couple. Within months they'd moved in together and two years later, on a cold dismal day in November they had married, being far too impatient to wait until Spring arrived with its much-improved weather and photographic opportunities.

Tapping away on her keyboard, Fliss told Ellie that she understood entirely how she was feeling, how truly delightful it was to be so completely in love and how Ellie must take heart from the fact that Fliss' own crush had been the real thing, resulting in a marriage that had endured for 18 years. A slightly smug smile tugged at the corner of her lips. Because it wasn't just any marriage. Felicity and Jasper Carmichael were the envy of many, their loving relationship, beautiful home and sparkling social life a testament to a highly successful relationship.

Pausing in the midst of her typing, Fliss glanced at the glittering circle of diamonds on her left hand. Jasper had presented it to her on their 15th wedding anniversary, a testament of his love he had said in front of the small crowd of friends invited to share the occasion; something that he wished he'd been able to present to Fliss when they were first married but which had been beyond the reach of a young journalist's salary. Everyone had applauded and Fliss had felt the tears roll down her cheek as she'd kissed him, sliding her arms around his neck and pulling him close. Her friends had fluttered around her, each catching her hand and admiring the diamond ring with only the slightest touch of envy showing. The champagne had flowed and Fliss had sat at the table, her eyes flitting over their family and friends feeling perfectly and completely content.

Sighing happily, she put her hand back on the keyboard to advise Ellie that her love for Logan had every chance to turn into the same success. It shouldn't be labelled as a mere crush until it had been fully explored. She would tell Ellie how much she and Jasper still loved each other, how the thought of life without each other was simply impossible. Ellie would want to know how strong their love was, how nothing had dimmed it over the years. Life with Jasper had been everything that Fliss could have hoped for and the same could be true for Ellie.

The light from the window landed on the diamonds and Fliss blinked, distracted by the glittering arc, the tiniest of frowns settling between her perfectly shaped eyebrows. Of course, there had to be sacrifices along the way. Life was full of compromise and marriage was a classic example. Sometimes one partner had to sacrifice slightly more than the other, that was the nature of life. It reflected the strength of your love when you were prepared to give up something you held dear for the benefit of your marriage.

The sun retreated and Fliss' ring stopped sparkling. Perhaps she should warn Ellie how important it was that you didn't expect everything to remain exactly as it was during those early days. Some of the passion would disappear over the years, the desire to spend every minute of the day together would wane, it was only natural. Fliss had written several emails to women advising that marriage like any other relationship, would evolve and change. It would become more sophisticated, more down to earth as it made way for deeper feelings. Those early days full of romance and butterflies couldn't last forever, it wasn't easy fitting all-consuming love into a busy working life. Shivering, Fliss lifted her head to look out of the window, searching for the sun which had disappeared behind the drifting clouds. Her diamonds had no sparkle at all now, they felt cold and heavy around her finger.

Perhaps it was too early for Ellie to think along those lines but as her fingers flashed across the keyboard and her thoughts crowded and shuffled for space, Fliss felt that she should still warn her. Because when Ellie and Logan's love changed, evolving into something far more practical, Ellie must be ready and understand that it wasn't failure. It was perfectly acceptable.

Jasper still came home with a kiss every night, although these days she was often in bed before he made it back. They still sat down to share a meal and catch up on each other's day whenever they could. It happened less and less recently, in fact Fliss was struggling to remember the last occasion, but they still talked. Jasper's busy life often took him away for days at a time and when he returned, the main subject of conversation was the interview he had completed and the laundry he needed done. The days when he had come bursting through the door to sweep Fliss upstairs declaring that he had missed her, were long gone. But that was okay, that was normal. Fliss herself was kept busy with work and yoga and meeting her friends for lunch. Perhaps a disadvantage of their successful lives was that they were both so occupied, always with so much to do and less time to spend with each other. It didn't mean that they didn't love each other anymore, just that there were other things demanding attention in their lives.

Giving an impatient tut, Fliss dragged her thoughts back to Ellie and tried to concentrate. What was needed here was positive thinking, encouragement to take a chance on a new relationship because the rewards could be so wonderful. Ellie needed to be inspired to take her courage in her hands and speak to Logan because it could result in years of happiness ahead and it was her job to give Ellie the confidence to embark on what could be a wonderful new adventure, not lecture her about the gradual decline of relationships.

But she was finding it strangely hard to focus. Normally thoughts of meeting Jasper and how very happy their lives had been left her with an internal glow, a huge satisfaction that her first instinct had been correct and that he was indeed the man for her, the one she would love forever. But for some reason, the glow was proving hard to find today. Instead of a feeling of warm contentment an alarm bell had begun to ring rather insistently in the deep recesses of Fliss' mind and it was proving impossible to ignore. But what was it trying to tell her, she mused in confusion?

She blinked again, but this time it wasn't the reflection from her ring that had distracted her, it was the tear that had wound its way down her creamy cheek and plopped unbidden onto her hand. Why on earth was she crying, she wondered, lifting her hand only to find more tears queuing to slide down her face in a steady stream. Whatever was happening?

With a sudden gasp, she pulled her fingers away from the keyboard. She needed to stop typing immediately. The intention was to encourage Ellie in the potential of her newfound romance, not deliver a lecture about how love was likely to fade as the years went by.

Searching for more pleasant memories to describe, Fliss tried to remember the last time she and Jasper had snuggled deep down into the settee with a bottle of wine and a night to themselves. Her husband was so busy of late, so occupied with work, when was the last time he had looked into her eyes and lost himself there? When was the last time they had gone out for the evening and enjoyed a meal, just the two of them? When was the last time they'd had a conversation that hadn't been interrupted by Jasper's phone? Describing to Ellie how happy they had been, how very much they loved each other, had made Fliss suddenly and acutely aware that, in truth, it had been some time since the Carmichael marriage had been quite as wonderful as she was proclaiming it to be. How strange that she hadn't realised until today.

Shaking her head, she felt more tears sliding down her face. Good Heavens, her marriage was in trouble and she hadn't even noticed! She was an agony aunt for goodness sake, she was meant to understand these things. How on earth had her husband managed to drift so far away without her even realising? Just when had this happened? Pressing a hand to her heart, Fliss closed her eyes, how could they have lost so much without even noticing?

'Are you ready for the meeting Fliss?'

Swallowing hard, Fliss pulled a tissue from the rose-patterned box on her desk and pressed it against her cheek. She needed to give this some serious consideration. She needed to think about what on earth she should do.

'Fliss?'

'Two minutes,' she trilled over her shoulder, 'then I'm all yours.'

Sliding her handbag from her bottom drawer, she pulled out her compact and inspected the damage. Not too bad. A little smudge under one green eye, a rather startled look that she needed to bring under control. A coat of '*Sun's Blessing*' on her lips, a tiny touch of concealer and no-one would be any the wiser that their agony aunt had just had a tiny meltdown regarding her own relationship

Of course she couldn't send the email she had drafted. She was meant to give advice, not confess she was in a pickle of her own! Standing up she smoothed her skirt over slim hips, catching a reflection of her tall willowy figure in the window. Whatever would Ellie from Leeds think if she were to receive the email Fliss had just written?

'Are you coming?' Vivian was waiting impatiently in the doorway of the meeting room.

'Yes, sorry,' answered Fliss. She would get the meeting out of the way and then write a sensible response to Ellie, full of encouragement and practical advice. 'I'm coming,' and then in an action which was entirely the result of many years habit, she reached down and pressed send before flipping her laptop closed.

14

....

FROM: Fliss Carmichael <agonyauntfliss@digitalrecorder.com>
To: Ellie Henshaw <Elliebellshenshaw@livewell.co.uk>
Date: 16/03/2020

....

Dear Ellie

It was wonderful to read your email and hear about how you feel, how happy you are and how you are so much in love with Logan. I certainly wouldn't dream of telling you that it's only a crush, who knows what may happen between the two of you. You feel so strongly about him that I think it's absolutely essential you gather up every shred of courage you have and speak to him. He may surprise you and be more aware of your existence than you realise but regardless, you need to be brave and have some sort of interaction to make him notice you. It doesn't have to be anything too complicated or taxing. The next time he walks across your office smile at him, speak to him, say 'Good Morning' or 'Hello', anything to make him lift his head and look at you. I'm a great believer in chemistry and I am certain that if you have a conversation, no matter how brief, you will know almost instantly if there is any sort of connection between the two of you. And let him know your name, he must begin to think of you as Ellie and not just someone who smiles at him in the corridor. Be brave, you must make it happen!

And to encourage you even further, I'm going to tell you something rather personal. I met my husband through exactly the same circumstances! We worked together in a large office and one day he walked past my desk and I fell in love, instantly, completely and wholeheartedly. Every time I saw him my heart beat that little bit faster, whenever he appeared my head emptied of all rational conversation. I felt so overwhelmingly happy simply watching him walk across the room. I was brave and spoke to him; one morning I looked up, gathered my courage and said 'Hello' and that, as they say, was that. He looked into my eyes, I looked into his and we were both completely lost in each other. So you see, it can happen. We've been married for 18 years and we're as happy as ever. I trust that gives you not only encouragement but some hope that your potential relationship with Logan could stand the test of time.

Of course, that overwhelming feeling of love doesn't always last. The butterflies, the sweaty palms, the shiver down the back, they can all disappear. They usually do as the years roll by but it's quite natural. People often ask me how to recover the romance in their marriage and I tell them that love endures, butterflies do not. It's not that you stop loving each other, it's just that a little of the excitement disappears, your life together becomes more practical, more about everyday demands and the often stressful business of living. My husband isn't quite the romantic he once was, he's an incredibly busy and successful journalist so there simply isn't the time for much swooning these days. That's perfectly normal, although I must admit when I read your email it reminded me of just how much our lives have changed over the last few years. In fact, the more I think about your email the more it's made me quite envious, remembering the sheer passion of those early days, the way he only had to look at me to make me dizzy with expectation. We couldn't bear to be apart and the highlight of our day was arriving home after work and spending time together.

But I suppose I can't expect that kind of connection to remain, not after so long. Or can I? Do you think a woman should simply give up after 18 years, be happy with her lot and say goodbye to the romance? Should I be content simply knowing that he loves me, even though these days he spends very little time looking into my eyes and a great deal of time looking at his phone? Is it wrong to want him to still notice me occasionally, have a conversion with me, spend some time with me?

Your email has made me feel rather peculiar and quite empty. I hadn't realised how distant my husband had become. It's not that we no longer love each other, but he has a very long 'to do' list these days and our marriage doesn't seem to be on it, which considering how much in love we once were is quite heart-breaking.

Oh Ellie, reading about how love is filling you with such happiness has left me feeling distraught. I've just realised that my marriage may be envied by some but it has become something of a sham. My husband seems to have drifted away from me and I hadn't noticed until today. I'm an agony aunt who has just realised that her relationship is in danger and I haven't a clue what to do about it!

Fliss Carmichael

This email has been sent by Fliss Carmichael, the online agony aunt of The Digital Recorder. All views expressed herein are her own and should not be taken as an instruction to proceed with any course of action without careful consideration of the potential consequences. The Digital Recorder claims no responsibility for any trauma, divorce proceedings or physical injury that may result from the advice contained herein. Thank you for contributing.

Chapter 2

Ellie Henshaw was trying to concentrate on her overflowing inbox and the pile of files teetering on the corner of her desk. Mr Goodfellow, the office manager, had already swept by to ask that they all give that little bit more effort during the day to prevent their backlog becoming more of a torrent.

'I know you all give 100%,' he had proclaimed with an insincere smile, 'but perhaps today we could squeeze it up to 110%? Thank you everybody,' and he was off, bustling down the corridor to repeat his message of teamwork to the less accommodating accounts department. Ellie had resisted the urge to inform him that 100% effort was the maximum anyone could provide despite his request and instead, she had put her head down and carried on working.

Trying to focus on the mass of emails waiting for her attention, Ellie was also keeping a close eye on her phone. It had been pushed behind the tower of files to make it clear to Mr Goodfellow, and anyone else who may wish to check, that it was of absolutely no interest at all to her, but not until she had spent several minutes placing it in such a way that she would immediately notice if a new message were to pop into her personal inbox.

Laura had told her not to expect a response. 'These agony aunts probably get thousands of emails a day,' she'd advised Ellie that morning. 'I bet they only reply to the really shocking ones.'

'What do you mean?'

'Oh, you know. Emails where *Justified from Wakefield* says that she knew her husband was having an affair with his secretary so she decided to start her own affair with the secretary's 18 year old son but now she's fallen in love

18

with him. Or when *'Fooled and Furious'* finds out that her husband has another wife somewhere in the neighbourhood because they bumped into each other in the supermarket and now they've become best friends and wonder if teaming up to make him suffer is considered acceptable.'

'Not this agony aunt,' Ellie had replied firmly. 'I looked at some of the emails and replies she'd published and there was nothing sensational, just the normal everyday type of problems.' There was a slight pause. 'Did a woman really run into her husband's other wife?'

'Yep. Decided to go to Tesco instead of Morrisons and they got talking in the bread aisle.'

'And what did the agony aunt say?'

'Told them to go for it and keep us all posted on what happened. They've got their own website now, *'Scorned of Doncaster'*.

Ellie wondered briefly if she had made a mistake. Laura had told her she was mad to send an email to an unknown woman asking for advice. 'I can tell you what to do Ells,' she'd insisted over a glass of wine after work. 'Stop dithering and go talk to him. Say hello and get it over and done with!'

Whilst knowing that Laura was making sense, Ellie's own much more reserved nature couldn't help feeling that professional advice was probably best and she had embarked on weeks of research and spent many hours reading page upon page of online advice before finally settling on 'Dear Fliss'. The Digital Recorder encouraged writers to submit their emails but advised that not all would receive a reply, especially if the subject had been covered before. Scouring the back pages of 'Dear Fliss', Ellie hadn't been able to see anything that covered the subject of unrequited love in the workplace so she had finally penned a request for guidance and was now impatiently waiting for a reply.

A quick check of her phone showed a stubbornly empty inbox and nibbling on an already distressed thumbnail, Ellie wondered if she should have mentioned Carl in her email. Maybe it would have given Fliss a more rounded view of the strength of Ellie's feelings. But she was writing for advice about Logan and how to capture his interest as they passed each other in the corridor. She wasn't asking for and didn't want any advice about Carl, so after careful thought all mention of him had been carefully erased from her email.

A bright light caught her eye. 'Laura!'

Ellie was staring at her phone and the email icon which was now flashing to show a new message had been received. 'Laura!'

'What?' Laura poked a head covered in tangled blonde curls over the small screen separating their desks. 'I'm busy giving 110% here,' she grumbled, sliding her nail file back in her drawer. 'What's wrong?'

'I've got an email.'

Looking distinctly unimpressed, Laura shrugged. 'And?'

'I think it must be from the Digital Recorder.'

'Have you opened it?'

'Not yet.'

'Could be from anyone then couldn't it?'

'But it could be from Dear Fliss.'

'I get emails from all sorts of places, half the time I've no idea who these people are, they just send me email after email about nothing!'

'I've told you before, press the unsubscribe button. And I don't get emails, I think this must be from her.'

They both stared at the phone.

'Well read it then!' demanded Laura. 'I need to know what she says. I bet she tells you to talk to him. Like I said you should. Except you didn't have to wait a week for me to answer.'

Ellie took a careful look around the office. It wouldn't be good if she were seen reading her personal emails, not on

20

a 110% day. There was no sign of Mr Goodfellow, although she could hear raised voices from the accounts department. Maybe his request for extra effort wasn't going down so well over there.

Sliding her phone discreetly closer, she tapped the icon and with another quick check around the office she let her eyes fall to her screen, giving a small yelp when she saw an email from the Digital Recorder.

'It's her!' she said to Laura in an urgent whisper. 'It's Fliss.'

'What does she say?'

Ellie was reading through the message, a smile beginning to lift her face.

'She said that she doesn't think it's a crush, it sounds like real love.'

A sniff drifted over the screen.

'Oh, Laura! She said that's exactly how she met her husband. At work! She fell for him in the office, 20 years ago and now they've been married for 18 years. Isn't that amazing?'

'Amazing.'

'She said I've got to be brave and initiate contact.'

'Initiate contact! You mean say Hello? Like I said you should? Like I've been telling you to do for weeks?'

'And I've got to make sure he knows my name.'

'Exactly what I said!' Laura looked thoughtful. 'Maybe I should look into being an agony aunt.'

Ellie didn't respond, reading the rest of the message in silence.

'What else has she said? Has she got some magic formula to get him to speak to you? Has she told you what to say? Ooh, has she sent you a script? Do I need to help? I've always fancied trying my hand at acting. What does she say?'

Frowning, Ellie re-read the last part of the message. 'Well, she says that reading my email made her realise that her marriage has changed quite a lot in the last couple of years and that she's not very happy.'

'She's unhappy?'

'Seems to be.'

'Why is she telling you how unhappy she is? I thought agony aunts were supposed to tell you how to deal with your problem?'

'So did I. Maybe it's a reciprocal sort of thing.'

'What?'

'You know, she helps me and I help her. Although I didn't think it worked like that.'

'It doesn't!'

'Well, she's asking me for help. She wants to know if I think she's being unreasonable expecting the butterflies to stay around after 20 years.'

'Butterflies? What butterflies? What on earth is she talking about? What has she said about Logan?'

Ellie took a moment to reply. The email had started with such hope and optimism, it was quite upsetting to see the swift arrival of so much sadness. She had expected only advice and encouragement, not a request for help.

'Ellie!'

Deciding to think about Fliss and her problem later, Ellie looked up to grin at an impatient Laura. 'Basically, she said that I should go for it. Workplace romances can be successful, hers was…'

'I thought you said she was unhappy?'

'Yes, but that's because of my email. Up until now she's been blissfully happy, or she thought she was. Anyway, she said I've got to speak to him, tell him my name, get him to look me in the eye and see if we have a connection.'

'A connection to what?'

'To each other of course.' A dreamy look filled Ellie's hazel eyes. 'Chemistry, instant attraction. Love.'

'Oh God, here we go again. Ells darling you really need to get over this. Love isn't all about fluttering hearts and swooning you know.'

22

'Well it should be,' answered Ellie firmly. 'Love should overwhelm you, make you go weak at the knees and consume your every thought!'

Sighing, Laura scratched her curls with a pencil. 'You're heading for disappointment. Again. You need to be more realistic. Accept that people can get on amazingly well and be in love and even get married without needing to pass out every time they smile at each other.'

'No.' Ellie shook her head. 'Never. I'd rather not get married at all if I have to abandon my idea of love. I want that feeling Laura, I want to feel a shiver run down my spine whenever he smiles at me, I want to feel those butterflies race around my stomach every time I think of him.'

'That's lust,' dismissed Laura. 'That's pure lust and it doesn't last.'

'No. It's love, true love, full of romance and passion and it's what I want.'

Laura sighed in despair. 'Well I think you're mad but at least I agree with your agony aunt. You need to speak to Logan.'

Ellie pushed her phone back behind the tower of files.

'She doesn't tell me how though,' she said disappointedly. 'I thought she might be a bit more specific but I still don't know how to start a conversation with him.'

Rolling her eyes, Laura checked the whereabouts of Mr Goodfellow and wheeled her chair round to Ellie's desk. 'For goodness sake, I don't know why you're making such a big deal about all this,' she huffed in exasperation. 'He's just a man, someone you want to get to know. You see him in the corridor, in the lift, walking up the stairs and you say "Hi Logan". That's it, that's as complicated as it gets.'

Ellie dropped her head. She knew it was a simple thing, a quick hello, a smile as he passed. But no-one seemed to understand the effect he had on her. Nobody appreciated just how overcome she felt every time he was close to her, how dizzy she felt just being in the same room. The power of speech deserted her well and truly in his presence and it wasn't until he had disappeared from view that she ever recovered sufficiently to think of something to say. Generally, she just stared at him, mouth hanging slightly open, eyes glazed.

'I know,' she said sadly. 'It should be easy. I've never had this trouble speaking to anyone before, which is why I think he's the one.'

'I certainly hope so,' grumbled Laura, 'I'd hate to have to go through all this again!'

'Sorry,' whispered Ellie, 'I know I should be braver. Fliss says I need to be strong. She says ....'

'If you'd listened to *me* you'd already be speaking to him,' interrupted Laura. 'Now, we need a plan.'

'A plan?'

'Yes. It's obvious you need help.'

'Fliss said ...'

'Fliss hasn't actually offered any proper help, has she? Okay, she said talk to him. But how? When? She hasn't helped at all if you ask me.'

'Well, she said ...'

'So *I'll* help you. And I think we need a plan. A way to get you two talking.'

Ellie couldn't help feeling a little nervous. Laura tended to be a great deal bolder than Ellie.

'What do you have in mind?' she asked nervously. 'Fliss says ...'

'Will you stop quoting bloody Fliss. She said you needed to start talking to him and I'm going to make sure that happens. I just need to think of a way.'

Pushing her chair back round to her desk, Laura recovered her nail file from the drawer, gazing into the distance as she pondered the problem.

'We need a situation where you can say hello and let him know your name,' she mused. 'You need to be together without anybody else around, apart from me of course.'

24

'You?'

'I'm going to have to be there Ellie because we both know full well that if it's just you and Logan, you'll give him a simpering smile and then stare at the floor for the next 5 minutes, too scared to open your mouth.'

Ellie didn't argue, she knew Laura was right.

'So …?'

'So give me time, I'll think of something. Fliss said you have to speak to him, well that's exactly what's going to happen. Just leave it all to me,' and ignoring her rather crowded to-do list, Laura pulled out her note pad and began formulating a plan.

Chapter 3

'How do I look?' asked a nervous Ellie for the hundredth time in the last 5 minutes.

'Gorgeous. Stop fiddling with your hair.'

Dragging her eyes away from the entrance door to their office block, Laura turned to give Ellie her full attention. She'd instructed her friend to ramp up the outfit today, dig out the heels and slap on the makeup. Ellie had responded in her own far subtler way and Laura had been forced to agree, somewhat reluctantly, that maybe Ellie just wasn't the sort to wear a see-through blouse over a black corset, the outfit Laura herself would have chosen. At least her friend had left the leggings at home and arrived in a flattering slimline skirt complete with a blouse that showed a hint of cleavage. Her brown hair shone like burnished chestnut falling in deep waves past her shoulders and her hazel eyes, always a barometer of her emotions, were flecked with both green and amber as they stared anxiously at her friend.

'You look lovely,' Laura said with a smile. 'Perfect.'

Not entirely reassured, Ellie continued to fuss with her hair while Laura turned her watchful eye back to the window and the view of the street beyond. She'd taken on board with enthusiasm the task of getting Ellie and Logan together in a semi-private situation where Ellie could finally introduce herself. Disappearing upstairs to Logan's office on the 7th floor, where the desks were full of people staring at screens with a single-minded focus, she had returned with the news that he always went for a coffee, flat white from Costa two doors down, at 10.45. His return time would depend entirely on the length of the queue and the attitude of the staff but, suggested Laura, if Ellie were in the lobby from 10.45 onwards then she would be right in Logan's path when he came back, cup in hand and

compulsively in Logan's direction as she tried to send Ellie a subliminal message.

Above his head, the bright red numbers indicated they had already reached floor 2 and Ellie tried to concentrate. All she had to do was say hello and introduce herself. It couldn't be easier really, just say, *'Hello, my name is Ellie'.* She'd been rehearsing it all morning, no stammering, no blushing, just, *'Hello, my name is Ellie'.* Sitting at her desk, she had said it quietly to herself over and over again until it was word perfect. Laura had snorted and pointed out that it was only 5 words and it should be pretty perfect but Ellie had continued to practice, *'Hello, my name is Ellie.'*

Except that now she was standing next to him her heart was hammering so hard it was making her breathless and her throat was so dry she didn't think she could say anything to anyone. Floor 3 began flashing and in a panic, she sent Laura a pleading look.

'Hello!' shouted Laura suddenly, making both Ellie and Logan jump. 'Hello,' she repeated, grinning at them both.

'Yes, hello,' Ellie said through dry lips. It sounded small and squeaky and she tried again. 'Hello,' she boomed.

Logan's eyes widened fractionally and he stepped backwards into the corner of the lift as he tried to keep both women in eyeshot.

'Hello,' he answered warily.

Number 4 shone brightly above the door and Ellie began to panic. The normally atrociously slow lift was moving too quickly, they would soon reach floor 5 and she would have wasted her opportunity. But she couldn't just blurt out her name, it would sound too contrived, strange. There had to be a better way of doing this, a more natural way and she threw Laura another helpless look.

With a roll of her eyes, Laura left her corner and moved to stand next to Ellie.

'Name?' she barked.

'Ellie.' It was that strange squeaky voice again but this time she let it go. 'Er, my name is Ellie.'

She had hoped to be staring into Logan's eyes when she finally introduced herself but he was watching Laura with horrified fascination. A large red 5 appeared above the door and there was a shudder as the lift slowed to a stop.

'Hello Ellie, my name is Laura.'

The doors began to open, the tiniest of gaps appearing.

'Hello, Laura.'

The only sound was the door making its soft swishy sound. Raising her eyebrow at Logan, Laura smiled encouragingly.

'So, she's Ellie and I'm Laura.'

'Er, I'm Logan.'

The doors slid open further, the gap widening and Laura let out a gusty sigh of relief. 'How wonderful,' she beamed, 'that's lovely. Hello Logan.'

She glared at Ellie as the doors squeaked their progress. 'Ellie!'

'Oh sorry. Hello Logan, how nice to meet you.'

'Er, yes. You too.'

'Well isn't this nice, all getting to know each other,' said Laura happily. 'Maybe we'll see you around Logan, do say hello, won't you. Come on Ellie, let's go.'

With the doors now fully open, Laura swung around to exit onto the 5th floor. But as she neared Logan, he flinched and took a quick step back, landing hard on Ellie's foot.

'Oh God, I'm so sorry!' A hint of pink appeared underneath his very designer stubble. 'Sorry I just …'

And then he stopped. Because as Logan's foot had landed on top of Ellie's much smaller one, his hand had brushed hers and the biggest crackle of electricity had surged between them, causing them both to instinctively jerk away before standing quite, quite still, looking directly into each other's eyes.

'Sorry,' he whispered, the smallest of smiles on his lips.

'It's okay … Logan,' breathed Ellie letting his name linger on her lips.

She could see him rubbing his hand, a look of wonder on his face.

'Did you feel …?'

She rubbed her own hand. 'Yes, I did.'

They continued to stare, neither of them moving and Ellie could feel her hand tingling. The doors began their relentless sweep together and as Ellie and Logan remained motionless, Laura's hand swooped inside the lift grabbing Ellie and jerking her out forcibly moments before the doors closed with a final creak.

'Bye Logan,' Ellie managed over her shoulder. 'Bye!' and then he was gone, leaving her rubbing the back of her hand in awe and already composing the email to Fliss describing the moment they had met and a connection had been well and truly made.

Laura clutched her head and groaned. 'Oh my God, what a disaster!'

'Wasn't that wonderful?' sighed Ellie.

Laura stared. 'Wonderful? Are you mad? That was the most embarrassing thing I've ever seen! Why on earth didn't you speak to him? What is it about that man that makes you lose all power of communication?'

Lifting her hand, Ellie stared at her fingers in wonder. 'Chemistry,' she said.

'Chemistry? That makes you unable to say hello to someone?'

'Fliss said that if I spoke to him, got him to look me in the eye, I would see if there was any chemistry between us.'

'Well you didn't speak to him, did you? I was the one having the conversation!'

'And she was right. There was chemistry, there is chemistry. I could feel it, we both did.'

'Really?' Laura shook her head. 'All I could see was two people who couldn't manage a sentence between them.'

'He touched me,' breathed Ellie.

Laura's eyebrows shot up. 'In the lift? Just now? That's a bit blatant, isn't it? You should report him! I'm surprised, he doesn't seem the type but it goes to show how careful you have to be…'

'No, he touched my hand.' Ellie lifted her hand so Laura could see her fingers. 'He touched my hand and there was electricity.'

They both stared at Ellie's fingers. Even Ellie had to admit they looked quite ordinary, no sign of the interaction with Logan visible.

'Could it have been the lift?' asked Laura as she obligingly inspected the proffered hand. 'Maybe it shorted out or something and …'

'It was chemistry. It was Logan. Fliss was right, it's meant to be.'

'Or it could just be static. Maybe he's wearing a cheap acrylic jumper or some plastic shoes that were sending out a lot of electricity and it's not actually meant to be. Maybe he shocks lots of people because of his cheap clothes?'

At Ellie's glare, she shrugged. 'Just saying. You have no idea what he's like, how can you be so sure he's 'the one'. After all, you thought Carl was 'the one' for a while.'

Ellie didn't want to talk about Carl. Maybe she should run the scenario by Fliss, make sure she had done the right thing but she would rather just concentrate on progressing things with Logan. The sight of Mr Goodfellow bearing down on the office prompted them both to scamper back to their desks where Ellie, her gaze still fixed on her pulsing fingers, made a half-hearted attempt to get on top of her ever-growing pile of tasks. But her mind wasn't really on the job. She couldn't stop thinking about Logan's eyes, which she had discovered were like liquid pools of silver-grey and in which she was certain she'd detected a glimmer of interest. He had stamped on her foot and then given her an electric shock and it was undoubtedly one of the most exciting 30 seconds in Ellie's life. The chemistry between the two of them was undeniable, this could turn into a 20-year marriage just like the Carmichael's.

Ellie frowned. She was still uncertain as to whether she was meant to respond to Fliss with advice. Having Googled agony aunts the previous evening, she hadn't come up with any evidence suggesting that the communication was intended to be two way. Was Fliss really asking for Ellie's help or had she simply been thinking out loud? What could Ellie possibly say that Fliss wouldn't already know? Or was that a thing in the world of agony aunts, mused Ellie. Perhaps they wanted opinions from someone with absolutely no experience. And still uncertain what she could say to an agony aunt who had suddenly realised she was unhappy, Ellie sighed and returned to the business of staring at her still tingling fingers.

FROM: Ellie Henshaw <Elliebellshenshaw@livewell.co.uk>
To: Fliss Carmichael <agonyauntfliss@digitalrecorder.com>
Date: 18/03/2020

Dear Fliss

Thank you so much for replying to my email. I know it seems a bit obvious, of course I need to speak to Logan. My friend, Laura, has been saying the same thing for weeks and now she's cross with me because I insisted on waiting to hear what you thought. But Laura is a lot more outgoing than I am and I suppose I wanted to hear from someone with experience that it was the right thing to do.

Anyway, I did it. I spoke to him! Laura said it was a disaster but I thought it went okay. It didn't go entirely as planned, I was in a lift with Logan and Laura and I was supposed to say hello and tell him my name. But I was so nervous and excited that Laura ended up having to do most of it. But we did speak and you were right, there was a connection, a moment of real, actual chemistry when his hand brushed mine and gave me an electric shock. We stood there, all tingly and looking into each other's eyes which I think is a positive sign although Laura isn't convinced. She says people who go around shocking other people are not necessarily a good thing but she doesn't believe in the whole chemistry thing to start with. Anyway, we said hello, I told him my name, our eyes met and we had a definite connection, so thank you so much for your advice.

I did wonder what you thought I should do next? Laura said that I should smile and chat to him now because we're officially friends. I think it might take a bit more than 30 seconds in a lift to become friends but Laura does know a bit more about such things than I do. If she was interested in him, they would be going out by now! But this is so important to me, I don't want to make a mistake or move too quickly, although Laura says that mooning over someone for weeks without saying anything could hardly be called moving too quickly. I suppose she's right, but what would you advise?

I was thinking about what you said in your email. About feeling that your husband is a bit remote these days and work seems to be more important than your marriage. I haven't been with anybody for as long as you two but I agree, just because you've been together all this time doesn't mean that it has to become ordinary. I want Logan to fall in love with me, I want us to be passionately in love and I hope that if we end up being married for 18 years, that never changes. So, I don't see why you should settle for a relationship that doesn't give you what you want anymore.

I'm not really sure what to suggest, I didn't realise that I was expected to advise you in return. But you told me to talk to Logan and I think that's what you should do. Talk to your husband and tell him how you feel. Maybe he just hasn't realised that you're drifting apart and how much you are beginning to miss his company. Or maybe he is feeling the same and wondering what to do about it. Follow the same advice you gave to me, take your courage in your hands and talk to your husband so you can discuss your feelings and fears.

I hope that helps and I'm sorry it's nothing more positive,

Regards

Ellie

Chapter 4

Fliss Carmichael took a sip of her drink and tried to relax. Waitresses were circulating with champagne which Fliss had gratefully accepted and canapes, which she had not. Over the years she had worked out that it was virtually impossible to eat a canape without incident. The filling often dribbled out to land on her chin or even worse on the front of her dress where it would remain for the rest of the evening. Sometimes she would take a bite only to have someone appear and ask how she was, an answer which she then had to supply through a mouth full of flaky pastry. The best approach, she had eventually decided, was to politely decline and so she stood, flaky pastry free, with her glass in one hand perusing the room.

It was a 50th birthday celebration for a work colleague of Jasper's and the room was filled with successful people, looking ever so slightly smug with their lot as they tried to steer the conversation towards a recent plaudit which they would then shrug away with practised humility. Over the years, as Jasper's star had risen ever higher, they were expected to attend an increasing number of such events which Fliss did with consummate professionalism. The advice of an agony aunt was invariably perceived as slightly beneath the gathered crowd of intellects, politicians and well-respected reporters but there was always at least one point in the proceedings where someone would ask her opinion, as a challenge if nothing else.

Tonight, Fliss clutched her still full champagne glass and remained by the wall. She didn't feel like circulating, she had no interest in the latest scandal and she would have preferred a little alone time, contemplating her own problems rather than taking on others. Since the moment she had pressed send on an email she had never intended should be read by anyone, she had been filled with a variety of conflicting emotions, not least of which was sheer horror. Holding her breath, she had opened her laptop, hoping that somehow she'd severed the connection too quickly and the email was still sitting in her drafts. But the Digital Recorder had lightning-fast broadband for a reason and despite Fliss' hopes, the email was now happily ensconced in her sent folder.

Fliss had wanted to scream out loud, shake her laptop and beg the email to return to her congested inbox. Instead, she had given in to her editor's increasingly loud demands that Fliss join them for the weekly meeting and had taken a seat at the large oval table, contributing nothing as she sat in complete if well-hidden panic. Her first instinct had been to immediately tell Vivian what had happened. When the complaint arrived at least they would be prepared. Perhaps they could speak to the legal team and start gathering advice. There again, Ellie may not complain, she may just show the email to everyone she knew and Fliss' lack of professionalism would be out there for all to see. In days gone by it would have taken some time for the mishap to reach the ears of her colleagues, giving her plenty of time to leave her job, move house and change her name. But with the advent of social media, it could be winging its way around the world in a matter of minutes. Trying to control her rapid breathing, Fliss had ventured down another path of possibilities; maybe Ellie wouldn't show the email to anyone else, not wanting others to know that she'd written to an agony aunt in the first place. There was a chance, albeit slim, that she would keep the whole incident to herself.

It was this scenario that had led to Fliss deciding to keep her faux pass quiet for the time being. That, and the fact that if she told Vivian she would also have to reveal what she had written and the world would then know that the marriage of Felicity and Jasper Carmichael, often lauded as near to perfect as it was possible to be, was, in fact, something of a sham. So she had remained silent, watching her inbox with growing anxiety.

Fliss hadn't set out to be an agony aunt. Having graduated from university she'd been lucky enough to find a position as a junior reporter on a local paper in Leeds, the same local paper where Jasper Carmichael had just been given his first opportunity. A few years later, when Fliss and Jasper's lives were firmly entrenched in each other, she had been offered a promotion, a tiny one but still a promotion, which involved working in Bristol. She had revelled in the glow of her opportunity for a whole 48 hours until Jasper had come home with news of a much bigger promotion, which involved him covering the night desk in Leeds for a short while at least. Of course, it had made sense for them to remain in Leeds and allow Jasper to make the most of his new role.

'Next time it's your turn,' he had said, wrapping his arms around his wife and pulling her back into bed. 'You'll get another chance Fliss, I'm sure of it and we'll make sure you can take it.'

Having said no to one promotion, another was rather slow in arriving and by the time it came, Jasper was well on his route to the top. Leaving Leeds just didn't make sense they agreed, so another missed opportunity for Fliss and by now her lack of willingness to take on a new role had sealed her fate. Talented and articulate but unwilling to move away from wherever Jasper Carmichael was currently hanging his hat, was the general opinion, a definite waste of talent but such was life.

Some months later, when the agony aunt called in sick unexpectedly one Monday morning, Fliss was thrown the post temporarily and to everyone's surprise, her naturally confident nature, innate kindness and inherent good sense made her immediately popular. A definite added attraction, as far as the paper was concerned, was that Felicity Carmichael looked nothing like an agony aunt might be expected to look. She was tall and slender, her creamy skin and heart-shaped face were the perfect foil for the cropped red hair and the ease with which she breezed into every room in a cloud of perfume, wearing a designer dress and always with a smile on her face, made her an instant hit. Several years later she was the resident agony aunt for the Digital Recorder and few who knew her could imagine that she deemed her role as something of a failure, a necessary sacrifice to the brighter light that was Jasper Carmichael.

When Fliss had read Ellie's email, the feelings of love described were so familiar and brought back such intense memories that for a moment Fliss had positively glowed with contentment. Happy that she could give such positive and rather personal advice, she had begun to write her response with a heart that was full of memories of her own obsession with a handsome young man. But even as she was typing words of encouragement, her mind had started questioning and probing, embarking on a little stocktake of its own with such reckless abandon that Fliss had no choice but to stop and start listening. And what it had to say had been quite uncomfortable.

Fliss had come to the astonishing conclusion that despite outward appearances, her marriage was in serious difficulties. The Carmichaels may still be a stalwart of glittering social events, their genuine affection for each other may still be obvious to anyone who met them and their almost perfect life a lesson for all, but underneath the glitz and the glamour, Fliss was horrified to realise that they had drifted far, far away from each other. They still shared a house and a bed, spent every morning drinking coffee together before they departed for work, wrapped their arms around each other almost by habit whenever they were close, but she couldn't remember the last time they had sat and had a meaningful conversation about anything that wasn't work-related. Their lives had become one long round of social encounters surrounded by other people and business meetings conducted by a work-obsessed Jasper.

It was a worrying situation, made all the more so because as an agony aunt, Fliss had absolutely no idea who she could ask for help without revealing that she did not, contrary to popular belief, hold all the answers and for possibly the first time in her life she was feeling very alone and completely bereft of suggestions.

Catching sight of Jasper in a corner of the room, Fliss stopped her rambling thoughts and watched him. He was still incredibly handsome. As he dipped his head nearer to the woman he was conversing with, Fliss admitted that he could still cause the butterflies to begin dancing in her stomach. His dark, almost black hair was as full as ever, his startling eyes, a bright shimmering blue with a line of intense black around the iris, were attention-grabbing. He weighed much the same today as when they had first met and the only thing that had outwardly changed was the confidence he now exuded. He had achieved his aim and was now a columnist, a serious columnist whose words were read and considered with the gravitas they deserved. He was respected and admired and when he walked towards a door, dressed in one of his Italian suits with his briefcase held firmly in one hand, someone would invariably appear to open it on his behalf, sure that whoever he was he must be important.

Fliss was proud of him. There was no doubt that she still loved him. The long hours he worked, the sheer effort he had put into becoming the best he could be, had inevitably kept him out of the house more and more often. He would arrive home and plant a kiss on her cheek, tell her how exhausted he was and describe his day. But she had begun to feel more like his secretary than his wife. Jasper was on a wonderful journey but at some point, he had left her behind.

'Gorgeous man your husband,' said a voice close to her ear and startled from her reverie, Fliss turned to find her friend Sylvia standing beside her.

'Well, if you like that sort of thing,' murmured Fliss. 'He's a little smooth for my tastes.'

Snorting into her glass, Sylvia grinned. 'Liar! I think that's part of the reason you two are such a success, you clearly still fancy the pants off each other.'

Fliss took a small sip of champagne. 'You think so?'

'Of course! It's obvious to everyone he adores you.'

At that moment, Jasper Carmichael broke free from the group he had been talking with and approached his wife, a smile on his face.

'Darling, you don't seem to have moved from that spot all evening. Everything okay?'

His free hand rested on her waist, his eyes looking into hers with concern.

'Hah!' exclaimed Sylvia. 'I think that proves my point.'

Looking from one woman to the other with one eyebrow cocked, Jasper waited.

'Sylvia was just telling me how I'm the envy of all my friends, for having a husband who adores me and can't keep his hands to himself.'

Laughing, Jasper drew Fliss closer so he could bury his face in her neck. As usual, she looked quite stunning, her cocktail dress carefully chosen to match her green eyes, her red hair cut in a short choppy bob. He kissed her gently next to her ear, his hand sliding around her waist a little further. 'Well she's right there!' he murmured.

Fliss smiled, enjoying the touch of Jasper's hands as he held her tight and Sylvia looked on with a mix of admiration and envy. Maybe she was wrong, perhaps she was feeling tired, a little down with life and imagining problems where there were none.

'I haven't seen much of you tonight,' she said, looking up into the blue eyes. 'I wanted to talk…'

'Oh, I spy Jonathan and I need to have a quick word with him. Excuse me, darling. I'll be straight back,' and with another fleeting kiss, he was gone, melting back into the crowd.

'Like I said, gorgeous,' sighed Sylvia. 'You're lucky we're good friends or I might be fluttering my eyelashes in his direction.'

'Mm,' Fliss watched Jasper make his way across the room to slap someone on the back. Within seconds they were holding an intense conversation. 'But I suppose all marriages change after a certain length of time, don't they?'

'Change. What do you mean?'

'Oh, you know.' Jasper had already moved on, starting a new conversation with a well-dressed man standing by the bar area, his promise to come straight back already forgotten. 'New priorities, work, lack of time, all that sort of thing.'

Her husband had disappeared and looking around the room she noticed Donna and James, two friends who had been together almost as long as she and Jasper. They were standing next to each other chatting to a group. As Fliss watched, she saw James's hand drift downwards to give his wife's bottom the slightest squeeze. Donna's hand pulled it back up to her waist but Fliss could tell from the lack of effort exerted that she wasn't in the slightest bit offended.

'That first flush of love, the rampant passion, the longing to be together. It changes over the years. It's natural, it's part of the development of a marriage,' murmured Fliss talking mainly to herself. 'Relationships change.'

'Well, you would know, being the agony aunt. But I always think that you and Jasper look as though the passion is still well and truly present in the Carmichael household. You always look very happy to be together.'

'Oh we are,' confirmed Fliss brightly, 'very happy.'

Jasper was good at placing a loving hand on his wife's waist, kissing her regardless of who might be present. But she couldn't help but wonder when he had last gazed into her eyes and seen nothing but his wife and not the person over her shoulder.

'Fliss, are you okay?'

Jerking herself back to the conversation, Fliss gave her friend a reassuring smile. 'Of course! Just a bit thoughtful tonight.'

Sylvia didn't look convinced and for a moment she watched Fliss' eyes roam restlessly around the room, searching for her husband.

'Have I spoken too soon? Are you worried about Jasper?'

'Of course not.' She tried to sound firm. Being an agony aunt, how could she ever admit to a breakdown in her relationship with her husband. No-one would trust her to advise others if she couldn't handle her own marriage.

'Really?' Sylvia was frowning, maybe Fliss hadn't been as convincing as she'd hoped.

Jasper suddenly burst back into sight. He was having a conversation with someone Fliss recognised as a work colleague and both Fliss and Sylvia watched as they were interrupted by a woman in a sparkling black dress who placed her hand on Jasper's arm to draw his attention. Laughing, Jasper kissed her on the cheek as he and his companion abandoned their talk to listen to what she had to say.

Sylvia watched as Fliss' gaze settled on her husband. 'Oh my God Fliss, are you worried that he's having an affair?'

The question was blunt and unexpected and for a moment Fliss was too shocked to speak. It hadn't occurred to her for a moment that Jasper would be unfaithful. She had always been supremely confident that her handsome husband would never betray her.

She shook her head. 'No!' she said firmly. 'Of course not.'

Sylvia nodded approvingly, sipping at her drink. 'Good.'

It was one thing Fliss had never worried about. Apart from anything else, Jasper was far too busy, he had enough difficulty finding time for his wife let alone fitting another woman into his life. It would never happen.

With a gasp of alarm, she put a hand against her mouth in horror. 'Is he having an affair?' she whispered. 'Is that why you asked me, to see if I knew? Does everyone know but me, is he...'

'Stop! Absolutely not.' A reassuring hand was placed on her arm. 'Anyone less likely than Jasper to cheat on his wife I have yet to find. He has eyes for no-one but you.'

Actually, thought Fliss, the main thing in Jasper's eye line these days was his phone.

'I didn't mean to worry you, I was just making sure you didn't have any silly ideas in your head. But I'm sure being an agony aunt you would know straight away if there was a problem.' Sylvia laughed. 'You would have it diagnosed and sorted out in no time at all!'

And that, thought Fliss, was her problem in a nutshell. Because she didn't have all the answers, she hadn't even realised that there was a problem until she had read Ellie's email. And now she needed to get to the bottom of her failing relationship and find a solution whilst telling no-one what was happening. Well, no-one apart from Ellie that was and smiling through stiff lips, Fliss continued to sip her champagne and wonder what on earth she was going to do.

Chapter 5

'Just the two of us?' asked Jasper.

Fliss couldn't work out whether he was surprised or disappointed.

'Yes. We don't often get the chance to spend time together these days, there's so much going on and we always seem to be surrounded by other people.'

Jasper finished knotting his tie and turned to smile at his wife. 'That sounds lovely. We haven't been out alone for some time.'

Relieved Fliss slipped on her shoes. She had wondered if Jasper would be disappointed by the suggestion. Not the going out part, he loved to socialise. But having to spend the entire evening with only his wife for company.

'Although I did promise Jack that the next time we were going to Giorgio's I would let him know,' he added, checking his appearance in the mirror. 'Apparently, it's his wife's favourite restaurant and he said they would love to meet us there. Shall I give him a ring and we can make a night of it?'

'What? No, that's not the two of us getting together, that's four of us going out!' Speaking more sharply than she'd intended, Fliss saw Jasper's eyebrows shoot upwards. 'Sorry, I just wanted to have a bit of time to ourselves tonight. Do you mind?'

'Of course not! I'm looking forward to it.' Jasper slipped on his jacket and came to press a kiss on the back of her neck. 'It was just a suggestion. A night out together sounds wonderful, just like the old days,' he added with a chuckle and another kiss. 'I'll catch up with Jack later in the week. Perhaps we should organise something on Friday, get a few people together and go for a meal. What do you think?'

Fliss tried to smile. 'Maybe we could get tonight out of the way before we start planning the next one?' she said lightly.

'Of course darling, let's concentrate on tonight!'

Reading Ellie's email suggesting that she talk to Jasper and tell him of her worries, she'd been forced to admit that it was eminently sensible advice and exactly what Fliss would have said herself if she'd been thinking clearly. Slightly ashamed that she had needed someone else to point her in the right direction, she had adopted the idea with enthusiasm. Communication was the key to any successful marriage, she knew that, so she needed to speak to Jasper and see if he felt that their relationship had changed of late. Perhaps, as Ellie had suggested, he was feeling exactly the same and would sigh in relief when Fliss brought up the subject and say that he also thought that action was needed and what did Fliss have in mind. They could have the problem sorted out in no time.

As a result, when Jasper arrived home that evening, she announced that she was taking him out for a meal. Their favourite restaurant had been booked, a nice quiet table in the corner requested, and whilst Jasper may think it was a spontaneous gesture, Fliss was feeling quietly confident that after her plan to have a good heart to heart, all would be back to normal.

After an enthusiastic welcome from the maître d' they were shown to the table Fliss had requested, quiet and tucked away from the noise and constant comings and goings of the main area.

'Wouldn't you rather have your usual table by the window,' asked Giorgio, pulling out Fliss' chair. 'Where you can see everybody else?'

'That would be great ...' began Jasper.

'No thank you,' answered Fliss firmly. 'This is perfect.'

At Jasper's raised eyebrow, she shrugged. 'It can get a little noisy,' she said. 'I wanted a chance to chat.'

He reached out and pulled one of her hands up to his mouth, kissing the back of her knuckles. 'That sounds far more interesting,' he said, so sincerely that Fliss immediately decided that she'd vastly overreacted to a busy few weeks. There was nothing wrong with their marriage!

Sipping at the white wine delivered with a flourish by Giorgio, Fliss smiled happily. This was going to be much easier than she had imagined.

'Isn't this lovely, just the two of us? We should make the effort to do this more often.'

'Indeed,' Jasper agreed as he reached for his phone. He always turned off both the sound and vibration whenever they were eating out. But his eagle eyes watched it all the time and a flash of light had told him a new message had arrived. 'It's wonderful,' he murmured absently, his attention taken by whatever he was reading.

Fliss remained silent for a moment then put her hand gently over his. 'Is it something important?'

'Not really, just a new press release from …. Oh, darling, I'm sorry! We're supposed to be having a night together.' Pulling a face, he pushed the phone a little closer to the centre of the table. 'I won't touch it again,' he promised, his intense blue eyes turning all their attention on Fliss. 'Now, what shall we talk about? Anything new happened in the world of agony?'

Fliss couldn't help smiling. She had been absolutely right, well, Ellie had been right. Communicating was so important, look at the improvement already. Maybe it wasn't all Jasper's fault, maybe she was also guilty of letting other things take priority in their lives.

'Nothing in particular. We just don't get much time to ourselves these days, I wanted us to be able to have a catch-up.'

Smiling across the table, Jasper lifted his glass. 'It has been a little manic lately, hasn't it?' he complained whilst

49

looking quite pleased with himself. 'This is such a good idea. You look beautiful tonight and it reminds me what a very lucky man I am.'

Fliss had never dreamt it could be so easy.

'You have been very busy recently,' she said magnanimously. 'But it is important that we make time for each other.'

'I couldn't agree more and tonight we have our opportunity so let's make the most of it!' and he raised his glass higher to toast his wife, almost throwing the contents over her as someone slapped him on the back.

'Fancy meeting you two here,' boomed a voice. 'You should have told us you were coming, we could have booked a table together.'

Ross Bannister grinned down at them, blowing a kiss in the direction of Fliss and grasping Jasper's hand.

'Why didn't you phone? Don't tell me you make a habit of sneaking down here without inviting us along?' he laughed.

Standing up, Jasper shook his hand with enthusiasm. 'No, of course not. Just tonight, Fliss booked it at the last minute.'

'Well it's not too late, come over. Freddie and Mags are here as well. In fact, Freddie said he wanted to speak to you about something.' Ross winked at Jasper. 'And seeing as he's heading up the new 'Audience with the Press' programme, I imagine it might be something you want to hear!'

Fliss saw the intense flash of desire on Jasper's face. She recognised it well because he used to look at her with the same expression. He sent a quick look in her direction but she gave him nothing in return, keeping her face bland as she twirled her wine glass between her fingers. The circle of diamonds knocked against it, giving off a radiant hue in the candlelight of the table.

'Really? What a shame I can't,' said Jasper, giving her a moment to contradict him before turning back to Ross. 'Special occasion you see, just the two of us tonight.'

'Ah! Date night eh? They can be important, got to keep the fires burning,' he chuckled sending a smile in Fliss' direction. 'Well, I'll leave you two love birds to it and you know where we are if you change your mind.'

Sitting back down, Jasper straightened his tie and fiddled with his napkin. Fliss could see the longing on his face.

'Thank you,' she murmured.

He looked up and she could tell his thoughts had been on an entirely different table.

'Thank you?'

'For not asking to join them.'

'Of course I wouldn't. You said you wanted tonight for us and here I am.'

Fliss reached out her hand but Jasper was looking over his shoulder towards the centre of the room and didn't notice.

'Actually, the something I wanted to talk to you about was us spending more time together.'

He brought his eyes back to hers. 'Sorry?'

'The amount of time we spend together, or rather, don't,' Fliss repeated a little louder.

'I'm not with you.'

'I know you're busy Jasper, very busy and probably going to get even busier.' As a well-regarded columnist, he had started to receive invites onto various chat shows and political debates on the television. Much as he grumbled about the time it took out of his already busy week, Fliss could tell that he loved it. 'I would never complain about the time you spend at work,' she clarified, 'but it does seem as though lately other things, well just about everything, seems to take priority over us.'

A light flashed on Jasper's phone and Fliss saw his hand twitch as he ignored it and picked up his glass instead. His eyes were pinned on the screen as though trying to divine the contents.

'I feel as though we're beginning to drift apart,' Fliss continued, trying not to look at the phone herself.

'You do?' For a moment she had his attention. 'But you know that I love you.'

'Of course. Well at least I think I do,' she said lightly. 'It's just that we don't seem to have the feeling of closeness we once had.'

'I'm busy at work darling, everything is going so well at the moment.'

'It's not that. You've always been busy, we've always been busy. This is different. I'm starting to feel as though there isn't room for our marriage in the midst of everything else and I think that it's important we make time for each other, more nights like this perhaps?'

His phone flashed again. 'Mm, good idea,' he murmured, his eyes flickering to the centre of the table where it sat.

Fliss put her glass down on the table with a small bang, jerking Jasper's attention back to her. 'Time when we can talk to each other and forget about everything else.'

Nodding, Jasper tried to hold her gaze as his phone flashed yet again. 'Absolutely darling. I'm sorry you feel like this. I hadn't realised, I'm as happy as ever,' he reassured her absently, his eyes back on his phone.

'Oh have a look,' snapped Fliss irritably. 'Maybe then you'll be able to concentrate on what I'm saying.'

She thought Jasper might decline but his hand was on the phone before she'd finished speaking, his thumb scrolling through his messages.

'It's from Freddie,' he laughed. 'Just making a joke about our date night.'

'I'm glad he finds it funny!'

'Not like that, he says he wishes he was on a date with you.'

'Really. Maybe I should accept, perhaps *he* would listen to me!'

Giorgio was approaching and without looking at the menu Fliss and Jasper both ordered their meals.

'I am sorry,' Jasper offered with an apologetic smile that didn't reach his eyes. 'It's just that Freddie has dropped a few hints about a permanent position on this new show of his and I'm really interested in the opportunity.'

Fliss sniffed, refusing to forgive him.

'I'm listening Fliss, really I am.'

'What did I say?'

'Er, you want us to spend more time together.'

'Why?'

'Why?'

'Yes, Jasper, why?'

'Because you er,' she could see him trawling through his memory. 'Because you feel that we're growing apart.' A slight grimace touched his face and his tone softened. 'Because I'm a fool and I haven't been paying you enough attention. Because you're worried that we might drift away from each other, even though that could never happen because I adore you as much now as I did the very first day I met you.'

Fliss couldn't help but soften.

'I want us to stop this before it becomes too bad,' she whispered, reaching across the table and taking his hand in hers, holding it tightly as she continued. 'Before we find it impossible to find our way back to each other.'

For a moment she thought she'd won. Because for a moment, a very brief moment, Jasper looked at her and only her in a way he hadn't for such a long time and Fliss Carmichael, agony aunt, felt a surge of relief that she'd taken the right action and stopped the decay of her marriage before it had any chance to grow.

'What's this I hear about you two preferring to stay over here in the corner?' Another hand slapped Jasper on the back and Fliss had to struggle not to roll her eyes in frustration.

'Freddie! Yes, tonight it's just me and Fliss, no business talk,' said Jasper with mock seriousness, sending a loving glance in his wife's direction as though the idea was his own.

'Well I can't say I blame you,' agreed Freddie, his eyes resting on Fliss and the black silk top that made her soft skin appear as creamy as a pearl, her red hair like fire beneath the restaurant lighting.

'I'm sorry Freddie,' she offered in an apologetic tone. 'If I don't take him out occasionally, I would never get to see him!'

Letting his eyes drop to the hand she was holding onto with a determined air, Freddie turned his gaze back to Jasper. 'You're a very lucky man,' he offered. 'There are lots of men out there whose wives would do anything to avoid spending a night together. Enjoy!' and with a chuckle, he wandered back to his own much noisier table.

Fliss tried to recover the moment. She waited until Freddie was out of sight and Jasper's eyes had, rather reluctantly, returned to their table and his wife. 'It's important that we don't forget about each other,' she said with a smile, albeit one that was becoming a little strained around the edges. 'With everything else that happens in our lives, we need to make sure that we save some time for each other.'

Forgetting about Freddie momentarily, Jasper smiled at his wife, his head tilted to one side as he inspected her face before shaking his head. 'I could never forget about you darling, you know you mean everything to me.'

Slightly mollified, Fliss began to relax just as Jasper's phone flashed again and this time it was in his hand and his thumb was scrolling down the screen before she had time to blink.

'Just Freddie again,' he chortled. 'Wants to know if we've finished the loving yet!'

'It would seem to be going that way!'

'He said when we're ready there's a cold bottle of champagne on their table and they've just asked for two more glasses.'

At her look, Jasper shook his head quickly. 'But of course, I want to stay here, with you,' he insisted. 'I can meet him another night.'

She saw his thumb moving against his phone, no doubt sending the bad news back to Freddie.

'Yesterday, someone asked me if you were having an affair,' she said coolly, watching his face.

'What? What on earth?' Dropping his phone which clattered against one of the plates, he stared at her in shock. 'An affair? Good God Fliss I would never … I wouldn't …'

'Oh don't worry,' she said harshly. 'I didn't think for a moment that you were. I can't imagine how you would find the time.'

'It's not about the time.' Jasper looked hurt. 'I love you, I would never have an affair.'

Fliss stared at him, looking for some tell-tale sign in the blue eyes. She had received enough emails over the years to know that when a husband lost interest in spending time with his wife, it often meant he was finding fulfilment elsewhere. She still thought it unlikely that Jasper was finding his in the arms of another woman, it was far more likely to be an email that had claimed his attention.

'Fliss,' he said beseechingly as her silence stretched. 'You do believe me, don't you?'

'I don't think you're having an affair, but I am trying to tell you that I think we have a problem,' she snapped as Jasper looked at her with a bewildered expression. 'It's as though our marriage has slipped down your priorities. Behind endless meetings with Ross and Freddie, behind socialising with colleagues and definitely way behind work.' After tonight, the distance that Fliss had felt opening between them was looking more like a chasm.

Jasper was hanging on to his phone as though it were some sort of lifebelt.

'Oh Fliss,' he said, the slightest tinge of impatience in his tone. 'Don't be silly. I love you my darling, more than ever. I admit,' he held his arms up in an apologetic manner, 'I am very busy at work but there's nothing wrong with our marriage, absolutely nothing at all! Please stop worrying.'

His phone flashed again and his fingers tightening tremulously around it as he tried to keep his eyes fixed on his wife. 'I love you,' he said slightly desperately. 'Very much.'

'Oh for goodness sake, let's go join them,' she growled. 'We might as well, you'll only spend the night messaging each other,' and with a last disappointed look at her husband, she stalked over to a large table in the centre of the room where the occupants cheered her arrival and held up a glass of champagne in her direction.

So much for a simple, straight forward solution, she thought grimly. She was going to have to dig much deeper into her reserves and come up with something else to bring her husband's attention back in her direction because talking was clearly not the answer!

FROM: Fliss Carmichael <agonyauntfliss@digitalrecorder.com>
To: Ellie Henshaw <Elliebellshenshaw@livewell.co.uk>
Date: 20/03/2020

Dear Ellie

I am so pleased to hear that my advice helped and for you to find actual chemistry, that's amazing! Now that you've made contact you must continue. I know that you find it hard to speak to him, I was the same many years ago, I used to go quite droopy whenever I saw my future husband across a crowded room. But you need to be brave and not rely on your friend to do all the work for you. You've introduced yourselves, which is good. He knows who you are and he'll remember that electric shock if nothing else!

Using names is far more intimate than shouting hello across a crowded office so from now on whenever you see him, make sure you use his name. Look him in the eye and say 'Good Morning Logan'. And smile! A smile really does say an awful lot about the person you are and how you are feeling. Make sure Logan knows that you're happy to see him, even if you're only walking past each other in the corridor.

As well as using his name, try and chat to him a little more and show that you're curious about him. Men like to think that they've stirred a woman's interest so ask a few questions. It doesn't have to be anything too complicated, for example, ask him what he likes to do outside of the office, does he have any hobbies, what kind of films does he like to watch, that sort of thing. All very casual but it helps to build a relationship between the two of you. Who knows, he might tell you he's about to go to the cinema and ask you along!

These are all small steps but you are getting closer to him all the time. Don't hide how you feel Ellie, there's nothing wrong with showing interest, someone has to make the first move. I was so relieved when my husband asked me out, because I'd decided that one way or another, I was going on a date with him and if he hadn't asked me, I was on the verge of asking him!

And now we've decided what your next step should be, I really must apologise for my last email. You are correct, it isn't normal to ask the person you are advising for help! I was typing as I was thinking and didn't mean to send the email. It must have been quite a shock for you to see all my ramblings when I should have been concentrating on your problem. But it was very kind of you to reply and offer me some advice, and very good advice it was too, exactly what I would have said myself!

It's funny how we are so much better at dealing with other people's problems isn't it? We listen to what is happening and often the issue is perfectly clear and we can see the path they should take. But when it's close to home it seems so confusing and uncertain. Thank you for taking an interest and just so you know, I did speak to my husband and I told him exactly how I was feeling. It was the right thing to do, we had a chat about how important it was to stay connected and how I felt we were drifting apart.

Unfortunately, he wasn't listening, which is a big part of the problem. I will be honest, it was a disappointing response. We've never had trouble talking to each other in the past and I was hoping for a more definite result. I will give things a little more thought and come up with another way of catching his attention. But enough of that, I won't start telling you my woes again!

Please don't worry about me, this is all about you and Logan. Stay strong Ellie, do what I've suggested and I'm sure that you two can get to know each other a little better. And then, who knows what may happen!

Fliss Carmichael

Chapter 6

'It's all a bit obvious isn't it?' asked Laura as she filed her nails. 'Do you need an agony aunt to tell you that the best way to get to know someone is to start talking to them?'

'You think she's wrong?'

'I think she's right. What I'm saying is, why on earth are you writing to someone you don't know and who quite honestly sounds as though she can't sort out her own life never mind help anyone else, when the answer is perfectly obvious. I told you weeks ago to start speaking to him and see what happened.'

It wasn't that Ellie thought Laura's advice was wrong, she had just decided that a second opinion might be a good idea, especially one from a professional. Laura wasn't necessarily the best of role models. Her idea of subtle was to lean across the table, using her elbows to push up her boobs and winking at some unsuspecting young man, giggling in delight if they turned bright red, which they invariably did.

When Ellie had finally gathered enough courage to admit that she had fallen head over heels for the tall, attractive young man who worked on the 7th floor, Laura had enthusiastically instructed her friend to say hello instead of hiding around a corner whenever she caught sight of him. Clapping her hands in excitement, she had offered to give Ellie a makeover to help catch his eye, which had been politely refused. Being very fond of her outgoing friend, Ellie had found it difficult to explain that she found the amount of blusher Laura considered essential for a normal day in the office to be positively frightening. She'd also refused Laura's breezy offer to pop upstairs and acquaint Logan with Ellie's rather repressed feelings and ask if he was interested, suggesting instead, that they wait to see what Fliss would advise.

'And she agrees with you,' she told Laura in a conciliatory tone. 'I've got to make sure I say hello every time I see him. And use his name. Then we'll start to build a connection. Doesn't sound too hard, after all, I managed to speak to him in the lift.'

They had agreed to stop discussing the meeting in the lift. With Laura insisting it had been an unmitigated disaster and Ellie holding her fingers aloft and insisting that a real connection had been made, they had eventually agreed to disagree.

But Laura had warned her that the next meeting between Ellie and Logan had to be a little more normal.

'I'm sure he thinks we're both lunatics,' she'd grumbled as Ellie gazed dreamily at her fingers. 'He might even report us to HR. It looked like we were trying to stalk him, all very creepy,' she'd complained, giving Ellie a cross glance. 'And stop rubbing your fingers! It was a bit of static not Cupid's arrow!'

But Ellie knew better. It was a sign, a big elemental sign that something was meant to be between herself and Logan and she couldn't wait to find out what it was.

'I'd better start practising,' giggled Ellie. 'Using his name and smiling. I wonder when I'll see him next.'

'Right now,' said Laura casually. 'He's about to walk into the office. Here's your chance. Head up, smile in place and just say, perfectly naturally, 'Hello Logan.' Even you should be able to do that Ellie. Ellie?'

Puzzled, Laura looked over at her friend's empty desk. Logan was walking in their direction his arms full of folders and a slightly nervous look on his face.

'Ellie, where are you?' whispered Laura furiously. 'He's coming over. He's coming to our desk. He's here. Where are you? Oh, hello Logan.'

Swivelling her chair around to block the view of her friend's desk and the figure she'd just spotted hiding beneath it, Laura jumped up to greet Logan by throwing her arms around him and turning him slightly sideways so he had no chance of seeing the crouching Ellie.

The hug wasn't entirely successful due to the volume of files Logan was carrying and as Laura's sleeve became tangled in a paperclip that was peeping out, they were obliged to step even closer to detangle her, a move that left a blush on his cheeks.

'Sorry,' beamed Laura, pushing him back a few steps so he was well away from Ellie's desk. 'Can I help you with anything?'

'I er, I've brought these files down for you. It's the contracts that you and er… you and er…'

'Ellie,' prompted Laura.

'Yes, that you and… er, Ellie were working on. We've finished the analysis and I was asked to return them and let you know that we're having a meeting this afternoon to discuss the findings.'

Laura rolled her eyes. As part of the administration team, she and Ellie were often dragged into meetings on the off chance that someone from another team may have a question to ask. They never did and the meetings usually dragged on interminably as they discussed matters that were of absolutely no interest to either of them.

'Another meeting,' she groaned. 'I hate those meetings.'

Logan nodded sympathetically, leaning forward to drop the files on Laura's desk and stepping back again quickly.

'Right okay, well I'll go …'

'But I'll tell you who loves them!'

'Er, loves them? Loves the …?'

'The meetings. Ellie!'

'Ellie?'

'Yes, Ellie. She loves those meetings.'

Logan's eyebrows raised. 'Does she?'

'Oh absolutely. But then Ellie's got that kind of brain. She's really into figures and statistics and er… well you know, all that kind of stuff.'

'Really?' Logan's eyebrows had reached their limit. 'I hadn't realised ...'

'Not many people do. She hides her light under her bush does our Ellie, I mean bushel,' she added hastily at Logan's expression.

'Fancy. Well, I must go ...'

'So she'll be really happy that we're having a meeting,' continued Laura, leaping in front of Logan to block his escape. 'It will be a chance for her to use her mind, dissect the er ... you know, the stuff that needs dissecting. Because she's got the same kind of brain as you.'

'Indeed.' Logan nodded politely and turned to go the long way around past Ellie's desk only to have his arm grabbed by Laura who pulled him firmly away.

'Must be nice to know that someone in the meeting will be interested,' she said, tugging him closer so he wouldn't discover the still hiding figure.

Flinching at her touch but seeing an opportunity for escape, he manoeuvred his body around the corner of her desk, ignoring the sharp edge which was now pressing into his thigh.

'Yes, lovely. I need to be off ...'

'You'll be in the meeting and you'll know that while everybody else might be bored silly and wish you'd shut up, Ellie will be watching you like a hawk and listening to everything you say!'

'Thanks, great to know.'

His long legs finally managed to clear the desk and with a little tug, he was free of Laura's grip, almost falling into the waste bin in his haste before he shot off at great speed, heading for the 7th floor without looking back.

Laura smiled happily as she rolled Ellie's chair backwards and pulled her out.

'Did you hear that Ellie? That's what's called thinking on your feet.'

Straightening up, Ellie rubbed her knees before sinking back into her chair.

'I'm not sure ...' she began warily. 'Maybe it wasn't the best thing to say.'

'Rubbish!' announced Laura, clapping her hands in glee. 'I made sure that he won't take his eyes off you in that meeting. Just remember to look interested. And what on earth were you doing under the table? I thought you were going to say hello!'

'I am.' Ellie nodded fervently. 'I am, just not right now. It has to be the perfect time and I wasn't quite ready.'

'Well you've got until this afternoon to get ready because like it or not you'll be in a meeting with Logan and this time you won't be able to hide under the desk so prepare yourself!'

It was almost impossible for Ellie to concentrate for the rest of the morning. Her heart was leaping with the joy of imagining herself in a room with Logan for an hour, but she was also racked with nerves at the prospect. It was so much easier for people like Laura, she decided as she read through a contract and made the necessary alterations. Laura was so bubbly and outgoing, it was a mystery to her why Ellie was so reserved. But it wasn't just her naturally shy nature that was causing the problem, pondered Ellie, it was far more complicated. She still remembered the first time she had seen Logan. He had been standing in the lobby with a group of friends, his head thrown back as he laughed at something that had been said. She had been battling with her umbrella which was refusing to retract and she had stood, windswept and ruffled, watching him with wide eyes. There had been something in the set of his chin and the plane of his face that had caught her attention and simply wouldn't let go. His hair was sticking up as a result of the wind and although she was too far away to see the colour of his eyes, she knew instinctively that they were kind and gentle. Her heart had been snatched by the tall, slender young man, and he had held it firmly in his hands ever since.

Ellie had spent the next few weeks watching for him, instinctively knowing when he was close by and her heart would hammer a tattoo as she peeped at him from beneath her eyelashes. After 3 weeks she had gone home one evening and sitting on her bed, still wearing her coat, she'd decided that this was no crush, this was love, true love. She had never felt like this before and it was an emotion far too intense to be ignored. So, with nothing more concrete than a certainty that they were meant to be together, she'd uprooted her entire life and changed the course of her future to the absolute horror of her family. Every day since had been spent hoping that when they finally met, he would fall in love with her just as she had fallen in love with him. That moment in the lift, that shock of electricity between them, it meant that Ellie had been right, she and Logan were a couple waiting to happen.

A few hours later, Ellie and Laura left their desks and made their way to the meeting room. Having allowed herself to be dragged into the ladies to be 'tidied up', Ellie had kept Laura firmly in hand and agreed to mascara but not to false lashes, had said yes to lipstick but no to the bright red 'Vampire's lust' and had let Laura apply a smudge of bronze colour to her pale cheeks but refused to let her contour new cheekbones. Taking a deep breath, thankful that she had pulled on a sparkly jumper over her leggings that morning, Ellie walked into the meeting room. It was important, advised Laura, that they chose their spot carefully. Normally they would shuffle to the end of the table, as far out of sight as possible and slump there until the ordeal was over. Today, Laura cast a careful eye around the room and then pointed to the very centre of the table, next to a large flip chart.

'I bet he'll be sat near there,' she whispered. 'He'll probably want to write on the board.'

Ellie nodded. She was so nervous her mouth felt like the Sahara Desert and her heart was hammering so loudly she could barely hear Laura above the racket it was making.

'Remember to speak,' instructed Laura firmly, pushing Ellie into a seat. 'No hiding, no going all shy. This is the man you've got a crush on...'

'It's not a crush,' interrupted Ellie automatically. 'I'm in love with him.'

'Whatever. But this is your chance. When he walks in you say *'Hi Logan'* and smile at him. That's all you have to do.'

Ellie nodded.

'You can do that can't you?'

'Hi Logan,' repeated Ellie obediently. It sounded quite nice hearing his name on her tongue.

'Good. Keep calm, don't go into one of your funks. Just say hello. And use his name.'

Laura had been doubtful about Fliss' advice that the use of names made the occasion more intimate. 'I can think of a lot of things that would make the occasion seem more intimate,' she had offered, 'and none of them include using their name every time you say hello.'

'It's a well know strategy,' Ellie had declared, hoping that Fliss was indeed correct.

Laura had tested the theory half an hour later when one of the young men from the IT team had arrived at her desk with a parcel. She'd taken it and flashed her dimples, offering a throaty, 'Thank you so much, *Joshua.*'

Josh had turned quite pink as Laura's tongue had rolled over his name. He'd stared at her longingly for a moment before turning around, tripping over his feet as he left and stopping to take one last glance over his shoulder as he retreated.

'Interesting,' Laura had said as she watched him leave. 'Definitely use Logan's name.'

'Are you okay?' she asked now as she sat next to Ellie, staring at the doorway opposite them.

Ellie nodded, saving her power of speech until it mattered. She must make sure she sounded normal this time and not squeaky and breathless.

'Good then – oh he's here. Ellie, he's here.'

Laura was squeezing Ellie's arm so hard that she was finding it hard not to yell and tugging hard, she was unprepared when Laura suddenly let go. Falling sideways she crashed to the floor, landing on her hands and knees under the table.

'Ow, that hurt …'

'Speak!' Laura was commanding in a loud whisper. 'What are you doing on the floor? Sit up, don't waste the opportunity. Use his name. SPEAK!'

'LOGAN,' yelled Ellie at the top of her voice, pushing the hair back from her pink face as she scrabbled to get back on her chair and sit upright. 'HELLO!'

The room came to a halt, the gentle conversation that had been drifting amongst the few inhabitants stopping as they all turned to stare.

Ellie saw Laura shake her head and she blushed furiously, wondering if anyone would think it odd if she retreated back under the table. A sharp nudge to her ribs made her continue.

'Hello Logan,' she said, her tone calm and controlled. 'How nice to see you again.'

Deciding she sounded like a hotel receptionist welcoming back a regular guest, she heard Laura give an anguished sigh but she ploughed on. 'Why don't you sit here?' Waving her arm in the direction of the empty seat to her side, she felt a sliver of pride. She must remember to tell Fliss that she had initiated more than just contact, she'd invited him to step closer.

Logan looked around uncomfortably. The room was filling up and several people were waiting for him to take a seat and move out of the doorway.

'Er thanks, Ellie.'

Yes! Ellie resisted the urge to do a victory punch. He had used her name. Surely that was progress? Something else to tell Fliss.

'But I have to sit over here,' he pointed to the end of the table where Ellie and Laura usually sat. 'I need to use the projector.'

Smiling to take the sting from his rejection, he shuffled to his chair, putting his laptop on the table and connecting it to the screen behind him. Of course he needed better technology than a flip chart, thought Ellie. You didn't present statistics and analytics on a bit of white paper.

She turned to glare at Laura who had the grace to look contrite.

'I'll sit with you,' offered Joshua from across the table.

'No, it's okay I …'

But he had already squeezed his rather wobbly beer belly through the gathering crowd and with a grunt he landed in the chair, leaning forward to look round Ellie and smile shyly at Laura, effectively blocking out any view of Logan. With a huff of resignation, Ellie had to resort to listening and although she didn't take in a word of what was said, she spent the next hour relishing the sound of Logan's confident voice as it filled the meeting room.

When the meeting finally came to an end and everybody began to pour out of the doors, Ellie was all for joining them as quickly as possible, only Laura's hand held her back.

'Wait,' her friend whispered. 'Not so quickly.'

Gathering her folders, Laura pushed her chair back in slow motion, shooed Josh out of the way and by the time she had walked around the table and reached the door, Ellie behind her, there were very few people left in the room, Logan being one of them. He was disconnecting his laptop but looked up to see them both hovering by the door, staring at him.

'Oh, Hi.'

Reluctant to speak, as a form of communication it didn't seem to be working for her, Ellie gave a smile instead. It was a big, wide smile, ever so slightly manic and Laura's eyes opened wide in alarm.

'Great meeting Logan. Ellie was just saying how interesting it all was. Very interesting. She was really interested.'

Laura poked her in the back and Ellie nodded fervently. 'Oh yes, very interesting.'

Picking up his laptop, Logan stood up. He was several inches taller than Ellie and as she looked up into his silvery grey eyes, she felt decidedly faint. 'Very, very interesting,' she murmured.

'Really? Are you familiar with SAS software then? I didn't realise you used it in the admin office.'

'Er, the SAS?' Good grief, is that what they'd been talking about. She should have paid more attention.

'Statistical Analysis Software,' prompted Logan. 'You're interested in it?'

Not in the slightest, thought Ellie.

'Oh, er, yes. I think I am.'

Logan glanced at his watch. 'I must dash,' he said apologetically. 'But I have some great articles which chart the progress of SAS in the workplace. There's a fascinating one about how it's revolutionised business intelligence and data management. If you're interested, I can send them over to you?'

Ellie wondered what on earth he was talking about. Maybe she'd gone blank again, which often happened when she bumped into Logan.

'She'd love to read them, Logan. Absolutely love to, wouldn't you Ellie?'

'Absolutely,' repeated Ellie faintly.

'Great, I'll email them over,' and with a smile he was gone, leaving Ellie standing in the meeting room trying to fathom how on earth the SAS played a role in the day to day life of the average office worker and whether she had just agreed to join.

Chapter 7

Gripping her glass of wine, Ellie rolled her shoulders and tried to relax.

'I suppose it could have been worse,' mused Laura. 'I mean you spoke to him and you used his name. Very loudly, which may be a good thing, who knows. Maybe the louder you say it the more connection you have,' she suggested hopefully.

'And he now thinks I have an overwhelming interest in statistical software,' groaned Ellie, who had logged straight onto Google when she arrived back at her desk and read with growing disbelief the highly specialised subject that was SAS in the workplace.

'Hmm.' Laura took a drink of her wine. 'But you don't have to actually read any of it. Just say you found it interesting.'

Within half an hour of the meeting ending, Logan had emailed Ellie several articles about his favourite subject with a little note saying that he hoped she found them as fascinating as he did. Ellie had ignored the articles, reading every word of the note several times over and unable to stop grinning with delight. When Laura wasn't looking, she'd pressed print so she could take a copy home and carry on looking at the way he'd started with a casual 'Hi Ellie' and finished with 'Logan'.

'What else would he put on the bottom of an email?' Laura had asked unhelpfully. 'I don't think you can read too much into it Ells.'

The note now sat at the bottom of her bag, already creased from the number of times she'd unravelled it to examine the words. Whatever Laura may say, he could have just written, '*here are the articles*' and not bothered with a *'Hi Ellie'* or signed it *'Logan'*. She couldn't wait to get home and read it again.

Unfortunately, Ellie had then moved on to the articles he'd attached and her mouth had fallen open at the complexity and sheer length of them, appalled that she'd managed to give Logan the impression that this was a subject that interested her and convinced that he would appear by her desk the following morning to carry out a quick spot test on what she had learned so far.

'You know,' continued Laura with relentless optimism, 'that's a really good sign. It means that he was thinking about you even after the meeting had finished. He could have forgotten all about the articles.'

'I wish he had,' Ellie muttered gloomily.

'But look on the bright side Ells! Look at the progress you've made.'

Ellie thought for a moment. She didn't think it was entirely what Fliss had meant when she'd advised Ellie to build a connection. But at least they'd spoken, he had used *her* name which was even better and they now had something in common. Well not exactly in common but at least it had resulted in a conversation.

'Why am I finding this so hard,' she sighed.

Laura watched her downcast friend and waved at the barman for a couple of top-ups. Reaching over, she tilted Ellie's glass upwards towards her lips, encouraging her to drink the contents. 'You're taking it all far too seriously honey,' she offered. 'I mean, come on! You've got a crush on a guy at work. It's no big deal, I get them all the time. They usually last a couple of weeks, maybe even a couple of months then someone else comes along. You're behaving like it's a scene out of Romeo and Juliet and you two are star crossed lovers, meant to find each other over the water cooler.'

'It's not a crush,' said Ellie firmly. 'It's love.'

'One-sided love. How can you say you're in love with someone you've never even met properly?'

'Love at first sight exists. You read all the time about people whose eyes meet across a crowded room and they fall instantly in love.'

'Yeah, but there's usually two of them and it's probably more a case of instant lust than true love.'

'It's love. Anyway, why are you having crushes? What about Gareth, I thought you loved him?'

'I do.' Two more glasses of wine arrived. 'But that doesn't stop me having a crush on someone else. It happens all the time. You see a hunky guy with gorgeous eyes and you can't stop thinking about him.'

Ellie gasped. 'Laura! You shouldn't feel like that about someone else when you're with Gareth! If you love him you should have eyes only for him.'

'You're a funny little soul Ells. You've been born in the wrong time. There's nothing wrong with fancying someone else, it's not as though I'm going to do anything about it. A little bit of swooning, a bit of flirting, it keeps the soul happy. You are taking the whole thing far too seriously.'

Shaking her head, Ellie wondered if Laura had any idea just how seriously Ellie had taken it. She would be shocked if she knew the truth.

'Well I think that if you love someone, truly love them, you shouldn't have those sorts of feelings for anyone else,' she muttered. 'And if it does happen you should ask yourself if you really are in love in the first place. It wouldn't be fair to stay with someone if you're not prepared to give them your entire heart.'

Laura put her glass down, her eyes opening wider as she leant across the table. 'Oh my God Ellie, is that why you and Carl ......'

'I need to ask you something,' jumped in Ellie quickly. 'What would you do if someone you've been with for a while started to lose interest? You know, if they stopped thinking about you like they used to, maybe they prefer to go out with their friends rather than have a romantic dinner with you?'

'Good grief! You're jumping the gun a bit. All he did was say hello and send you an email. He needs to show a lot more interest before you can worry about him losing any!'

'Not Logan. I mean in general.'

'You mean if the relationship starts to flag a bit?'

'Yes, sort of.'

'Is this about your agony aunt?'

'Not exactly. Well maybe a bit, I just wondered what you would do.'

Laura took a thoughtful sip of her wine. 'Well, underwear has always worked for me,' she announced, digging into her bag of crisps and munching. 'There was a spell when Gareth was spending more time at the pub than he was spending with me. It was because they were showing the World Cup matches but even so, I was getting pretty fed up with him slipping out for a pint nearly every night and not coming home for hours.'

Ellie listened, wide-eyed.

'So I bought some really nice underwear, not the sort of thing that you would wear every day. In fact,' she pulled a face, 'I have to say it wasn't particularly comfortable. I brought it home and left the bag on the kitchen table. I saw him looking through it, he didn't say anything but he did look surprised. And a bit shocked.'

'And? asked Ellie, her drink forgotten as she imagined Gareth, solid, salt of the earth, football loving Gareth, coming face to face with the sort of lingerie she could imagine Laura taking home.

'I didn't say anything and after tea, I asked him if he was going down the pub to watch the match.' Finishing her crisps, she licked her fingers. 'I told him I didn't mind because I was thinking of meeting you for a drink and maybe we'd go dancing afterwards.'

'Me?' squeaked Ellie.

'Yes. Then I picked the bag up and told him I was going upstairs to get changed.'

'And?'

'Let's just say he didn't go to the pub.'

'Good job I wasn't waiting for you,' grinned Ellie.

'Of course, it wouldn't work every night. We ended up getting sky with the sports package so he could watch the matches at home, but it certainly got his interest back where it belonged.'

Somehow, Ellie couldn't see that sort of approach working with the sophisticated Fliss Carmichael. Only the previous day Ellie had seen a photograph of Fliss and her husband at a party, arm in arm as they raised a glass of champagne to someone in the distance, both looking the epitome of cool elegance. But maybe it was worth mentioning. Perhaps Fliss would appreciate hearing what worked for others.

'Ellie, why did you stop seeing Carl?'

Twiddling her glass, Ellie peered into its contents as though searching for something. 'I told you, I decided there didn't seem to be any point continuing with a relationship that wasn't going anywhere.'

Laura was watching her friend carefully. 'But you didn't finish with him because you'd developed a crush on Logan, did you?'

'Of course not!'

'Because that would have been stupid Ells. To finish a relationship just because you liked the look of someone you didn't even know.'

'I wouldn't do that, don't be silly.'

Laura didn't look convinced. 'You and Carl seemed perfectly happy together.'

'You were the one who told me he was boring!'

Laura shrugged. 'Well, he was. But just because I found him boring doesn't mean that you should finish with him. You were together for a long time. And you can be a bit boring yourself you know, which is probably why you got on so well.'

'Boring!'

'Well, quiet then.'

Ellie had once described her perfect idea of a romantic weekend; a quaint little hotel deep in the countryside, a cosy room, long walks across the fields, a blazing fire, a glass of wine. Laura had stared at her open mouthed and declared that it sounded as dull as ditch water and not a patch on the weekend she had spent in Ibiza with Gareth, where they had partied all night and slept all day, waking as the sun disappeared to start all over again.

'Just because I don't like to spend every Saturday night at Karaoke doesn't make me boring. Or quiet.'

Laura sniffed. 'But you can be a bit odd, all that romance stuff you read, watching swoony films nonstop. You're not exactly the life and soul of the room you know. Not that I mind,' she added hastily. 'I love you regardless, I'm just saying, some people might find you a bit quiet. Anyway, you and Carl seemed quite happy and then all of a sudden you ended things.'

'It just didn't seem right,' sighed Ellie. 'I wasn't in love with him.'

'You told me you were.'

'Yes, well, I thought I was but then I realised I wasn't. Not enough, not the true, deep love you should feel for someone you plan on spending the rest of your life with.'

'And it had nothing to do with Logan, some random guy who you saw getting into a lift and decided you were in love with?'

'No!'

'Because it would be so like you to decide that you were madly in love with a tall, dark stranger. You'd probably decide that he'd captured your heart and therefore you were destined to be together, or some other nonsense.'

'Don't be silly.'

'Maybe you've fallen for Logan on the rebound? A sort of substitute because Carl is no longer in your life.'

'It wasn't like that,' defended Ellie. 'I realised that my relationship with Carl wasn't what I wanted so I ended it. It's nothing more complicated.'

'Is he still following you around?'

Carl often turned up unexpectedly where Ellie was. She was in no doubt that her mother was letting him know where her errant daughter may be found, Susan Henshaw had been devastated when Ellie announced that she was ending things with Carl. Both her parents considered him to be a thoroughly decent young man and entirely suitable for their dreamy daughter, someone to keep her feet firmly on the ground.

'Yes,' sighed Ellie. 'He says he wants to talk but I've said all I need to say. It's over. I hate that I've hurt him so much but there isn't any point talking, I won't change my mind.'

Only the previous evening her mother had told her that it wasn't too late, Ellie could admit that she had made a mistake and everything could get back to normal. Carl would understand because he was that kind of person, her mother had remonstrated. He knew that Ellie was impulsive and he would forgive her in a heartbeat.

'Sounds like he's still in love with you Ells darling. I think he'd like you to go back to him. Oh, maybe he's even decided he wants to marry you! Although typical man, they always leave it too late to ask, don't they?'

Spotting Gareth walking towards them, Ellie was saved from answering and she stood up to put on her coat and brace herself for the cold evening air, refusing Laura's request to stay and have another drink with them rather than going home alone. She didn't tell Laura but she actually loved her quiet evenings at home. Nothing to distract her but thoughts of Logan, planning how their house would look, what they would call their children, how happy they would be. It was time well spent as far as Ellie was concerned.

Saying goodbye, she left the pub, deciding that something else she wouldn't tell Laura was the truth about Carl. That was something better kept to herself, or maybe herself and her agony aunt, but definitely not to be shared with Laura.

....
FROM: Ellie Henshaw <Elliebellshenshaw@livewell.co.uk>
To: Fliss Carmichael < agonyauntfliss@digitalrecorder.com>
Date: 26/03/2020

....

Dear Fliss

My friend Laura says that once you've received an email from an agony aunt you stop writing and if that's what I'm supposed to do then I'm sorry that I keep sending you more questions. It's just that you seem to understand exactly how I'm feeling and everything you've told me to do so far has worked. This is so important to me. I truly am head over heels in love with this man, despite what anyone else says, and you are the only person who has accepted how I feel and hasn't tried to tell me that it's a crush that I'll get over.

I have given up so much for the opportunity to be with him and I have to make sure that I give our potential relationship a chance, I want him to look into my eyes and fall in love with me, just like you and your husband did. I didn't tell you the whole story in my first email. You see, I was actually with someone else, for quite a long time. I thought it was love, we were on the verge of marriage but when I saw Logan I realised that if I could feel like that about a man I'd never even met, then I wasn't really in love, so I ended things. Nobody would understand the decision I made so I kept the reason to myself, even Laura doesn't know the truth. So, it's not just about me and Logan, it's about what I let go for the chance to be with him.

After introducing myself in the lift, I had a wonderful opportunity to speak to him because we were in another meeting together. Laura said it was like watching a car crash in slow motion, but I thought that it went okay. I used his name as you advised. Laura said I yelled it and it was so embarrassing that she nearly left. It was a little bit on the loud side but I wanted to make sure he heard me. Laura told him I was really interested in statistics because that's what he does. She was trying to help but her help doesn't always work out and now he thinks I'm interested in some software and he's sent me loads of articles to read. It's all very boring and I'm worried that he's going to ask me a question about it. But Laura said if he does, I just flutter my eyelashes and ask him what he's doing that night. She finds that sort of thing really easy but I always get embarrassed and end up saying something stupid and I'm just not sure what to do next.

I know you said that agony aunts don't ask for advice, but I think that's unfair. Who is supposed to help you? Everybody needs someone to confide in and I actually feel quite responsible for your unhappiness. If I hadn't sent my email about Logan, you may not have started thinking about the past and how much things have changed. I've not had much experience in this sort of thing but you are right, other people can often see what your problem is far more clearly than you can yourself and I'll be happy if anything I say helps you.

I think that your husband is still in love with you, it's almost as though he's just forgotten how he feels. Laura said that when Gareth, that's Laura's boyfriend, forgot about her during the 2018 World Cup, she bought some new lingerie, just to give him a gentle reminder. I'm sorry if that's not the sort of advice that you should give someone you don't know, and as an agony aunt, you've probably thought about it already. And I don't mean it to be embarrassing but according to Laura, all men need a nudge every now and then and I thought I would mention it, just in case it helps.

I'll carry on trying to talk to Logan, I just hope he doesn't want to talk about the SAS because I haven't read any of the articles all the way through yet.

Thank you

Ellie

Chapter 8

As soon as they arrived home from the restaurant, Fliss announced that she was tired and was going straight to bed. Looking mildly surprised, Jasper had one foot on the bottom step as though to join her when his phone flashed. Attention diverted, he wandered into his study to check the email he'd just received and Fliss knew that was the last she would see of him for some time.

Perversely pleased that she wasn't expected to make small talk, she still slammed the bedroom door behind her in displeasure. The evening had been a disaster, for Fliss at least. Jasper had looked surprised but totally unworried by her declaration that they were drifting apart. Her worries had been dismissed with a shake of the head and a smile and the rest of the evening had been hijacked by the conversation of their friends, which Jasper had seemed to enjoy far more than a conversation with his wife about his failures in their relationship.

It was a couple of hours before Jasper finally made it upstairs and although Fliss was still wide awake, she lay very still as he moved quietly around the bedroom before sliding into bed next to her. Tossing and turning, her mind racing with possibilities, she finally fell asleep in the early hours of the morning and when she eventually woke up, Jasper was long gone, his pillow already cold.

Fliss had arranged to meet a friend for lunch and for a moment she considered cancelling. A day spent at home without the need to be sociable appealed and wandering downstairs, she made herself a coffee and curled up in the living room, staring out into the garden and warming her hands on her cup.

Jasper had been adamant that nothing had changed, that he was the same loving husband he had always been and there was absolutely nothing for Fliss to worry about. But failing to keep her husband's attention long enough to explain why she was worried about his lack of attention, had left Fliss even more anxious. Was she being unreasonable expecting him to stop looking at his phone occasionally and speak to her without interruption?

She thought of all the emails she'd received over the years from women describing how their husbands were suddenly spending more time at the gym, had started to use moisturiser for the very first time, were going out running or had all manner of new interests that gave them a good reason to be out of the house. Only with hindsight did the wife realise that the driving force behind the sudden desire to keep their skin well hydrated was, in fact, another woman. The thought of Jasper having an affair had been easy to dismiss, she trusted him implicitly and despite everything else, she truly believed he still loved her. But was she being naïve, wondered Fliss? Was she behaving like the classic deceived wife, insisting to all and sundry, including herself, that her husband would always remain faithful?

Wandering back upstairs, Fliss found herself opening Jasper's wardrobe, staring at the array of suits and trailing her hand along the sleeves. There had been nothing to make her suspicious. If Jasper came home late, she knew exactly where he had been. If he was entertaining or attending a social event, Fliss was often by his side. It wasn't that they didn't spend time together, he was there in body, it was his spirit that seemed to have deserted her. These days when Jasper looked at her, she got the impression he was going over his day's schedule or drafting an email in his head.

Leaning forward, she sniffed tentatively, resting her nose against the nearest jacket and letting it slide along the line of suits. Nothing. No perfume she didn't recognise, no unusual scent. She stared into the wardrobe for a few more minutes, no tell-tale blonde hairs clinging to a lapel, no strange messages peeping out of a breast pocket. Slamming the door, she shook her head. What on earth was she doing, her husband wasn't having an affair!

Diverted by a text buzzing on her phone, she read Penny's message checking that lunch was still on and began typing an excuse why she couldn't make it before pausing and staring out of the window. Jasper wasn't having an affair, of that she was certain. Well, fairly certain. But it never hurt to be absolutely sure and deleting her reply saying that she had a headache, she wrote back to say she was looking forward to seeing her friend.

Penny had divorced her husband two years previously after finding out that the gym he was visiting most evenings was actually the apartment of his aerobics' instructor and was little more than a treadmill positioned conveniently by her bed. A chat with Penny might be just the thing she needed and putting down her phone she headed for the shower.

Penny was already at their table when Fliss arrived. Compensating for a growing feeling of inadequacy, Fliss had applied her makeup with care, highlighting her green eyes and outlining her lips in a bright red that almost matched her hair. She wore fitted trousers that made the most of her long, long legs and a casual top that highlighted the creamy skin of her neck.

'You look fantastic Fliss!'

Ignoring the menu, she ordered a glass of wine and Penny's eyebrows shot upwards. 'Not like you to drink during the day,' she commented lightly. 'But if you're going to hit the wine, let's make it a bottle.'

The waiter was called, a bottle delivered and Penny sat back in her chair with a small sigh of contentment.

'It's lovely to see you. So, update me! It's been ages since we've been able to meet, what's been happening?'

Shrugging, Fliss kept her tone light. She would save her worries to herself and Ellie for now.

'Same old, same old,' she said instead. 'Jasper is as manically busy as ever, we've been out virtually every night this week and the one night we stayed at home he watched back to back runs of the Andrew Neil show so he was up to date with every possible opinion of every possible subject.'

Penny laughed, raising a glass to her friend in sympathy. 'Jasper has always been very dedicated to the job,' she agreed. 'If it was any other husband you'd probably be worried right now.'

Fliss cocked her head. 'Any other husband?'

'Other than Jasper I mean. It must help to know that he's still totally besotted, can't keep his eyes, or his hands, off you. He may be busy but at least you know he's not up to anything, he'll always come home even if it is very late. Unlike some other people I could mention,' added Penny bitterly.

When Penny's husband had stopped coming home altogether, claiming he'd been exhausted from his work out and had crashed at a hotel close to the gym, Fliss had gently told her friend that it was time to confront him and demand the truth. It had become clear to her that Darren was being unfaithful, if only she could see the problem with her own marriage as clearly.

'Besotted? Hardly! We've been together for such a long time. I don't think people stay besotted for this long, do they?'

Jasper had told her the previous night that he still loved her. He had insisted that he was as happy as ever. That should be enough. But it was like a loose tooth, Fliss couldn't stop probing and worrying at it, there was something wrong and she needed to get to the bottom of it somehow.

'I mean, relationships change, don't they?' she murmured. 'Time moves on and passion, well it tends to disappear.

Other things become more important, work for example. You tend to spend less time together but it's natural, it isn't a sign that there's anything to worry about.'

Penny's eyes grew wide. 'Are you having trouble with Jasper?'

'What? No, I just meant …'

'Oh God, I would never have believed it, you and Jasper of all people. I thought you would last forever.'

'There's no trouble!' interrupted Fliss hastily. 'None at all.'

She didn't want the rumour mill to begin churning out gossip about the state of the Carmichael's marriage.

Penny relaxed, sitting back even as she gave Fliss a searching glance. 'Sure? Because I sometimes wonder if you keep it all to yourself because you think it would reflect badly on you, as an agony aunt, if you admitted you were having problems of your own.'

Fliss felt a sting of colour in her cheeks, perhaps Penny knew her better than she'd realised. And she was right, after all, what kind of agony aunt had to ask someone else for advice?

'Nothing is wrong,' she said as cheerily as possible. 'I was just saying that after being married for 18 years, things do change. But nothing to worry about.'

'I thought I didn't have to worry about Darren,' sighed Penny. 'I was convinced that we were as happy as ever, that he was going to the gym because he genuinely wanted to look after himself. Unbelievably, I took it as a compliment! I thought he was doing it for both of us. I can't believe how stupid I was!'

'You mustn't blame yourself, I always thought you and Darren were happy.'

Snorting, Penny emptied her glass and topped them both up. 'So did I. Hindsight is such a wonderful thing, don't you think? Now I look back all the signs were there, I just ignored them. I was convinced I had nothing to worry about and that our marriage was as strong as ever.'

'Signs?' asked Fliss with interest.

'Oh, I get it!' Penny nodded her head wisely. 'You need to give someone some advice and you want me to help.'

She was right in a way, thought Fliss.

'Do you mind talking about it?'

'Not really,' sighed Penny. 'If I'd realised what was happening sooner maybe I could have saved my marriage.'

'You mentioned signs, what sort of signs?'

'He was just busier than usual, you know. Busy at work, busy going to the gym. I didn't think it was a problem. But I should have paid more attention to why and then maybe he wouldn't have gone off with that gym bunny of his.'

Fliss felt a tendril of worry begin to wrap around her stomach. If she had to describe Jasper it would be busy. Very definitely busy.

'And what do you think you should have done?' she asked cautiously.

'At first, I thought he was trying to keep himself fit. He lost weight and started to tone up. I was foolish enough to think that he was doing it for us but it was because he was bored. Bored of me and our marriage, it was all the same old routine and he was fed up with it. If I'd understood I could have swallowed my pride and taken action.'

'Action?' Fliss' eyes were wide. 'What kind of action?'

'I could have spiced things up a little, you know in the bedroom.' Penny's cheeks had gone quite pink. 'It's not something I'd ever had to worry about before. To be honest, it never seemed to be a problem. But if I thought it was needed and would stop Darren leaving, I could have done, well something a bit different maybe.'

Almost as embarrassed as her friend, Fliss took a hasty sip of wine.

'But do you think it would have helped?' she asked. 'Would it have stopped him leaving?'

'It might have done. If he hadn't started going to the gym then he wouldn't have fallen for *her* and we'd still be happy.'

85

Fliss doubted it somehow. She couldn't help feeling, with a dose of her own hindsight, that Darren was a serial philanderer and sooner or later the allure of someone else, with or without a treadmill next to the bed, would have tempted him away from his marriage.

They sat back and allowed the waiter to place the salads they'd ordered on the table. When he left Penny leaned forward, lowering her voice confidentially. 'If I could have stopped him leaving, I'm sure we'd have been okay in the long term because I happen to know that he's unhappy with gym bunny.'

'Really? Who told you?'

'Darren works with someone called Gary and I know his wife vaguely, she goes to the same yoga class. Anyway, she winked at me the other week and said it looked like Darren had learned his lesson the hard way.'

'What lesson?'

'Well, now he's living with her, his new girlfriend isn't quite as interesting as she used to be. Leaves her underwear over the radiators and piles the sink with plates. Darren hates that, we always had to have an empty sink. And he says the underwear drives him mad. Also turns out that she doesn't wear a G string every day, which seems to have come as a surprise to him. He really thought she wore bloody uncomfortable bits of floss because she wanted to and not just because he was visiting her that night! Anyway, when the G strings ran out it was the same grey knickers that the rest of us wear. He told Gary it was depressing.'

'He's not happy?'

'Apparently not and...' Penny paused for dramatic effect. 'Neither is she! Her aunt works at the launderette that my sister's cleaner goes to and it turns out gym bunny has been saying that his snoring is taking some getting used to and she objects to him arriving home from work and sitting on the settee, farting and watching TV for the rest of the night. When he was only over there a few nights a week he was a lot more – active.'

'Do you think he wants to come back?'

Penny grinned. 'I think he might.'

'And you'd be okay with that?'

'Good God no! Wouldn't dream of taking back the two-faced cheating bastard. But I won't tell him until he's finished putting up the shelves in the garage. And fixed the lock on the back door. In fact, the living room could do with a coat of paint. I might as well get something out of it.'

Leaving the majority of her salad, Penny filled up their glasses again. 'The thing is,' she said, leaning forward again and fixing her gaze on Fliss. 'If you're advising someone before it's got to the stage where the marriage falls apart, tell them not to presume it's okay just because their husband says it is. If their gut says something is wrong, it probably is and they need to take action before it's too late.'

'Action in the er, in the bedroom?'

'Can't hurt, can it? It might just stop him in his tracks, give him something to think about.'

When Fliss had read Ellie's email about the power of lingerie, she had been sceptical. She had never needed any artificial means to grab and hold Jasper's attention and the idea of resorting to racy underwear was not something that sat comfortably with her. There again, neither was the prospect of losing her husband. She'd advised other women in the past to try anything they felt might entice their partner back into their lives so perhaps it was time Fliss followed a little of the same advice.

The meeting with Penny had certainly given her something to think about and as she emptied her glass, she decided she may have to go on a little shopping expedition after lunch. Maybe it was time she took Ellie's advice more seriously and started pulling out all the stops in her efforts to capture Jasper's attention. Hopefully, even Freddie and his potential new job opportunity wouldn't be able to compete with a G string worn in the right circumstances.

Chapter 9

With a couple of glasses of wine under her belt, Fliss managed to overcome her natural reservation and found herself in a delightful lingerie shop she had used before. But this time, instead of browsing the tasteful satin underwear she had previously purchased, she made her way somewhat warily to the far end of the shop where the lighting was subtly different and the walls were bedecked with a very different selection of corsets and suspenders. Staring at the display in horror, she immediately decided that she'd made a mistake. Despite what Ellie and Penny may say, this wasn't something Fliss was comfortable with, there had to be another way of catching Jasper's waning attention without resorting to leather and red frills.

Turning to leave, she found herself face to face with a petite woman wearing horn-rimmed glasses, a calm smile and with a total lack of judgement on her face.

'Can I help?'

'Oh, I don't think so, I'm not sure, I don't …'

'We have some lovely items,' the woman said holding out her hand as if to emphasise the point, 'and if you're looking for something to make a statement, then these are ideal.'

Is that what she wanted, wondered Fliss desperately? To make a statement? Surely she would be better off just saying, 'Jasper, I feel you're moving on without me'. That was a statement. Wouldn't it make the point much more efficiently than underwear? Shaking her head, she clutched her bag a little more firmly to her body. There had to be another way. She needed to leave before she humiliated herself any further.

But then her thoughts flew back to the previous evening when she had tried to do exactly that. Sitting opposite Jasper she had told him, quite clearly in her opinion, that she felt there was a growing problem in their marriage. It hadn't been a success. Nibbling her lip she thought about Ellie's advice and Penny's regrets that she hadn't visited a shop exactly like this one.

Staring at the exit longingly, she remained where she was.

'I think it's important that er, statements, should still be tasteful,' she said in an embarrassed half-whisper, her eyes wandering to the display only to encounter a peephole bra and flying back to the sales assistant with speed.

'Of course,' agreed the woman calmly. 'A woman such as yourself,' she cast an experienced eye over Fliss' willowy figure, 'needs to keep to a certain standard.'

Fliss swallowed. Was there a standard for seducing one's husband?

'I'm really not sure,' she said anxiously. 'I don't know what …'

'That's why I'm here to help. I'm sure we can find exactly what you're looking for. Now,' the woman put her hands together in a business-like way that made Fliss relax a tiny, tiny smidgen. 'What exactly do you need?'

Fliss' eyes rolled over the display and swiftly away again. 'Oh, I don't know. Something to er... something to catch the eye?' she suggested, her cheeks beginning to turn the same colour as her hair.

'Married?' asked the woman, casting a look at Fliss' hand and the circle of diamonds resting there.

'Yes.'

'And is this for your husband?'

'Of course!'

The sales assistant held up her hand. 'I don't judge, I just need to understand what you need.'

Blushing even deeper, Fliss nodded. 'Yes. It's for my husband.'

'Roving eye?'

'I beg your pardon?'

'Has he got a roving eye.'

'Roving? Oh no, well I don't think so.'

'I see. Lost interest?'

'No! Well, sort of I suppose. I mean we still, he still, it's not like we don't …'

Oh ground, please open up and swallow me, prayed Fliss.

'I understand. Attention elsewhere and needs bringing back?'

Fliss nodded. It seemed there was a description for it after all. 'Yes, I think that er... covers it.'

'Right. What level do you want to go in at?'

Fliss stared.

'Are we looking at a little gentle seduction, an eye-catching display of your natural assets to bring your husband's attention back where it belongs.'

Feeling her cheeks flame as the assistant cast an eye over her assets, Fliss gulped and cast her eye towards the exit again.

'Or are we talking a major effort, something designed to make your husband forget all about anything else for a while and remain close to your side for some time to come?'

What seduction level was she, thought Fliss in a panic? If level 1 was a matching set of lacy underwear what was level 5, some serious, eye goggling apparatus that could leave them both in need of the first aid box?

'I don't know,' she said faintly.

'Okay. So are you thinking …' the woman rifled through the rails and pulled out a black PVC affair with slashes in the most inappropriate places and what looked like clamps hanging down from the chest area.

'Oh goodness me no!' Fliss put out a hand and held onto the wall to steady herself. She would rather put up with a growing distance in her marriage than dress up like that when she was making the Sunday roast. And what was she supposed to hang from the clamps, she doubted they were for tea towels.

'Okay, so more like ...' more rifling and this time an ivory satin corset was held out, ruched and decorated tastefully with small bows and lots of lace.

'Well ...' reaching out a hand Fliss touched the material. It was soft and smooth. In fact, it wasn't too dissimilar from the sort of thing that Fliss might normally wear, just a little more explicit. 'Yes, I think maybe ...'

'It would suit you.' The woman had stepped back and was looking at Fliss through half-closed eyes. 'You have the perfect skin to set this off superbly and it is very tasteful.'

Slightly uncomfortable at being imagined semi-naked, Fliss snatched at the corset.

'Okay, I'll have this,' she mumbled and desperate to be out of the shop and somewhere her cheeks could cool down, she pulled out her credit card and almost threw it at the sales assistant.

Safely back home, Fliss had another glass of wine to calm her trembling hands and finally gathered enough courage to try on the corset. It had been appallingly expensive and she decided that the art of seduction must be big business. But the sales assistant had been right, it did look amazing against Fliss' creamy skin and was exactly the right side of provocative. All she had to do now was wait for Jasper to arrive home. She didn't know which one of them would be the most shocked when she whipped off her dressing gown and revealed her new satin creation, but the longer she thought about it, the less likely it was that she would be able to go through with her plan. There was no point waiting, tonight would be the night. Tempted to have more wine, Fliss had a cup of tea instead. She'd had enough Dutch courage, any more and Jasper would arrive home to find her asleep on the bed and the corset on the floor beside her where she doubted it would have the same effect.

Jasper was working late again. He was meeting Freddie to discuss the new programme and he was confident that a permanent post was about to be offered. Fliss had sent him a good luck message earlier in the evening and then spent the rest of the night curled up on the settee, her stomach a quivering mass of nerves as she waited for him to return home. When the message pinged on her phone to tell her he was on his way, she headed straight up to the bedroom before she changed her mind. Pulling on the corset, she spent a moment or two examining herself in the mirror. Her figure was slim and taut, much like it had been when she and Jasper had first met. Her breasts were still full and high and her legs were long and shapely, all shown off to their very best as the corset pulled her in and pushed her out in all the right places.

Slipping a silk dressing gown over her goosebumps, she brushed her hair and checked her makeup. Not a smudge in sight, not a hair out of place. All she needed now was Jasper. Her heart was thumping uncomfortably in her chest. What if he thought she was being ridiculous, dressing up like this? What if he looked at her with indifference, could she bear to see his eyes wander over her half-clothed figure and then back to his phone? With a gulp, she jumped to her feet. This was a terrible idea, it wasn't what their marriage needed, she would change now and climb into her fleecy pyjamas before Jasper arrived home.

The sound of his car pulling up outside stopped her in her tracks. There were so many laces and hooks on the corset it would take her hours to get changed. The moment had arrived, whether she was ready or not and with a squeal of alarm she dashed to the bedroom door, her ear pressed against it listening for sounds of Jasper downstairs.

The front door slammed and another opened somewhere in the house. Perhaps he had gone into his study. Maybe he needed to send an email after the meeting he'd just had with Freddie, or perhaps he'd brought home some work. Straining to hear what was happening, Fliss pushed the bedroom door open and peered across the landing. There was a light reflected from downstairs, it was coming from the kitchen. Was he making himself a drink before coming to bed? Had the meal been dreadful and he was making a sandwich? Nibbling on one long red nail, Fliss stood uncertainly in the bedroom doorway. Should she wait for him to come upstairs? She could be waiting for some time, he may work in his study for several more hours. Was it acceptable during seduction to throw yourself semi-clothed across your husband's desk or would he be slightly miffed that you had creased some important paperwork?

Tiptoeing uncertainly onto the landing, Fliss decided he was definitely in the kitchen, not a room she had considered when playing out various seduction scenes in her head. It was a tad cold in there, lots of tiles, granite surfaces and metal. If she was going to lounge against a wall, letting her dressing gown slip from one shoulder as she sent her husband a tempting look, she would prefer to be somewhere warmer.

Fliss waited for him to move to another room, wondering what was taking him so long. The least he could do was co-operate in his seduction and come upstairs to find his beautiful, sexy wife laid casually across their very comfortable bed. Fidgeting with impatience, she crept to the top of the staircase. The kitchen was the first door to the right and she could hear Jasper rattling around. He must be hungry, she decided. She'd heard the fridge open so maybe he was making a sandwich after all. Wrinkling her nose, she tried to decide what to do. What if he had a ham sandwich in his hand as she erupted on the scene, trying to look alluring. Did it matter? Could a seduction be carried out if one of them was holding a sandwich or would empty hands be needed to fully participate? Maybe if he was really hungry, he would prefer a ham sandwich to his wife, even if she was wearing a corset. The kitchen and the possibility of food becoming involved was not ideal but there was only so long Fliss could dither around on the landing and apart from anything else, she was freezing.

Shivering, she decided that she had prevaricated enough. She was going downstairs and if Jasper was determined to stay in the kitchen then she would have to join him there, dealing with the ham sandwich in whatever way seemed proper once she arrived. She was cold and her nerve was failing. If she didn't do this now she would have wasted over a hundred pounds and still have a problem with her marriage.

Taking a deep breath and wishing she had pulled on some socks, Fliss slipped quietly down the stairs, her nerves hammering in her chest as she pushed the kitchen door gently so it opened enough to let her slip inside and lounge in the doorframe.

The fridge door was wide open and Jasper was looking inside its depths.

'Hello sexy,' she purred. This had better be worth it, she thought, gritting her teeth and feeling gut-wrenchingly uncomfortable. 'I've been waiting for you.'

The rustling noise in the fridge stopped and Fliss waited for Jasper to peer round the door.

'I've missed you,' she cooed, getting into her role a little more. 'Now you're here I expect you to make it up to me.'

Silence. His feet were visible beneath the fridge door but he was standing very still, no doubt waiting to see what she would say next, leaving her to whisper and flirt whilst he played hard to get. The problem was, she wasn't used to it.

'Come on then, you sexy man,' she tried, racking her brain for something slightly more tempting, 'come and see what you've been missing.'

Nothing. Fliss bit her lip, she could do with some input, it was proving more difficult than she'd imagined standing half-naked in the kitchen and flirting with someone hiding behind a fridge. Perhaps Jasper didn't understand he had to join in, after all, this was fairly new to both of them.

'So,' she carried on with more determination than allure, 'are you going to, er, have a look?'

Not exactly sexy but she was beginning to lose the flow. 'I can promise it will be worth it,' she added desperately.

The fridge door started to move slowly and Fliss let out a sigh of relief. It would be much better if this were more of a two-person conversation. She hoped he would leave the ham in the fridge. She didn't need anything else to worry about.

'Come on then,' she encouraged, keeping her voice low and husky which was hurting her throat slightly. 'Come out, where I can see you. I've got exciting things planned for us tonight.'

'Fliss.'

At last, a little interaction.

'That's right, it's me. Now come and get me you, er, you big boy.'

'Fliss?'

'Yes,' she said a touch of impatience creeping in. 'Yes, it's me.'

'Fliss!'

About to close the fridge door herself and haul Jasper out into the open in an attempt to get this seduction moving a touch quicker, she took a step forward only to stop. The voice was coming from behind her.

Peeping over her shoulder, Fliss found her husband standing in the entrance hall, his mouth hanging open as he stared wide-eyed at his scantily clad wife draped seductively against the kitchen door. This was more like the kind of reaction she'd been waiting for and spinning round, Fliss gave him what she hoped was a come-hither smile.

'There you are,' she said throatily. 'I've been waiting for you.'

Wiggling, she allowed her silk dressing gown to slip from one shoulder, swishing it to one side so he could see her corset in all its glory. He looked shocked, very shocked, and hoping that was a good reaction, Fliss took a step towards him, tripping slightly over feet that were now so cold they'd started to go numb.

Then she stopped. If Jasper was in the hallway, who on earth was in their kitchen. And now she thought about it, Jasper looked less shocked and more horrified. Was that a natural reaction when your wife presented herself in a cream silk corset?

There was a small squeak from behind her, and turning slowly she saw the fridge door finally close and Freddie's alarmed face appear, red and slightly sweaty.

'Freddy!' Frozen in the doorway, she watched as his eyes unwillingly travelled down her scantily clad body before shooting back to her face, half closing in fright. Frantically she pulled the dressing gown around her, wrapping it tightly across her body and tying the belt several times in ever bigger knots. 'What on earth are you doing in our kitchen?'

'I'm sorry Fliss, I wanted some information that Jasper had and he said …'

'Felicity! What on earth are you doing?' Jasper had walked into the kitchen, his face pale as he stepped between his wife and Freddie, giving them both an indignant look.

Meeting Freddie's eyes over Jasper's shoulder, her cheeks filled with hot colour as she recalled the conversation they had been having. Correction, the conversation Fliss had been having whilst Freddie hid behind the fridge door, no doubt traumatised.

'I thought it was you. In the kitchen,' qualified Fliss.

'But why are you dressed like that?' asked Jasper, quite perplexed. He looked at Freddie who was staring down at the floor and at Fliss, staring at her blue toes with the edges of the cream silk corset peeping from the top of her dressing gown. 'Oh! Oh, I see.'

Nobody spoke. Eyes shifted around the room looking anywhere but at each other. Freddie was holding a carton of orange from the fridge, Jasper was holding a sheet of paper and Fliss was holding what was left of her shattered dignity.

'Well,' she said cheerfully. 'Nice to see you, Freddie. Give my love to Mags, won't you? Jasper, I'll see you upstairs, don't work too late darling,' and turning on her heel, she fled up the stairs as fast as she could, slamming the bedroom door behind her before letting out a howl of embarrassment that shook the windows.

FROM: Fliss Carmichael <agonyauntfliss@digitalrecorder.com>
To: Ellie Henshaw <Elliebellshenshaw@livewell.co.uk>
Date: 31/03/2020

Dear Ellie

Your friend is correct, usually, one email is all that is needed for an agony aunt, but I really don't mind that you've carried on writing to me. Your situation is so close to my heart that I'm very interested to hear how it's going and it sounds like you've made real progress, I'm so proud of you. Having a conversation about things that interest each other is a major stepping stone to creating a friendship that will hopefully turn into much more. But it's also very important that you are truthful. I know it can be tempting to tell people that we enjoy watching programmes that we don't actually like or that we follow sports that in truth we hate. If you are attracted to someone you want to find something in common, it helps make them feel closer to us but beware, because it can cause conflict later in the relationship. I did once encounter a poor woman who had told her new partner how much she enjoyed watching darts. He was delighted to find someone who shared his interests and thought they were both happy spending every Saturday night watching repeats of his favourite matches. 20 years later she finally snapped and stabbed him with one of his own darts. I'm telling you this as a cautionary tale and no names will be divulged but it proves how important it is to make sure that we show our true selves to any prospective partner.

Your friend Laura seems very enthusiastic on your behalf but it may be a good idea to ask her to be less forward in giving your opinion to others. You need to build a relationship with Logan based on what you both like and not what your friend claims you like. And that's exactly what you need to do next, continue to build on your budding friendship. Find out what he likes to do outside of work, apart from being a member of the SAS. See if there's an opportunity for you to engage with each other away from the office. Perhaps without Laura?

You mentioned your previous relationship and I hope I've misunderstood but it sounded as though you had left your partner because you had fallen in love with Logan. That does worry me. It is only a possibility that you and Logan will become a couple, not a certainty. To leave someone you were in love with because you saw a man from afar and developed strong feelings for him is very impetuous. I can't help feeling that I should have asked you more questions before I encouraged you to pursue a relationship with Logan, I do hope that you've thought it through.

And last but not least, thank you for your suggestion. You are absolutely right, although I spend my day giving help to others, finding the right solution for myself is proving difficult. It's actually quite comforting to have someone think of me and how I might resolve my own problem so I don't mind at all that you've taken an interest

I did try the lingerie. Jasper was quite shocked, not in the way I had expected and it didn't go entirely to plan. But the good news is that my husband has now been offered the job he wanted. I'm hoping that it was given to him for the right reasons and not in any way due to my lingerie. It was a good idea in principle but I don't think that it entirely suited our situation. I hope that you're right and he does still love me just as much as he always has. It's certainly what he keeps saying, although that may be because he wants me to stop talking to him so he can read his emails.

I sincerely hope things work out for you Ellie, good luck in the next stage of your romance.

Fliss Carmichael
x

Chapter 10

It was raining. And not just a little shower but pounding rain that bounced 6 inches back into the air as it hit the pavement and when Ellie finally opened the door and fell into the lobby, she was soaked. It was also windy. Her umbrella had given up at the first hurdle and was currently in a bin close to her flat. Her hair was stuck to her head and water ran in rivulets down her cheeks which were pink, both from the sting of raindrops and from exertion as she had bent her head and fought the wind.

'Hello, Ellie.'

She had been staring at her feet in their inadequate kitten heel shoes, which were now so wet they squished out water as she walked. Wondering if they would dry if she wedged them down the back of the radiator and sat at her desk in bare feet, she had paid no attention to the solitary figure waiting for the lift. At the sound of his voice, her heart gave a painful thump and her breath caught in her throat. Telling herself to calm down, she looked up and smiled.

'Hello, Logan.'

They both turned back to track the progress of the lift in silence allowing Ellie to take a quick peep at her reflection in the mirrored wall on one side of the lobby. Oh dear.

'Awful weather isn't it?' offered Logan.

'Mm.'

'Luckily my bus stop is close to the office.'

'That is lucky.'

Another pause.

'Is yours further away?'

Ellie supposed that her appearance had given him a clue.

'Yes.'

'No brolly today?'

'It blew inside out. First corner.'

'What a shame.'

The lift arrived and standing back, Logan held out his hand encouraging Ellie to enter first.

What lovely manners, she thought even as she considered shaking her head and fleeing towards the steps. Just the two of them in a lift was her dream come true but the prospect had made her knees acquire a definite wobble. If she had time for one of Laura's mini-makeovers she may feel more confident but instead, she had to make do with trying to flatten down her windswept hair as Logan turned his back.

Not asking which floor she needed, Logan pressed 5 and 7 and Ellie felt a little wriggle of pleasure that he'd remembered. Although, she admitted to herself, he was unlikely to forget given his previous experience in the lift with her.

Staring back down at her feet, Ellie racked her brains to think of something to say. She wasn't normally stuck for words. Most of her school reports made mention of her inability to stop chattering and her mother had always said that she could talk the hind leg off a donkey. But somehow, in the presence of Logan, her legs turned to jelly and her mind turned to mush. She tried to recall the advice Fliss had given, establish a rapport, find out what Logan liked to do away from work. This was the perfect opportunity to discover more about him, as long as she steered clear of any discussion about the SAS.

'Did you have time to read any of those articles?'

Too late.

'Er, I started the first article,' she began truthfully. 'I haven't had time to read any more.'

Also true. After the first paragraph, it had been abandoned in favour of watching *Escape to the Country*.

'They can be a bit heavy.'

More silence. The numbers were shooting along at speed and they were already at level 4. She couldn't waste this opportunity, she must speak. Her heart was hammering and her palms were sweating. What could she say?

'What did you do last night?' She really must learn to control her volume level when Logan was around. She had sounded loud and quite demanding.

'I …' he pulled a face as he tried to remember.

Above his head number 5 appeared and Ellie resisted the urge to grab him by the lapels and insist on an answer.

'Yes?' she encouraged.

'I … er…' A nervous twitch began to pull at the corner of his eye.

The lift shuddered to a halt and the doors began sliding slowly open.

Reluctantly Ellie stepped forward. 'I have to go,' she said giving him a look of disappointment.

'Sorry, I er, I was trying to remember. I went for a drink with some friends after work and then watched TV, I think.'

Not very informative but watching TV could be something they had in common. She should ask him which TV programme he'd watched, maybe he'd also been engrossed in *Escape to the Country*. Perhaps he was a fan like Ellie and it would be something they could talk about. He would see her in the lift and say, 'Hey Ellie, what did you think about last night's episode then. Wasn't that kitchen to die for?' It could become their thing.

She was in the entrance of the lift, her foot wedged against the door so it wouldn't begin to close. Mr Goodfellow was already doing his rounds of the office. He wasn't far away, heading directly towards her desk and she really needed to be sat there when he arrived.

'What was it?'

'Sorry?'

'Which programme,' she asked urgently.

'Programme?'

103

'Which programme did you watch?' She looked over her shoulder to check Mr Goodfellow's location. 'What was it?'

His eye twitched again as he desperately tried to remember. 'I, er … it was…'

'Yes?'

'A film! I remember! I watched *Black Hawk Down.*'

His shoulders sagged with relief as he slumped against the lift walls and grinned at Ellie. 'It's one of my favourite films and I watched the DVD again.'

Ellie couldn't help feeling let down. It wasn't *Escape to the Country*. It wasn't even *Fantasy Homes by the Sea* or *Love it or List it*. Maybe it was a film about bird watching in the countryside and he'd watched it because he loved nature, which could be seen as a vague connection to Ellie's obsession with moving to a thatched cottage situated deep in the countryside, but only a few minutes from the nearest Tesco. And Boots. Ellie didn't want to live very far away from a Boots.

'That's a shame,' she said disappointedly.

Logan looked confused, 'I enjoyed it.'

'Do you like hawks?' she asked optimistically.

'Hawks? Like … bird hawks?'

Were there any other kind, wondered Ellie. 'Yes. Do you like them?'

Logan looked baffled. 'I suppose so.'

Mr Goodfellow was bustling ever closer to her desk, she needed to get out of the lift but she was reluctant to move her foot and let the door shut. Chewing on her lip, she tried to think of a witty close to the conversation, something bright and funny that would make Logan chuckle all the way up to floor 7 and remember her with a smile.

'Well, bye,' she said, moving her foot and letting the doors begin closing. She stuck her face in the gap where she could still see Logan's face peering out. 'Bye!' she shouted, then sprinted to her chair so she was in place when Mr Goodfellow arrived, casting his beady eye over the team.

Laura was fidgeting at her desk.

'Was that Logan in the lift with you?' she asked excitedly.

Ellie nodded. She was busy googling Black Hawk Down. 'Yes, and I spoke to him!'

'Finally! What did you talk about?'

'I asked him what he did last night.'

Laura nodded, then frowned. 'Why?'

'Because I need to find out what he likes to do outside of work. See if there's any overlapping interest, something we could share.'

'Oh right. Things in common.'

'That's right.'

'And what *did* he do last night?'

'He watched Black Hawk Down. I thought it might be about birdwatching,' Ellie turned away from Google. 'But I don't think it is.'

Laura nodded sagely. 'Big war film, my Gareth loves it. It's about helicopters and fighting and men being real men.'

Ellie's face was disappointed. 'Not really my sort of thing.'

'Well, you can always say it's one of your favourites. Just read the reviews and then you can have a conversation about it. Gareth still thinks my favourite film is Terminator. I haven't had the heart to tell him I've never actually seen it.'

Ellie thought back to Fliss' email and shook her head. 'Best not,' she murmured. 'He already thinks I'm interested in statistical software,' she continued giving Laura a slightly disapproving glance. 'I think he needs to get to know the real me. I just need an opportunity to talk to him for a little bit longer and find out more about him, what he likes, what he doesn't like. There must be something that we have in common and that we can chat about.'

They both knuckled down to work and it was a couple of hours later that Ellie heard an excited Laura whisper, 'Look who's here.'

Logan was at the far end of the office, chatting to Mr Goodfellow. Ellie hadn't seen him arrive but one way or another he was going to have to walk past her desk to leave. The butterflies arrived full flight in her stomach.

'Brush your hair,' whispered Laura from behind the screen.

'My hair?' Ellie whipped out her compact and gasped in distress. She had been so caught up in her unexpected meeting with Logan that morning, she'd forgotten how wet she'd become. Her hair was still a mess, windblown and tangled. She had a smudge of mascara on one cheek and her lipstick hadn't survived her commute.

Frantically she ducked down and scrabbled through her bag for a brush and a tissue.

'Logan!' she heard Laura say enthusiastically.

Rubbing at her cheek and reapplying some lipstick, Ellie kept her head down as she grappled with her hair.

'Oh, er, hello Laura.'

'So, Black Hawk Down eh?'

'Sorry?'

'Ellie mentioned that you watched it last night.'

'Did she? Yes, I did. Sorry, Laura, I have to get …'

'What other films do you like?'

The brush became tangled in Ellie's still very damp hair and flinching she took it a little slower. It wasn't easy crouching next to her chair. She kept banging her head on her desk and her elbow was in her drawer.

'Films. Well, er, all sorts I suppose but I've got to…'

'Yes, but which ones Logan. Do you like romance?'

'Not really I …'

'Top Gun? Have you ever watched Top Gun?'

'Well yes, everybody has at some point haven't they?'

'That's a romance! So, you see, you do like romances.'

'If you say so …'

106

'And what about when you're not watching TV. What do you like to do?'

'Do?'

'Yes Logan!' Laura's voice was a little impatient and as Ellie gave herself a final check in her mirror, she could see Logan's feet moving around restlessly on the carpet.

'Yes, what do you do? Any sports?'

'Er, I play football on Saturday for …'

'Excellent! Hobbies?'

'Well, no, I don't have time …'

'No hobbies, okay. Social life?'

'What?'

'Pub, meals, friends? Do you have friends?'

'Of course I have friends!'

'And do you meet these friends in pubs?'

'Well, yes …'

'Good, good. Which one?'

'Which pub?'

'Yes, which pub.'

'I er, it depends on the night of the week. Sorry, Laura, I have to go …'

Finally happy with her appearance, Ellie stood up, plopping herself back on her chair. Logan jumped at her sudden appearance and peered warily under her desk.

'Ellie! There you are,' her friend said enthusiastically, as though Ellie appearing from under her desk was a common occurrence. 'Logan was just telling me all about the things he likes to do outside of work.'

'I think he needs to get back to his office,' said Ellie, examining Logan's face.

'Yes, in a minute. So, Logan, we didn't get to the bottom of which pub you go to when you meet your friends. On Friday for example, which pub would you be in on Friday night?'

Logan held the files he was holding out in front of him like a shield. 'Friday?' he asked weakly.

'Yes, where will you be going on Friday?'

Clearing his throat, he looked around, probably searching for the emergency exits thought Ellie.

'Laura, I think Logan needs to …'

'This Friday Logan! Where will you be?' Laura's voice brooked no arguments.

'A group of us from work go to the Flying Horse on Friday,' he advised inching backwards. 'Just for a couple of drinks.'

'What an amazing coincidence. The Flying Horse is exactly where Ellie and I were planning on going this Friday!'

'Were you?' asked Logan in surprise.

'Were we?' asked Ellie even more surprised.

'Yes! We've been told we should join you there, great night apparently.'

'It is?' The surprise level just kept increasing.

'Yes! You'll see us there this Friday, can't wait,' and waving him away with one hand, Laura pulled out her notebook and started writing.

Smiling apologetically, Ellie watched him walk towards the doors where he took the steps two at a time, seemingly in a hurry to reach the safety of the 7th floor.

'Laura, it sounded like you were interviewing him for goodness sake.'

'I was. You wanted to know what he liked and what he did, and know you do.' With a flourish, Laura tore off a sheet of paper and handed it to Ellie. 'There you go. You must be able to find something in common and in the meantime, remember to wear your glad rags on Friday because we are going to The Flying Horse after work,' and looking extraordinarily pleased with herself, Laura cracked her knuckles and started clearing her inbox.

Chapter 11

When 5:00 o'clock arrived on Friday evening, Ellie almost passed out from a mixture of fear and anticipation. She had spent the day failing to concentrate on anything but the thought of meeting Logan in The Flying Horse that evening and as the clock finally indicted that the working day was over, she and Laura flew into the Ladies to examine Ellie's appearance.

Her hair was still in the soft waves she had created by getting up an hour earlier than usual and her normally subdued day time makeup was being critically surveyed by Laura.

'You need more eyeliner, more mascara and more lippie,' she instructed. 'And undo a button of your blouse, you look like a librarian. Did you bring your other shoes?' She was rifling through the large plastic bag Ellie had brought with her containing anything that she may need including her straighteners, a spare skirt in case she spilt coffee on the one she was wearing, a spare blouse in case the coffee dribbled rather than spilt, a pair of shoes that had a much higher heel than Ellie normally wore at work, 2 packs of tights because the desks at work were cheap and nasty and they often lay in wait to snag on the unwary leg, plus all the makeup she possessed.

Ten minutes later, she was declared satisfactory by Laura.

'Are you sure you need to wear your coat?'

'It's minus 2 degrees out there, of course I need my coat!'

'Okay, as soon as we arrive at the pub take it off. And give it to me, don't have it over your arm.'

'Why not?'

'Because I don't want anything stopping him from seeing you. You, not your bloody awful coat.'

Slightly offended, Ellie pulled her oversize coat snuggly around her. It may be several years old and not exactly the height of fashion when purchased but it kept her warm which she felt was a more important quality.

'I'll carry your coat and your plastic bag,' instructed Laura. 'Make sure you stand up straight so he can see what a lovely figure you've got …'

'Laura!'

'What? You want him to notice you, don't you?'

'Yes but there's more to me than my figure!'

'Well, he can work that out later. I'll carry everything, you have your handbag and nothing else, no clutter.'

Nodding, Ellie pulled on her woollen hat only to have it snatched off by Laura.

'Are you mad! You can't turn up in that monstrosity.'

'It keeps my head warm,' protested Ellie.

'Well if all goes to plan you'll have Logan to keep you warm,' muttered Laura, shoving the hat in the plastic bag and turning Ellie in the direction of the door. 'Come on, let's do this.'

The Flying Horse was a few streets away from the office and it only took a couple of minutes for them to arrive. As they approached the main door, they spotted some of the accounts team and a couple of the IT group entering the building.

'Mm,' said Laura as they stepped inside the porch. 'Why do so many people come here for a Friday drink and why didn't we know anything about it?'

Ellie wondered if she should point out that Laura often described their co-workers as losers and dropouts and quite deliberately made Ellie go for a drink where, in Laura's words, the conversation would not send you to sleep. Pushing Ellie out of sight of the main bar, Laura pulled off her friend's coat, fluffed up her hair and ran a critical eye over her outfit. 'I don't suppose you'd consider undoing another button?'

110

'No.'

'Okay, it was worth a try. Let's get in there.'

Ellie would have preferred for Laura to walk in ahead of her. Her friend would not waste time dithering in the doorway or have to pluck up her courage before barging into the centre of the large group, all of whom were vaguely familiar. But Laura was weighed down, Ellie's coat over her arm along with her own, her handbag slung over one shoulder and Ellie's plastic bag tucked under one arm with her umbrella swinging from her fingers and she could barely see where she was going, let alone lead the cavalry charge. So it was left to Ellie to walk as confidently as she could towards the large group of work colleagues gathered around the bar.

'Ellie!' came a welcoming voice from the crowd. It was Joshua, large and pink-cheeked, beer in hand. 'Fancy seeing you here. Didn't know you were a Flying Horser. Is that Laura behind you?'

Several people turned to smile and shout out a greeting as Ellie stood, unencumbered with anything other than a neat handbag draped over one shoulder, her slim waist shown to its advantage by her fitted skirt, her hair laying in burnished waves across the shoulders of her blouse which had precisely one button open. She thought she detected a couple of admiring glances from various directions, they were more used to seeing her in leggings and a jumper with her hair still windblown from the morning and an absence of lipstick.

Laura meanwhile was hardly visible, laden down with their coats, bags and scarves.

'Does she often act as your pack mule?' laughed one of the IT team, receiving a glare from Laura in return as she hauled her small pile onto an empty chair.

'I'll get the drinks,' she muttered in Ellie's ear as she brushed past. 'You stay here and try to look interesting.'

Adopting what she hoped was an interesting expression, Ellie stayed where she was, peeping from beneath her lashes and hoping to spot a familiar face in the crowd around her.

'You came,' said a soft voice by her side and turning, she found Logan at her shoulder.

'Yes, yes we came,' nodded Ellie somewhat unnecessarily.

They smiled at each other and tried to look relaxed as they examined the crowd until Ellie dared a peep of the corner of her eye in his direction and found that Logan was doing the same. Blushing they averted their eyes hastily.

Ellie was trawling her memory for something interesting to say. Laura had given her the rundown on *Black Hawk Down* earlier in the day but she was struggling to remember anything of the plot. She'd never had this problem conversing with Carl. But there again, she had never felt this way about him. She heard Logan clear his throat and wondered if he was having the same difficulty. Whenever she'd seen him in the lobby he had been chatting to his friends, even laughing, throwing back his head and showing even white teeth. Was it a good sign that he seemed to be struggling as much as Ellie? Or did it mean that he found her boring and difficult to speak to? Was her lack of Karaoke experience holding her back?

Laura returned, erupting through the crowd with two glasses of white wine in her hand.

'Logan!' she exclaimed, sending a beam of triumph in Ellie's direction. 'Fancy seeing you here.'

He frowned. 'But I told you I came every Friday,' he pointed out. 'And you said ...'

'It's great to see you,' interrupted Laura. 'Really great. I told Ellie that we might bump into you tonight. I'd heard that you came here as well.'

'Yes, I told you ...'

'Lovely! Well, Ellie was all for going somewhere else.' Ellie, about to take a sip of wine, stared at her friend in astonishment. 'You're lucky that I could talk her into coming. All our friends wanted her to go to The Leaning

Wagon tonight. They'll be missing her there now! Life and soul of the evening is our Ellie.'

Logan looked at Ellie in surprise and she cringed. Laura had made it sound as though she were the star performer at a Thank God it's Friday event.

'Right,' he murmured faintly, taking a deep drink from his pint and looking at Ellie curiously. 'I see.'

Looking pleased with herself, Laura sent a little wink in Ellie's direction. 'Leave it to me, honey,' she whispered, 'I'll make sure tonight is a success.'

The crowd was growing bigger by the minute, newcomers pushing to get through to the bar and shoulders rubbing as everyone jostled for space. Holding onto her wine and wondering what to say next, Ellie stumbled slightly as someone knocked against her, losing her balance as she clung onto her handbag and her glass.

Logan's arm shot out to stop her from falling and she was thrown against him, an electric shock zipping its way down her body. With a gasp she tried to right herself but something was pressing against her, stopping her from moving and pushing her against Logan's chest. Looking over her shoulder she found it was Laura, leaning against her with one hand in the small of Ellie's back keeping her firmly in the circle of Logan's arms.

'Whoops, sorry you two!' said Laura happily. 'I lost my balance for a minute there.'

Ellie's heart was thumping so hard she was surprised Logan couldn't feel it. Her breath was coming in short bursts and her entire body tingled as she relished the feel of his skin against her own. Laura moved her weight and suddenly Ellie was free. She didn't move. She could smell his aftershave and feel the warmth of his body, maybe she would stay here for a while.

'Sorry Ellie,' he said quietly, still holding her close. 'I thought you were going to fall.' His face was serious, his eyes looking deeply into her own and as Ellie gazed back she felt as though they were the only two people in the room. The swirl of chatter and laughter drifted away, the crowds around them vanished and it was just Logan and herself, pressed against each other, staring into each other's eyes. Clinging onto the moment, she prayed it would last forever.

'Logan! There you are, I was beginning to think you weren't coming tonight.'

Ellie let her hand linger on his chest a moment longer, imprinting the feeling in her thoughts so she could relive it, again and again, later in the evening.

'Logan! It's so crowded, I couldn't find you.'

His eyes were still tangled with Ellie's but the voice wouldn't stop, it wouldn't go away.

'Logan.'

He blinked as though to release himself and Ellie wanted to cry out for him to stay exactly where he was.

'Logan!'

A young woman appeared at their side, shining blonde hair, carefully arranged around a face that was peering over Ellie's shoulder and gazing adoringly at Logan.

Ellie heard Laura give a disparaging sniff. 'Hello, Harriet.'

'Laura. You don't usually come here on a Friday.'

'We're always here,' answered Laura in a disinterested tone.

'I've never seen you.'

'Well, I've never seen you either.'

'Me! I'm always here.'

'Really? Then why have I never seen you?'

The two glared at each other until Harriet blinked, looking away with a shrug and laying her hand on Logan's arm.

'Hello, Logan.' She spoke in a soft breathy voice that Ellie immediately envied. 'There's a lot of us here tonight isn't there? There's barely room to stand.' Stepping closer she tossed her head so blonde hair drifted onto his shoulder.

'Oh look! There's a table free over there,' she nodded her head in the direction of an empty table at one side of the room. 'Shall we grab it?' she asked, fluttering her lashes coquettishly.

'Bloody Harriet from accounts,' whispered Laura behind Ellie. 'Right cow! If she's got her sights on Logan, we're in trouble. She won't be struggling for things to say to him.'

'Logan?' The breathy voice sounded a little more strident now. 'Logan, shall we go sit at that table?'

'You need to do something, don't let her take Logan anywhere! You won't get him back!' Laura said urgently in Ellie's ear.

'Logan, let's sit down somewhere we can talk.' The breathiness had returned as she tugged his arm giggling softly. 'Come on.'

Logan's eyes finally left Ellie's, the arm that had been around her shoulders slid away and the room seemed suddenly chilly.

'Excellent idea Harriet.' Laura shoved Ellie in the direction of the empty table at the side of the room. 'Come on everybody, let's sit down!'

There was a short scuffle as Laura stood in front of Harriet who brought her elbow up to land viciously in Laura's ribs making her double over and gasp and giving Harriet the vital seconds she needed to sidestep Ellie and plant herself on the chair next to Logan, a victorious grin on her face.

A furious Laura dragged two chairs opposite them and shoved Ellie into the one facing Logan, their knees almost touching beneath the table and their eyes on a collision course. Setting his pint down on the table, Logan gave her a shy smile.

His mouth opened and Ellie thought he was about to say something to her.

'I watched the film you mentioned,' said Harriet in the breathy little voice, leaning against him so she could speak softly into his ear. Ellie noticed Laura's knuckles whiten. 'It was really interesting.'

Ellie wondered if it was *Black Hawk Down*. A few more people joined them at the table, relieving the pressure at the bar and Ellie was vaguely aware of someone pulling up a chair and sitting on her other side.

'Did you like it?' asked Logan, his attention suddenly back on Harriet.

Ellie leaned forward, she wanted to hear Harriet's reply.

'Do you like films?' asked the figure next to her. Ellie tutted, she hadn't been able to catch Harriet answer but she was giggling again and had her hand firmly back on Logan's sleeve.

'Sometimes,' she answered over her shoulder. She watched Logan lean closer to Harriet so he could hear her better,

'My name's Jeff.'

Ellie was trying to eavesdrop. Why was Harriet using that silly little girl voice and half whispering? It was impossible to work out what she was saying.

'I work with Logan.'

Laura was clearly having the same problem. 'Speak up Harriet,' she yelled across the table making everybody jump. 'We can't hear you.'

'You're Ellie, aren't you?'

Harriet glared, her lips thinning. 'We were having a private conversation actually,' she snapped and Logan's cheeks went pink as everyone looked at him.

'We were just talking about films we'd seen,' supplied Logan hastily as Laura kept her eyes fixed beadily on Harriet.

'Logan's mentioned you.'

At last, he had Ellie's attention and she turned back to Jeff's slightly receding hairline and developing beer belly.

'Really?'

'Yeah. Something about you being interested in what we do upstairs.'

116

Oh God, another conversation about SAS.

'Right,' she murmured.

'Not many people think statistical analysis is interesting,' continued Jeff thoughtfully. 'It's nice to meet someone who realises how fascinating it is.'

'What else did Logan say?'

'What about?'

'About me! Did he say anything else about me?'

It sounded desperate but Ellie needed all the help she could get and as a work colleague, maybe Jeff could give her some valuable insight into Logan.

'No.'

Or maybe not.

Losing interest, Ellie returned to watching Harriet and Logan. She needed to have a conversation with him. If Fliss knew that right now she was sitting in a pub with Logan only feet away, she would tell Ellie to make sure she spoke to him, initiated contact, made him look into her eyes.

'How's the football going Logan?' asked Harriet.

Damn, thought Ellie. Exactly the question she should have asked.

Jeff snorted. 'Bloody awful,' he answered. 'We haven't won in weeks.'

Ignoring him, Harriet kept her eyes pinned on Logan.

'We're having a bad spell,' he admitted with a grimace. 'That's all.'

'You interested in football Ellie?' It was Jeff again. Was it Ellie's imagination or had his chair moved ever so slightly nearer to her own?

'Not really.'

His face fell. 'What do you like?'

She liked watching Logan and being able to hear what he said, which was becoming increasingly difficult with Jeff chattering in her ear.

'Oh, er all sorts of things.'

Harriet had adopted the little whispery tone again and Logan had been forced to lean closer to hear what she was saying.

Turning sideways Ellie looked at Jeff. 'Do you know Logan well?'

'Logan? Yeah, we're mates.'

Very informative. 'And what does he like to do.'

At Jeff's raised eyebrows she carried on. 'I mean, you two, as friends. What do you like to do, together, you and Logan?'

Shrugging his shoulders Jeff looked thoughtfully into his pint. 'Loads of things.'

'Like what? What does he ... what do you like?'

Fidgeting slightly under Ellie's rather direct stare, Jeff seemed to be struggling for an answer. 'Well we both play football in the local business league,' he said proudly.

'Yes, football. And what else?'

'Well, erm, well, let's see ...'

Ellie was beginning to suspect that Logan and Jeff had less in common that Jeff had led her to believe.

'Okay,' she sighed. 'Tell me about the football.'

His face brightened. 'We train every Tuesday night, at least we're supposed to but we usually end up at the pub.' Which could explain the lack of winning matches thought Ellie. 'And we play every Saturday.'

Her mind began to race with possibilities and her eyes rested on Jeff's rather round face as she explored them.

'Do many people come to watch you?'

He shook his head. 'No, not really. Other teams have supporters. One of the insurance firms have just about every member of their staff turn up to cheer them on. A couple of the IT boys sometimes come to watch us and somebody from accounts once came. But generally, there's no-one there.'

Ellie tilted her head thoughtfully. 'That's not very encouraging,' she murmured.

'You're right,' said Jeff with feeling. 'It would be nice to get some support.'

On the other side of her, Laura was becoming fidgety with the lack of interaction between Logan and Ellie. Turning her back on Jeff, Ellie caught her eye and mouthed 'football' in her direction.

Pulling a face Laura raised her eyebrows. 'What?' she whispered.

'Football. Mention football again. Discreetly.'

Looking baffled, Laura obliged.

'Football!' she said loudly across the table. Everybody stopped and waited for her to continue. She looked at Ellie and shrugged her shoulders.

For a moment Ellie wondered if Fliss could be right and that having Laura with her was not a good idea.

Grimacing Ellie jumped in. 'Jeff tells me that no-one from work turns up to support you at your football matches.'

Logan shook his head. 'Unfortunately not,' he agreed with a sigh as Jeff puffed himself up with pride at being quoted by Ellie.

'That's a shame,' she continued, seeing Laura catch on and give her an encouraging wink. 'Perhaps you'd do better if you had some fellow workers watching?'

'Absolutely!' agreed Laura. 'Couldn't agree more.'

Even Harriet was sitting up a little straighter, her eyes narrowing as she listened.

'Wow,' said Jeff with a grin. 'I'm glad you agree, it makes me feel better already.'

Ellie ignored him, her eyes were fixed on Logan and she willed him to meet her gaze. Her hands were becoming clammy, her heart racing. Look at me, she willed him, look at me.

'It's really nice of you to be so interested,' Jeff added, looking pleased with himself. 'And especially since we've only just met …'

119

'I think that someone should go to the next match,' suggested Ellie, forcing the words out of a dry mouth.

'You are amazing,' continued Jeff. 'Absolutely amazing to think of us ...'

'So I'll come and watch you,' she finished in a rush. 'I'll come and be your supporter,' she said, her eyes still pinned on Logan's face, waiting for his reaction.

She saw Laura's approving smile. She caught a glimpse of Harriet's furious expression but her eyes didn't move from Logan.

'Brilliant! It's a date!' shouted Jeff. 'Ellie you're a star!'

'What?' Ellie swung a bemused look at Jeff. 'What? No, I didn't mean ...'

'What a good idea Ellie,' said Harriet quickly, the breathy little voice suddenly loud and clear. 'And if you're going to support Jeff, I'll support Logan. What do you think?' She placed a hand very firmly on his arm, her nails digging in. 'Is that a date Logan?' and smiling happily she picked up her wine glass and tipped it gratefully in Ellie's direction.

FROM: Ellie Henshaw <Elliebellshenshaw@livewell.co.uk>
To: Fliss Carmichael <agonyauntfliss@digitalrecorder.com>
Date: 02/04/2020

Dear Fliss

I'm so glad that you don't mind me continuing writing to you. Laura says the advice you give is just common sense and it's exactly what she told me to do weeks ago. She said if I left it to her she could get Logan to ask me out in no time at all. But her plans don't always work out and I would prefer to follow advice from someone who knows what they're talking about. I also feel that you and I have an extra connection because you've been through the same thing.

I've tried to follow through with everything that you've suggested. I had another conversation with Logan in the lift. This time it was just the two of us and I didn't shout at him or act as though I was about to attack him. He remembered my name, which made me absurdly happy and he asked about the SAS articles. I think at some point I will have to explain that it was just a misunderstanding because I can't make any sense of them at all and I think you were right, we must get to know each other honestly. I wouldn't want it to become a problem in 20 years like your dart lady.

I found out that he goes to The Flying Horse every Friday night with a group of people from the office, so I went along. Actually, Laura was the one who found out and she arranged for us both to go along, so I could talk to him, meet him outside of work and build up a connection, like you suggested.

It didn't go entirely to plan. There's a girl called Harriet from our accounts department who also goes and Laura has found out since that she's had her eye on Logan for ages. Harriet and Laura got into a bit of a scuffle but I didn't mind because Logan and I were having a good chat. We didn't say much, in fact, it was less of a chat and more of a moment but we were definitely connecting. I offered to watch Logan play football, I thought it would give us a joint interest outside of work and be something just the two of us would be involved in. I'm not sure what went wrong but I ended up agreeing to go on a date with someone called Jeff. Then Harriet told Logan that she would go watch him play football so now Logan and I are going on a date, we'll be at the same event at the same time, we'll just be with other people. I must admit, it's not how I imagined it!

Maybe I should have told you about Carl in my first email. I was with him for a while, two years, well, nearly three. The day I saw Logan, I fell in love with him and I understood that I wasn't meant to be with Carl. He hadn't proposed but everyone expected us to get married, even Carl. My parents would talk about the wedding as though it was never in doubt, Carl would talk about our house, our future even our children as though we were already married. I began to wonder if he ever intended to ask me or whether I would wake up one day and find that the date had been set, the dress chosen and all I had to do was turn up. But when I saw Logan I realised that I couldn't marry Carl, not if I could have those sorts of feelings for another man. I know it sounds crazy, maybe it is crazy, but Logan has the kind of effect on me that no-one else ever has.

Carl didn't take it very well, in fact, he doesn't believe I mean it. He's convinced I'm just having a wobble about our relationship and that I'll change my mind. I suppose I didn't mention him to you because I wanted to concentrate on Logan. And yes, it was impetuous, but I thought it was the best thing for both of us, to end things before they became even more complicated. I don't regret what I did, although I do regret that I hurt him.

I'm sorry that the lingerie thing didn't work out. To be honest, it was Laura's suggestion and she said it always works like a dream for her. But I don't think that you should give up. You told me how much your husband means to you, how very much in love you were. I don't think that it's wrong to try and rescue those feeling. He probably feels just the same about you but so many things happen in life, they take up our time and our thoughts and we sometimes let go of the one thing that's most important to us in an attempt to balance everything else. Maybe he's just forgotten how things used to be between you and he needs a reminder of the love you not only had for each other but showed to each other.

I hope you don't think this is a rude question, but I was wondering if you and your husband have a family? You've never mentioned children so I presumed that it was just the two of you. I can imagine that worrying about all this with a family to consider as well as each other must be difficult. Do children make a marriage stronger I wonder? Or just more difficult.

Anyway, all I can suggest is that you remind him how things used to be between you both when work wasn't the most important thing in his life. Not by wearing lingerie, but in the way you behaved towards each other, maybe a younger more carefree version of yourselves, things you would do or say to each other. Sorry if that sounds a bit drippy, this is all new to me but maybe it's worth a try. You're helping me so much that I would love to be able to offer you something in return.

Thank you again for listening

Ellie

Chapter 12

Waving goodbye to Jasper, Fliss was relieved to have the house to herself for an hour and, making herself another coffee, she curled up in her favourite spot and thought long and hard about her marriage. Ellie's advice was simple and straightforward and, thought Fliss, to the point. Jasper still loved her, she loved him. Perhaps this was exactly what was needed, a gentle reminder of how things used to be between the two of them and maybe then he would begin to understand how much the balance had changed. She would do exactly what Ellie advised and work on resetting her marriage to a happier time, she would think back to all the romantic gestures they used to make, all the everyday things that had made them who they were and hope they served to give Jasper the incentive he needed. The lingerie would stay in the back of the wardrobe, which would be a huge relief to Fliss and she would concentrate on reminding him how much they used to enjoy each other's company.

Thinking about the incident in the kitchen with her beautiful satin corset and Freddie's panicked eyes, brought the colour flooding back into her cheeks. It had been positively mortifying and she was in no rush to try lingerie as a solution to anything ever again.

By the time Jasper had said goodbye to a startled Freddie and gone upstairs to find his wife, Fliss had been buried beneath the most sensible pair of pyjamas she could find with her large fleecy dressing gown wrapped around her body.

He had stared at his wife with bemused eyes. 'Whatever were you thinking?'

Fliss had been sitting at her dressing table, brushing her hair energetically, her cheeks still pink with embarrassment as she'd met Jasper's gaze through her mirror. 'I thought it would be a nice welcome home for you.'

'Well Freddie certainly appreciated it.' Jasper had sat at the bottom of the bed and watched her. 'I don't know which one of us was the most surprised.'

'I was making an effort,' she'd said stiffly. 'Something we both need to do!'

'What for?'

'Jasper! Didn't you hear anything I said the other evening? About how worried I was that we were drifting apart, how things between us seem different?'

He had shaken his head with a slight hint of impatience. 'I was listening, darling and I told you, there is nothing to worry about! I couldn't love you any more than I do, I really think you're letting your imagination run away with you. Work is ….'

'It's nothing to do with work,' Fliss had snapped. 'Well, maybe a little. I don't mind you being busy, but these days you don't seem to think about anything else. There doesn't seem to be an us anymore.'

'Nonsense!'

'Why won't you even consider that there may be a problem?'

'Because there isn't. We are exactly the same as we've always been, I love you, you love me, we're happy. I know I've been very busy lately but there are all sorts of opportunities coming along that I'm trying to take advantage of.'

'You've been busy all our married life, this is different, it's something I can't put my finger on …'

'We go out far more than most other couples I know.'

'Yes, because you need to catch up on something work-related or have a business meeting over a meal, that's not *us* going out ….'

'We have some amazing holidays.'

'The last three holidays we've had have been with other people!'

'The Broadhurst's let us stay in that magnificent villa of theirs for a fortnight, we could hardly ask them to move out so we could be alone.'

'But what about *us* Jasper. What happened to us? What happened to the couple who used to be quite happy spending an evening together, not surrounded by other people but quite alone?'

'This is ridiculous Fliss, there is nothing wrong with our relationship!'

And he had stalked into the bathroom, leaving Fliss frustrated and unhappy and with no choice but to jump into bed and try and pretend that the last hour had never happened.

Jumping up and shaking off the memory, Fliss tried to be positive. There were other ways she could work on Jasper, other ways she could remind him how their relationship used to be and wondering if she would have an aversion to cream satin for the rest of her life, she went upstairs to get changed.

When Jasper came home that evening, the house was full of the rich aroma of beef bourguignon and there was a bottle of red wine next to a couple of glasses on the kitchen table. Fliss had left the corset at the back of the wardrobe and was dressed in jeans and a top as she cooked and stirred and listened to Michael Bublé describe how very much he loved her.

'Hello darling,' she called out as he appeared in the doorway. 'I hope you're hungry, I've made lots!' and she reached up to place a warm kiss on his lips.

Seasoning the casserole, she turned back to him in time to see the wince.

'Sorry darling, I had a huge and very late lunch. I didn't think to let you know,' he apologised. 'You don't usually make anything without checking.'

He was right. In years gone by, she would make something delicious and have it ready for when her

126

handsome husband walked through the door. They would open a bottle of wine and sit at the table chatting for hours. These days they went out far more and if they did have a rare evening at home, Fliss would check with Jasper before she made any effort in the kitchen.

'It's okay, I should have asked.' She dropped the lid back on her casserole dish a little more forcefully than she had intended. 'Not to worry, it often tastes better the next day.'

'Oh, don't forget, we're having dinner with the Bensons tomorrow, I need to talk to Barney about an idea I have for an article,' he reminded, his back to her as he looked through the post she had placed on the dresser.

Fliss forced another smile. 'How lovely,' she said insincerely. 'Can't wait. Why don't we go earlier and have a drink before the Benson's arrive, just the two of us?'

'Okay, if you want to.' Jasper gave her a distracted smile and turned to leave the kitchen. 'By the way, I have to go back out tonight,' he threw over his shoulder. 'The piece I'm writing on local councils needs a bit more of a punch and I've just managed to get an interview with one of the treasurers. He should give me a few interesting quotes but he can only do tonight.'

He was halfway upstairs, his words floating down to a tense Fliss who was now sloshing wine into one of the glasses.

'Can't be helped,' she muttered through gritted teeth.

His wardrobe door opened and closed and she could hear him moving around upstairs as she emptied her glass.

'Sorry if I've spoiled any plans.' He was back, having changed his shirt and tie. 'I would have gone straight there but I needed to pick up some paperwork first.'

He walked past Fliss and into his study, returning with a folder. 'You hadn't arranged anything had you?' he asked, looking through the papers in his hand rather than at Fliss.

'Just a pleasant evening at home. A home-cooked meal, a bottle of wine, a little time together.'

Grabbing his briefcase and adding the file, he reached over to give her a kiss on the cheek while looking at his phone. 'Good, then I haven't ruined anything important. Don't wait up.'

The following day, making an excuse to leave the office she sat in her car in the underground car park with her phone in her hand nibbling on her bottom lip anxiously. In the early days of their relationship, they used to phone each other countless times. Fliss would call just to say hello and hear his voice and Jasper often phoned to tell his wife how he was missing her and very much looking forward to seeing her that evening.

She dialled his number.

'Jasper Carmichael,' came his disembodied voice.

'It's me silly,' giggled Fliss.

'Oh hello, darling. Anything wrong?'

'No. I just wanted to hear your voice I suppose.'

'My voice? You can't hear me?'

'I didn't say I couldn't hear you, I said I wanted to hear you.'

'I can hear you okay.'

Fliss gave up. 'It was a shame about last night.'

Her voice was low and intimate, mainly because she didn't want anybody else in the car park to overhear her conversation. She could imagine the office gossip if it was discovered that Fliss Carmichael was making suggestive calls to her husband when she should be solving the issues of a distraught nation.

'Last night?'

'You having to go out.'

'Oh right, yes. Did you want something?'

'Well only the obvious,' said Fliss with another little giggle.

'What's obvious?'

Closing her eyes, Fliss wondered if making a sexy call to your husband whilst hiding in your car should be this difficult.

'You. That's what I want,' she persisted, becoming a little impatient and losing the sexy tone briefly. She took a breath and lowered her voice. 'I just wanted to hear your voice darling, I missed you last night and I just can't stop thinking about what we could have done ....'

She heard a bang and a couple of blips and then Jasper's voice returned. 'I was on loudspeaker,' he explained. 'It was a bad connection. Freddie said it sounded like a sex chat call!'

'Freddie?'

'Yes, he's just popped by the office to discuss a few things. So, what did you want?'

In the cold, half-empty car park, Fliss turned hot with embarrassment.

'Freddie heard me?'

'Yes, we both did, at least we were trying to. What were you saying?'

'Or, er nothing.' Goodness me, Freddie must think she was sex-starved. 'Er nothing, just checking the arrangements for tonight. With the Bensons.'

'I put it on the calendar,' answered Jasper. 'It's all there.'

'Of course. I'll check it, sorry to disturb you. Bye,' and ending the call as quickly as she could, Fliss flew back into her office, refusing to contemplate what Freddie must be imagining.

That evening they met the Bensons and Fliss sat through a meal she didn't really want to eat and watched her charming husband laugh and joke and generally hold court around the table. When she reminded Jasper of her idea of drinks beforehand, he agreed but then arrived home late and immediately made a phone call while Fliss sat waiting, dressed and ready to go. In the end, they'd arrived only 5 minutes before the Bensons and the champagne Jasper ordered arrived just in time to be enjoyed by all the party. Lifting a glass in her direction, he sent her an admiring glance, squeezing her hand lovingly when someone mentioned how pretty her dress was, kissing the top of her head as he helped her pull her coat on and taking the time on the drive back to tell her how lovely she looked. They were the picture of a happy and contented couple.

When they arrived home, Fliss stood silently in the hallway as Jasper dropped another kiss on her cheek and told her again how beautiful she looked before wandering into his study and opening his laptop. After 5 minutes, she hung up her coat, went upstairs to bed and was asleep before he finally finished work for the evening.

Making sure she was up early the next morning, Fliss spent half an hour in her own study and by the time Jasper came downstairs, she had finished her task and had a cup of coffee waiting for him.

'Morning,' she said brightly, kissing him as he reached out for his cup.

'Morning,' he smiled, kissing her back. 'You look nice!'

The slim-fitting emerald dress emphasised her creamy complexion and clung to her still tiny waist. She was already wearing her heels, which would normally be slipped on just as she left the house and she was wearing a little more makeup than she usually employed for a day in the office.

'Thank you,' she said examining her dress and smoothing out a non-existent wrinkle. 'I thought ...'

Looking up she found that Jasper had already moved away and was scrolling through his phone. Walking around the kitchen table, Fliss stood in front of him. 'I wondered if you wanted to meet for lunch?' she continued.

'Lunch?' He didn't look up. Something had caught his attention and a small frown appeared on his forehead. 'That sounds lovely. Excellent idea.'

Fliss smiled. She would book a table at the lovely little bistro they often visited, it was perfect for a quick weekday lunch.

'But I don't think I can do today. Rain check?'

She wondered if it would be totally unreasonable to take his phone and throw it out of the kitchen window. Not too far, somewhere he would be able to retrieve it fairly quickly after they'd had a proper conversation.

'Shame,' she said instead. 'It's been a long time since we met for lunch.'

'Yes,' murmured Jasper, his thumbs deftly tapping his screen and sending a message to someone he obviously found more interesting than his wife. 'We'll arrange something soon,' and he dropped a kiss on her forehead and was gone. Glaring at the back of his head, Fliss kicked off her shoes and watched them hit the wall and roll under the table. Perhaps she should have suggested inviting Freddie, that would have guaranteed his interest. She could only hope that the rest of her plans for the day were more successful.

It was an hour later when her phone rang. Seeing Jasper's name on the screen she looked around to see who else was in the office and answered, a smile on her lips.

'Hello, darling.'

'What were you thinking?'

The smile disappeared. It wasn't the reaction she had expected.

'Didn't you like it?' she asked warily.

'Like it? Have you gone crazy?'

'It was just a little surprise.'

'It was certainly that! For both of us.'

'Both... both of you?'

'Yes, both of us. I was in a really important meeting with Freddie about the new show. The first proper meeting we've had about the format of each session, how I would lead it, how I would be the anchor that holds it all together.'

'Oh.' Fliss voice was small. 'You always go to your office first thing and…'

'Not today! Today I went straight to the meeting and you imagine how I felt when I opened my diary and out fell a hundred little red hearts all saying '*I love you.*' It was certainly a surprise.'

'There wasn't a hundred,' Fliss said defensively. 'There were 18. One for each year we've been married.'

'It seemed like a hundred when they were all pouring out and falling over my desk and the floor and Freddie. It was so embarrassing. You should have seen his face!'

Fliss could imagine. So far this week he'd seen her parading around the kitchen in her underwear, heard her tell her husband how much she wanted him during a failed attempt at a sex call and now this.

'What did he say?' She didn't really want to know but something made her ask anyway.

'He said I'm a very lucky man,' Jasper told her begrudgingly. 'He said Mags would never do anything like that.'

Fliss could tell from Jasper's tone that he wished his own wife hadn't bothered.

'I used to leave you little messages all the time.' Her voice was sad. She was staring out of the window at the rain splattering against the glass and wondering why this all seemed so very hard. The one thing she had always relied on was the ability to talk to her husband about anything. 'You used to keep them in your desk drawer,' she reminded him, wondering where they had all gone. Probably dropped in the bin during the clear out resulting from his last promotion. Bigger office, bigger desk, bigger drawers and no place for the silly love notes Fliss used to leave in his diary each morning.

There was a long pause.

'I still have them actually.'

132

Fliss was surprised. 'You do?'

'Of course.' Fliss heard a sigh whisper down the line. 'I'm sorry, it was just a surprise and it was in front of Freddie.'

'I wanted to remind you of....' Suddenly Fliss couldn't go through with another conversation about how she felt their relationship had changed, Jasper clearly wasn't listening.

'Remind me of what?'

'Oh, nothing. Sorry I embarrassed you.'

'Freddie said I'm lucky and I am.' Another faint sigh. 'Look, why don't I take you out tomorrow?'

'With Freddie?'

'No.'

'With Ross?'

'No.'

'With the Bensons?'

'Not with anybody, just the two of us.'

She couldn't help the grin that started to spread across her face. 'Sounds lovely,' she agreed. Maybe the hearts had worked after all. 'I look forward to it,' and she put the phone down and got back to answering 'D*isgusted of Huddersfield*' feeling far more optimistic.

Chapter 13

Fliss worked hard and cleared her desk so she could leave work early and have plenty of time to prepare for the evening ahead. She took a long bath filled with her favourite scented bubbles and rubbed vast quantities of body butter into her skin until it felt soft as silk. Her short red hair was carefully styled and she spent a long time applying her makeup before she slid into a black dress with a slightly daring split along one thigh, allowing a glimpse of long legs dressed in sheer stockings.

Lipstick and perfume were applied and finally, Fliss was happy. Walking carefully down the stairs in sky-high heels, she left her coat and bag on the hallway table before perching on the very edge of the settee, legs crossed at the ankle so as not to crease her dress and waited patiently for the sound of car tyres on the gravel. A table had been reserved and a taxi booked to collect them in, Fliss checked her watch, 25 minutes. Jasper was cutting it a little fine but he always went to work in a suit and tie so wouldn't have to get changed. As long as he was home before the taxi arrived, all would be well and taking several calming breaths, Fliss continued to wait.

15 minutes later she was slightly less patient and fidgeting a great deal more. Where on earth was he, she wondered crossly? Why hadn't he left work early to make sure he was home in time? Maybe not 3 hours earlier as Fliss had done, she doubted he would want to spend an hour meditating in a bath full of bubbles or shave his legs, but early enough so she wouldn't be sat anxiously waiting for him. Glancing at her watch again, Fliss decided that if he didn't arrive home soon, she would phone and suggest that she took the taxi alone and they meet in town. It was that or take the taxi driver hostage until Jasper finally arrived.

Another 5 minutes passed and she abandoned the settee to pace angrily around the living room, constantly walking to the front door and peering out of the glass pane to see if her husband's car was about to pull into their driveway. Her phone was clutched in her hand but so far she'd resisted the urge to call, if he was driving he might pull over to answer making him even later. She was clenching her teeth so hard her head was beginning to throb but suddenly she saw car headlights shine through the hedge and gave a huge sigh of relief. He was here. Thank Goodness!

At the same moment her phone rang, making her jump and pulling on her coat she pressed answer, as she peeped out, waiting for Jasper's figure to arrive at the front door.

'Fliss darling,' came his slightly breathless voice. 'I'm so sorry!'

Staring at her phone, she took another look outside. The car by the front door was now near enough for her to see Zoom Taxi Service written on the front door.

'Where are you?' she asked, grabbing her bag and checking her hair in the mirror. 'Are you still at the office?'

'Yes, I tried to get away but …'

'It doesn't matter.' She was trying to sound understanding but decided reasonable was the best she could manage. 'The taxi has just arrived, I'll meet you in the restaurant.'

'Sorry darling …. I'm afraid that's not possible.'

The taxi blared his horn, impatient after 40 seconds of waiting.

'What do you mean?' Reasonable was now also out of the question and Fliss' voice had taken on a note of decided hostility.

'A last-minute meeting was called. I know you were looking forward to us going out tonight, I was looking forward to it as well but I had to go to the meeting …'

'Are you still there?'

'It's just winding up.'

'Then I'll wait in the restaurant and you can come along after it's finished.' Fliss stood in the hallway staring at her reflection in the mirror. Her pale face stared back. 'I'm sure the restaurant won't mind if you're a little late.'

'Yes, well, er … I'm not sure how much longer it will last ….'

'I'll wait,' said Fliss in a firm voice. 'You said it was winding up.'

'Yes, it is...'

'Then we can meet at the restaurant.'

'I'm sorry darling but we can't. I've already cancelled the table.'

The taxi sounded his horn again.

'You've cancelled the reservation?'

'Yes. I thought it was for the best. We can always go out another night, can't we? When I don't have meetings to worry about and …'

'When?'

'Well, I can't do tomorrow but …

'When did you cancel the table?'

'Oh, about an hour ago when ….'

'You cancelled the table and then you phoned me?'

'Well, I realised I was unlikely to make it and …'

'You cancelled the table and left me standing here for the last hour, knowing I would be getting ready, knowing I *would* be ready. And you didn't phone me?'

'Ah, sorry. I was trying to find the time to give you a ring and it's been really busy.'

The horn blared out and throwing open the front door, Fliss stormed over to the waiting driver.

'JUST A MINUTE!' she screamed, resisting the temptation to kick the door to reinforce her message. 'Just wait a minute!'

'I'm sorry Fliss! I should have phoned you earlier I know but …'

'I wasn't talking to you.' Taking a deep breath, Fliss walked back towards the house. 'I was talking to the taxi driver. Who, unlike you, is here. He arrived on time and is currently waiting to take me to a restaurant which you cancelled an hour ago because you decided you *might* still be in a meeting.'

'I can tell you're upset,' began Jasper in an injured tone, 'but it wasn't quite like that.'

'Really? Well, we can talk about it when you get home.' Fliss looked back at the driver who had defiantly set the clock but was keeping his hands away from the horn.

'Yes, of course, although I might be a bit late.'

'What?'

If Jasper had been able to see the expression on his wife's face he may not have continued.

'Bearing in mind that I had to cancel the restaurant ...'

'You didn't *have* to cancel, you *chose* to cancel.'

'Yes, well, bearing in mind that the reservation is now cancelled, I agreed to meet Freddie so we can go over a few details about the new show.'

'Freddie. You're meeting Freddie?'

'Yes, I'll try not to be home too late darling. And I'll make this up to you, we'll rearrange ... oh, I've got to go. See you later,' and the line went dead, leaving Fliss with her phone still pressed to her ear and a wave of anger beginning to gather in her chest.

She was still wearing her coat, her bag was in her hand and a taxi sat outside her front door. Her mind started to swirl with possibilities. Could she be mistaken, was she foolishly hanging onto the belief that her husband would remain as faithful as she had been all these years? What other explanation could there be for his behaviour? Was Jasper having an affair?

The taxi driver was watching her, he had locked his door when she'd erupted from the house shouting and now he was keeping a careful eye on her as she stood, undecided in the doorway. Slipping her phone into her bag, Fliss locked the door behind her. The taxi driver opened his window an inch.

'Do you still want to go to the restaurant?' he asked.

Fliss waited for him to unlock the back door so she could slide in. 'Slight change of plan,' she murmured, giving him the address of Jasper's office along with a pleasant smile. No doubt he would go back to the office and tell everyone what an absolute tyrant Fliss Carmichael was. It would probably be in the paper tomorrow.

'So sorry to keep you waiting,' she said politely and he pulled out of the drive with Fliss sitting in the back, suddenly terrified of what she may be about to discover.

The taxi driver dropped her on the corner of the street where Jasper worked. Shivering a little in the cold night air, Fliss pulled her black coat a little closer around her. If she'd realised she might be carrying out surveillance tonight, she would have chosen something warmer.

Trying to look inconspicuous in her cocktail dress and high heels, she dodged from lamp post to lamp post, spending a moment or two behind a bus stop and using a convenient street sign for cover as she crept along the street. She was wary of getting too close in case Jasper walked out, straight into her arms, but her shoes were intended for show only and it would be impossible to set too brisk a pace once her errant husband finally appeared. It was essential she wasn't too far away when he made his appearance so she continued to shuffle forward, holding her beaded clutch bag in her hand and hanging onto the edges of her coat in the other.

When she was as close as she dared, a conveniently large 4x4 provided an ideal vantage point and tiptoeing behind it, she peered through the windows, able to see the entrance to the office. A passing car slowed down and the front window rolled down to reveal two young men who both whistled appreciatively.

'Hello gorgeous,' shouted one as they crawled by. 'Need a lift anywhere?'

Waving them impatiently away with her bag, Fliss crouched down lower as they drove off, conscious that the security guard on the door was now peering out into the street. He looked out curiously, his eyes scanning the parked cars and Fliss wondered if he'd caught a glimpse of the top of her red hair as she'd dropped below the level of the window. She stayed there for a moment or two and then slowly straightened up. He had disappeared, probably gone back inside to make a cup of hot tea and warm his hands thought Fliss blowing on her own cold fingers.

She stopped mid blow. Jasper was walking towards the door, phone in hand, laughing at something being said. Probably about his foolish wife buying his explanation for cancelling their table, Fliss decided angrily. She pressed her nose against the window of the car, ready to duck down again if he looked in her direction and watched him open the door and run lightly down the steps onto the pavement.

'Can I help you with something?'

Jumping in shock, Fliss swallowed a yelp and spun around to find the security guard, not inside warming his hands on a cup of tea, but standing on the road beside her and watching with interest as she bobbed up and down next to the 4x4.

'Oh! No thank you, I'm fine,' she whispered, giving him a reassuring smile before looking anxiously back to see if Jasper had noticed her. Still engrossed in his phone call, he had turned left and was now walking briskly down the street.

'Are you sure? You see, it looks to me like you're watching this building.' The guard, who Fliss realised now he was a little closer was built like a colossus, pointed in the direction of the office block. 'And as it's my job to make sure everybody in this building remains safe, I'd like to know exactly what you're doing.'

Watching her husband disappearing down the street, Fliss tried to wriggle around the enormous figure standing in her way, but he took a step to the right, effectively blocking out much of the street and all of the light.

'Watching the building? Nonsense.' She looked over her shoulder anxiously. Once Jasper was at the end of the street, she would have no idea which direction he had taken unless she was there to follow him.

'So you are …?'

'So I am … I am actually …I'm admiring this car!' Fliss patted the driver's door. 'I'm thinking of buying one.' The security guard's eyebrows shot up. 'For my husband,' Fliss qualified. 'As a present. And I saw this and thought I'd er … check it out.'

The look he gave her could only be described as disbelieving but as he flicked his eyes to the side giving the car a quick once over, Fliss neatly sidestepped his vast frame and leapt onto the pavement.

'And now I have to go,' she said breathlessly, hoping he didn't decide to follow her. There was no way she could outrun his giant strides. 'Because I'm meeting my husband and I need to tell him all about this car and how nice it is and …bye!' and she was off, sprinting down the street as fast as she could in impossibly high heels and a coat that was wafting behind her and acting as the very opposite of aerodynamic.

Reaching the corner, gasping for breath, Fliss was just in time to see Jasper turn right and disappear up the next street and weaving her way through pedestrians who comprised a mix of late workers and early revellers, Fliss shot after him. A couple more turns and then hanging onto a lamp post and holding the stitch she had in her side, a panting Fliss watched her husband walk into the foyer of the Royal Hotel, a 5-star city establishment within 5 minutes' walk of his office.

Sliding discreetly through the door in his wake and still breathing heavily, she was forced to leap behind a large palm tree as Jasper stopped, looked around and then made his way to an empty seat by the window. Sitting down he immediately took his phone out of his pocket, carrying out another quick examination of the lobby area before making a call.

Desperately trying to get her breathing back under control, Fliss peered through the palm fronds and watched as her husband caught the attention of a waiter and ordered a drink. Deciding she was a little too close for comfort, she took a couple of careful steps backwards, weaving in and out of the greenery until she found another palm tree, slightly more generous in its foliage and a little further away from where Jasper sat. Standing on tiptoe she parted the leaves until she had a good view of the lobby and in particular, her husband.

'Can I help you madam?' asked a polite voice by her ear and Fliss whipped round to see a waiter by her side, the pair of them under the eagle eyes of the hotel manager who was keeping a respectable distance.

'No thank you,' whispered Fliss. 'I'm waiting for someone.'

'Then can I find you somewhere to sit? There are plenty of seats available.'

'Oh that's kind, but no, thank you. I've been sitting all day, I think I'll stand.'

'Okay,' he looked over his shoulder at the hotel manager. 'Then would you like to stand by the bar? Your, er, friend will be able to see you more easily.'

'No! No, thank you but I … I …' Fliss had a quick look through the leaves to make sure Jasper was still in situ, 'I love the smell of these fronds you see,' she improvised wildly. 'They're very calming after a long day, don't you think?'

The young man looked doubtful but obligingly stepped forward and took a sniff at the palm leaf Fliss was now holding in her hand.

'I can't smell anything,' he admitted. 'In fact, I'm not sure they're real.'

'What?' Fliss took a closer look. If they were fake, they were very good and for a moment she forgot about Jasper and his potential affair and stroked the palm tree, trying to work out if it were genuine. 'But they look so realistic. Are you sure they're fake?'

Fliss and the waiter both leaned closer to take a better look.

'Can I help you, madam?' At the sight of his waiter and the strange women both now huddled in the palm tree, sniffing its leaves, the Hotel Manager had abandoned his remote observation and was standing haughtily by their side.

'No, thank you. I'm waiting for someone,' Fliss responded a little snippily. Undercover work was all about blending in and remaining unnoticed as you kept eyes on your target. Several people in the lobby were now watching the red-haired woman and her obsession with the palm tree with growing interest. 'I'm sure he'll be here soon and, in the meantime, I'm quite happy standing here.'

'I see.' The hotel manager looked at her suspiciously. Her hair was a little windblown from her jogging, her lipstick a tad smudged and her coat had started to slide away from one shoulder as she nestled into the tree. 'I think madam may have made a mistake. This is not that kind of establishment.'

'What kind of establishment?' whispered Fliss, bobbing down quickly as Jasper suddenly looked over in her direction.

'The kind where women wait for men.' The Hotel Manager looking down at her disparagingly. 'I think it would be best if Madam left, now.'

Fliss turned to look at him, still half crouched behind the plant. 'What on earth are you talking about?' she demanded in outrage. 'I told you I'm waiting for someone!'

'Who?'

'Well,' Fliss screwed up her face as she considered how much to tell him. 'A man …'

'Okay, I need you to leave. Now.' He had dispensed with both the Madam and the plum accent and the look he gave her was far from flattering.

'Not like that, how dare you! Not just a man, my husband.'

He stopped, uncertainty clouding his face.

'I'm sorry Madam, you're waiting for your husband?'

At least the Madam had returned. 'Yes, well not exactly. I'm looking to see what kind of woman my husband might like …'

'That's it, out.'

A wave of his hand brought a security guard to his side, nowhere near as big as the last one Fliss had encountered but still large enough to give cause for concern.

'Let go of me!' Her voice was rising and she saw Jasper look round with a slightly puzzled look on his face at the familiar tone.

Dodging back behind the palm tree, Fliss took the security guard by surprise and caught off balance he fell into the branches with her, keeping a tight hold of her arm and they wrestled together in the foliage.

Keeping one eye on Jasper whose gaze passed the shuddering tree but with no idea that his wife was huddled in its depths, Fliss struggled to free herself. 'Keep your voices down for goodness sake,' she whispered angrily as she was dragged out of the leaves and pulled towards the reception desk. 'And take your hands off me! I told you, I'm waiting for my husband.'

'You said you were here to procure a woman for your husband,' argued the Manager. 'Quite a different thing.'

'I said no such thing! Let me go! My husband is here, get off me immediately.'

A small crowd was now gathering, all stopping to watch as a protesting woman was dragged past reception and towards the door. At least they were providing effective cover between herself and Jasper, thought Fliss, still trying to pull away from the security guard.

143

'I insist that you let me go,' she demanded, struggling against the detaining arms, 'I just want to see my husband that's all.'

Wriggling around, desperately trying to escape, her coat had slipped completely off one shoulder, the tempting split at the side of her black dress was now gaping and the neckline was pulled taught revealing a great deal more cleavage than usual. Fliss sent a silent prayer upwards that she wouldn't bump into anyone she knew.

'I just want to see my husband,' she wailed. 'Let me go, let me go to him,' and with an almighty tug she was free, leaving her coat in the grip of the security guard as she tottered forwards, straight into the arms of an astonished Freddie.

'Fliss? Goodness me. You certainly don't like to be parted from Jasper for very long, do you? Heavens what a very lucky man he is!'

....
FROM: Fliss Carmichael <agonyauntfliss@digitalrecorder.com>
To: Ellie Henshaw <Elliebellshenshaw@livewell.co.uk>
Date: 08/04/2020
....

Dear Ellie

Your friend is quite right, a lot of what I am telling you is common sense but it's surprising how hard it is for us to be sensible when we're struggling to find the best way to handle a problem. I am so pleased that you were able to take my advice and are now having conversations with Logan but I have to admit, I am quite concerned about how things are progressing. If I've understood correctly, you are going on a double date with Logan but not as his girlfriend? I really can't see that arrangement working out and I think the best course of action would be complete honesty before the situation becomes any worse. I'm sure that Jeff would understand if you gently explained that you hadn't meant to ask him out in any way. The Logan and Harriet situation is difficult. You can't tell Logan not to go out with Harriet but maybe it would be good if you explained that you had wanted to watch him play football and not arrange a date with Jeff. I find that once a misunderstanding takes root it can become a whole lot worse before it gets better and this could be quite problematic if you don't take swift action. And please don't take this the wrong way but I can't help feeling that your friend, whilst her heart might be in the right place, is not helping as much as she may believe she is. I would recommend that you continue contact with Logan but without Laura being involved.

I understand what you're saying about Carl, although I admit I still have reservations. Maybe the feelings you had for Logan were exacerbated by the perception that you were being rushed into a marriage with Carl, one you weren't necessarily ready for. I know how you feel about Logan and I would never tell you that it wasn't real and meaningful but please be careful Ellie. You've turned away from a man who loved you on the off chance that you could form a relationship with Logan. If it doesn't work out you could end up

145

alone. Make sure this is what you want before you continue but of course I'll carry on helping you in any way I can.

I don't find it rude that you ask whether Jasper and I have a family and no, we don't have any children. It was a decision we made a few years ago. We have a very full life, lots of friends, socialising, dashing here and there, and of course work. As a couple we sat down and agreed that a family was probably not for us, we were happy as we were. Maybe that's part of the reason that I feel as I do. We sacrificed a family because we enjoyed our lives and as a result, I suppose I expected my marriage to bring me absolute happiness and that's no longer happening.

Which is why your advice was perfect and I am trying to remind Jasper how life was between us when we sat down and made that decision. I've spent the last few days trying to reset the clock back to a happier time in our lives, happier for me at least. It's not been entirely successful, almost everything I've planned has gone wrong and most people I know would be quite shocked at the way I've been behaving! I won't go into too many details but my husband's new boss thinks I'm a sex-mad obsessive and I've been banned from a local hotel. The only person who doesn't seem to have noticed any of my efforts is Jasper! But it was excellent advice and I'll continue with the plan, I'm sure it will work if I try a little harder.

In the meantime, please make sure that you clear up this misunderstanding with Logan and Jeff. I know I said that you needed to meet him outside of work over a shared interest, but I didn't envisage that being done whilst you both dated different people!

Good Luck
Fliss x

146

Chapter 14

It was freezing cold and Ellie had layered herself with scarves and gloves and two pairs of socks to watch Logan and Jeff play football. The pitch was at a local sports centre where the facilities included an assortment of playing fields and little else and Ellie joined the scattering of unenthusiastic spectators who stood in clumps around the pitch.

Harriet had been much braver and there was a marked absence of any woolly layers, something Ellie thought she may now be regretting as her lipstick struggled to cover the blue tinge to her lips. They huddled together, neither having any real interest in the match being played despite the enthusiasm they were trying to project, and watched as the players began to run around in no discernible pattern that Ellie could spot.

'You know, I meant to thank you for setting this up,' said Harriet through chattering teeth. 'It was a wonderful idea.' Ellie glanced around the desolate playing fields, the rubbish drifting around in the stiff wind and the grey skies which looked as cold as Ellie felt. 'I've been trying to get Logan to ask me out for ages so this was perfect.'

Logan hadn't actually asked Harriet out, but Ellie decided not to labour the point.

'He's gorgeous, isn't he?' giggled Harriet. 'I mean Jeff is nice too,' she added generously. 'But Logan is dishy.' She shivered and Ellie wondered if it was with delight or cold.

'I'm not interested in Jeff.' Ellie didn't want there to be any more misunderstandings. 'This isn't a date, I just thought it would be nice to support our work's team.'

'Really? You're here just to cheer them on?'

It sounded unlikely, even to Ellie, but she nodded. 'Oh yes, I'm a great believer in er, supporting each other. You know, if someone at work is doing something, like football, everyone else should, well, support them.'

Harriet looked surprised. 'I didn't realise. I thought you suggested it because you fancied one of the boys.' It was clear that Harriet couldn't imagine any other reason why someone would voluntarily watch a football match, especially on a raw Saturday morning in April. 'What other teams have you supported?'

'What else?' Ellie frowned. 'Oh, all sorts,' she said vaguely. 'Erm, the chess team.' One of the young men in IT played chess online and she'd watched over his shoulder for 30 seconds one afternoon while standing at his desk asking for help. 'And the er, quiz team.' Laura had once persuaded Ellie to join her at a local pub where they took part in a quiz to win a spa weekend away. It had been a fairly humiliating experience except for the specialist round in which they scored top points after it transpired that Laura had an encyclopaedic knowledge of anything makeup related.

'We have a quiz team? Well, that has to be better than standing here freezing to death. I wonder if I could persuade Logan to ditch the football and start quizzing. It would be a lot warmer.'

Harriet watched as a panting Logan came thundering towards them, only to trip over a clod of earth on the uneven pitch and fall flat on his face, allowing the ball to be scooped up by an equally breathless member of the opposition.

'Oh well done,' shouted Harriet clapping her hands. 'Well done Logan, great play.'

Ellie didn't know anything about football, but she had a feeling that Harriet's praise was misplaced.

'Isn't he clever?' asked Harriet with a grin. 'Although I'd still rather support him in a quiz, more choice of outfits indoors.'

'I think he enjoys football.' Ellie watched him haul himself to his feet and dash across the pitch to join in a melee in the penalty box. The ground was sodden with the recent rain and Jeff came splashing up the pitch to join the rest of his team, only to go skidding through the mud and grab at Logan's shorts before they both landed in a heap. Ellie and Harriet were treated to a flash of Calvin Klein underpants before Logan managed to pull his shorts back up his muddy body.

'You really don't fancy either of the boys then?' asked Harriet, waiting until Logan was once more clothed before taking her eyes away from him. 'I had wondered whether you had your eye on Logan until you agreed to go out with Jeff.'

'I am not going out with Jeff,' reminded Ellie. 'I've told you, I'm here to support the team.'

A wayward kick sent the ball heading straight in their direction and as one they squealed and jumped out of the way. A couple of young men nearby sniggered and one of them collected the ball and threw it back onto the pitch. Maybe that's what spectators were meant to do, thought Ellie, but the ball was filthy, splattered with mud and grass and she had no intention of touching it with her new gloves.

'It's important that the team feel we appreciate their efforts,' she confirmed, ignoring the mocking look.

'Hmm. So you don't fancy Logan?'

Put on the spot, Ellie pretended to be enchanted with the game for a moment as the players scuffled and pushed and tried to stay upright on the wet pitch. Technically she didn't fancy Logan, she loved him. But maybe this wasn't the right time to make such a statement.

'Oh fantastic move Jeff, well done,' she shouted instead. Jeff, who was bending over with his hands on his knees gasping desperately for air, looked up in surprise. He grinned at Ellie only to grunt in pain as the ball hit him squarely in the middle of his back and he lurched forward as the rest of the players ran past, hard to separate in their mud-soaked kits.

'He's good isn't he?' she pointed out to Harriet, trying to move her away from the subject of Logan. 'It's obvious he's a natural.'

Regaining his balance, Jeff went lumbering after his team only to find the direction of play had changed and they were all charging back towards him. He crouched low in the centre of the herd and covered his head with his hands until the danger had passed. Waiting until he looked up again, Ellie gave him a big thumbs up and a little whoop.

Satisfied that Ellie was more interested in Jeff than she was willing to admit, Harriet watched the rest of the match, her eyes pinned on Logan and cheering loudly whenever the ball went within 6 feet of him.

It was a moment of intense relief to both of them when the final whistle sounded and defeated again, Logan and Jeff trundled off in the direction of the changing rooms and a cold shower. They'd told the two women that they would meet them back in the clubhouse after they had changed and not waiting a moment longer than necessary, Ellie and Harriet shot off in search of warmth and wine.

A table of shrivelled sandwiches, a quiche sitting in a pool of liquid and a selection of greasy sausage rolls were set out on the table. Deciding not to risk a bout of food poisoning, Ellie declined to join the queue of supporters who were helping themselves to large platefuls as they trickled past in the direction of the bar and any radiator that was pumping out a modicum of heat.

'Yoohoo,' yelled Harriet suddenly, making Ellie spill her wine and she looked up to see Jeff and Logan bearing down on them.

Smiling widely, Harriet moved up to make room for Logan. 'Come and sit here, next to me,' she cooed in delight.

'Er, I'll just get a drink, do you want anything?'

His gaze rested on Ellie and she tried to recall all the advice Fliss had sent her. Use his name, it makes a connection 'Hello Logan.' Talk about his interests, it promotes intimacy 'You did well today.' Ask questions to show you are intrigued by them. 'Er, did you enjoy it?'

Harriet was staring at her, and Ellie wondered it had sounded too formal. She would have to practise.

'It was okay.'

'Have you thought about quizzing?' asked Harriet.

'Quizzing?'

'Yes, it's a lot warmer.'

A bemused Logan shook his head. 'I hadn't ...'

'It could be fun!' beamed Harriet. 'Think about it.'

'Right, okay. So, any drinks?'

Shaking their heads, Ellie and Harriet waited patiently for them to return, nursing their own lukewarm wine. Both men sat on stools on the opposite side of the table and Ellie saw Harriet's lips thin a little as Logan failed to take advantage of the empty seat by her side.

Jeff was grinning across the table at Ellie who was studiously avoiding his eyes and for a moment there was a pained silence.

'So, you do this every week?' asked Harriet, her lips still blue under her pale pink lipstick.

Logan nodded. 'Pretty much.'

'I see.'

'Have you ever won a match?' asked Ellie with interest. After all, there had to be some incentive to spending every Saturday rolling around in a cold wet field.

Logan screwed up his face and Jeff looked nonplussed.

'Well... I'm pretty sure we won a match last season. In fact, we might have won two.'

'But then our goalie left,' said Jeff. 'Got a new job in Bradford. Someone told me he didn't really want the job, he just couldn't face playing football for us anymore.'

'But you still play, every week?' Ellie asked Logan.

'Yep. I know we're rubbish.' He looked down at his pint. 'We may be bad footballers but we're a team at the end of the day and we have to stick together.'

Ellie stared at him, admiring his steely resolve as he shrugged his shoulders and took a deep drink of his lager.

And afterwards?' asked Harriet, slightly less impressed by Logan's loyalty.

'After?'

'Yes, after. Do you all go out? Dancing, clubbing, for a meal?'

Ellie looked around at the thin crowd of supporters. The majority of the company team were gathered around the buffet, obviously treating it as a free meal for the day. A few had jumped straight in their cars, probably preferring a warm shower at home. The small group of men sitting at the table next to them were slowly working their way down their drinks and Ellie hadn't heard them exchange a single word so far. None looked to be the sort to have a quick change of clothes in the car ready to go on a rave.

'We just go home,' advised Logan. 'We play our match, eat some sandwiches and then go home.'

Harriet's face fell. She had been hoping for more. 'So this is it?'

Jeff and Logan both looked at her. 'Er, yes. This is us playing football.'

'And you haven't thought about quizzing?'

Logan looked baffled. 'I'm not sure …'

'Ellie has been to watch the quiz team you know. And the chess team, she's very supportive in general.'

Avoiding the three pairs of eyes now staring at her, Ellie took a sip of wine and tried to look nonchalant.

'I didn't even know we had a quiz team,' said Jeff, scratching his chin thoughtfully. 'When do they do their stuff then Ellie?'

'Oh, er, I don't think they're doing any, er, quizzing right now. Does anyone want any more to eat? Logan, would you like another sausage roll?'

'No thanks. Why aren't they quizzing?'

'I think … I don't think … I'm not sure. Harriet, would you like some quiche?'

'Who is in the team?' chipped in Jeff. 'I could ask them. I quite like a good quiz.'

'I can't remember any names.'

'Which department do they work in?'

'Do you know, I'm not sure. Would you like a sandwich Jeff? You must be hungry after all that running.'

'I'm fine thanks. Maybe I could just ask around.'

'No! I mean, there's no need because no one is on the team, not at the moment.'

Jeff raised his eyebrows, waiting.

'I mean, there isn't a team right now. They've er, disbanded.'

'Why? Didn't they have enough players?'

He could be very insistent, decided Ellie. Not always a good quality.

Sighing, she rubbed at the pain that was beginning to thump along her forehead. 'No, not that. They had all the players they needed, it's because of the er, season.'

'What, Spring?'

'Not that kind of season, I mean the quizzing season. It's over you see. And the team has to disband and not come together again until the new season starts. To avoid any accusations of cheating.'

Jeff's mouth was hanging open in amazement. 'I didn't know there was a season for quizzing.'

'Of course there is. You have a football season, don't you?' asked Ellie, hoping that she was right.

'Well, yes but …'

'All sports have a season. Including quizzing. That's why no-one is doing it at the moment. Quizzing that is. No-one is quizzing because it's not quizzing season.'

Silence fell over the table as they all considered the possibilities.

'Well why don't we all go for a meal later,' Harriet said eventually. 'Maybe a curry?'

She was looking at Logan but Jeff's face brightened. 'That sounds like a great idea! Shall we join them, Ellie?'

Cringing inside Ellie shook her head. According to both Laura and Fliss, she needed to break up this happy little foursome as quickly as she could.

'Sorry,' she apologised. 'I can't …'

'It doesn't have to be a curry,' Jeff jumped in. 'Maybe you'd prefer a pizza?'

'No, I like curry it's just that I can't. …'

'I know a great place.' There was a note of desperation beginning to creep into Jeff's voice. 'Me and Logan sometimes go there on a Friday night. I'm sure you'll love it.'

'I'm really sorry Jeff but I …'

'Please come Ellie!' All pretence was lost as Jeff's smile grew bigger and slightly out of control. 'You'll enjoy it!'

Feeling awful and struggling to meet his eyes, Ellie wriggled around in her seat. 'I only planned on watching the football Jeff, nothing else. I just came along to support the team.' Her voice wobbled slightly and peeping under her eyelashes, she could see Jeff's hopeful gaze begin to fade. 'It's not a date or anything, I try and support all my colleagues.'

Hurt eyes met hers. 'I see. Like the quiz team?'

Ellie swallowed hard. 'Yes, like the quiz team. I wanted to come and watch you and Logan,' she placed a slight emphasis on Logan's name, 'play football and be, you know, supportive.'

There was a glimmer of understanding beginning to appear on Jeff's chubby face and she could see Logan out of the corner of her eye, his pint half raised to his mouth as he listened.

'I see,' said Jeff stiffly. 'And that support doesn't extend to coming for a meal with me?'

'I'd rather not. Sorry.'

154

Jeff's face was despondent and Ellie wondered if it had been the wrong thing to say, or at least the wrong thing to say in the pub in front of the others. Except that Logan was now looking at her with a very strange expression on his face, an expression that Ellie could only describe as hopeful and for some reason, it was making her feel quite peculiar.

'I don't think Ellie wants to go for a meal Jeff,' he said, keeping his eyes fixed on hers. 'Don't make it hard for her. I don't think I fancy going out myself, to be honest.'

There was an angry gasp from Harriet. 'Why?' she demanded. 'It doesn't matter if Ellie doesn't want to join in, we can still go.' She cast a brief look at a clearly devastated Jeff, his round face drooping onto his chest as he stared at the table. 'And Jeff as well,' Harriet added reluctantly. 'As long as he doesn't feel uncomfortable being with the two of us.'

'I don't mind.'

'Really? You won't feel like a gooseberry?'

'No. I'll come with you.'

'It could be difficult for you, not having your own partner.'

Sniffing, Jeff cast another hurt look in Ellie's direction. 'I have nothing else to do tonight. I'll come.'

'Like I said, I don't feel like going out tonight,' repeated Logan. 'I pulled a muscle playing today, a night in would suit me.'

Ellie couldn't drag her eyes away from his face, the smudge of mud still on his chin and those delicious silvery grey eyes that kept winging in her direction and making her heart thump that little bit faster.

'Then maybe me and Harriet will go?' asked Jeff hopefully, his face cheering up and his cheeks wobbling a little.

'Absolutely not!' Harriet adjusted her outraged expression. 'I mean, maybe not,' she said a little quieter. Leaning over the table, she tried to insert herself into

Logan's line of sight. 'But if you don't feel like going out, we could get a takeaway and stay in?'

He shuffled his empty pint glass on the table mat. 'I don't think …'

'Jeff can come!' offered Harriet in desperation. 'I'll collect it and come around to your house. You don't have to go anywhere then.'

Both she and Jeff were looking hopefully at Logan. His eyes flickered across the table at Ellie's distraught face and then back down to his pint.

'Go on mate,' encourage Jeff. 'It sounds great. That's not a date or anything,' he cast another reproachful glance at Ellie, 'it's just a takeaway with friends.'

'Ellie,' asked Logan gently. 'What do you think about a takeaway? No dates, just with friends.'

Ellie's breath caught in her throat. Logan had just asked her if she would like to join him for a takeaway at his house. Her hands were trembling under the table and her stomach was on a rollercoaster of delight as she stared into his eyes. Of course, there was the small matter of Jeff and Harriet but as far as Ellie was concerned it was most definitely an invitation from Logan to her. Logan asking Ellie out.

'A takeaway. With friends,' she murmured. She wondered anxiously what Fliss would tell her to do. She knew what Laura's advice would be. 'I, er … I…'

'Hello, Ellie.'

Blinking, it took Ellie a moment to work out where the voice was coming from and reluctantly dragging her eyes away from Logan, she turned round to gape at the figure standing by her side.

'What are you doing here?' he asked. 'I didn't know you were interested in football?'

She saw Harriet give him a quick assessment, her eyes running up and down the compact frame, the sandy blond hair, the pleasant open face with its smattering of freckles across the nose and the clear, light blue eyes.

'Carl!'

All eyes had moved away from her, swinging in Carl's direction as he stood relaxed, at ease and with, she realised in surprise, a slightly proprietorial air about him.

They were all waiting for her to answer. 'Oh, er, my office has a team. I came to support them.'

'Right.' Nodding his head, Carl turned his gaze on Logan and Jeff, completely ignoring Harriet. 'Did you win?'

At the shake of heads, he looked sympathetic. 'Shame. Do you need a lift home, Ellie? Now the match has finished?'

Cheeks flaming, Ellie glared at him. 'Of course not!' she snapped. 'I can find my own way home.'

Watching the exchange, Logan put down his glass and stood up to face Carl. 'You didn't introduce us, Ellie,' he said calmly. 'Is this a friend of yours?'

'This is Carl,' she said reluctantly. 'He's....'

Carl interrupted, thrusting his hand out towards Logan to give him a friendly shake.

'My name's Carl,' he said affably. 'And I'm Ellie's fiancé. Pleased to meet you all.'

Chapter 15

Ellie gasped, turning to face the shocked faces sitting at the table.

'No, he isn't!'

'Pre-wedding jitters,' threw in Carl. 'We're having a break. You know what it's like.'

None of them appeared to have the remotest idea what it was like although Harriet was watching the exchange with huge eyes, soaking in every word.

'No!' said Ellie crossly. 'We are not having a break. We used to go out and now we don't. There's nothing temporary about it.'

Carl didn't look at all upset. He just shrugged his shoulders and smiled. 'Okay, Ellie. Whatever you want to call it. By the way, your mum said not to be too late back because she's made chicken pie for tea,' and with a smile that encompassed everyone, he strolled away, leaving Ellie floundering with her mouth opening and closing like a fish.

'You have a fiancé?' asked Harriet in amazement.

'No, I don't! We used to go out, that's all.'

'How long?'

'What?'

'How long for?'

Ellie didn't want to answer. She watched Carl put his empty glass on the bar and walk towards the door.

'How long did you two go out?' asked Harriet again.

'Two years,' muttered Ellie. 'Well, nearly three I suppose.'

'Three years! You went out with him for three years? And were you engaged?'

'No! Not exactly.'

'How exactly?'

It was a good question, decided Ellie. There had been no proposal, no bended knee, no romantic meal out. Just a growing acceptance by Carl and her family that at some point the knot would be well and truly tied and romantic, head in the clouds Ellie would come crashing back to reality with a husband and a mortgage.

'Carl wanted us to get married,' she said truthfully. 'But we didn't get engaged. Not officially.'

'And are you still together?'

Ellie wanted Harriet to shut up and go away. She wanted them all to go away so she could speak to Logan and make sure he understood exactly what she was saying. He hadn't looked at her since Carl had left, he hadn't looked at anyone, simply staring into his empty glass with a slightly dazed expression.

'No! We've split up. Carl is just reluctant to accept facts, that's all.'

'Mm, he must think he's still in with a chance,' suggested Harriet. 'Is that why you didn't want to go out with Jeff tonight?'

Oh God, could this get any worse, wondered Ellie. She hadn't given Carl a second thought when she'd turned Jeff down, the only man in her thoughts had been Logan.

'Of course not,' she snapped. 'I came to support L .... I came to support my colleague. I'm not going out with Carl anymore.'

Harriet reached over to pat Jeff on the back of his podgy hand. 'Never mind Jeff. You can still share a take away with me and Logan tonight.' She peeped upwards at Logan from beneath her eyelashes. 'It sounds like Ellie is busy but we don't have to change our plans.'

Logan stood up, collecting the glasses from the table.

'I'll get more drinks, shall I?' he asked, leaning over to grab Ellie's glass and looking directly into her eyes briefly. Was that disappointment she could see there? Confusion, anger? She couldn't really make it out. 'And yeah, I'm up for a takeaway,' he announced, ignoring Harriet's happy squeal as he held the glasses up high.

'Who wants what?'

Ellie refused a drink and watching Logan's stiff back as he walked to the bar, she began pulling on her coat and her many layers of scarves and hats and gloves. The afternoon had been a strange mix of highs and lows and her instinct was telling her to leave before it became any worse. For once she wished that Laura was by her side. Her behaviour may often be eccentric but she would take Harriet in hand right now and make Logan sit back down to listen to Ellie.

Saying goodbye to Jeff, who pretended not to hear her, and Harriet, who clearly didn't care whether Ellie stayed or left, she went to stand next to Logan.

'I'm going now,' she said quietly.

'Right. Thanks for watching.' He didn't turn around and Ellie fought the urge to put her hand on his arm, feel the touch of his skin.

'I'm not going out with Carl anymore.'

'You said.'

'I haven't been for a while.'

She hoped he wouldn't ask for a more detailed timeframe because it wasn't very long at all. Just since Ellie had walked into the office one day and found Logan, laughing at something a friend had said, his head thrown back and the dimple in his chin clear to see. Although she would like to explain what had happened, she thought it may be too early in their very tentative relationship to tell him that the reason she had ended things with Carl was because she had fallen in love with Logan.

Logan grunted, waving an empty glass in the direction of the bartender.

'He just can't accept that we're over and sometimes he turns up and …' It all sounded so silly. 'And we were never engaged. I don't know why he said that.'

Although she did really. Carl may not have been the sort to go down on one knee and produce a heart-shaped jewellery box containing an antique engagement ring, a particular fantasy of Ellie's, but he had made his feelings quite clear. Until Ellie had ended things, telling him that despite everything she had said and done to the contrary over the last few years, she didn't think she loved him enough to spend the rest of her life with him.

She was still talking to the back of Logan's head and closing her eyes, Ellie felt the few moments of hope that had engulfed her heart only minutes before, well and truly evaporate. 'Well, goodbye,' she said, 'see you on Monday,' and receiving no response she turned in the direction of the door and headed for home.

Ellie's mother was in the kitchen, putting the finishing touches to the pie she was just about to put into the oven. Throwing her coat over the pile that already sat on one of the scuffed chairs, Ellie placed her hands on her hips and gave her mother a hard look.

'Carl turned up,' she announced. 'I wonder how he knew where I was? Did you tell him?'

Susan Henshaw bent down to put the pie on the middle shelf before standing up to meet her daughters glare. 'Yes, I did,' she said calmly. 'I told him that you were going to a match to cheer on someone from your office and he'd better get round there to stop you taking it any further.'

Her mouth dropping open, Ellie gasped. 'Mother! How could you! How many times do I have to tell you that Carl and I are over, finished? You must stop interfering like this, I can't have Carl following me, turning up unexpectedly. It's got to stop.'

Susan didn't look at all perturbed by Ellie's words. Wiping down the surface she pulled off her apron and flicked on the kettle.

'And how many times do I have to tell you that you're making a mistake?' she said. 'You're lucky Carl realises how confused you are and is prepared to wait for you to come to your senses. But he won't wait forever you know, one day he'll give up and go find someone else.'

That moment couldn't come soon enough for Ellie.

'Mum, I haven't made a mistake. It's what I want …'

'Oh Ellie, you don't know what you want! That's the trouble.'

'That's not true. I know I want love…'

Her mother snorted. 'And there you go! Always the romantic. But love isn't like that Ellie. It's not all hearts and flowers and big romantic gestures. You won't find anyone who loves you more than Carl does, just because he doesn't come home every night with a red rose between his teeth doesn't mean he doesn't love you!'

Sitting down at one of the empty chairs, Ellie tried again. 'I know he loves me, mum. But it's not just about how Carl feels. It's about how I feel.'

Bringing two cups of tea over to the table, Susan sat down and faced her daughter. 'You've always been the same you know,' she said with a small smile. 'Even as a little girl, it was always knights on white chargers, hearts and flowers. You sent most of your time with your head in the clouds, dreaming of the day when a prince would arrive and rescue you.'

Ellie had grown up in a household where love was not in short supply but it was delivered in a brisk, no-nonsense fashion. Her father would come home from work and go upstairs to get changed while her mother put the evening meal on the table. After he had eaten, he would always rub his stomach and say it had been smashing and her mother would tell him to go sit in the living room and she would bring him a cup of tea. As far as Ellie was concerned, that was the limit of any conversation they had. If they went out, which they usually did on a Saturday night visiting the local pub for an hour or so, they would invariably part company as they walked through the door, her father standing at the bar to discuss the day's sports or the cost

162

of his last car service and her mother sitting with the small group of women who would chat about the cost of food and the state of the local shopping centre.

There was never any physical contact that Ellie could see. The walk home from the pub would be made side by side but their hands would not be entwined; her father would take her mother's elbow if he felt she needed any support and she would tug on his sleeve if she wanted to catch his attention. They sat side by side on the settee most evenings and watched TV, making the occasional comment but usually in silence. There were no raised voices, no uncomfortable moments. Both her parents made it clear that they loved both Ellie and her older brother but hugs and kisses were not traditionally shared. She presumed that they had been in love once, enough to marry and raise a family but there were no outward signs of anything other than a respectful affection towards each other.

As a teenager, she had found herself enchanted with the idea of something far more romantic. She would watch couples in the street as they wrapped their arms around each other and kissed in doorways. Her imagination was captured by tales of people sacrificing all for love, crossing mountains and valleys to be close. In Ellie's opinion, the tragedy of Romeo and Juliet was most definitely worth the despair because to feel such sorrow meant they must have also felt the very pinnacle of love. It wasn't long before she decided that she wanted to feel the dizzy heights of such romance, she wanted a man who adored her, who would arrive home each evening to wrap his arms around her and tell her how much he had missed her.

Ellie had met Carl when she'd joined her parents at the pub one evening, sitting next to her mother and listening to the chatter ebb and flow around her. Carl had walked over to say hello to her mother and offered to buy Ellie a drink. As he placed half a pint of lager on the table and Ellie accepted it with a smile, it appeared that the deal had

163

been struck. Ellie and Carl were now going out. A no-nonsense young man, solid and hard-working, he immediately met with the approval of her parents. Indeed, Ellie would have to admit, he had met with her approval. The romantic fantasies of her youth were forgotten and Carl was enough to make her heart beat a little faster. She would lean out of the window of her family's terraced house to see him walking down the street and then race downstairs to be the one to open the door for him. They went to the pictures, the pub and even out for the occasional meal, although much like her father, Carl thought it a waste of money paying someone else to cook his food. After 18 months, they had moved into a flat together and although Ellie's father had raised an unhappy eyebrow at the turn of events, her mother had tutted and told him to be quiet.

'It's the way things are now Dave,' she'd scolded. 'They'll get married when they're ready.'

Carl had never proposed and if he had, Ellie would probably have said yes. She loved him. Not in the earth-shattering romantic way she had once longed for, but it was still love. Talk of marriage had become frequent whenever they visited her parents and Ellie had come to understand that it was something seen as inevitable, the next step in their relationship. At some point, Carl would take her out one Saturday morning and they would stop outside a jeweller's shop. He would point at the rings and say, 'so which one do you like then?' and Ellie would be engaged.

Except that moment had never arrived. Instead, Ellie had arrived at work one day and seen Logan standing by the lift. She had stared at his lean shape, his strong jaw and his slender hands. She had watched his profile as he talked and laughed and she had fallen head over heels in love, just as she had always imagined that she would. Suddenly, Carl and his steady love was no longer enough. The idea of marrying him and settling down to the sort of lives her parents enjoyed, filled Ellie with dismay. All the romantic thoughts she used to have as a young girl came flooding back, that desire for the kind of love that swept her off her feet become absolutely necessary. Deciding that if she truly loved Carl she wouldn't feel like that about another person, she had eventually told him that their relationship was over. Trying to explain to his shocked and bewildered face that she simply didn't love him enough to continue a relationship, was one of the hardest things Ellie had ever had to do. Explaining to her equally shocked parents that she wanted more, had been the second hardest.

'More?' her father had questioned. 'More of what?'

'More love,' she had told him.

He had turned to her mother, standing in the kitchen and holding one hand to her heart as she listened to her only daughter. 'What's she on about Susan? What does she want?'

Despite telling her daughter she was being ridiculous, Ellie always suspected she had spotted a moment of understanding in her mother's eyes and that despite her proclamations that she had no idea what Ellie was doing, her mother had, in fact, understood exactly what her daughter meant. No mention was made of Logan's dark hair or his dimple. Ellie felt that it was enough to say that she wanted to end the relationship without revealing that her decision came after falling instantly, truly, madly and deeply in love with someone she had never even spoken to.

Ellie picked up her tea and took a sip.

'Life is hard Ellie,' her mother said softly. 'You were lucky to find someone like Carl to love, someone who loved you back. He's a good man. Oh, he may not be fancy and keep whisking you off to restaurants and spout poetry at you. But he's a good, kind-hearted man and he thinks the world of you.'

165

Carl had told Ellie that he loved her several months into their relationship. Ellie had been thrilled with the realisation that she was now part of a couple, two people in love. But having said it once, Carl didn't see the need to repeat himself and Ellie could count on the fingers of one hand how many times the declaration had been made.

'I know mum,' she said sadly. 'I do know. But I don't love him, not enough.'

But Susan shook her head stubbornly. 'You're making a mistake,' she warned her daughter. 'You're mistaking romance for love. Love is deep and steady and strong. It's not beating hearts and infatuation. This is just a wobble and you'll wake up one morning and understand what you've thrown away. Let's hope it's not too late and Carl is still around,' and sighing, she left the table to check on her chicken pie now browning nicely in the oven.

Dear Fliss

I am so grateful that you've carried on writing to me, it's reassuring having someone on my side. I know you were anxious about the football thing, I must admit I was pretty worried myself, so I thought I would give you an update. It was very difficult but I made sure that Jeff knew I wasn't there as his date and although he was upset, I think that Logan was really pleased. But then Carl turned up and told everybody I was his fiancée and it all went hideously wrong. I was just beginning to feel as though I was having a breakthrough with Logan. It was strange because Jeff and Harriet were both there, but he was looking at me in a very peculiar way that made me feel quite hopeful. But after Carl left, he wouldn't speak to me, not properly. I'm not sure that he believes it's really over between me and Carl. I tried to explain but he acted as though he didn't want to listen to me. Even though we don't know each other, it was as though I disappointed him in some way and that hurts even more than him not speaking to me. Laura says that she should have gone with me and whenever she leaves me to sort things out for myself, it all goes wrong. Maybe she's right, I certainly came away feeling quite miserable.

I was really angry with Carl, I can't seem to make him understand that it is truly over. But I also feel sorry for him. I did love him and he is actually a wonderful person. But once I saw Logan, I understood that it wasn't the relationship that I wanted, the one that would keep me happy and content for the rest of my life. I didn't tell Carl the truth. It seemed cruel to let him know that I loved someone who I'd never even spoken to, more than I loved him and I don't want Carl to be hurt. Even if things don't work out with Logan, and at times I think it's very unlikely, I still think that it was for the best that I understood how I felt about Carl before we got married

167

But I do wish things were going better with Logan. I realise that you can't expect someone to fall in love with you just because you want them to and perhaps I was hoping for too much. No matter what I do, something always seems to go wrong between us, I'm beginning to worry that we're just not meant to be together, something I never thought I would say.

It sounds as though things are going just as badly for you. But don't give up Fliss, there's too much at stake. I think you are right to persevere and try to remind your husband of happier times when life was simpler. I remember when Carl and I first moved in together, just making him tea and toast on a morning seemed so romantic! Everything was special because it was new and exciting and I can understand how that could fade years later. But all those little things that you used to enjoy together, the silly little things that made you laugh and feel like you were the only couple in the world, try and bring those back into your lives.

How very brave you both were, deciding that you were complete enough as a couple and didn't need a family. It shows a real honesty about your relationship. So many people do what is expected of them rather than what they truly want to do, and that alone should encourage you to carry on trying with your husband and overcome your current issues. It sounds to me like you belong to each other.

Good luck and thank you for everything

Ellie

Chapter 16

When Jasper finally returned from his meeting at the Royal Hotel, Fliss could hear him whistling cheerfully downstairs before he came creeping into the bedroom in case she was asleep. He seemed very relaxed for someone who had just discovered that his wife had been ejected from a public place for soliciting, witnessed by his new boss who was now more than likely convinced that Fliss was sex-starved and quite, quite besotted with her husband.

Sitting up in bed, her make up removed, Fliss waited, her face pale and tense.

'Oh darling, I am truly sorry about tonight,' Jasper said as he tiptoed into the room and saw her waiting for him. 'Maybe I jumped the gun a little cancelling the restaurant but I thought we might be at that blessed meeting all night.'

'It's okay,' she offered in a small voice. After all, in the general scheme of things, it wasn't the worst thing to have happened to Fliss that evening.

'I ended up meeting Freddie at the Royal,' continued Jasper as he pulled off his shirt and disappeared into the bathroom to drop it into the laundry basket.

Fliss nibbled on her lip, here it came. Appearing in the bedroom again, Jasper paused before he hung up his suit.

'It was a bit strange,' he said looking over at her. 'Freddie was convinced he'd seen you in the doorway of the hotel. Being thrown out!' He laughed and carried on sliding his trousers onto the hanger. 'Said you were half-dressed and shouting how you just wanted to be with your husband or some such thing.'

Fliss stretched her face into a smile, her hands were clenched so tightly under the covers her nails were in danger of drawing blood.

'I told him it wasn't possible, that I'd just spoken to you at home. He took me to the window to point you out but whoever it was had gone.'

Actually, she had been hiding behind a bus shelter across the road, much to the interest of the homeless man who had been in the process of settling down for the night. Momentarily tempted by the cider bottle he had held out silently in her direction, she'd waved it away and remained crouched as low as she could manage, watching as Jasper and Freddie appeared at the window of the hotel and peered out into the street, looking first one way and then the other until Freddie shrugged and they walked away. Only then had Fliss left, running towards the nearest taxi rank as quickly as she could manage.

'I think he's still convinced it was you,' chuckled Jasper, finishing in the bathroom and sliding into bed. 'I am sorry about tonight, we'll try again later in the week, shall we?' and letting his head fall onto his pillow with a contented sigh, he was asleep before Fliss even had time to agree.

The following morning, Fliss climbed out of bed at the crack of dawn, which wasn't hard because she'd hardly slept a wink all night and when her eyes did finally close, she'd had a strange dream which involved a pole, very little clothing and Freddie looking equally shocked and fascinated. Waking up sweating, despite the cold temperature outside, Fliss had gone downstairs and made a cup of coffee, an essential for any serious thinking.

The previous evening had been nothing short of mortifying, even if it had answered her question regarding Jasper's loyalty. It would seem that the only serious competition she had for his affections was Freddie, and of course the job. There was no other woman. The plan could continue and she would remind Jasper, with renewed determination, just what they'd once had and hopefully jolt him into seeing how much had changed. She just needed to remain clothed and stay away from Freddie.

So when Jasper came downstairs a few hours later, he found his wife in the kitchen in pair of cut-off jeans and bare feet, singing happily as she made pancakes in what she hoped was a faithful recreation of the Fliss of years gone by, the one who had never had any trouble capturing her husband's attention. She had spent a considerable amount of time applying a subtle layer of makeup that made her look as though she hadn't bothered applying any at all and her hair had been carefully fluffed to produce a just got out of bed look. Her feet were almost blue with cold and she was desperate to slide them into her fluffy slippers but the Fliss from old had been far more relaxed about such things and hadn't possessed any slippers, fluffy or otherwise.

'You're up early. Are those pancakes you're making?'

As usual, Jasper was immaculately dressed, his shirt professionally pressed, his pinstriped suit lint-free and without any unwanted creases.

'Your favourite,' grinned Fliss. 'I thought you deserved a treat.'

Jasper was staring at his phone and it was a moment before he looked up, a slightly vacant expression on his face. 'What? Oh, pancakes. Yes, I did used to like them but I don't think I've got time this morning. I have an early meeting and ….'

'Nonsense. They're nearly ready, sit down.'

'Fliss I really …'

'I always made you pancakes in the morning, remember?'

'Yes I do and they were lovely.'

'You used to say that you couldn't get through a day at work without your pancakes!'

'But …'

'They're ready. Here we go,' and stepping back Fliss flicked the frying pan upwards, tossing the pancake high into the air. It had been her party trick, or rather her kitchen trick. One magnificent toss upwards before she slid a perfect pancake onto Jasper's plate. But it had been some time since she'd been in pancake mode. And as she took a step backwards, Jasper had taken a step forwards, their elbows crashing together which meant that as the pancake went sailing into the air, it adopted a slight lilt and in a move worthy of a spin bowler, completely changed direction flying over Fliss' head to land squarely on Jasper's shoulder.

Gasping, Fliss put her hand to her mouth, looking with horrified eyes at the pancake now decorating Jasper's suit, a greasy stain already beginning to grow across his lapel.

'What on earth,' yelled Jasper, leaping back but far too late to avoid the pancake attack. 'Fliss! For God's sake, look at my suit!'

'I'm sorry,' she whispered, grabbing a tea towel to remove the offending pancake. 'I'm so sorry, I tossed it a little too high and …'

'I'm going to have to get changed which means I'm going to be late,' grumbled Jasper, rubbing at his suit with a grimace. 'And I'll have to take this to the dry cleaners, I wanted to wear it later in the week.'

'I'll take it for you,' Fliss offered. 'I'm sorry, it was an accident.'

'Well, it wouldn't have happened if you'd listened to me in the first place. I didn't even want a pancake!' and taking off the greasy jacket, Jasper went bounding up the stairs chuntering on every step.

Shoulders drooping, Fliss threw the remains of the soggy pancake in the bin. Not the best start to the day she decided, trying to find a smile to put in place as she heard his footsteps coming back down the stairs.

'I've made you a coffee,' she said cheerfully as he came back into the kitchen. 'You can knock it back before you go.'

172

'Thank you but I really am running late now. I'll grab some at work,' and with a last glance at his phone, he was gone, the only sound his car starting up and the swish of gravel as he left the drive.

Goodness me thought Fliss. It really shouldn't be this hard being nice to your husband. No wonder so many people didn't bother! Cleaning the kitchen of pancake, she hoped his mood wouldn't stop him from appreciating the surprise waiting for him when he arrived at his office and tonight, she was going to make toad in the hole, his absolute favourite meal. They were going to eat at the kitchen table, not in the formal dining room. They would chat and talk about their day, as they always used to, they would open a bottle of wine and relax in each other's company. They would have a lovely time whether Jasper wanted one or not! She would make him remember how much they had always enjoyed each other's company, how happy they had been to spend an evening together without work colleagues or friends surrounding them. He would remember, even if she had to tie him to the chair and keep him there until it happened. And feeling a little more optimistic, Fliss wandered upstairs to get changed and put something warmer on her feet.

The call came just after Fliss arrived at work and was musing over an email from *Confused of Oxford* who couldn't understand why his new wife was refusing to visit her mother in law or accept any of the excellent advice she had been offering the newlyweds. Surely, he argued, that having someone tell you the order in which you should do the washing up after the evening meal was helpful, far better than finding out you'd been washing your plates incorrectly all your life.

'What the bloody hell is going on with you Fliss!' raged Jasper.

Somewhat surprised, Fliss pressed the phone to her ear so no-one else in the office could hear his angry rant. 'What?'

'What on earth did you think you were doing?'

He had to be talking about the little surprise she'd arranged for him, but it was a strange reaction. Perhaps he was talking about something else entirely.

'Doing about…?'

'You don't seem to be yourself at all. All these strange things that keep happening, like prancing around the kitchen nude and throwing pancakes over me.'

'I wasn't naked,' she said stiffly. 'And I didn't throw the pancake over you, it sort of jumped. I did apologise …'

'I don't care about the pancake,' yelled Jasper, making Fliss jump.

'You brought the subject up …'

'I'm talking about the bloody silly thing you put in my briefcase this morning.'

Fliss pouted. It was hardly silly. It was a romantic gesture, a cute little light-hearted moment that was intended to make Jasper smile and think of his wife.

'Silly?' she began indignantly. 'It wasn't silly …are you listening to me? Who are you talking to?'

'The police.'

'The police? Why are you talking to the police? What's happened, are you okay?'

'I'm fine. Just about. And the police are here to talk to me about why I drove into a hedge.'

'Hedge? What hedge?'

Fliss had forgotten about keeping her phone call discreet and was now on her feet, already reaching out for her handbag.

'Have you had an accident?' she demanded, her voice rising with concern. 'I'm on my way, where are you, what happened?'

She could hear voices in the background and Jasper talking in muted tones before he returned to Fliss.

174

'Yes, I did have an accident,' he snapped. 'Is it any wonder? What on earth were you thinking putting that ridiculous thing in my briefcase?'

Fliss halted on her way to the door. The rest of the office had watched with concern as she'd leapt to her feet and she could feel Vivian's anxious eyes on her. Her instinct had been to dash to Jasper's side but suddenly she was having second thoughts.

'In your briefcase? The er, thing in your briefcase?' she asked quietly wanting to clarify that they were talking about the same thing in the same briefcase.

'Go, go,' Vivian was mouthing in her direction, shooing her towards the door. 'I hope he's okay, go on.'

'Yes, my briefcase.'

'Right, that thing.' Waving at all the gestures of goodwill that were erupting around her, Fliss gave her colleagues a nervous smile and made a quick escape. 'It was a gesture. A romantic gesture for the man I love,' she added. 'Because I feel that perhaps we're both so busy at the moment that we don't give each other the attention we once did so I decided that I would show you how much I love you.'

'In my briefcase?' demanded Jasper in outrage. 'You couldn't have just told me when I got home?'

'Well that's part of the problem isn't it,' Fliss snapped back. 'Getting you to stay at home and listen to me isn't as easy as it sounds.'

She had arrived at her car and throwing her bag on the passenger seat, she started the engine. 'I'm on my way, where are you,' and listening to the address Jasper gave her, Fliss ended the call and shot off to collect her husband.

Two police officers were talking to Jasper when she pulled up behind his Mercedes which had its nose pressed into a hedge at the side of the road. Walking towards them, she ignored the officers for a moment and reached up to slide her arms around Jasper's neck.

175

'Are you okay?' she asked, scanning him for any signs of injury and finding none. 'Are you hurt?'

'I'm okay.' He didn't hug her back and reluctantly Fliss let him go, turning to look at the car instead. It seemed to have veered off the road, sliding down a small embankment into the hedgerow. A recovery truck was pulling up behind the police car, the driver already tutting and shaking his head.

Jasper gave Fliss an exasperated look. 'Fortunately, no-one else was involved but I'll probably get fined,' he said in a sharp voice, leaving no doubt that the fault was entirely hers.

'Driving without due care and attention,' interrupted one of the officers. 'Driving without paying full attention to the road. Touching a remote device whilst driving …'

'I wasn't touching a remote device! It was my briefcase!'

The officer looked at him from beneath bushy eyebrows and continued. 'Failing to exercise complete control over a vehicle in your possession, failure to …'

'Okay, okay,' snapped Jasper with another angry glare in Fliss' direction.

'Er, your briefcase?' she asked, taking a tiny step back. Both officers turned to look at her, the younger, female policewoman letting her eyes roam over Fliss' rosy cheeks.

'Yes. Apparently, your husband suddenly worried that he had forgotten to put his diary in his case,' she informed Fliss. 'So he flicked it open to check.'

Flinching Fliss nodded. 'I see,' she said shakily. 'And ….'

'And the little…. surprise you'd left in there for him did its job. It surprised him to the point where he thought he'd been attacked by something and drove off the road.'

Fliss sent a weak smile in Jasper's direction but there was a total lack of amusement on his face.

'Of course, Mr Carmichael should have pulled over and brought his vehicle to a halt before opening his briefcase,' advised the first officer, who seemed to be quite enjoying the situation. 'As it was, he took his eyes off the road and

176

endangered the lives of himself and others by opening said case which was on the passenger seat next to him.'

'I see.' Fliss did see. She could understand that if Jasper hadn't been sat at his desk when he opened his briefcase, then the cute little jack in the box which was designed to pop out and wave its small 'I love you' flag could have been very distracting. Distracting enough to make him veer off the road.

'Well, officer. I feel I should confess and tell you that I was the one who put the, the er … surprise in my husband's briefcase this morning.'

Fliss' legs had become quite wobbly as she spoke and she was trying to remember the last time she had watched police interceptors on the TV. Were they likely to arrest her immediately she wondered, would she be bundled into the back of the car and taken away? She had a quick look round for a camera, please God let this not appear on any programme. Agony aunts weren't supposed to get arrested. In fact, she was fairly certain there was a clause in her contract about breaches of the peace.

'That may be, Mrs Carmichael. But it was your husband who chose to open his briefcase whilst driving and put himself and others ….'

'Yes, yes,' interrupted Jasper testily. 'I get the message!'

The bushy eyebrows waggled in his direction but at that moment the recovery driver shouted over that he was ready to pull the car from the rather prickly hedgerow and would they all move out of the way. Stepping back, Fliss found herself standing next to the young female officer who turned to give her a sympathetic look.

'I thought it was cute,' she murmured. 'Sometimes they just need a reminder don't they, especially when you've been together for a while.' Fliss wondered if it were so obvious that she and Jasper were no longer newlyweds. 'Take a tip from me,' continued the WPC in a hushed voice. 'Try some nice underwear, works a treat every time,' and with a supportive smile, she wandered off to where her colleague was advising Jasper of the charges that would be brought.

Chapter 17

When Jasper came home that night, Fliss was waiting in the kitchen. She'd made toad in the hole as planned but she doubted that Jasper would be happy to sit at the kitchen table laughing as they reconnected over old memories.

The wine had been opened and Fliss, pale-faced and tense, had already poured them both a glass. For a moment Jasper simply stood in the doorway and then with a sigh he sank onto one of the chairs.

'What's going on Fliss?' he asked wearily.

'It was me at the Royal Hotel last night.'

For the first time in many, many months, Fliss was confident that she had her husband's undivided attention as Jasper stared at her in astonishment.

'What? You were there, Freddie saw you?'

She nodded.

'But I don't understand. Freddie said you were half-dressed and shouting and they threw you out!'

She nodded again.

'But I'd just spoken to you, at home. I mean, why, how … why were you at the hotel?'

'Because yet again you had a reason for us not spending time together and I suddenly wondered, well I thought…' Fliss let her head fall back slightly as she closed her eyes. What exactly had she allowed herself to believe?

'I wondered if you were having an affair,' she said quietly.

Jasper's mouth fell open. 'Oh not this again, I've already told you it's a ridiculous idea! I love you, I love being married to you, I am not having an affair!'

He banged his hand on the table and the glasses rocked slightly.

'But you don't seem to love being married to me anymore Jasper. You are so involved with anything and anybody that isn't me.'

A look of exasperation came across the table. 'I'm busy! I have an extremely busy schedule and …'

'No. It's more than that, I've been trying to tell you for weeks that I feel that somethings not quite right with us at the moment. Something has changed, I don't know what but you, me, *we're* different and you don't seem to want to listen. I know you're busy. I understand busy, and this isn't it. This is … I don't know what this is which is why I've been trying to reach out to you.'

'You followed me to the Royal Hotel to reach out to me?'

'I followed you to the hotel to make sure that there was no-one else in your life. I wore sexy underwear in the hope that you might look up from your phone for a few minutes and remember who I was. I filled your diary with hearts and put a jack in the box in your briefcase because I wanted you to stop for a moment and bring your mind back to our marriage.'

Jasper was staring across the table as though he had never seen her before. 'I don't understand,' he was shaking his head. 'I don't understand why you would feel like this.'

Fliss watched him. She didn't understand it herself, but she needed to do something about it before it was too late.

Running a hand through his hair, Jasper sighed again. 'I truly don't know what has brought this on darling. I don't know what to say other than I am happy, with you. Nothing has changed as far as I'm concerned, nothing at all.' At Fliss' impatient sigh, Jasper held his hand up. 'But, if you're unhappy, if you feel this strongly then I'm listening.'

He looked fidgety and she could see his hands clenching compulsively around the phone he hadn't looked at since arriving home. Keeping silent, she let him take the lead for once.

'Why don't I take you out.'

Fliss snorted. 'We've tried that!'

'Okay, how about a night away? Me and you, no distractions, plenty of time to talk.'

Fliss held her breath. 'Really?'

'Really.'

Feeling a smile begin to break through, Fliss nodded. 'Sounds wonderful.'

'How about the Park Hotel? We'll drive up Friday afternoon, book a table, stay overnight in that lovely suite we had last time. Clear the air, have a break. What do you think?'

Jumping to her feet, Fliss didn't care about the red wine that erupted from her glass over the table as she threw her arms around her husband's neck. 'I think it sounds wonderful, I love you!' she said, burying her head into his shoulder. It was the sort of thing they had done regularly, once upon a time, taken off for a night or two, nothing to do but relax, walk, eat, sleep - just the two of them.

Jasper untangled her arms from his neck so he could look into her eyes. 'And I love you my darling, I confess I don't know why you suddenly feel so unsure about that fact but we need to do something before I have another accident!'

Blushing as she remembered the jack in the box Fliss grinned. 'I can't wait,' she murmured, leaning over to kiss her husband. 'I absolutely cannot wait!'

When Friday afternoon arrived, Fliss had packed a small overnight bag and was grinning from ear to ear at the thought of some quality time spent with her husband. Jasper arrived home, as promised, much earlier than normal and Fliss, who had spent the morning waiting for the phone to ring with news of another meeting, sighed in relief when she saw his repaired car pull into the driveway amid a swish of gravel.

'Hello, darling. Do you want to get changed or are you happy to drive there in your suit?' She had insisted that he pack before going to work that morning and even put his suitcase in the back of the car to save time later.

Jasper had placed his briefcase on the floor and was pulling off his tie as Fliss came dancing down the stairs, dressed and ready to leave.

'I was going to get changed,' he said, finding his arm being taken to steer him away from the kitchen. 'And maybe have a cup of coffee before ….'

'Oh, no need for that! We'll be there in an hour, you can have a drink when we arrive.'

'Okay, I suppose …'

'And you look so handsome in your suit. Why don't you wear it for the drive and get changed when we're at the hotel?'

Looking startled at the speed of their exit, Jasper allowed himself to be pushed in the direction of the drive and the car he had just parked.

'Well I could, are we in a hurry?' he asked in bewilderment as Fliss picked up her handbag.

'Not at all. Just looking forward to getting there.' And it wasn't going to be spoilt by anything, thought Fliss with determination. No last-minute calls or emergency meetings. The sooner she got Jasper out of the house and on the way to the hotel, the better.

'I'm just popping next door to feed Jenny's cat. She's not home until later tonight and I promised I'd give it some lunch. I've never known a cat who needs 3 meals plus snacks every day but it will only take me two minutes.' She had already closed all the doors that opened from their hallway, in particular the one to Jasper's study, to limit any distractions. 'My suitcase is next to the front door. Lock up, get the car started and pick me up from the bottom of Jenny's drive,' she instructed and pointing him firmly in the direction of the doorway, Fliss set off at a jog to their neighbour's house.

There was a brief moment of panic as, cat fed, Fliss stood in the drive and waited for Jasper to appear.

Deciding that she would put more than a jack in the box in his briefcase if he'd gone into his study to catch up on some work, she waited impatiently. He seemed to take an inordinate amount of time to pull out of one driveway and into another but hearing the sound of gravel she relaxed and seconds later he appeared, smiling at her from the front seat.

'Sorry,' he said as she opened the door. 'Quick call.' He saw her face darken and hastily added, 'Really quick call. Just reminding everybody I'm off with my darling wife and will be totally incommunicado!'

Mollified, Fliss sank into the passenger seat. 'Have you put your phone away?' she asked.

'Yes.'

'Answering service on?'

'Absolutely.'

'Out of office on your emails?'

'Yep.'

'Lovely!' Sighing with happiness, Fliss turned to give her husband a huge smile. 'How absolutely lovely!' and then sat back to watch the country lanes fly by as they drove to their hotel and their night of togetherness.

Checking in, Fliss looked around in delight. It was a while since they had visited and she'd forgotten how utterly charming it was. A huge fire blazed merrily away in a drawing room to one side of the reception area, comfortable chairs scattered around inviting bodies to come and relax deep inside their snug depths. On the other side was a small intimate bar with lots of highly polished wood, soft lighting and a welcoming air and Fliss hugged herself with joy. This was the moment she had been waiting for. When devoid of any interruptions she and Jasper could sit in front of the fire with a glass of red wine and open up their hearts. This was the night when everything would get sorted and their marriage recovered. Fliss could feel it in her bones, tonight everything would be put right again.

'Where's my suitcase?' she asked, looking around.

Having signed them in, Jasper was holding the key to their room in one hand, a satisfyingly big brass affair rather than an impersonal plastic card, and his suitcase in the other hand.

He looked at Fliss blankly. 'Your case?'

'Yes. Where is my suitcase?'

Looking down at the clearly empty floor around them, Jasper shrugged his shoulders.

'Er, I don't know. Where did you put it?'

'*I* put it by the door and asked *you* to put it in the car.'

She couldn't fail to see the flash of horror that passed over his face.

'Ah, yes. I remember.'

'Is it still in the car?' she asked hopefully.

'Er, well, I don't think so, shall we have a look?'

'Did you put it in the car Jasper?'

Screwing up his face, he stared upwards at the ceiling, giving a great deal of thought to the question. 'Hmm, in the car, did I put it in the car. Let me just think, did I ….'

'Jasper! Did you put my case in the car or not?'

'Not exactly.'

'How exactly?'

'Not at all.'

'You left it in the house?'

'Oh no!'

Fliss let her shoulders relax.

'I took it out of the house and put it on the drive while I made my call.'

'And?'

'And that's where it is now. I drove around to Jenny's to collect you and I forgot to put it in the car.'

He had stopped looking up at the ceiling and was now concentrating on the red and cream carpet in the lobby. Fliss looked down at herself. She hadn't been to work that morning and unlike Jasper who was still dressed in his suit, she was wearing a pair of leggings, a t-shirt and trainers, all

184

worn for comfort and travelling rather than style and totally inappropriate to be worn at an expensive restaurant such as the one in the hotel.

'My bag is on the driveway of our house?' Fliss felt that the situation warranted clarification. 'It's not in the car, or even in the house. It's on our drive?'

'Er, yes. It is. But don't worry, it's not a problem because I am going to drive back now and collect it.' She could tell he was trying hard to rescue a tricky situation. 'And you are going upstairs to have a delicious long soak in the bath. I booked the same room we had last time, the one with the freestanding bath in front of the window where you can lay neck deep in bubbles and see nothing but fields and trees for miles. And I ordered a bottle of champagne which will be upstairs, waiting. You can have a glass while you're in the bath. You have a drink and I'll be back before you know it.'

He wouldn't be back before she knew it. He would be back in a minimum of two hours. And that was providing that her bag was still on the driveway and hadn't been liberated by someone passing by.

'We could cancel the reservation and just eat in our room.'

'Absolutely not! I know you were looking forward to the meal and quite frankly I was looking forward to seeing you in that dress you packed. I'll go straight back home now and you go upstairs and have a bath. Then we'll get on with the business of having a lovely time.'

With few alternative options available, Fliss let Jasper dump his bag in their room and shoot off while she tried desperately hard not to think unkind thoughts and set about following his directions, sliding into a bath filled to the top with gloriously scented bubbles and a chilled glass of champagne in her hand as she gazed off into the distance.

Feeling the tension fall away from her shoulders and the worries drift out of her head, Fliss stayed in the bath until her skin was wrinkled and the water had turned cool. Pulling on the thick white robe emblazoned with the hotel's logo, she poured herself another glass of champagne and relaxed on the bed. Jasper would be back soon, she would get changed, slipping into the beautiful dress currently laying in her suitcase and they would walk down the huge staircase hand in hand looking exactly like a couple in love.

An hour went by and Fliss took up a spot in the bay window of their room, which conveniently looked out over the approach to the hotel. Dusk was beginning to fall and she could see thousands of fairy lights coming to life along the tree lined driveway as she watched for Jasper's car. Her stomach was growling, other than a slice of toast with her morning coffee she'd had nothing but champagne.

A further hour passed and it was now pitch black apart from the myriad of lights wound around the tree branches and the illuminated fountain by the front door which was casting an eerie wash of silvery-blue across the entrance to the hotel. The bottle of champagne was empty, the minibar had been stripped of nuts and snacks and it took Fliss several attempts to text Jasper and ask how far away he was as she fought against the growing tide of hunger and irritation at his absence.

The response came back quickly, a grovelling apology, an admission that on his return to the house he'd been 'caught up in something' but an assurance that he was now on his way and would soon be there, complete with her case. Pulling a face, Fliss held a hand to her stomach, if she didn't eat something soon she would fall over. When Jasper arrived, all he would find would be his comatose wife. Not the romantic evening she had planned.

Waiting another 45 minutes, Fliss sent a further text, slightly less coherent than her last and with several typing errors, demanding to know when he would arrive. The reply took a little longer this time and she had an image of

186

him speeding desperately through the night, trying to make up for lost time. It would be very soon he said, only another hour or so.

Throwing the phone on the bed, Fliss debated whether to order room service and forget about the restaurant reservation. She was hungry and the champagne had gone to her head. At this rate when Jasper finally arrived, she wouldn't be capable of holding a simple conversation with him let alone dissect their marriage. Frowning, she recovered her phone. An hour, he had said, he would be there in an hour. It had taken them an hour to drive here earlier that afternoon which meant, calculated an outraged Fliss, that he was currently still at their home and nowhere near the romantic hotel suite or his wife, the wife he had promised faithfully would be the sole focus of his attention for the entire weekend.

Staring at the phone, Fliss felt the anger begin to grow. Why had she let him leave in the first place, she chastised herself. She should have known the minute she was out of sight, she would also be out of mind. Despite anything he might say to the contrary, her husband didn't want to spend a romantic evening with her talking about their relationship, he didn't want to talk to her at all.

Well, enough was enough. Throwing the bathrobe to the floor and tripping over the empty champagne bottle which went spinning under the bed, Fliss pulled on her leggings and t-shirt. It took several attempts and she ended up with both legs down one legging for a while, hopping around the room as she tried to work out what the problem was. As far as she was concerned, Jasper had just blown his last chance. When he made it back to the hotel, he would find the room empty as she so often had of late and he could sit here and wonder where his wife was and why she hadn't waited for him. Who knew, it might actually make him think about what was going wrong in their lives and with a last regretful look around the beautiful suite, Fliss grabbed her phone and walked out.

FROM: Fliss Carmichael <agonyauntfliss@digitalrecorder.com>
To: Ellie Henshaw <Elliebellshenshaw@livewell.co.uk>
Date: 17/04/2020

Hi Ellie

I'm so proud of you for putting the record straight with Jeff. It takes tremendous courage to be completely honest but it is kinder to Jeff in the long run, to tell him the truth about how you feel rather than to let him keep hoping. There are few things more debilitating than losing hope.

The next step and I know that you won't want to hear this, is to be equally open with Logan. You shouldn't waste any more time hoping that you'll bump into each other in the lift, or hanging around football pitches. It seems to me that you've given up a great deal to be with him. Carl was your future and you've changed the course of your destiny because you fell in love with someone else. Make it count for something. Logan must understand exactly what is happening with Carl. Don't let any more misunderstandings occur, don't let anything else come between you both. It's not been the smoothest of paths and whilst I normally advise caution with such things, I can't help feeling where you are concerned it might be an idea to simply tell him exactly how you feel and leave absolutely no room for any more confusion. Every time you seem to be making progress, something comes along and spoils things so don't waste any more time Ellie, make him listen to you and be honest. Tell him how you feel before anything else goes wrong!

If it's any consolation, I'm finding my own path to be a bit rocky at the moment. It doesn't seem to matter how hard I try, I can't seem to reach Jasper. We had arranged a special night away, a lovely hotel suite, a restaurant and an evening to ourselves. I'm afraid it didn't go very well, in fact, it was a disaster. It's as though trying to get him to recognise how things have changed is only serving to make me see how bad they've become.

Deciding that our future didn't depend on a family was a hard decision to make, but Jasper and I were happy as a couple and it seemed the right course for us at the time. Actually, there is something that very few people know. Two years ago, I found out I was pregnant and then I had a miscarriage. The pregnancy was unexpected, we'd never made any firm decisions one way or another about a family, we both thought it would happen one day. Then I found out I was expecting a baby and suddenly our lives moved onto a whole new level. We were excited, terrified, worried, happy. We kept it very much to ourselves in the early months, it was a delicious secret shared only between the two of us. But then I lost the baby. And the excitement and happiness disappeared, only the terror and the worry remained. It took a while for me to get back to my old self. When Jasper and I discussed the future, the thought of going through such pain and heartbreak again petrified both of us and we agreed that we were blissfully happy as we were. Jasper pointed out that we didn't really have time to fit in a family anyway, we were far too busy with our lives, so we chose to remain a couple, no family, just the two of us.

I have never regretted our decision but now Jasper seems to have forgotten how we felt and why we made that choice and it's making me angry. You're the first person I've ever really discussed this with and it's surprisingly liberating to get it off my chest. It's also making me think far more deeply about our life together and I've come to the realisation that I shouldn't have to save our marriage by myself. There'll be no more games, no more ploys to get Jasper to look up from his phone once in a while, I think it's time he understood the danger we are facing. My overwhelming fear is that he won't feel motivated enough to do anything about it and the thought of not having Jasper by my side is something that I find quite terrifying.

Sending you courage,

Fliss x

This email has been sent by Fliss Carmichael, the online agony aunt of The Digital Recorder. All views expressed herein are her own and should not be taken as an instruction to proceed with any course of action without careful consideration of the potential consequences. The Digital Recorder claims no responsibility for any trauma, divorce proceedings or physical injury that may result from the advice contained herein. Thank you for contributing.

Chapter 18

By the time Ellie arrived at work on Monday morning, Laura was pulling her hair out, desperate to hear how the encounter had gone.

'Did you tell Jeff you weren't at football because of him?' demanded Laura. 'Did you tell Logan that you fancied him? Did you tell Harriet to back off? Did you make sure everybody understood that it's Logan you want?'

Throwing her bag into her bottom drawer, Ellie flicked on her computer, wondering where to start.

'Not exactly,' she answered wearily.

'Not exactly? Which bit did you not exactly do?'

'Well, I did tell Jeff I was there only as a supporter.'

'That's a start,' encouraged Laura.

'And I refused to go for a meal with him.'

'Good.'

'Even though Logan would have been there.'

'Logan? You refused to go for a meal with Logan?'

'Yes, because I would have gone with Jeff, not Logan.'

'I see. But to refuse to go with Logan, that's not good.'

'Then Harriet said she'd get a takeaway and take it round to Logan's.'

'Oh, that's bad. That's really bad.'

'Logan didn't seem interested.'

'Ah, now that *is* good.'

'I think he was on the point of refusing.'

'That's really good! What do you mean, on the point of refusing? Did he actually refuse?'

'No, he asked me if I would join them.'

'Wonderful!'

'But then Carl turned up and told them all he was my fiancé.'

'Oh that's bad, that's very bad. What on earth did Logan say?'

'He didn't say a lot. I mean I told everybody that Carl was my ex but Logan just seemed disappointed.'

'Disappointed?'

'Yes.'

'Logan was disappointed that you had a fiancé?

'I don't have a ...'

'Yes, I know,' interrupted Laura. 'But he was disappointed to think that you *may* have a fiancé?'

'He seemed to be,' sighed Ellie. 'He barely looked at me when I was saying goodbye.'

'Now that *is* good. That's very good!'

'Good? How can that be good?'

'Because Ells darling, even though you were supposed to be there with Jeff and Logan was supposed to be there with Harriet, I think he must have wanted to be there with you and he was upset when he thought you were already engaged to someone else.'

Ellie sat in her chair thinking. Surely the very fact that she was supposed to be there with Jeff meant Logan already thought she was taken. She opened her mouth to argue but Laura ploughed on.

'It makes sense, really it does. Logan probably knew you didn't want to go out with Jeff, he was going along with it all so he could be close to you.'

Ellie was doubtful. There had been nothing in Logan's behaviour to give her any indication that he had a hidden desire to be close to her.

'Now, suddenly,' continued Laura in an excited tone, 'suddenly his plans are dashed! He finds out that not only does Jeff want to ask you out but there's someone else in the game.'

'The game?'

'The game of love! He was disappointed Ellie, what does that tell you?'

Pulling a face, Ellie tried to think. 'I'm not sure,' she eventually admitted. 'I've been thinking about it all weekend and I have no idea.'

'It means,' Laura paused for dramatic effect. 'It means that he's interested in you! He is actually interested. In you. Oh, Ells, it's not one-sided crush anymore, it's a possible reciprocal double interest scenario. I think part of the reason Logan finds it as hard as you do to hold a conversation is because he's got a crush on you. Isn't that wonderful?'

Ellie was staring. She had no idea how Laura had reached this conclusion although she had to admit to liking the outcome. If only she had the same very positive outlook on life that her friend possessed.

'Really?' she asked, still unsure. 'You think that Logan is interested in me?'

'Of course. Why else would he be disappointed? And now you know exactly what to do next.'

'I do?'

'Yes. You need to tell Logan what happened. That you fancy the pants off him and you went to football for one reason only, because you wanted to be with him. God knows, I can't imagine any other reason you'd want to spend a cold Saturday afternoon watching grown men playing games.'

'That's what Fliss said as well,' admitted Ellie begrudgingly. 'But I can't, I really can't. It's taken me this long to pluck up enough courage to say hello. Now you both want me to tell him how I feel and see what happens?'

'Did Fliss tell you to let him how you feel?'

'Yes but I can't, I…'

'You know, the more I hear about this agony aunt business the more convinced I am that I would be really good at the job,' mused Laura, forgetting about Ellie for a moment. 'Everything she tells you I've already suggested.'

'But neither of you seem to understand how hard it would be for me. Laura, are you listening? I can't just suddenly declare undying love for him because you think he's upset that I may have a fiancé.'

'Yes you can. Well, not necessarily the undying love bit. That could scare him off for good. But you need to be honest with him, and you can be. Because now you know he's interested in you.'

'But I don't know that,' Ellie whispered in anguish. 'I don't know that he has any interest me at all, not really.'

'Then,' said Laura with a stern look from under knotted eyebrows, 'you've been wasting your time mooning over him and telling me how much you loved him.'

'I haven't …'

'Yes, you have. If the opportunity comes along and you waste it, then it was all for nothing. Including Carl.'

'Carl?'

'Yes. Carl. Because whatever you say to the contrary Ells, I am beginning to believe that you ditched the man you had been with for three years simply because you saw someone across a crowded room and couldn't get him out of your head. You fooled yourself into believing that Logan was the love of your life, *the one*, the man who would be bringing you a rose with your morning cup of tea in 20 years, who would hold your hand when you walked down the street, who would stare into your eyes every night and tell you he loved you.'

Ellie didn't speak, A single tear had escaped from the corner of her eye and was making its way slowly down her cheek as Laura, her down to earth friend who snorted at the idea of true love and happy ever after, described exactly how Ellie felt.

'I think you left Carl because you had fallen in love with Logan and if you don't do something about it now, you've ruined not only your own life but Carl's as well and all for something that you're not prepared to fight for.'

Perhaps Laura would make a good agony aunt, it was almost word for word what Fliss had said.

'But what can I do?' sniffed Ellie, not denying Laura's claim. 'What can I do about it?'

'You can be brave and tell him what you think Ells. Be really brave, walk up to Logan and tell him exactly what is going on inside that head of yours. You'll have to because there's no way he's going to work it out for himself.'

Laura spun her chair around and shuffled back to her desk, leaving Ellie sitting in silence, her head full of thoughts. It had been hard enough getting this far with Logan, the thought of boldly walking up to him and baring her soul made her feel quite weak. But Laura was right. And Fliss. If she didn't take her opportunity with Logan, then it had all been a waste of time. She and Carl could still be together, maybe even planning a wedding. If she didn't at least try to let Logan know how she felt, then she could end up miserable and alone forever. It was time for Ellie to become braver than she had ever thought possible, she just wasn't entirely sure how she could manage it and with a quaking heart she started her work for the day, her mind a turmoil of emotion.

A few hours later, Laura rolled her chair around to Ellie's desk.

'Well?' she demanded.

Ellie shifted uncomfortably. 'I just need the right moment and …'

'Oh for goodness sake, you're always waiting for the right moment. Think about how many opportunities you've missed, how many okay moments that have passed by while you've been waiting for the perfect one to arrive. And let's face it, Ells, you usually muck it up anyway. Stop dithering and get on with letting Logan know the truth.'

Ellie wanted to argue, but she knew Laura was right.

'I can't just walk up to his desk and start a conversation about how much I like him!'

'Why not?'

'Because it's … it's… inappropriate.'

'More inappropriate than agreeing to go on a date with one of his mates, or having him think that you're secretly engaged to Carl?'

'Not exactly. But it's still ….'

'Ellie, stop telling me about it and start telling Logan.'

'It's not that easy …'

'I mean right now, stop talking to me and talk to him.'

'But you don't understand ….'

'Now Ellie! He's just about to get in the lift, go talk to him. Now!'

Looking across the office, Ellie could see Logan walking towards the bank of lifts, a pile of files in his arms as per usual. The doors were already starting to open, Ellie had precious little time to reach him if she wanted a conversation about Saturday and the arrival of her fiancé.

'Go!' squealed Laura, 'quickly.'

Almost vaulting over Laura's desk, Ellie wound her way through the tables and filing cabinets that marked out the administration corner, cannoned off a couple of colleagues walking by and headed for the lift in Logan's wake.

'Logan,' she yelled, slightly out of breath from her exertion. 'Logan, I need to speak to you!'

Hearing her voice, he looked up in surprise and then held his hand against the door so it wouldn't shut, allowing Ellie to leap inside.

'Thank you,' she gasped, slipping in and standing in front of him. 'I need to speak to you, quite urgently.'

He smiled and nodded. 'What is it? Do you need help with something?'

'Not exactly.'

'Is it SAS? Have you been reading about it?'

'Er no.'

'Okay, do you want me to stop by your desk later and ….?'

'No! I need to talk to you now. There's something I need to tell you,'

He blinked, looking a little worried even as he nodded his head. 'What is it?'

She'd been rehearsing ever since Laura had delivered her early morning pep talk. In her head, she had practised how

197

she would tell him with a little apologetic grin about the original mix up at The Flying Horse, how she had wanted to go to the football to watch Logan, not Jeff, how Carl was very definitely her ex and not her fiancé. She had it all sorted out in her head, now she needed to stop thinking about it and start talking.

Taking a deep breath she opened her mouth. 'Logan …'

Someone cleared their throat, a small but definite clearing of the vocal cords and Ellie froze, her mouth still hanging open. Because it hadn't been Logan. She was standing directly in front of him, staring right at him, and he had made no move whatsoever. Which meant only one thing and cautiously, Ellie shuffled fractionally sideways so she could look over her shoulder.

Mr Goodfellow stared back. And not just Mr Goodfellow but the CEO of StaySafe Insurance Group, the Director of Human Resources and the Administration Director, all standing behind her and to a man, waiting to hear what Ellie had to say.

'I … er … I…'

Her cheeks were suffused with colour and she was praying very hard that the ground would simply open up and swallow her, immediately. Her eyes flew to the large red numbers above the lift doors. Never had they moved so slowly. They were still only on floor 6.

'I … er… oh ….'

'What is it Ellie?' asked Logan gently. 'What did you want to say?'

Perhaps the lift would fail. It could shudder to a creaking, groaning halt and then plummet to the basement as they all screamed in fright and were thrown around its confined interior. It would be infinitely preferable to this, decided Ellie.

'I don't know,' she whispered, shaking her head violently. 'It's completely gone out of my head.'

'But you said it was important,' piped up Mr Goodfellow. 'Can't you remember what you wanted?'

'Nope.' Ellie shook her head and held her hands aloft to emphasise the point. 'Gone. Completely gone.'

'It was only a minute ago you jumped in the lift yelling his name. And now you can't remember why?'

'No. Nope. Sorry. No.'

They were all staring at her, even Logan who was looking almost as embarrassed as Ellie.

Tutting, Mr Goodfellow shook his head. 'Well can you remember what it was about in general?' he demanded. 'What sort of thing are we talking? Statistics? Interpretations? Analytics?' he barked.

Love, the unrequited sort, misunderstandings and mishaps, thought Ellie.

'Sorry, it's gone,' she apologised. 'Completely.'

The lift shuddered to a halt and the doors slid open. No-one moved, the CEO was looking at Ellie with an interest verging on the concerned and Mr Goodfellow was rolling his eyes in irritation.

'I er …' Logan waved his hand towards the door. 'I …er…I need to get out.'

'Right! Of course, you do,' babbled Ellie, jumping out of his way. 'Of course, please, don't let me hold you up.'

She pressed herself against the wall and let Logan exit the lift.

'Are you ….?'

'No! No, I'm sure it will come back to me later. I don't think it was important actually, now I come to think of it. It was just a little question I wanted to ask, nothing urgent at all. Bye Logan, sorry for … well bye!'

The lift doors closed and silence reigned. In desperation, Ellie started humming, a cheerful little tune that was meant to put everyone at their ease and show how very relaxed she was about the incident. The lift shuddered to a halt once more and one by one they all stepped out, the CEO giving her a searching glance as he walked past.

'Are you getting out Ellie?' asked Mr Goodfellow.

'No, no. I'm going up a few more floors.' She wanted the doors to close and everyone to disappear.

'There are no more floors Ellie. You've reached the top of the building.'

'I have? Well, I wonder where my floor went. I must have missed it.'

'Which floor did you want my dear?' It was the Human Resources Director, clearly worried that he had overlooked supporting a very vulnerable employee.

'Floor? Which floor. Hmm, that's a good question. Which floor?'

Ellie was scanning the panel which listed each department to be found in the StaySafe Insurance Group.

'I'm not sure which floor I wanted,' she stuttered, her eyes skimming the names for somewhere she could reasonably be heading. 'I wanted er, I wanted the IT department.'

The CEO reached forward to pat Ellie on the arm. 'You'll find them on floor 5, my dear,' he said in a gentle tone. 'Stay in the lift and press number 5.'

'Floor 5,' thundered Mr Goodfellow. 'The floor you work on Ellie! 6 feet away from your desk.'

Chapter 19

When Ellie returned, Laura was jigging around in her seat waiting for an update.

'Did you see him, did you speak to him?' she asked excitedly.

'Er, no.'

'Oh Ellie, you didn't chicken out again did you?'

'He wasn't in the lift alone.'

'So?'

'Mr Goodfellow was there plus a bunch of senior management! I couldn't say anything in front of them all.'

'You could have said you needed a word with him, could he come to your desk when he was free.'

Ah, thought Ellie. Yes, she could have said exactly that. How easy it would have been. 'I suppose so,' she mumbled. 'I was too embarrassed to think of anything.'

'Well you'll just have to try again,' said Laura firmly. 'But one way or another, you need to speak to him before you go home today. You can't afford to let this go on.'

Another hour went by with no sign of Logan and Laura swung her chair round to face her friend.

'You'll have to go lurk,' she instructed. 'You can't wait for him to appear.'

'Lurk?'

'Yes. Go up to the 7th floor and hang around. Find things to do on that floor and watch for an opportunity. He's bound to leave his desk eventually, he'll need to go to the toilet at some point.'

'I'm not hanging outside the men's toilet on the off chance that Logan will use it!'

'Okay, then stay away from the toilet but just …lurk, hang around where he might appear.'

Ellie didn't need an explanation of lurking, she had become an expert over the last few weeks. It wasn't uncommon for her to linger in the lobby, fumbling with her brolly and checking her handbag, generally delaying the moment she would have to jump in the lift in the vain hope that Logan would appear and they could travel up to the 5th floor together. Some mornings she had taken the lift, only to trot back down the stairs and repeat the whole process again. And she wasn't the only one employing similar tactics. Only the previous day she had walked in to find Harriet hovering by the lift. Smiling politely at each other they had taken the journey up to the 5th floor where Ellie had gone straight to the ladies, hung around for a few minutes then belted down the stairs to hover in the lobby for Logan's arrival, only to find Harriet standing by the lifts once more.

'Oh, er, I thought I'd left my brolly behind,' Ellie had said with pink cheeks.

'Yes, me too.'

They'd both looked around the empty lobby before shrugging their shoulders and getting back into the lift and up to the 5th floor.

Laura had no idea just what an accomplished lurker Ellie had become over the weeks.

'Go on Ellie, everybody does it, it will increase your chances of bumping into him.'

'Okay, okay. But I can't stay up there too long. Mr Goodfellow has got his eye on me at the moment. Actually, if he asks where I am, tell him I'm in IT. He won't be surprised.'

On the 7th floor, Ellie began her lurking. Walking up the steps, slowly so she didn't overexert herself and end up panting and red-faced, she fluffed up her hair, straightened her skirt and walked casually from the staircase down the long corridor. Desks were arranged to one side, nothing more than a few screens marking where one section ended and another began and at the end of the corridor was another staircase. Rows of heads were visible, all studiously bent over a keyboard or staring at a monitor. They seemed to work a great deal harder than anyone on floor 5, thought Ellie. No-one would be able to lurk around administration without being noticed, usually by a bored Laura who would yell their name and ask what they wanted.

Keeping her gaze fixed straight ahead so it would appear to the untrained eye as though she were simply passing through, Ellie squinted sideways and managed to catch sight of Logan's inky black hair approximately halfway down the office. At least she knew where he was and reaching the end of the corridor she shot down the stairs, belted along the 6th-floor corridor and then back up the stairs to re-emerge back on the 7th floor. No-one so much as blinked in her direction and trying to look supremely indifferent to all around her, she walked slowly along the length of the corridor once more, refusing to look in Logan's direction but knowing the exact moment she passed his desk. It was on her fourth journey down, along and back up the stairs, that she emerged from the staircase and gave a small gasp. A few steps ahead of her, walking slowly and trying to look just as supremely indifferent, was Harriet.

Hugging the doorway, Ellie watched Harriet's progression along the corridor. She was looking forwards, her head never turning to seek out Logan's desk or check his profile but Ellie knew she was peeping out of the corner of her eye, it was exactly what Ellie had been doing.

At that moment, a movement to her right caught Ellie's attention and with another gasp, she saw Logan stand up and stretch. Holding her breath, she watched as he wiggled his shoulders to ease the tension of spending long hours at his computer and then weaved his way around the desks and onto the corridor. Harriet was several feet in front of him, Ellie several feet behind him and not waiting to see what Harriet did next, Ellie leapt forwards, almost jogging to close the gap between them.

'Logan!' she said in a subdued but urgent whisper. 'Logan!'

He stopped and turned just as an equally determined voice came floating down the corridor.

'Logan! Logan!'

Harriet was waving her arm, looking thoroughly surprised to find him tucked away on the 7th floor.

'Logan!' said Ellie firmly. 'I want to speak to you!'

'Logan! What are you doing up here?' trilled Harriet from her less advantageous position further ahead.

Logan's head swivelled from Ellie to Harriet and back to Ellie.

'Hi Ellie, have you remembered what you wanted me to help with?' he asked.

'Oh yes, I have, I've remembered.'

He took a few steps in her direction and Ellie saw the thunderous expression appear on Harriet's face. Abandoning her insouciance, she set off at a pace down the corridor in their direction, her face determined.

'And?'

'Er, you were right. It was about the SAS!' Ellie improvised. 'I wanted to ask you a question about it.'

'Logan!' Harriet had reached them, triple jumping the last few feet to grab hold of Logan's arm. 'How lovely to bump into you. I had totally forgotten that you worked on this floor!'

'Hello Harriet,' he said politely.

'It's such a coincidence bumping into you like this,' Harriet continued, pulling on his arm slightly to make him face her. 'I'd actually wanted to ask you something.'

'Really? That is a coincidence, Ellie has come to ask me something as well. Is yours work related?' asked Logan with a small frown.

'Work related? Of course not!'

'Ah, Ellie's is. Do you mind if I talk to her first? It seems pretty urgent.'

If looks could kill, Ellie would have dropped to the floor immediately.

'Work related?' Harriet asked, in disbelief.

'Yes.' Ellie smiled. 'Logan knows I'm interested in SAS and he very kindly gave me some articles to read.'

'You're interested in the SAS, Really?'

Logan smiled. 'It's not the SAS Harriet, I don't think Ellie is remotely interested in them. It's SAS, Statistical Analysis System software.'

Harriet stared. 'Statistical Analy ... what?'

'Statistical Analysis Systems,' laughed Logan. 'It is a bit of a mouthful.'

'And Ellie is interested in it?'

'Yes, it's actually unusual to find anyone who knows what it is let alone has an interest.'

'I bet it is. And you're going to speak to her now, about .... about it?'

'Yes, can I catch up with you later Harriet? Do you mind?'

Ellie suspected that Harriet would know all about SAS by the time she spoke to Logan again. Good luck to her, she thought, it was the most uninteresting subject Ellie had ever encountered.

'No problem at all,' cooed Harriet. 'Although I might stick around and listen actually. It sounds pretty cool.'

Logan looked questioningly at Ellie who smiled sympathetically. 'It is pretty cool Harriet but if you don't mind, I really need to speak to Logan at my desk. That's where, the er, the SAS question is.'

Defeated, Harriet hung onto her smile, her teeth bared at Ellie. 'Is it indeed? Well then, whenever you're free Logan perhaps you could come and chat to me at *my* desk, about the question *I* want to ask!'

Harriet walked stiffly away, back down the staircase and Ellie wondered how many laps she had completed before she'd managed to encounter Logan. It would appear Ellie wasn't the only lurker in the building.

'So what is the question?' asked Logan intrigued as they turned towards the staircase. 'You say it's at your desk? Have you been trying to…'

'I lied.'

They were on one of the half-landings of the staircase, the 7th floor a few steps above them, the 6th floor a few steps below. Logan stopped, his eyebrows raised.

'Lied about?'

'Lied about SAS. I haven't read any of the articles. I don't understand a word of it actually.'

'I see. So you don't want to talk to me …'

'Yes! I just needed Harriet to leave.' Emboldened by her own honesty, Ellie took a deep breath. 'I needed to tell you something, quite important. You see, the night at The Flying Horse when I said I would come and watch the football, it was you I wanted to watch. Actually, no. If I'm being completely honest and I think I should be,' how proud Laura and Fliss would be, she thought as she continued, 'I didn't want to watch anyone playing football but I wanted to come along and support you. Then Jeff jumped in and I just didn't want to tell him to get lost. I thought it would be embarrassing for all of us if I said that I … that it…' Her cheeks couldn't go any pinker. 'That it was you that I wanted to go with.'

'You wanted to support me?'

'Yes.'

'Why?'

'Why? Because I er…well I like you.'

Her heart thumped alarmingly at the admission, and she thought that her legs would give way completely as she hung onto the handrail and watched him consider her words. How nice it would be if at this point Logan admitted to deep-rooted and long-held feelings for her. How he spent his days not caught up in the excitement of analysis but in thoughts of Ellie from administration who he kept catching sight of in the lift and walking slowly along the corridor of floor 7.

But Logan didn't say anything, his own cheeks adopting a flush of colour as he waited for Ellie to continue.

'And then Carl appeared and said I was his fiancée.' She peeped up to see a closed expression on Logan's face. 'But he's not, I'm not. I did go out with him for a while, quite a long while actually. But we never agreed to get married.'

'He seemed quite insistent.'

'I know. He is insistent, he still wants us to get married. But it's over. And I need you to understand because, well because….'

Ellie struggled to remember why she was humiliating herself in this way, before recalling Fliss' advice and Laura's stern words that Logan would end up with Harriet if Ellie didn't throw a little honesty at the situation.

'Because I like you. Very much.' She wouldn't embarrass both of them by blurting out a declaration of love on the staircase. Just like would do for now. 'And I felt it was important that you know.'

Checking to see the effect her words may have had, she met Logan's lovely silver-grey eyes looking down at her in surprise and, was that a hint of excitement she could spot in those dark irises?

'I see.' He didn't appear blown over with emotion, and there was no equally heartfelt declaration coming back her way, but he didn't look appalled. Perhaps he was just a generally restrained sort of person. It was an excellent quality, she decided, restraint and calm in times of stress and unexpected encounters on the staircase.

'Look,' he ran a hand through his hair and Ellie had to stop herself from smoothing down the wayward strands he'd created. 'This isn't really the place for all this.' They both cast an eye around the rather echoey staircase. 'But I am glad that you've er… spoken to me. Why don't we meet up for a drink and a …chat? Just the two of us. No Laura.'

'No Laura,' agreed Ellie unable to control the grin that appeared as he carried on.

'The Flying Horse?'

'The Flying Horse.'

'5:30, straight after work?'

'5:30 it is.'

'Okay, see you later and Ellie,' he looked at her, a small smile tugging at the corner of his lips, 'I'm looking forward to seeing you,' and then he was gone, sprinting back up the staircase and leaving Ellie hugging herself with bliss. It had finally happened, the humiliation, the despair, the uncertainty, all worth it. She had a date with Logan!

FROM: Ellie Henshaw   <Elliebellshenshaw@livewell.co.uk>
To: Fliss Carmichael   <agonyauntfliss@digitalrecorder.com>
Date: 20/04/2020

Dear Fliss

I just had to write a quick email and say thank you, thank you, thank you. I did everything you suggested and I have a date with Logan! A proper date, the two of us in a pub with each other, no-one else.

It's all down to you and your fantastic advice and I couldn't wait to let you know that it has finally worked out. I told him about the misunderstandings, about how I felt. I actually admitted that I liked him! He didn't run away or look appalled, he said we should go out and talk so we're meeting after work and I'm so excited, I feel as though I'm walking on a very fluffy cloud somewhere in a rosy pink sky. Tonight we'll get to sit and talk, with no-one else to interfere or get involved. I know that we're going to find so much in common, I just know that it's going to be wonderful and exciting and everything that I've been dreaming of.

Laura said I shouldn't get too excited and that something will go wrong but I don't think so, not this time. Standing there and telling him how I felt was one of the hardest things I've ever had to do and I refuse to let that go to waste. And you were right, I've given up so much, it's time to make sure it wasn't all in vain.

I also had to say how very sorry I was to hear about your baby. I cried when I read your email, it was so beautiful and sad. I can understand why two people would decide not to put themselves through that again. But I also can't help wondering whether you should sit down and talk about it now it's all less raw and frightening. Maybe it was the right choice then but not necessarily the right one for you now? Could it be part of the reason you feel unhappy, why your marriage isn't giving you what you want anymore? I'm sorry if I am upsetting you in any way talking about something so painful and personal. I'm sure that you know exactly

what you are doing but sometimes our unhappiness comes from unexpected places and needs some examining.
Thank you again for your wonderful advice, I have to go now because Laura wants to give me a makeover! Don't worry, I'll let you know what happens!

Your very grateful friend

Ellie

Chapter 20

Fliss was sitting at the kitchen table drinking coffee when Jasper appeared in the doorway, dressed in a suit, his phone inevitably in one hand. He had eventually arrived back at the hotel with Fliss' suitcase the previous evening only to find the room empty and his wife missing. Checking with reception who knew nothing about Mrs Carmichael's whereabouts and were reluctant to call the police without a little more investigation, he'd made several increasingly distraught calls, all of which Fliss had ignored. Not receiving any response, he had left a final message saying that he could only presume Fliss had returned to the house for some urgent reason and jumping back in his car, he had driven home as quickly as possible and arrived back to the sight of his wife fast asleep in bed, her phone turned off and laying on the floor. The bottle of champagne she had downed on an empty stomach had made it impossible for Jasper to wake her up enough to demand an explanation and eventually he had given up and climbed in beside her.

With a throbbing head and a mouth as dry as the Sahara Desert, Fliss glared at Jasper as he walked into the kitchen.

'You stayed at home to work,' she said furiously. 'You left me in the hotel and you stayed at home to work.'

Fully expecting an apology for her unexpected departure, Jasper took a step back looking startled at the unaccustomed venom in her voice. 'No,' he said defensively. 'I drove home to collect your suitcase and I …'

'My suitcase which you had left on the driveway! Because you were on the phone, as usual.'

'Well, yes it was my fault that's why I offered to drive back…'

211

Noting his appearance, Fliss' eyes narrowed. 'Are you going into work today?'

'Work? Well, yes but only ....'

'It's Saturday and you told your office you would be away for the weekend. Why are you going to work?'

'Ah, yes, well ... when I realised that you had left the hotel and returned home without letting me know,' said Jasper with an aggrieved air, 'I agreed to attend a meeting today that I ....'

'When?'

'When. In about 45 minutes so I ...'

'When did you arrange this meeting? It was after 11.00 when you got back last night.'

Fliss saw his face tense and his feet began to slide backwards, one hand behind him as he groped for the kitchen door.

'Was it? I had spoken to someone earlier and ...'

'You arranged it yesterday afternoon, didn't you?' Fliss stood up, walking towards her retreating husband, her eyes full of icy rage as she watched him flounder. 'You arranged this when you came back to the house to collect my case, didn't you?'

'Well,' Jasper straightened his tie nervously. 'I did make a couple of calls and a meeting had been suggested for today but I told them I didn't think that it was possible ...'

'Why did you come into the house?'

'The house?' He cleared his throat. 'Er, this house?'

'Yesterday. All you had to do was pull into the drive, collect my bag and drive back to the hotel. Why did you come into the house?'

Panic was building in Jasper's eyes. His probing hand had finally found the kitchen door handle and he was gripping it behind his back.

'I remembered a call I'd meant to make before we left, just a quick one,' he added hastily at his wife's murderous expression. 'So I popped into my study and then I saw an email that I had to respond to and ....'

'And you were going to break the news this morning, at the hotel? You were going to tell me that something had come up and you had to go to a meeting.'

'No! Absolutely not. If we'd been at the hotel, of course I would have phoned and told them I couldn't go.' He had managed to open the door and was walking backwards out of the kitchen, trying to put sufficient space between himself and the fireball in front of him. 'I wouldn't have interrupted our break.'

'You wouldn't have had to tell them you couldn't go unless you had told them in the first place that you could!'

Jasper screwed up his face and Fliss could see him testing her theory in his head. 'Ah, well, I had indicated that I would *like* to have gone if the circumstances had been different but as they clearly weren't different, I couldn't. But then the circumstances became different and I could go, so I let them know,' he finished weakly. He had made it into the hallway and was continuing his slow reversing in the direction of the front door.

Standing in the middle of the kitchen, the fight suddenly left Fliss' body.

'We need to talk Jasper,' she said quietly, lifting her hand to interrupt him. 'No romantic dinners, no overnight stays in a hotel. We will talk, here, in our house. And for once you will stop thinking about everyone and everything else and listen to what I am saying to you.'

Jasper nodded. 'Yes, excellent idea, I agree, that's what we'll do.' He hovered, indecision on his face and Fliss saw him cast a quick glance at the clock. 'Er, would that be after my meeting?' he asked hopefully. 'I'll have my meeting and then come home so we can talk?'

'After your meeting Jasper. Straight after your meeting.'

'Yes! Understood, straight after my meeting. Actually, I just need to call into …. no, no! Straight after the meeting, that's a much better idea, bye darling!' and he was heading for the door at speed before Fliss added anything more to the conversation.

With the house to herself, Fliss curled up in her favourite chair by the fire, her hands wrapped around another cup of coffee. She still blushed at the memory of herself in her cream silk corset, whispering sweet nothings to Freddie. She would never be able to walk into the Royal Hotel again after being evicted under suspicion of being at best a madam and at worst a manic stalker. Then there were the love hearts in Jasper's briefcase, the jack in the box, the accident, the police. Fliss felt that she had put in as much effort as she could possibly manage into recovering her marriage but the subtle approach seems to be causing her nothing but grief and embarrassment. And underneath it all was a growing feeling of resentment. Sacrifices were almost inevitable in a marriage, but why did they all have to be made by Fliss? And the ultimate sacrifice of all, the decision they had taken to remain a couple and preserve their happiness seemed to have backfired. It was meant to be the two of them, together forever. Fliss was feeling decidedly lonely these days, lonely and empty.

When Jasper arrived home later in the afternoon, Fliss' head had stopped aching quite so much and she had made several decisions. Going into his study to leave his briefcase on the desk, Jasper came straight back out, an unusual occurrence these days, and joined her in the living room.

'I'm not happy,' Fliss started without any preamble, watching as Jasper's eyebrows shot up his forehead at her directness. 'I love you Jasper, but our marriage has changed. You seem to have lost interest and I am beginning to feel lonely.'

His mouth fell open in shock and ignoring him, Fliss marched onwards. 'This is not about how busy you are with work, it's about how busy you *make* yourself with work. It's become an obsession. It's all you think about and sometimes I feel it's all you care about.'

No! Fliss I ....'

214

'You don't even look me in the eye any more, you're always looking down at that blessed phone. You say the right things Jasper, you behave as though you still love me but there's a distance between us that's growing.'

'But I love you ...'

Fliss didn't want any interruptions. If Jasper started telling her how much he loved her then she would start to believe him and convince herself that the problem was over, so she ignored his interruption and continued.

'I've tried to reignite the romance but you don't seem to have even noticed.' Freddie certainly had, thought Fliss grimly. He had been a witness to most of her failed attempts. 'This isn't how it was meant to be Jasper. We said that we didn't need a family, we were happy to remain just the two of us. Except that now I seem to be on my own.'

The barb struck home and Jasper flinched, his eyes veering away, a muscle twitching in his jaw. The decision made two years ago had not been mentioned by either of them since.

'So I've decided it's time I stopped trying.'

Jasper's face paled and Fliss could see a bead of sweat begin to form on his forehead. 'Stop trying?' he whispered. 'You mean you....'

'I don't see why I should bother anymore.'

'What? Oh no! I didn't realise you were so unhappy, I...'

'I mean, it's time *you* put a little more effort into our marriage.'

'Oh God.' Jasper doubled over, his breath coming out in a short sharp gasp. 'I thought you were saying...' His hand was shaking slightly as he held it out to her. 'Fliss I love you.'

Ignoring the hand, she continued to sit up straight in her chair.

'And I love you,' she said calmly. 'But love isn't always enough.' Fliss had always felt that love was absolutely enough. That with love you could achieve anything, with

215

love you could survive anything. She wondered if she had been wrong her entire life, or maybe love, or the lack of love, wasn't the problem in her marriage.

'But what else is there?' asked Jasper bewildered. 'If we love each other, why isn't that enough?'

It was a good question, thought Fliss. 'Because I've never doubted you before,' she answered slowly. 'I've never once wondered if you were having an affair or if you were bored of my company.' She held up a hand to stop his denial. 'And now I wonder about all of those things. Because our relationship has changed. Right now I get the impression you would rather spend your time with Freddie, or the Benson's or Ross or just about anybody else but me. Your phone is now the most important thing in your life.'

Jaspers eyes opened wide, the emotions racing across his shocked face. 'That's not true. I don't…'

'Really? We couldn't even spend a night away in a hotel without you needing to arrange a meeting.'

His head dropped slightly. 'I'm sorry, I ….'

'What's gone wrong? Is our relationship so bad that you don't want to spend time with me anymore?'

'No! I want to be with you forever. It's just that work….'

'Stop blaming it all on work Jasper! It's you I'm worried about, you and me. The couple we used to be.'

'Aren't we a couple anymore?'

'No. Not really. And it worries me that if we don't do something now, we may never be the people we once were. It's time to stop putting work first, second and last and let's get back to the business of being in love.'

Silence fell in the room and Fliss could hear the clock in the hallway ticking rhythmically as Jasper stared at the empty fireplace. She wondered where his phone was, for once it wasn't gripped tightly in his hand. She could see the struggle in his face, the reluctant knowledge that maybe his wife had a point worth considering.

'What do you want me to do?' His voice was quiet, his face still pale with shock and it was the first time that Fliss

216

felt he was listening to what she had to say. Were they finally making progress?

'I don't know,' she said honestly. 'I just want to feel as though I'm a part of your life again. I want you to occasionally stop thinking about work and look at me as though you can see me.'

Jasper moved restlessly in his chair. 'I am genuinely very busy at work …'

'I know! And I don't mind. But not every minute of every day. It's not as though I'm talking about hiking around Asia for a couple of months without a phone signal.'

Jasper gave a genuine gasp of horror at the thought, his skin turning grey. 'I can't do that! I can't…'

Fliss could almost see his heart palpitating through his jacket. 'Relax, that's not what I'm asking.'

His breathing slowed a little and Fliss reached forward to pat his hand reassuringly. 'Surely we can spend the odd night together without you panicking about work?'

'Yes, of course.' The tremor in his hand eased.

'And we can start doing things together again like we used to?'

No family equalled a life in which they could please themselves, do whatever they wanted whenever the mood overcame them. Those were Jasper's words, he had whispered them to Fliss as he had held her hand one night. It was the first time he'd suggested that maybe not having a family could be a good thing for their marriage.

'Of course we can my darling. Of course. I'm sorry…'

Holding up her hand, Fliss shook her head. 'It's not about blaming each other, we've both let this happen. But let's stop it now, while we can, let's start again.'

'What exactly do want me to do?'

'Do? I just want you to be interested again. For a brief period once or twice a week. Let's arrange a proper date night, one night each week, regardless of what is happening at work. You forget about work and your only appointment will be with me.'

'Just the two of us?'

'It's not much of a date otherwise.'

'An assignation with my wife?'

'Yes, what do you think?'

He reached out a hand, which was taken by Fliss and squeezed gently. 'I think that sounds fantastic,' he said with such conviction that Fliss couldn't help but smile.

'No work, no phones.'

'No phones? What if ...'

'No phones Jasper!'

'Of course. No phones.'

'And maybe the occasional lunch? We always used to meet at least once a week, I don't know why we stopped?'

'I don't know why we stopped either but I agree, we should start again.'

'And we need to stay home more in the evenings, together. You don't have to accept every single invitation to a meal out or a birthday celebration, especially from people we hardly know!'

'I thought you liked going out? It's not as though I go without you.'

Fliss pulled a face. He did always include her but she still didn't see any more of him. He liked to go because he could talk about work and wander around the room arranging meetings.

'We go out too much Jasper. It would be nice to have an occasional evening at home.'

'On date night?'

'No, as well as date night!' she snapped. 'Unless you're saying that the thought of spending two evenings with me is too much for you to handle?'

'No, no, of course not darling. Just checking. It all sounds perfect to me.'

'Are you sure about this ...'

'Absolutely sure. I can't believe you've been feeling like this,' and still looking a little shaky, he stood up and poured them both a very generous brandy. 'Let's do it my darling, let's get back to the business of being in love.'

Chapter 21

The smell of something cooking woke Fliss on Monday morning and sliding out of bed she went downstairs to investigate. With a later start than Jasper, Fliss was usually the one who made the coffee and threw in some toast whilst Jasper got ready for work. After he left Fliss would wander upstairs to get dressed at her leisure before heading off to deal with the mountain of emails addressed to 'Dear Fliss'.

Sniffing the air, she pulled on her dressing gown and went downstairs to find Jasper, fully dressed and wearing a frilly apron over his crisp white shirt, standing at the cooker.

'Morning.'

'Morning darling. I've made some coffee and I thought I'd whip up a few pancakes for you before I left for work.'

Fliss stayed in the kitchen doorway.

'You're making pancakes?'

'You're always the one that makes breakfast so I thought I'd step in for a change.'

Taking the proffered coffee, Fliss approached her beautiful range cooker warily. Jasper was right, it was always Fliss who cooked, especially their morning pancakes. Partly because she enjoyed whipping up a batch and making Jasper eat several before he set off for an intense day's work. And partly because Jasper couldn't cook. Not in the slightest.

Leaning forward and screwing up her nose slightly, she inspected the contents of the pan.

'Pancakes?'

'Yes, although I may have the consistency a little wrong.'

Staring down at the charred mush that resembled scrambled eggs, Fliss thought that the consistency was the least of Jasper's worries.

'I'm sure they'll still taste nice,' she said kindly.

'Do you think so?'

Jasper gave a vigorous shake so that the uncooked mix laying on top trickled sideways to join in with the embers below.

'Which flour did you use?' asked Fliss with interest, wondering why there seemed to be so much raw egg rolling around.

'There's flour in pancakes?'

They both looked down. The egg was rapidly turning black and most of it was now stuck to the bottom of the pan.

'Shall I take over?'

'Maybe it's for the best, although it's taken longer than I thought and I won't have time to eat any.'

Lucky you thought Fliss removing the pan from the heat. She would throw it away after Jasper had left for work.

'Sorry darling, I thought it would be nice for you to have someone else make breakfast. I messed it up, didn't I?'

Watching Jasper struggle out of the frilly apron, Fliss gave in and untied the knot, sliding her arms around his neck.

'It's the thought that counts,' she said, reaching up to kiss him. 'And it was a very nice thought.'

Jasper had never made her breakfast before. Should she point out that she wasn't expecting him to suddenly start sharing the cooking or come home early to do the ironing. The problem in their marriage went far deeper than household chores.

But he was looking down into her eyes in a way he hadn't for such a long time and Fliss decided not to spoil the moment and let him wrap his arms around her instead.

'I'll try not to be home late tonight,' he murmured in her ear, sending a frisson of delight down her spine. 'I do have a meeting at 4:00 but I'll wrap it up as quickly as I can.'

'Do you have any plans for tonight?'

'Ross invited me to meet someone he's lined up to do some research work for us.' A little of her delight faded. 'But I've told him I can't do tonight. I have someone very important that I need to meet with.'

Fliss pulled away slightly. 'Oh,' she said in disappointment. 'Who?'

Pulling her back in his arms, Jasper leant down to press a quick but firm kiss on her lips. 'You of course! Now I need to get off or I *will* be late home,' and with another kiss, he threw the apron on the kitchen table and headed out of the door.

Hugging herself happily, even though it had taken scalding hot water and a good long scrub to rescue the pan, Fliss grinned as she got dressed. It was two minutes of togetherness. Only two minutes, but it had been precious time when Jasper had looked at his wife instead of his phone and it already felt wonderful!

Her inbox was full of pleas for help, both realistic and outrageous and with a sigh, Fliss set to work. It was all very well dishing out advice, she thought reading an email from *Outraged of Leicester* who had found an exchange of sexy texts between his wife and her boss on her phone, but in reality, the solutions she had been dispensing over the years were probably worthless. She now knew from experience that telling someone to try sexy underwear or to make a romantic gesture wasn't anywhere near as straight forward or as easy as it sounded. *Outraged of Leicester* was asking if he should make sure his wife was being fulfilled at home to the point where she no longer had the energy to send a cheeky text to anyone else. Fliss decided she would advise him to sit down and talk to his wife before he got out his thong. He could save himself a lot of embarrassment, and energy.

Looking down the long list of emails waiting for her attention, Fliss remembered the conversation she'd had with Jasper when she'd been offered the job. They'd agreed that in the short term it would be an easy way to keep the mortgage payments going while Jasper broke into the world of reporting and that as soon as their situation allowed, Fliss would stop being an agony aunt and return to her long-held ambition to become a writer. Except that moment never seemed to arrive and as Jasper climbed the ladder, ever higher and with a great deal of speed, it had been silently agreed that Fliss would continue with the job and allow him to fly. Gazing out of the window, Fliss watched the clouds scuttle by and allowed herself a moment of fantasy where she kissed Jasper goodbye each morning and instead of slipping on a Karen Millen dress and a pair of Jimmy Choo shoes, she would stay in her comfy leggings and retreat to her own study to write.

'Fliss. Fliss!'

Turning around, Fliss found an Interflora man standing behind her desk next to a grinning Vivian.

'Well someone has a romantic husband,' announced her editor. 'What's this in aid of?'

A huge bunch of roses were being held out as everyone in the office crowded round to sniff and admire.

'Oh, how lovely!'

'They smell divine! Is it an anniversary?'

Fliss buried her nose in the deep red, velvety blooms. They did smell delicious.

'No,' she answered, smiling at her colleagues. 'I told Jasper that it was no good just saying he loved me, he had to start showing it.'

They all stared back.

'And he sent you flowers?'

Fliss nodded.

'That's all it took? You just told him to be more romantic?'

That wasn't quite all it had taken, thought Fliss, but maybe some of the details were best kept to herself.

She nodded instead. 'I told him on Saturday.'

'And he's sent you a lovely bunch of roses on Monday. Wow, that means he actually listened to you. What a result! The only way I would get a bouquet like this is if I sent it to myself,' said one of the women with feeling.

'Well, Fliss is an agony aunt,' reminded Vivian. 'She will have known exactly what to say to him I expect.'

Blushing slightly, Fliss went in search of a vase and left her colleagues chuntering about the lack of romance in their lives. It may not have been quite as easy as she had suggested, but it did seem to have worked and with a happy grin she returned to the stack of emails about the woes of life and love.

Although Jasper had promised to be home at a reasonable time, Fliss wasn't holding out much hope. She had found over the last few years that it needed more than good intentions to prise her husband from his office before he had squeezed every last second from his working day. So she was surprised to hear tyres rushing through the gravel only 30 minutes after she had arrived home. She was upstairs changing when she heard the door slam and running downstairs she found Jasper standing by the front door, frantically scrolling through his phone as though he were trying to memorise its contents before putting it to rest.

'You are early!' she exclaimed in surprise.

'As promised.' Jasper was still staring down at his phone and Fliss could see the internal struggle he was experiencing before he laid it gently down on the hall table, giving it one last longing look. 'And I'm going to make the evening meal, I've brought some steak home.'

Fliss couldn't hide her surprise. Not only did Jasper not cook but she would have bet the contents of her bank account that he had no idea where to buy the ingredients for an evening meal.

'Sally went to the supermarket for me,' he admitted with a grin. His long-suffering PA was used to his inefficiencies with the practicalities of life. 'I told her I needed something easy.'

'And you're going to cook it?'

'Yes. I'm going to pour you a glass of wine and get changed. Then I'm going to slap on a couple of steaks while you sit down and put your feet up. No work for me tonight, just an evening with my beautiful wife.'

'Shall I help …'

'No. Now, which wine shall we have?'

30 minutes later, Fliss was sitting in the living room listening to music and wondering why she hadn't been firm with Jasper the minute she had felt that their marriage was disintegrating. All that silly nonsense she had gone through trying to catch his attention when all she had to do was be honest with him. Okay, this wasn't actually what she had meant when she'd told Jasper to try harder in their marriage. She had no burning desire to wake up to a cooked breakfast every morning, but it was a start. If she could wean him away from his phone a little more each day, who knew, maybe in a few weeks they would be back to the Jasper and Fliss of old and sighing with happiness, she took a sip of wine and relaxed back into the cushions.

A few minutes later she frowned. The delicious smells that had been drifting her way from the kitchen had subtly changed. The aroma had become acrid, less tempting and more of a warning. Jumping to her feet she dashed into the kitchen to find it empty, no sign of Jasper but with two very overcooked steaks on full heat in a pan with some black onions and massacred mushrooms and smoke drifting from the oven.

'Jasper!' she yelled, grabbing the pan and removing it from the heat. 'Jasper where on earth are you?'

Turning off the oven and checking inside to find a tray of burnt oven chips and with steaks now so well cooked they resembled shoe leather, Fliss peered into the hall. Jasper's study remained dark and unused and there was no sound from upstairs. He seemed to have vanished halfway through cooking the meal. About to turn back into the kitchen, Fliss noticed a small beam of light coming from the large cupboard in the hallway. Full of coats, boots and umbrellas, it was in heavy use during the cold winter months and thinking that she must have forgotten to turn off the light, she flung open the door only to give a small yelp.

'Jasper! Didn't you hear me shouting? The steaks have burnt. What *are* you doing in here?'

Her husband was huddled in one corner, his back turned to the door and hearing her voice he stiffened, keeping very still for a moment before shuffling around slowly.

'What have you been doing?' asked Fliss in bewilderment, looking round the coat filled cupboard. 'Couldn't you smell the food burning?'

Biting his lip, Jasper looked down shamefaced. 'Sorry. I just wanted to … er, I needed to make a quick … I thought I'd just be a minute.'

Looking down, Fliss noticed that the hand held firmly behind his back was clutching his phone.

'You hid in the cupboard to use your phone?'

Jasper nodded. 'Sorry, it was just a quick check of my emails. I didn't want you to think… you know.'

Fliss wasn't sure whether to laugh or cry. Her husband, all 6' 1" of him, stood in front of her, his head firmly lowered as he tried to hide his phone, for all the world like a naughty schoolboy facing the headmistress.

'Jasper, I didn't say you shouldn't use your phone at home. I suggested that perhaps when we went on a date we make it a phone-free evening.'

'I know, I know. I don't want you to think I'm more interested in work than you but there was an email I wanted to check and ….'

Stopping his ramble by leaning forwards and kissing him on the cheek, Fliss leant her head on his shoulder.

'We'll get the balance right again,' she said, more to comfort herself than her husband. 'It may just take a little bit more practice. Now, the steak is ruined and the chips are burnt, why don't we order a takeaway,' and she led her husband out of the cupboard thinking that she may have been somewhat previous with her self congratulations. This could take a great deal more work than she'd imagined.

The takeaway arrived, their glasses were refilled and they were soon on the settee watching *A Cat On A Hot Tin Roof.* Jasper had apologised profusely for burning the steaks and for hiding in the cupboard with his phone, and for checking his emails quickly after they had finished eating. Trying to stay patient, Fliss had repeatedly told him that none of it was a problem, if he needed to use his phone he could do so without hiding.

Holding hands on the settee, Fliss tried to relax. This is what she had wanted, her husband's attention once in a while, a little time spent together without the constant presence of other people. She wondered why the achievement didn't feel quite as satisfying as she had expected.

The film stopped, replaced by an advert for mobile phones which brought a snort from Fliss and Jasper stretched out his arms and declared that he would take a quick toilet break. Fliss saw his hand slide down the side of the settee where he'd secreted his phone and slip it discreetly into his pocket. It was the third time he'd declared he needed the toilet, in other circumstances Fliss would have been phoning the doctor to arrange an emergency appointment.

'Do you need to check your emails?'

'No! Of course not,' denied Jasper, just as his pocket began to vibrate slightly. 'I've told you, no work tonight.' His trouser pocket began to glow as the vibration

227

increased and he slapped his hand against his phone, trying to disguise the flashing light.

'Won't be long,' he shouted and leapt from the room, crashing into the door in his haste.

Fliss had been watching him throughout the film. He had tucked his phone out of view and whenever he though her attention was sufficiently engaged he would slide it fractionally upwards so he could check his messages. If Fliss left the room she knew it was in his hand within a nanosecond.

He was trying, she accepted. Her fingers had been wrapped in his for much of the evening and he had been determined that he wouldn't retreat to his office to spend the rest of the evening working. But should it take so much effort? Should he find it such a struggle to spend the evening with her?

Waiting for him to return Fliss shivered, missing the warmth of his body and wondering why she didn't feel happier.

'Did I miss anything?'

He was back, sliding next to her on the settee and gathering her close to him.

Fliss hadn't even realised the film had resumed and with a smile, she shook her head.

'Nothing, but I was cold without you.'

Wrapping his arm more tightly around her, Jasper kissed her softly. 'You'll never be without me, darling. Never. It will be me and you to the end, just the two of us.'

Dearest Ellie

I couldn't be happier for you! A date with Logan, how wonderful. It looks as though things may work out for you after all, although I can't take all the credit. I can't help feeling that if you were meant to be then it would have happened sooner or later, without any input from me. You've been very brave Ellie, I know that none of this has been easy for a naturally reserved person such as yourself but you've been determined from the beginning to make it work.

Now that you have a date, and let's hope it's the first of many, please be careful. I know Laura is a very dear friend and she has helped you a great deal but don't be tempted to embark on any mad schemes that she may come up with. I confess, I'm still worried about how you ended your relationship with Carl, it was a huge leap of faith to decide he wasn't the man for you and that Logan was. Don't be too impetuous with your new relationship, make sure that it's everything that you want before you make any rash decisions.

Please don't ever be worried about what you say to me. You frequently stop me in my tracks and make me think about how I feel and the direction I'm taking. But you are exactly what I need, someone who I can be truthful with, someone who makes me look deep inside myself.

Jasper is trying so hard to change. He says he won't use his phone so much when he comes home, although that just means he hides it from me! He is trying to limit the amount of work he does in the evening and at the weekend but I know it's a struggle. And that's the bit that hurts, because it shouldn't be so difficult. It didn't used to be.

But what is more frightening is that for the very first time, I am thinking about the decision we made about not having a family. I was so sure, so certain it was the right thing to do and now I can't stop wondering. I watch other people who are just as in love as Jasper and I and they seem to cope with a family and careers and a busy life. Their children are thoroughly loved and wanted. Were we naïve to think that we could only remain the people we were if we stayed as a couple? I still don't regret what we decided, but I have started to reconsider. And that's almost as frightening because if there's one thing I am absolutely certain of, it's that Jasper is happy and content and as sure now as he was 2 years ago that we did the right thing, I don't think his faith has been shaken in the slightest.

I should be happy that he seems to have finally realised that we have a problem and we need to take action. I should be happy because he's trying so hard. I should be happy because we've spent more time together these past few days than we have in the past year. I should be happy. I'm trying to be happy, I'm acting as though I'm happy. But deep, deep down I know it isn't working. Maybe you were right Ellie, maybe the source of unhappiness isn't always as obvious as it seems and I think I may still have to find mine.

Have a wonderful time on your date, I hope everything goes well and you and Logan are soon the couple of your dreams,

All my love
Fliss
x

This email has been sent by Fliss Carmichael, the online agony aunt of The Digital Recorder. All views expressed herein are her own and should not be taken as an instruction to proceed with any course of action without careful consideration of the potential consequences. The Digital Recorder claims no responsibility for any trauma, divorce proceedings or physical injury that may result from the advice contained herein. Thank you for contributing.

Chapter 22

'**A** date?' exclaimed Laura. 'A proper date, not one of your strange affairs when you both just happen to be in the same place but you're with someone and Logan's with someone and ...'

'A proper date. Just the two of us. I told him I liked him, a lot, and we're going to the Flying Horse tonight to talk about it.'

'See how easy that was? If only you'd done that weeks ago when I told you to, never mind messing around with your agony aunt nonsense. Now, do you need me to be there, just in case it all goes wrong again? Shall I ...'

'No,' interrupted Ellie hastily. 'I've got it covered this time.'

'Mm, are you sure? Because you do seem to get it wrong an awful lot where Logan is concerned. Shall I come and sit somewhere nearby so I can come to the rescue? Or I could wait outside and you can text me if you're struggling. Oh! It could be like that film, we could both wear a wire and I'll hide outside and listen to everything and tell you what to say!'

'No! Thank you but I think I need to do this one on my own.' She would never say it to Laura but there was a definite tendency for her plans to become disasters. Tonight, Ellie wanted a much simpler affair. 'Nothing will go wrong. This could be my last chance so I have to get it right.'

It had been a difficult journey, she would never have believed that getting to know someone could have been quite so difficult. In her head she had smiled at Logan in the lift one morning and he had smiled back and then shyly asked her name. She'd answered and from then on it had simply been a matter of waiting. A few days later they would be chatting away whenever they met, the short jump from the lobby to the 5th floor not giving them enough time and eager to find out more about her, Logan would ask her for a drink. They would talk to each other for hours, amazed at how much in common they had, how many of their likes and dislikes overlapped and by the end of the evening, they would both know that they were meant to be. It hadn't worked out quite like that, but tonight was her chance. He would see the true Ellie, no elaborate plans, no plots and subplots, just Ellie and Logan.

For the rest of the afternoon, Laura tried to coach her friend with various scenarios beginning by giving Ellie a rundown on the current state of the football league.

'Why on earth would I need to know that?'

'Because when men struggle for something to say, they always fall back on football. You know the sort of thing, *'what do you think about VAR?'* or *'do you think Liverpool should have signed Takumi Minamino?'*'

'Who?'

Exactly! I read the sporting news every couple of nights so I know what Gareth is talking about.'

'Carl knew I wasn't interested in football, he didn't expect me to talk about it.'

'Lucky you. But Logan might get stuck and once they get stuck, they come out with the football chat.'

A little later, Laura sent Ellie some of the articles about SAS with several statements highlighted.

Ellie stared at them. 'What on earth ....?'

'Just in case he starts talking about SAS again. At least you'll know what he means.'

'But who read them?'

'I did. Actually, it's quite interesting once you get past all the twaddle at the beginning.'

Staring at her friend, Ellie wondered, not for the first time, what a lot went on inside that curly blonde head.

'I've already told him I don't understand it.'

'You have?'

'Yes. There didn't seem much point pretending.'

'Didn't he mind? Men like to think that woman are interested in what they do at work.'

'Of course not. He said it was an acquired taste.'

'Gareth is always giving me chapter and verse of what he did during the day. It bores me stiff but he seems to need to get it off his chest. I think I probably know as much about his job as I do my own!'

'Carl once asked if I knew anything about accountancy and when I said no, he never mentioned it again.'

A little later, Laura pulled out her make up bag. 'Right,' she declared, 'what's it to be? Sexy and flirty or shy and retiring. I don't have any false lashes with me but I can sort out your eyebrows. And I have a fantastic new lipstick …'

'No thank you. I've decided I'm going just as I am.'

'What do you mean?'

'No makeover. I want Logan to see me exactly as I am, get to know the real me.'

'Well, he can get to know the real you, once he's asked you out. And the chances of him asking you out are greatly increased by you having a makeover.'

But Ellie shook her head. 'No. Not this time.'

'You mean you're going, like that?'

Ellie could have taken umbrage at Laura's shocked tone as she cast her eye in horror over her make up free face and shiny but unfussy hair but she was far too happy. Instead, she just smiled.

'Yes, just like this.'

Laura chewed on her lip anxiously. 'There's a lovely blouse in the window of Topshop,' she advised. 'It's sort of semi see-through but they've put it over the cutest little vest top and it would suit you. Shall I dash out and get it for you?'

233

Ellie continued to type. She loved the bright yellow daisy strewn jumper she was wearing, even if it appeared Laura did not.

'No thank you,' she said breezily. 'I'm happy going like this.'

At around 5 o'clock, Laura sent Ellie a list of films with a brief description next to each one.

'What are these?'

'Men films. You know, the ones they all quote from. The sort of films we find very tedious but they love to watch. Over and over again.'

'Really? Carl was always happy to watch whatever I watched. He never admitted it but I think he actually enjoyed Pride and Prejudice and he definitely liked Emma.'

'I can't help wondering why you ended things with Carl,' Laura replied tartly,' if he was so bloody perfect why did you walk out?'

They worked in silence for the next 10 minutes until Laura relented and came over to throw her arms around Ellie. 'Have a lovely evening,' she whispered in her ear. 'Are you sure you don't want me to come …'

'No, really I don't. I'll be okay,' she reassured her friend. 'This is the night, I just know it,' and pulling on her winter coat and her woolly hat, she set off for The Flying Horse.

At 5:20 Ellie was in the pub. Logan had sent her a text to say he was running a few minutes late, some work emergency. He must have gotten her number from Laura and with a grin, Ellie stroked the words on her screen. He was texting her like a real boyfriend would. He was sending her a text about their date. Maybe soon he would be sending little messages saying things like, *'How about pizza tonight?'* or *'Love You'* or *'Can't wait to see you later'*.

Unable to believe how happy a short text could make her, she ordered a glass of wine at the bar and sat down at a table for two in the corner, away from the crowds. She couldn't stop smiling and as workers began to trickle in after a hard day at the office, she wanted to hold her phone aloft and let them all know that she was waiting for Logan, the man she was meeting tonight for a date.

'Hello, Ellie.'

Almost knocking her glass over in excitement, Ellie looked up with a smile, only for it to disappear.

'Carl! What are you doing here?'

Looking round to see if Logan was anywhere to be seen, she slammed her phone on the table in frustration. She had been quite clear with her mother that she had to stop letting Carl know where she was. Although she thought with a frown, she hadn't told her mother that she was meeting Logan tonight so how did Carl know?

'We both work in the same area, Ellie. It's just a coincidence.' He nodded his head in the direction of the bar and Ellie saw two of his work colleagues who she vaguely knew waving at her from across the room.

She nodded stiffly in their direction.

'I see. Well, have a nice evening,' and she looked back down at her phone.

'No Laura?'

'No.'

'Here by yourself?'

'No.'

Carl looked at the table which contained one glass and at the empty chair next to Ellie and raised his eyebrows.

'I'm waiting for someone.'

'Someone?'

'Yes.'

'A man?'

'Carl, please go back to your friends and leave me alone.'

'Is it a man? Are you meeting a man?'

'Yes I am.'

At the pain in his face, Ellie's attitude immediately softened. 'You must have expected it to happen at some point,' she said softly. 'I told you to get out there and meet someone else. Someone better suited to you than I was.'

'There is no-one better suited to me than you.' His voice was low and so intense that Ellie couldn't help her heart from giving a little leap. He sat down heavily in the empty chair at her side. 'I love you, and you deciding you don't love me doesn't alter that.'

'Carl I …'

'No Ellie, let me speak. I've listened to you, I've let you tell me over and over how we're not right for each other, that you need something different, something more romantic, more flowery, more whatever. But I believe we are right for each other. I love you, with all my heart, with all my soul. I'm not the sort to tell you every day, but if you need me to, I can and I will. I'm not the sort to come home with my arms stuffed with flowers but if you need me to, I can and I will. I'm not the type who holds your hand all the time, who kisses you when we're walking down a street, but if you need me to, I will. I will do all of those things because I love you.'

Ellie felt tears wet her cheek. They were rolling down her face as she listened to the man she had once been in love with.

'But don't you see,' she said, wiping her cheeks, 'I don't want you to have to change into somebody else, somebody that you're not, I want you to be you.'

'But you don't want me?'

She had, for almost three years she'd been perfectly happy to be with Carl. She had abandoned her idea of love as the hype of books and films. She'd felt safe and protected, she had loved him in a solid, ordinary kind of a way.

'No, I don't.'

She reached across the table to grab his hand, her heart breaking at the expression on his face. 'I don't want to hurt you, Carl, I loved you, I still love you in a way and I never, ever want to hurt you. But it's over between us and I think you should move on and find someone who is perfect for you, someone who will love you the way you are, the true you.'

'And is that who you're meeting tonight? Someone perfect for you?'

When Ellie had broken off her relationship with Carl, she had been very careful to tell him only that she felt they were together more from habit than from love. She hadn't wanted to hurt him any more than she already had by telling him that she'd fallen in love with someone else, head over heels, heartbreakingly in love.

'I don't know him very well yet, but I'm hoping to get to know him. And yes, I think he could be the one for me.' Her heart cracked a little at the pain in his eyes and she squeezed his hand. 'I'm so sorry Carl, so very sorry I've hurt you.'

Nodding, he smiled through the pain. 'As long as you end up happy Ellie. I think I always knew you needed more than I could offer. I couldn't believe how lucky I was to find you, to have you in my life.'

Good grief thought Ellie, if he carried on like this she would be apologising and begging him to take her back. Why couldn't he be angry and bitter and storm off into the sunset to find a new life for himself?

'But be careful Ellie, love is more than a bunch of roses now and then or a romantic meal for two on Friday night. Don't expect too much from your new man, he may end up disappointing you, just like I have.' They were still holding hands and squeezing her fingers gently, he leaned across the table to give her one last lingering kiss. 'Goodbye, I hope you find what you're looking for,' he whispered and standing up he walked away, watched by Ellie, tears rolling unchecked down her face

'I thought you said it was over between the two of you?'

Spinning around and almost toppling off her chair, Ellie found Harriet standing next to the table, a smug smile on her rather narrow lips and a delighted look in her eye. And behind her, looking shocked and disappointed, stood Logan.

'It is! I didn't know he would be here and he wanted to say goodbye and ….'

'He turns up a lot, doesn't he? For an ex I mean. It does look to everyone else like you're still an item.'

'Well, we're not. What are you doing here?'

'Oh just popped in for a drink, thought I'd see if any of the crowd were here.' Tossing her blonde hair, Harriet turned to place a possessive hand on Logan's arm. 'And look who I found!'

Searching out Logan's eyes over Harriet's shoulder, Ellie looked at him beseechingly. 'Logan, I'm sorry, I didn't know he would be here and we were just …'

'Shall we move on Logan?' interrupted Harriet, tugging on his sleeve. 'We don't want to be playing gooseberry with Ellie and her fiancé, let's leave them to it and go somewhere else.'

'He's not my fiancé! We're not even going out anymore.'

But Logan wasn't looking at her, his eyes were pinned on Carl who was leaning over the bar, his back in their direction as he ordered a drink.

'You're right Harriet, we don't want to interfere. Bye Ellie,' and letting Harriet slide her hand into his, he turned around and walked away.

Chapter 23

The following morning, there was no lurking as Ellie arrived at work and threw herself into the waiting lift. She didn't want to bump into anyone, not Logan, not Harriet, not even Jeff. She had spent much of the previous evening weeping and her eyes were red and puffy. She'd shed tears over the hurt she'd caused Carl and even more tears over the seemingly impossible task of getting to know Logan better without disaster falling. After concluding that maybe she and Logan were not destined to be together after all, the tears had doubled, falling down her cheeks like a waterfall. Today she wanted to go straight to her desk without having to explain herself to anybody.

'Hello Ellie.'

It was Logan, in the doorway to the lift, looking a little pale and bleary eyed himself.

'Hello.'

He reached over to press number 5 and the doors began their slow swish together.

For once, Ellie felt far too defeated to be embarrassed by his closeness and she let a small sigh drift into the space between them. 'We don't seem to have much luck getting together, do we?' she asked quietly. 'But I didn't know Carl would be there last night, and I certainly didn't invite him. It's over between us, he's just having a problem accepting that and moving on.'

The numbers seemed to be flying along this morning. They were already at floor 3.

'And I know that Harriet said that you should leave us to it, but I wish you'd stayed and talked to me. I'm just sorry it became so confusing.'

'I'm sorry too.'

Floor 4 flashed on the screen.

'Is it too late? Could we try again?' asked Ellie.

The regret in Logan's eyes was unmistakable. Was that a good thing or a bad thing, Ellie wondered. What exactly was he regretting?

'The thing is Ellie...'

Floor 5. The doors started their slow parting and Ellie could see Laura already sitting at her desk, looking impatiently at her watch, waiting for Ellie to update her on the previous evening.

'The thing is…'

'Are you getting out?' asked Mr Goodfellow, giving Ellie a sharp glance as he walked in to stand next to Logan. 'This is floor 5 Ellie.'

'Yes, yes I'm getting out.'

What was the thing? What was the thing that Logan wanted to tell her?

'Come on then!' barked Mr Goodfellow, 'let's get a move on.'

'Yes, okay. Er, see you later Logan?' and before she could say anymore, the doors were closing, leaving Ellie staring through the gap, her eyes fixed on Logan's anguished face until he disappeared.

'Come on, tell all. What happened? Are you two dating now? Is it official? What did he say? Oh Ells darling, whatever is the matter?'

Scooping the weeping Ellie into her arms and ignoring the curious looks from the rest of the department, Laura swept her into the ladies and held her tightly as Ellie sobbed on her shoulder.

'Carl was there,' she wailed, wiping her eyes with the tissue Laura provided.

'Again! You need to report him, he's becoming a stalker.'

'He wasn't following me this time, he was there with friends from work.'

'That's what he says. What happened, surely Logan didn't believe you two were still together?'

'He was so lovely, so caring, so …romantic.'

'Logan?'

240

'No, Carl.'

'But I thought you said that Carl didn't have a romantic bone in his body? Isn't that part of the reason you broke up?'

'Yes. But last night he said things, said lovely things that ….' Ellie hiccoughed and blew her nose.

'Oh my God, don't tell me you want to go back to Carl? What about Logan? Did you tell him that Carl is history? What happened Ellie, for goodness sake get to the details!'

'No. None of that. It's over between me and Carl, it was just very moving what he said and I was upset because he was upset and I was holding his hand …'

'You were what!'

'I was holding his hand and then he kissed me …'

'He kissed you! Oh my God, he kissed you? We are still talking about Carl? Carl kissed you?'

'Yes, I think he finally realised that it was over. But Logan was there with Harriet …'

'Harriet? Bloody Harriet? Where did she come into the story?'

'She said she'd just popped in to see if anyone else was there. Anyway, she was with Logan and they both saw the kiss and …what's wrong?'

Laura was pulling a face, a mixture of horror and regret. 'I'm sorry, I think that might have been my fault. I was so excited that you and Logan were finally about to get it together that I told Amy in accounts that you were going on a date, to The Flying Horse. I knew she'd tell Harriet, but I thought it would make her back off, not come and join you!'

'You told her where we were?'

'No, I told Amy, she told Harriet. Sorry.'

'Well, I don't suppose it matters.' Ellie couldn't help wondering if she and Logan might be dating, married and expecting their first child by now if her lovely, caring friend Laura hadn't been so determined to help them get together. 'Anyway, Harriet dragged him off and said they would leave me and Carl alone.'

'Bloody cow!' raged Laura. 'Typical bloody Harriet!'

'He didn't have to go with her,' Ellie pointed out reasonably. 'He could have stuck around to see what I had to say.'

'Yes well, bloody Harriet stopped him. I bet he wanted to and she wouldn't let him. I bet she ...'

'Never mind,' said Ellie wearily. 'I saw him in the lift this morning and tried to explain it all to him.'

'Good for you. What happened?'

'I realised that 5 floors in a lift isn't long enough to discuss anything important. In fact, I think I might stop speaking to anybody in the lift ever again. It hasn't gone at all well.'

'Don't give up,' implored Laura. 'Don't give up on him. I'm sure it can still be rescued. You just need to speak to him again. You could go to the 7th floor and ...'

'No.' Ellie was shaking her head firmly. 'No. No more half conversations in lifts or lurking in the corridor. The moment will come and if it does I'll take it. But no more plans Laura. No more.'

They went back to their desks and despite her red eyes and occasional sniffle, Ellie tried to ignore the sadness in her heart and get down to some work. Stretching her shoulders an hour later she looked up and saw a profile she knew well. It was Logan, walking along the corridor. Her heart gave a little jerk and she wondered if he would look in her direction. But he disappeared from view and refusing to let the tears come again, Ellie bent back over her desk.

'Don't look now but Logan is here,' came a whispered instruction a few minutes later.

Sure enough, there he was again, walking slowly along the corridor once more, eyes in front, the usual collection of files in his arms absent.

242

Ellie watched as he arrived at the staircase, paused slightly and then took them two at a time back up towards floor 7. A movement at the other side of the office caught her eye and she saw Harriet erupt from the small group of desks that housed the accounts department and arrive at the foot of the stairs just in time to see Logan disappear. Her shoulders slumped and with an irritated toss of blonde hair, she looked around to see if anyone was watching and then set off up the stairs herself.

Wondering what had transpired last night after they had left The Flying Horse, Ellie allowed herself a little daydream. Perhaps Logan had told Harriet that he was sure Ellie had broken things off with Carl and that it was all a misunderstanding. Maybe he had drunk his pint and then told Harriet that he was going home, to think about Ellie, the person he knew he should be with. Or, thought Ellie grimly, he could have told Harriet that Ellie couldn't be trusted and he was fed up with her leading him on. Perhaps they had ordered a bottle of wine and stayed together until closing time. Knowing Ellie's luck, that was a far more likely scenario she decided.

'He's back,' hissed Laura.

Turning her head, Ellie saw Logan appear again walking slowly along, eyes to the front. It was so soon after his last appearance that he must have gone up to the 6th floor and straight back down again. Harriet must have failed to catch up with him.

'What on earth is he doing?' asked Laura with interest.

They both watched as he said a casual 'Hi' to one of the IT team before pausing, ever, ever so briefly where the admin desks began and then continued to walk towards the stairs.

A flash of blonde hair appeared and both Laura and Ellie swivelled round to see Harriet emerge several feet behind Logan and walking as quickly as she could to catch up with him. Reaching the stairs, he paused then shot up, leaving Harriet no chance of closing the gap.

Fascinated, they transferred their gaze to Harriet who was now panting slightly as she reached the stairs and stopping briefly to catch her breath, set off as quickly as her high heels and much shorter legs would allow.

'Well,' began a fascinated Laura, 'well, well …'

She stopped. Logan had appeared again at the opposite end of the corridor.

She gasped in excitement. 'You know what he's doing, don't you?' she demanded of an open-mouthed Ellie. 'You know what's going on?'

'Do you think he wants to talk to Harriet and doesn't know she's following him?'

'He's lurking!' Laura almost shouted. Lowering her voice, she rolled her chair to Ellie's desk and grabbed her arm. 'He's lurking,' she said again in an over exuberant whisper.

'You think he's trying to see Harriet …'

'Bugger Harriet! He's trying to see you!'

They watched as Logan repeated the same format, walking slowly along the corridor. But this time when he reached the administration section he stopped the pretence and his head turned sideways, seeking out Ellie's desk. For a long moment, their eyes met before he blushed bright red and swung his eyes back round to the front, his steps suddenly quickening as he made for the stairs.

'He's looking for *you*,' repeated Laura. 'He's hoping to bump into you.'

'No! You think so?'

They were clutching each other's arms and Ellie frowned. 'Before I got out of the lift he said something.'

'What?'

'Well nothing much but it made me think.'

'What? What?'

Laura was jigging in her chair with excitement. 'What did he say.'

'He said '*the thing is*'.'

'The thing is what? What is the thing?'

'I don't know because Mr Goodfellow got in and I had to get out so he never told me what the thing was.'

She looked expectantly into her friend's confused face.

'But he had something to tell me because he started saying 'the thing is' and he wouldn't have said that if there wasn't a thing to say, would he?'

'Oh my God, you're right. I wonder what he wanted to tell you. Oh look, she's back.'

Harriet had appeared again, looking quite exhausted as she hung onto the handrail searching desperately for any sign of Logan.

'She's pretty determined,' said Laura with reluctant admiration, 'I'll give her that.'

Taking a few deep breaths, Harriet started to make her way along the corridor on slightly shaky legs before hauling herself back up the staircase, one steep step at a time.

They waited. But after several minutes there was no further sign of Logan. Either he had abandoned his lurking for the day or, a far more likely option decided Ellie, he had finally been cornered by Harriet.

For the rest of the morning, Ellie continued to work, one eye on her monitor and the other on the corridor to check for any further sign of Logan. Laura had moved both the filing cabinet and waste bin to the side and instructed her that at the next sighting, Ellie had to leave her desk pronto and intercept his progress.

'He wants to talk to you Ells,' she had said, clearing all obstacles from her potential path. 'Stand up and pretend you're going to IT or something, give him a chance to get the thing off his chest.'

But he hadn't appeared and by early afternoon, Laura was beginning to lose patience.

'Maybe you should go to …'

'No. I've told you, I'm not doing any more lurking, following or planning. If it's meant to happen, it will.'

'But he's clearly got something to tell you. He said so.'

'Then he'll have to come and find me. He can come to my desk and tell me.'

'But Ellie …'

'No. Not this time,' and Ellie had turned back to her computer and carried on working.

'Don't you need to know what he wants to say?' an exasperated Laura had asked after another hour had passed with no sign of Logan.

'Yes. But I'll wait until he tells me. I'm not chasing him all over the building.'

When her friend stood up, wriggling her shoulders and saying that she needed to stretch her legs, Ellie looked at her suspiciously.

'Where to?'

'Not to the 7th floor. I've been working hard, I just need to talk a short stroll.'

Laura had spent most of the day gazing at the staircase, waiting for Logan to appear and pestering Ellie to go find him. She had worked even less than she usually did.

'Don't interfere,' warned Ellie. 'I'm serious Laura, no more disastrous plans.'

'Relax! I'm not going anywhere near him. I'll bring you a coffee back,' she promised and disappeared down the corridor leaving Ellie gazing anxiously after her.

Ten minutes later she was back, a coffee in each hand.

'And?'

'I told you, I just needed to stretch my legs and make a coffee.'

Ellie looked at her disbelievingly. 'You mean you didn't go find Logan?'

'Of course not. Ellie ….'

'You didn't try and speak to him about last night?'

'I told you I wouldn't. Ellie I …'

'I know what you said but I can't believe you actually resisted the temptation.'

'Well, I did. Ellie, I need to tell you something.'

Stopping her typing, Ellie wriggled her own aching shoulders and shifted her chair so she had a better view of Laura.

'What's wrong?'

It was rare for her friend to look so serious, not unless she'd laddered her last pair of tights or forgotten to bring her favourite lipstick.

'It's just something I've found out. And I need to tell you.'

She put one of the coffees in front of Ellie.

'What's wrong. You look so serious. Has something happened? Is it Gareth?'

'No, nothing like that. It's just that, well it's ... I know what the thing is.'

'Thing, what thing?'

Composing herself, Laura took one of Ellie's hands in hers and looked into her friend's eyes.

'I know what Logan wanted to tell you this morning. I know why he's been lurking, trying to speak to you. I know what the thing is.'

There was a knot of unease beginning to form in Ellie's stomach. A definite feeling that this wasn't going to be good news.

'Go on,' she whispered.

Pulling a sympathetic face, Laura rubbed the back of Ellie's hand.

'It's about Harriet,' she began gently. 'It's about Logan and Harriet.'

'Oh for goodness sake just tell me!'

'Okay. Well, the thing is – oh that's what Logan said this morning, isn't it. Well,' she continued hurriedly at Ellie's glare, 'the thing is that last night when you all left the pub, Logan and Harriet went somewhere else. They had quite a lot to drink by all accounts. Josh saw them later on and he said that Logan was well and truly drunk. But the thing is ...'

'If you say that one more time I swear ...'

247

'Sorry! The thing …. sorry! Well, what happened is that last night, when he was very drunk and upset because let's not forget he'd just seen you kissing your ex-boyfriend and thought you were stringing him along …'

'Laura!'

'Sorry! So last night, when he was drunk and upset, Logan asked Harriet out.'

There was always background noise in the office, even if no-one was talking there was the noise of a keyboard being used or the printer whirring away. But for a moment, Ellie would swear that it was completely silent, except for the frantic beating of her heart.

'What?'

'Actually, I suspect Harriet asked him out and he was just too drunk to say no but …'

As the tears started to roll down Ellie's face for the countless time that day, Laura stopped her chattering and pulled her friend closer to wrap her arms around her shaking shoulders.

'I'm so sorry Ellie, but Logan and Harriet are going out.'

FROM: *Ellie Henshaw* <Elliebellshenshaw@livewell.co.uk>
To: *Fliss Carmichael* <agonyauntfliss@digitalrecorder.com>
Date: 24/04/2020

Dear Fliss

I just thought I would let you know that it's over between Logan and myself. Unfortunately, despite all the really good advice that you gave me, it turned out that it wasn't meant to be. We never had the date because Carl was there and Logan saw me talking to him. Well, I suppose it was a little bit more than talking because I was holding his hand and he kissed me, but we were saying goodbye. I tried to tell Logan what was happening, but he looked so upset and then he went to have a drink with Harriet instead. Thinking back, did I give in too easily, should I have insisted that he stayed and talked to me? Or maybe he should have just trusted me. Anyway, he got drunk and asked Harriet out. So now it's over, not that it ever really started. No happy ever after for us.

I've done a lot of thinking over the last few days. I was wrong about so much, about love and about life. I even started to wonder for a while if I had made a mistake ending things with Carl. Although I was very angry that he turned up at the pub at such a crucial time, he said such warm, lovely things that I couldn't help but be moved. But after a great deal of thought, I decided that I had done the right thing. If I had truly loved him, I wouldn't have fallen for Logan and been prepared to walk away from our relationship. If I loved him enough then I wouldn't have had eyes for anybody else so it was better to end our relationship before I hurt him even more.

I hope that Logan is happy with Harriet. That's quite hard to say but I do hope that he finds love, however it comes to pass. So now it's all over. And it hurts

I hope you and your husband resolve your problems. I've concluded that life is never easy but love does make it more bearable and I hope the love you two once felt for each can be recovered. I'm so sorry if my emails and questions have distressed you in any way. Sometimes

249

things happen, like you see the back of a head or someone asks you about a decision you made two years ago and it sets the ball rolling in a direction you don't really want to follow. Reflecting on the past can often change the course of our future, and I hope that both of us manage to find a future that is every bit as bright as we wish for. Don't give up on your husband, but be sure you understand what it is you want from him.

Thank you for all your advice and for caring so much. I'm not sure what I expected when I wrote my first email to you but I certainly hadn't expected friendship or such support.

Thank you for everything you tried to do for me,

Your friend

Ellie

Chapter 24

The next few days passed in a flurry of flowers and chocolates as Jasper decided to show his wife how much he still loved her and Fliss' desk at work was becoming quite crowded with the blooms that appeared on an almost daily basis. Vivian had perched on the only free millimetre the previous morning and looked pointedly at the latest offering, a vase of beautiful and expensive orchids, filling the room with their rich scent.

'Everything okay?' she'd asked discreetly.

'Of course, what do you mean?'

'Oh, nothing. It's just that the last time I saw an effort like this, it was followed a few weeks later by a divorce.'

'Vivian!'

'Sorry, just saying, that's all.'

'It's not like that, not at all. Jasper is simply trying to be a little more attentive. We're trying to inject the romance back into our lives,' explained a defensive Fliss.

Vivian held her hands up in the air. 'Then I'm pleased for you. Just checking.'

Inspecting the latest arrangement and looking for a space to set it amongst the rest of the bouquets scattered over her desk, and the filing cabinet, and her colleague's desk and the printer cabinet, Fliss wrinkled her nose. Maybe Jasper was going a little overboard with his daily declarations of love. But you could never have too many flowers, she decided, searching for her phone which had disappeared between the roses from Monday and the beautiful little plant pot engraved with a heart and overflowing with forget-me-nots from Wednesday.

She had arranged to meet Jasper for lunch and had been checking her phone regularly, waiting for the message to advise he had been caught up with work and wouldn't be able to make it. In the early hours of the morning, she had woken up and found a cold space next to her instead of a gently snoring husband. Pulling on her dressing gown she'd gone downstairs to find him at his desk, typing away.

Looking guilty, and tired, he'd admitted that he had really needed to catch up on some work that evening but had instead remained on the settee with Fliss. Kissing him on the head, Fliss had led him back to bed, promising that the following evening she would cook something for them both and he could spend the entire evening in his study.

Despite not coming to bed until after 4 in the morning, he was still up before Fliss and she had arrived in the kitchen to see him staring down at something that was so burnt and shrivelled, Fliss had trouble putting a name to it.

'Bacon. I decided not to try the pancakes again.'

Tipping the contents of the pan into the bin, Fliss had pushed Jasper into a seat and handed him a coffee.

'Darling, this is not what I meant when I said you had to start paying attention to me again!'

The day after the pancakes, she had been greeted with porridge. It was only after she'd taken a mouthful and gagged, that Jasper had admitted he hadn't really known what to do with porridge and checking on Google, he'd found an 'authentic' recipe that was made with water and salt.

'Please, stop getting up early to make me breakfast.' There was undoubted relief on Jasper's face. 'And if you need to work when you come home, just say so.' More relief.

'But you said …'

'I said that we needed to spend time together again, not that you had to turn into the husband of the year and stop working if I was within 50 feet of you. Now, I'm going to make us both some toast while you finish getting ready and tomorrow, leave the breakfast to me!'

Jasper had kissed her gratefully and sighing Fliss had scrubbed out yet another pan. At this rate, she'd need a new set. On his way out of the door, he'd suggested they meet for lunch, a chance to chat as they shared a bite to eat at one of their favourite restaurants in the centre of Leeds. Fliss had agreed but was fully expecting that a business meeting would take priority and had spent the morning keeping a careful eye on her messages.

When 12.30 arrived and nothing had been heard from Jasper, Fliss closed her laptop and pulled on her coat.

'I'm going to meet Jasper for lunch,' she told Vivian.

Her editor sniffed. 'Most couples I know relish having a whole day without their partners getting involved in their lives.'

'Well Jasper and I are not like that,' Fliss told her loftily. 'We've decided to spend more time together actually.'

'If you're having problems …'

'We are not having problems!' That wasn't entirely true, thought Fliss, but not the sort Vivian was imagining. 'There is no divorce, no separation, we're just reconnecting.'

'Reconnecting?'

'Yes, we're reminding ourselves of why we got married in the first place and how much we enjoy each other's company.'

'Well, you're the agony aunt but it sounds like a lot of mumbo jumbo to me. And no-one sends flowers every day unless they feel guilty about something,' and shrugging, Viv turned away and walked back to her office leaving Fliss glaring crossly at her back.

Walking briskly to the restaurant, Fliss arrived early and was pleasantly surprised to find Jasper already there, standing by the bar in the main dining area, checking his phone as per usual.

'Hello darling,' she murmured, standing behind him and caressing his free arm.

'Fliss! You're early!'

Giggling as he jumped and spun around, Fliss reached up to kiss him. 'I am, as are you! Couldn't you wait to see me?' There was a spare barstool next to him and Fliss slid upwards and turned it slightly so she was facing him. 'Have you ordered anything?'

'No, what are you doing?'

'Doing?' Fliss stared at him in amusement. 'I'm sitting down. Why do you look so surprised, did you think I would be late?'

'No, of course not. But let's not sit here,' grabbing his wife's arm he gave a little tug which brought Fliss shooting off the stool and crashing into his chest.

'Jasper! What on earth …'

'It's noisy out here. I've asked for a table in the other room.'

'Okay, if you want to. But I'm quite happy to stay here …'

'No! I want us to sit at a table.' He was looking over his shoulder rather than at Fliss and grabbing the coat she was halfway through removing, he scooped it up along with her handbag. 'Come on, let's get settled.'

Taking her hand, he pulled her briskly in the direction of the smaller dining room next door.

'For goodness sake Jasper, not so fast. Ow!'

Apologising to one of the diners who she practically knocked over as she was hauled along in Jasper's wake, Fliss tried to pull back and slow him down. 'Jasper!' she hissed. 'What is wrong with you? Let go of me!'

Finally releasing the grip he'd kept on her hand, Jasper stopped by a small table for two, set in the farthest corner of the room and so dimly lit Fliss had to peer to see where the chairs were.

'Why are you in such a hurry? Are you too busy to have lunch today?'

'Absolutely not. Sorry. I just didn't want to miss getting a nice, quiet table.'

Fliss looked around. The majority of diners were in the other room and Fliss and Jasper were surrounded by empty tables. She would need a torch to read the menu the lighting was so low. 'Are you sure? You're acting very strangely.'

Sinking down into one of the chairs, Jasper reached a hand across the table and smiled. 'I'm so sorry darling. I had my heart set on one of these tables. It thought it would be romantic.'

Thinking that dark didn't necessarily equal romantic, Fliss forgave him anyway and smiled. 'And you have time for lunch?'

'Of course! Now, why don't we have a glass of wine?'

Mollified, Fliss pulled the menu closer and squinting through the darkness she tried to read the wine list.

'Oh don't bother with that, I'll go and tell the waiter what we want.'

Fliss looked up in surprise. 'But the waiter will come to the table and …'

'I think we should have a drink straight away, maybe a glass of champagne to celebrate how well this is all going. You know us, er, finding each other again.'

Fliss resisted the temptation to point out that she had never lost Jasper. He, on the other hand, had not only mislaid his wife but had been making no effort to find out where she was.

'You wait here,' Jasper continued. 'I'll find a waiter and tell him that we're celebrating,' and with a smile and a swift kiss, he was gone, weaving his way across the room with the same speed with which he had entered.

Bewildered by his haste, Fliss took advantage of his absence and pulled out her compact to check her lipstick and run a hand through her choppy hair. Lunch, she had imagined, would be a quick sandwich, a chat and back to work. If Jasper was talking champagne and celebrations, she might be phoning Viv and asking for the afternoon off.

10 minutes later she was on the verge of leaving her seat to see where he had gotten to when she spotted him walking back towards their table.

'Sorry, sorry,' he offered, slightly out of breath. 'I couldn't find a waiter and when I did he was really keen to discuss er, vintage etc.'

'Vintage?'

'Yes. It turns out he knows a lot about champagne and when I mentioned this was a celebration, he insisted on going through the full list with me and making sure we had the very best glass for the occasion.'

Fliss couldn't help but look surprised. They had been to this restaurant many times before and she couldn't remember the waiters ever saying anything other than 'okay' whenever she had ordered a glass of champagne.

'Which did you choose?'

Jasper stopped reading the menu. 'Choose?'

'Yes, After the recommendation, which vintage did you choose?'

'Do you know, I can't remember. I'll go ask him …'

'No! Sit down. He'll be here shortly and we'll find out.'

Almost before Fliss had finished the sentence, a waiter appeared by their side holding a tray containing two glasses.

He didn't have the steadiest of hands and the glasses had been placed too close to each other so they trembled and tinkled as he came to a halt.

'Champagne?'

Jasper nodded and Fliss stared. He didn't look like a waiter with an encyclopaedic knowledge of champagne. In fact, he didn't look as though he would have an encyclopaedic knowledge of anything much. He was barely old enough to be employed, his chin was covered in painful red acne and his mouth hung open slightly, as though the task of carrying two glasses was more responsibility than he was comfortable with.

'What is it?' asked Fliss, willing to give him the benefit of the doubt.

He stared at her blankly.

'Which one did you choose?' she tried again.

Another long pause as he looked down at the glasses and back at Fliss.

'Champagne.'

'Yes, I know.' Fliss smiled so he didn't feel she was being a difficult customer. 'I just wondered which one you had brought us. My husband said you know a great deal about the subject and had recommended a vintage you thought we would enjoy. I just wondered which one it was.'

In slow motion, the young waiter blinked, his head swivelling to look first at Jasper, who was sitting on the very edge of his seat with his head bowed, then back down at the glasses on his tray before returning his blank stare to Fliss.

'It's champagne.'

'Yes but …'

'Thank you,' interrupted Jasper. 'Thank you so much.'

The waiter carefully placed a glass in front of Fliss and one in front of Jasper before crossing his arms and staring at the centre of the table.

'We'll be ready to order in a minute or so.'

The waiter nodded.

'So if you could come back?' suggested Jasper gently.

'You don't want to order now?'

'No. If you could give us a few minutes?'

Nodding again, the waiter tucked his tray underneath one arm and with a shrug of his shoulders, shuffled away.

'I thought you said he was an expert on champagne?' asked Fliss in confusion. 'He didn't seem to know anything about it!'

'It wasn't him that I spoke to,' said Jasper, gazing across the room as though searching for someone. 'I don't know where that waiter has gone. Perhaps I'll go find him and I can ask which …'

'Oh, it doesn't matter. I'm sure it will be delicious.'

'No, no, I'm going to find out. I want you to know what we are drinking for our celebration. Hold tight darling, won't be long,' and he shot off like a hare out of a trap,

257

covering the ground at speed and almost cannoning off the back of their young waiter who was making much slower progress.

Fliss wondered if Jasper was okay. He worked so very hard, perhaps it was starting to take its toll. Sipping at her champagne and thinking it tasted very much like every other glass of champagne she had ever ordered in this restaurant, she pondered his weird behaviour. He certainly didn't seem himself today, maybe he was anxious about the opportunities that had opened up to him lately. Leading the chat show was something he'd been thrilled about, but maybe deep down he was more anxious than he was prepared to admit. He worked such long hours, putting himself under such pressure, perhaps it was all proving too much for him.

Suddenly worried, Fliss peered across the room. She could see plenty of waiters but no sign of her husband. Where was Jasper? Was he in the throes of a breakdown whilst all Fliss could do was insist that he pay her more attention? Could it be that the problems affecting their marriage ran far deeper than being too absorbed in his work? Could Jasper be ill and she hadn't even noticed?

Feeling her own anxiety levels begin to rise, Fliss took another sip of her champagne. She must be a really dreadful agony aunt, she decided. She hadn't noticed that her marriage was in trouble and now she had completely overlooked that her husband was ill and in need of help, not her constant nagging. Emptying her glass, she put it back on the table with a shaky hand. Where on earth had he disappeared to?

Chapter 25

There was no sign of Jasper. Their waiter was lurking in a corner, watching her beadily as Fliss looked anxiously around the room. Where could he be? How long did it take to ask a waiter for the name of a drink? Deciding that she needed to find him, Fliss stood up only to see him dashing through the large archway between the two rooms, skidding to a halt so as not to crash into the table in front of him and almost sprinting back to their table.

'Darling, are you alright?'

Jasper gazed at his wife in surprise. 'Alright?'

'Yes, is there something you need to tell me?'

'Oh I couldn't find the waiter and then when I did he was busy so he said he'd write it down and give it to us before we left …'

'Not about the drink! I mean you, are you okay? You're behaving so strangely, is there anything wrong. You're not, ill?'

'Ill? Good grief no, I'm okay.'

'Am I asking too much of you? Am I being unreasonable?'

'No, of course not. Really, Fliss, I'm okay. I've just had a busy morning that's all.'

Reaching out to take his hand, Fliss waved away the waiter who had materialised at their side. 'As long as you're okay,' she whispered. 'That's the most important thing.'

With a small sigh, the waiter wandered off again leaving Jasper and Fliss holding hands across the table. Fliss thought he looked tense, almost nervous and she tried again. 'You would tell me if there was something wrong with you?'

'You would be the first person I would tell. Now stop worrying about me and let's look at the menu, oh!'

Slapping his hand against his forehead, Jasper rolled his eyes wildly. 'I forgot to ask what the specials were. I'll just go check.'

He tried to stand up, despite Fliss hanging tightly onto his arm and she pulled hard to make him sit back down.

'Relax, please. We'll ask the waiter,' she turned around to catch his eye but he was still walking at a snail's pace back to the corner he inhabited.

'No need,' insisted Jasper brightly. 'They're all written on a board next to the bar. Really, I won't be a minute,' and pulling his hand free he set off once again, his long, loping stride covering the floor as quickly as he could.

Remaining at the table, Fliss clutched her heart. She didn't care what he said, this was not normal behaviour. There was something seriously wrong and it seemed to be something he didn't want to share which made her even more anxious.

The waiter had finally made it back to his position, Fliss waved her arm and beckoned him back to the table.

'Are you ready to order?' he began hopefully.

'No, but I'd like another glass please.' Fliss pushed her empty glass towards him, still pondering the hundred and one things that could be wrong with Jasper.

'Another glass?'

'Yes.' How could she have not noticed anything before? Maybe this was the reason for his distance, he was dying and he was trying to wean Fliss away from him before he left her.

'One glass?'

'Yes.' Jasper's glass was still full, there was no point ordering him another one yet. In fact, he hadn't taken so much as a sip, was that because he was ill and on medication, wondered Fliss? Had he been told not to drink?

The waiter didn't move, his eyes fixed on the glass as though looking for inspiration.

'Just a glass?'

Pausing in her distress, Fliss watched him pick up the glass and inspect it closely. 'Well,' she began carefully. 'Obviously, I would like something in the glass.'

'Oh. So not just a glass then.'

Her fingers gripped the edge of the table, she was too grief stricken to cope with this at the moment.

'I would like another drink,' she said slowly. 'I have had one drink and I would like my glass refilling with another.'

'With another ...?'

'What?'

He bowed his head towards the glass. 'You would like it filling with ...?'

Fliss stopped worrying about Jasper and wondered if she were in some sort of danger herself.

'With champagne.'

'So, you would like another glass of champagne?'

Making sure her phone was within reach and wondering just how long it actually took to press nine three times, Fliss nodded.

'I would like another glass of champagne, please.'

A smile broke out from the acne. 'Of course madam. And can I get you anything else?'

Was he kidding, thought Fliss? It had taken ten minutes to establish that she wanted a drink. How long was it likely to take to order a meal?

'No thank you. Not at the moment,' she enunciated carefully and with a satisfied smile, he disappeared, hopefully, to get Fliss another drink. As the waiter left, Jasper arrived, sinking into his seat with a gasp.

'Shall I order you another drink?' he asked spotting her empty glass. 'I can go ....'

'No!' yelped Fliss. 'Sorry, I didn't mean to shout. I've already ordered one.'

She inspected Jasper's face. Did he look pale, she wondered, he was definitely sweaty, his forehead was damp with perspiration. In fact, rather than looking pale, he had a flush of colour on each cheek. Was he running a temperature?

'Are you hungry?' she asked, wondering if he had any appetite. Jasper not being hungry was a sure sign that there was something wrong.

'Actually, I'm not very hungry,' admitted Jasper, ignoring his champagne and filling his water glass instead.

Fliss swallowed her wail. This was serious, very serious. She could feel her eyes filling with tears. 'Really?' she asked, her lip trembling. 'Not at all?'

Jasper grabbed one of the menus. 'Well, I'm sure I could manage something. And you can have whatever you want. Don't be upset, I'm just happy to be here with you,' he said alarmed at her reaction.

Sniffing, Fliss looked down. The light was so low it was hard to see anything on the menu. 'Did you check the specials board?' she asked. 'Anything you think I might like?'

Jasper froze, menu in hand. 'Actually,' he began slowly, 'it was all so boring I can't remember anything! Definitely nothing you would have liked darling, I checked it carefully.'

Fliss closed her eyes. His memory was clearly starting to go. Had it been going for a while, was this all part of the problem. Was he constantly checking his phone because he couldn't remember what he had to do next?

'Don't worry,' she whispered, placing a hand gently over his. 'It doesn't matter.'

The waiter arrived, her glass sliding around on his tray. 'Are you ready to order yet?'

Fliss took the glass directly from the tray, she really couldn't wait for him to lift it up, oh so carefully and slowly and set it down on the table. Placing a hand on his arm, she held on to him tightly, ignoring the alarm on his face as she lifted her glass, draining it in one long drink.

'No food yet,' she said, wiping her mouth and placing the glass back on the tray. 'But I'll have another glass, please.

262

With champagne. A glass, full of champagne and given to me.'

Releasing her grip on his arm, she watched with interest as he shot off. He had quite a turn of pace when motivated, she decided.

Jasper was staring at his wife in concern. 'I think I should be asking you if you're alright,' he said watching her slump back in her chair. 'Anything wrong?'

How brave, thought Fliss. How wonderfully brave and selfless. 'No,' she whispered, 'nothing at all.'

'Are you thirsty? Would you like some water?'

'No thank you, *I'm* okay.'

They sat for a few minutes, neither speaking as they fiddled with their serviettes, Fliss watching Jasper like a hawk and Jasper peering over his shoulder as though he expected someone to appear behind him any minute.

'Is that lettuce on your tie?'

Fliss leaned forward to get a better look. 'I think it's actually rocket. How did that get there?'

Jasper's eyes were glassy, the beads of sweat on his forehead had become small rivulets that coursed down the side of his face and his skin had a waxy sheen. Fliss held her breath, he was clearly seriously ill. Why wouldn't he tell her what was wrong with him?

'Jasper,' she whispered, her voice trembling. 'What is it? How did the lettuce get on your tie?'

She waited as he swallowed, moved his knife and fork around the table and put them back where they had started. He hadn't met her eyes and with growing trepidation, Fliss wondered if she should take him straight to the hospital.

'The lettuce?' His face was contorting with the effort of replying and his eyes were now swivelling from side to side. 'Yes, the er, lettuce.' He looked down at the tiny sprig of green on his otherwise spotless blue tie. 'I … actually …I can't remember.'

'You can't remember?' This was worse than Fliss had contemplated. Whatever was wrong with Jasper, he was deteriorating rapidly.

'Shall I take you home darling? You can have a lie down and see if you feel any better ….'

'No! I don't want to go home.' He looked at his wife hopefully. 'Unless you want to go? You could go and I'll grab a sandwich here and see you later.'

'But you said you weren't hungry?'

'Did I? Well, my appetite seems to have come back. You could go and I'll stay ….'

'Jasper, I don't want to go home. I feel perfectly well. It's you I'm worried about.'

'Oh.' His face fell and he looked over his shoulder again. 'I've told you, I'm okay.'

'Do you want to order some food then?'

'Er, yes, I suppose so. I'll go and get …'

'Jasper sit down!' Fliss spoke a little louder than she had intended and the occupants of the next table turned in their seats, a large lady in a bright pink dress giving Fliss a startled look. 'Please sit down,' she said in a hushed tone. 'You've been dashing around ever since we arrived. Relax, the waiter will be back in a moment and he'll take our order.'

Sitting back in his seat Jasper looked anything but relaxed and Fliss was relieved to see their waiter heading over to their table with her champagne.

'Have you decided what you'd like to eat?' she asked gently, having barely glanced at the menu herself.

'No, I haven't. I don't know what I want. Maybe I should go and …'

'Sit!'

The couple at the table gave her another look and started whispering. Fliss closed her eyes and struggled for composure. 'Read the menu darling and decide what you want. The chicken salad sounds nice, I think you ordered that last time we came here.'

'Salad?' Jasper was holding the menu, his eyes anywhere but in front of him as he fidgeted and looked around.

'Yes, salad.'

Maybe this was a sign of things to come. If Jasper continued to deteriorate at this rate she would soon have to do everything for him, including choosing his meals.

'Shall I order one for you?'

The waiter had arrived with Fliss' champagne taking care to stand out of reach as he picked up the glass and transferred it to the table. Jasper hadn't answered and deciding to make the decision for him, Fliss smiled at the waiter.

'Two chicken salads please.'

'Two?'

'Yes, two.'

'Two for you?'

'Yes, well one for each of us.'

'You both want a chicken salad?'

Fliss clucked in irritation. She was all for encouraging the youth of the UK to get a job but really, they should have provided some training before letting this young man loose on their customers.

'Yes. I want a chicken salad and my husband wants a chicken salad. That's one each, please.'

The waiter nodded slowly before shuffling around to direct his gaze at Jasper.

'Another chicken salad?'

Quite alarmed now at the colour of Jasper's face, Fliss couldn't help but snap.

'For goodness sake, he doesn't want *another* chicken salad, he just wants *a* chicken salad. We want one each!'

The waiter was still staring at Jasper who nodded his head in agreement. 'That's right,' he said nervously. 'I want a chicken salad.'

'So you want another ...'

'Please just get two salads!' Fliss shouted. 'Now!'

There was a general tutting and a hum of disapproval from the nearby tables and Fliss closed her eyes in mortification. 'Please,' she said equally loudly. She needed them all to hear. 'We would like two chicken salads, please.'

Looking unhappy, the waiter started on his tortuously slow journey away from the table only to be stopped by Fliss calling him back.

'Just a minute.' Lifting up her glass she drank the contents in one deft swallow.

'And another glass.'

'A glass of ...'

'Another glass full to the brim with champagne and brought to me at this table,' agreed Fliss, ignoring the chastising look from the pink dress lady.

Jasper was half out of his chair once again and Fliss reached out, trying to grab his hand before he disappeared and persuade him to sit back down. 'The waiter will bring us some food soon,' she said in a comforting tone. 'Just sit down and wait.'

'No, I have to go!'

Fliss stood up. 'You feel bad? You need to go home? I'll call us a cab, you shouldn't drive ...'

'No!' Jasper sat back down abruptly and Fliss followed his lead, slumping back into her seat. 'I didn't mean I wanted to leave, I er .. I er ....'

'What is it darling? What do you need?'

'I need to go to the toilet!' He was on his feet again, his voice echoing around the room and Fliss saw another stare coming from the pink dress lady, only this one had an edge of sympathy.

'Okay. Do you need me to help you?'

Jasper looked at her in astonishment. 'Of course not,' he answered in shock. 'I won't be long,' and he was striding across the room once more to disappear from sight.

Fliss' champagne arrived and she held the cold glass against her cheeks. Tears were beginning to form in her eyes again and all she really wanted to do was get Jasper home so she could take his temperature and get some medical advice. Her stomach was in knots, there was no room for a chicken salad no matter how tasty it was. She took out her phone and began researching whatever could be wrong with him, only to put it away again with a gasp. It was nothing good.

Time ticked by with no sign of Jasper and with mounting concern, Fliss considered her options. She could burst into the men's toilets and look for her husband, no doubt now unconscious and laying on a cold tiled floor. Or maybe she could ask someone to go in on her behalf and check the situation, saving embarrassment for any other occupants. Perhaps one of the staff members would go if she explained the circumstances.

Still debating her course of action, Fliss became aware of the waiter, back by her side with his tray now containing a glass of champagne and two chicken salads.

Grabbing the tray, Fliss placed it onto the table, far less carefully than he was intending and grabbed his arm. A look of panic crossed his face as he tried to pull away.

'I'll get it straight away,' he mumbled, trying to walk backwards.

'Get what?'

'Another glass of champagne. I'll go get it now.' He gave a little tug of his arm.

'I don't want another drink.' Not exactly true thought Fliss, but there were other things she needed to do first. 'I need you to go to the toilet for me.'

The panic turned to raging anxiety as with a much firmer tug he tried to free himself.

'The toilet?' he asked as they both struggled for possession of his arm. 'I'm afraid I can't do that madam. You'll have to go yourself.'

Pink dress lady had stopped all pretence of eating her own lunch and was now enthralled at the exchange between Fliss and the waiter.

'You don't understand,' panted Fliss, standing up and keeping a firm hold of him despite his efforts. 'It's not for me! I'm worried about my husband. He went to the toilet and he hasn't come back yet. I want you to check if he's okay.'

The struggle continued as the waiter looked at her in confusion.

'But he's not in the toilet.'

'He isn't feeling very well,' continued Fliss, now having to dig her heels in quite firmly to keep a grip on the flailing arm. 'I think he may have passed out.'

'He hasn't passed out.'

'You don't know that. He may be unconscious, on the floor. Oh, please go in there and check for me.'

'He isn't there,' panted the young man, his face now scarlet as he tugged and pulled in an effort to get free.

'Yes, he is, he went about 10 minutes ago, probably longer. I need you to …'

'He isn't in the toilet!' shouted the waiter. 'He's eating his salad.'

With an enormous effort, he was free, his white shirt pulled out of his waistband and the sleeve hanging over his hand where Fliss had been tugging.

Looking at the empty seat opposite her, complete with an untouched chicken salad, Fliss wondered if she was the one who wasn't very well. Everybody was behaving so strangely. Was she running a temperature and hallucinating? She sat down, passing a trembling hand to her forehead.

Pink dress lady had moved her chair to get a better view and was almost sitting at Fliss' table, and the waiter, who Fliss had just noticed was wearing a small gold name badge proclaiming him to be Edward, was poised for flight as Fliss took a deep breath.

'But he isn't eating his salad, is he?' she asked gently. 'He isn't eating his salad because he isn't here.' She stared pointedly at the empty space. 'Is he?'

Edward, understandably nervous, watched her every movement carefully.

'Not *that* chicken salad,' he agreed. 'He isn't eating *that* chicken salad.'

Fliss nodded her head slowly to emphasise her words. 'And if he's not eating his salad, he could be in the toilet, couldn't he. Unconscious. On the floor.'

'He's not in the toilet, he's eating his salad. Not that one!' he added hastily as Fliss eyes narrowed. 'He's not eating that chicken salad because he's not here.' He was speaking in the slow measured tone one would use for the elderly or the insane. 'He's eating his other chicken salad.'

Staring at him Fliss wondered if she should just call the manager and be done with it but she decided to try one last time.

'This is his salad,' she began. 'And my husband is not eating this salad because he's not here. There is no other salad.' She glanced down at her plate, 'other than my salad,' she said. 'And he's not eating that salad either because he's in the toilet.'

There was a hint of pity mixed with the exasperated look Edward was giving her. 'But he is eating his other chicken salad, in the other room.'

Fliss sat up a little straighter. 'What other salad?'

'His salad. The one in the other room.'

Silence fell. Fliss thought back to Jasper's strange behaviour ever since she'd arrived, his edginess, his almost permanent absence from the table. Leaning forward, the pink dress lady moved Edward gently to one side slightly so she could see Fliss more clearly. 'He has been coming and going a great deal since you sat down,' she said.

Edward joined in. 'That's because he is sat at a table in the other room as well. With his chicken salad. The one he's eating.'

'Oh my word, he's sitting at two tables at the same time?' gasped pink dress. 'Is it …' she lowered her voice to a whisper, 'another woman?'

'Oh no,' answered Edward.

Looking vaguely disappointed she raised her eyebrows delicately. 'So who is he with?'

'It looks like a business meeting.'

Interest lost, pink dress lady shrugged her pink shoulders. 'Still very strange behaviour,' she muttered before turning back to her dining companion to relate all that she had found out.

'Where?' asked Fliss quietly.

'Er maybe I should go tell him to come back …'

'Where?'

'I could tell him that you want …'

Standing up Fliss pushed him to one side. She didn't need the waiter's help to find her husband and with her head held high, she stalked, as firmly as she could after several glasses of champagne, out of the small dining area and into the main room. The search didn't take long and she saw Jasper almost immediately, sitting at a table in the window with Freddie and Ross. Edward, moving more quickly than he had all day, barrelled into her back as she stopped.

'Shall I ask him to …' he bleated but Fliss was on the move again, covering the ground at a pace. She was still a few feet away when Jasper looked up, mid-laugh at a comment made by Freddie and saw his wife bearing down on him, fire and brimstone flashing from her eyes.

Leaping to his feet, he caught the bowl of chicken salad he had almost emptied and it tipped sideways onto the table.

'Steady on old chap,' shouted Freddie, laughing as he made a grab for it. 'What's the hurry?'

'Fliss!' gulped Jasper. 'Darling, I was just coming to ….'

'How could you! How could you Jasper?'

'I'm sorry I…'

'You left me. You left me to have lunch with Freddie and Ross!'

'Not exactly…'

270

'She's very keen,' she heard Freddie mutter. 'Doesn't like him to leave her even to go to work.'

'Fliss I can explain, I …'

'Don't bother, I know exactly what happened,' and with a glare, she turned on her heel and for the second time in their married life, she walked away.

My dearest Ellie

I can't believe that it went so wrong so quickly. Your last email was so full of optimism and happiness that it's hard to grasp it's now over. I think the constant problem between yourself and Logan has been one misunderstanding followed by another. You don't seem to have been able to meet and talk to each other without interference from others. Are you sure that nothing can be rescued, a frank and honest chat, an admission that things haven't gone to plan and a plea to start again? I am so very sorry that your dream failed to materialise, it seems unfair when you had placed so much hope and belief in its success.

But don't give up on love Ellie. It didn't work out for you this time but never, ever give up on love. It's the one thing I think is truly necessary in everybody's life, at least once, even if for a short burst. Love and happiness and the contentment that they bring is something that everyone deserves to feel and I hope and pray that you will feel both, soon.

I will miss your emails, your updates and your thoughts. It's made me question everything about myself and that's a good thing, even if the answers didn't bring the solace expected. The trouble with examining your actions carefully, unpicking them, reassessing them, is that you never know what you're going to find under the surface. You were so right, the cause of unhappiness is not always what you may expect. I've come to the rather frightening understanding that the cause of my unhappiness can't be laid solely on Jasper's shoulders. I followed his lead and thought the life we were embarking upon was the one I wanted to live. It turns out, that's not the case. Regrets are pointless, they don't change the past so I don't regret the decisions we made but I have come to realise that I no longer agree with them. I don't doubt that Jasper loves me and I don't doubt that I love him.

272

But I also understand, deep down, that I'm ready for more, I need more. I told you once that honesty was the only way you could move forward with Logan and I think now it's time I applied that to my own situation.

My very best wishes for the future Ellie, I hope that you find the love you deserve,

Your friend

Fliss

Chapter 26

Ellie left work at the usual time, her coat wrapped around her against the still chill winds and her woolly hat, so despised by Laura, firmly in place to keep her head warm. She had moved out of the flat she'd shared with Carl as soon as she ended the relationship, despite his assurances that she could stay as long as she wanted. The only place she'd managed to find at such short notice was a less than desirable flat which was tiny and damp with cardboard thin walls through which she could hear her next-door neighbours and their regular arguments followed by even louder reconciliations. The thought of going home to the cold and unfriendly rooms made her heart sink but she refused to return to her parents, tail between her legs and she was persevering until she found somewhere better.

Pausing at the door, she gazed out into the dark drizzly evening and wondered if she should have accepted Laura's invite for a drink. Anything was better than going back to an empty house and spending the evening feeling sorry for herself. Last night had been bad enough but what was there to look forward to now? Her dream of a life with Logan were shattered. There would be no happy ending, no 18 years of blissful married life like Fliss and her husband.

'It's a bit unpleasant out there isn't it.'

Logan was standing beside her, no Harriet in sight and Ellie couldn't help but smile at the irony of bumping into him so easily now it was all over.

'Pretty miserable,' she agreed.

'Do you have far to walk? I've got an umbrella with me.'

'No, not far.'

'Have you got a new umbrella yet?'

Ellie didn't reply.

'You said yours had been blown inside out a few days ago.'

He had been listening. The morning she had arrived, wet through and windswept, he had listened when she'd told him her umbrella had given up on her.

'No, I haven't had time yet.'

'Then let me walk you to your bus stop otherwise you'll get wet.'

Now he wanted to walk her home? Now he had asked Harriet out he wanted to walk her home? Why did life events frequently arrive in the wrong order?

'Er no, thank you but I'm alright.'

He smiled down at her. His eyes were less red-rimmed than they had been that morning and he had recovered some of the colour in his face.

'I don't mind,' he insisted. 'We could maybe stop for a drink and have a chat.'

'No!' She may have been desperate to manipulate a date with Logan over the past weeks, but he was going out with Harriet now and Ellie had no intention of pursuing him anymore. 'I don't think that would be appropriate,' she said stiffly.

'Not … I'm sorry I don't …'

'No drink, thank you. And I don't need you to walk me anywhere. I'll be just fine.' She wondered if he wanted to tell her in person that he was going out with Harriet.

'Then take my umbrella please,' he said quietly. 'I don't want you walking home in the rain.'

Had Laura put him up to this, wondered Ellie? Or was it because he was going out with Harriet that he no longer needed to worry about the crazy woman in administration who followed him around and attacked him in lifts.

'Won't Harriet mind?' she asked, watching his reaction carefully.

He looked puzzled. 'Why on earth would she? It's not her umbrella.'

No, thought Ellie. But you are her boyfriend.

'Really it's only a few streets away. I'll be okay. I like the rain,' she lied.

Stepping away from him, she felt the oversized drops begin to lash at her the moment she moved away from the cover of the doorway. Her phone was buzzing in her pocket and she pulled it out. The rain had suddenly taken a turn for the worse, the drizzle becoming a torrent and Ellie was beginning to regret her decision.

It was her mother. She never called Ellie during the day in case she disturbed her at work but she'd sent a message and Ellie read it, her face white with shock.

'What's wrong?' asked Logan, taking her elbow and pulling her back underneath the shelter of the doorway. 'What's happened?'

'My dad, he's had a heart attack. He's in Leeds infirmary.'

The phone almost fell from her hand and Logan grabbed at it before it hit the soaking wet street. She gazed around as though looking for something. 'I need to go there, I need to go to him, I don't know …'

Logan was already in action. Shoving the brolly into Ellie's numb hand he'd stepped out into the street and was frantically flagging down a taxi.

The rain was hitting the brolly and bouncing up into the air and Ellie's shoes were already wet through but she didn't care, she didn't even notice the drops trickling down her neck.

'Ellie!' Logan was calling her name and was standing by a taxi, the door open as he beckoned for her to get in.

Giving him back the brolly she expected him to disappear but he climbed in next to her, shoving the closed brolly by their feet.

'We'll be there in a few minutes,' he reassured. 'It's not far from here. Do you know which ward he's in?'

276

Ellie nodded. The message from her mother was short but succinct.

The taxi set off and Ellie watched the streets roll by through the rain misted window, imagining her mother writing the short message. Feeling a sob rise in her throat she realised that Logan was holding her hand tightly in his own and even though she felt that she should snatch it away she couldn't help but be soothed by the constant caress of his thumb on the back of her hand and the warmth of his fingers against hers. They arrived in less than ten minutes, the driver at Logan's request dropping Ellie as close as he could to the Accident and Emergency unit. Logan climbed out, his hair immediately soaking wet in the pouring rain. Helping Ellie out, he pressed the umbrella into her hands. 'For later,' he said.

Jumping over the puddle that was already forming by the kerb, Ellie stopped. 'The taxi, I …'

'I'll get the taxi fare. I hope your dad is okay Ellie. Look after yourself,' and leaning down he pressed a gentle kiss onto her cheek, his stormy grey eyes looking into her soul before he climbed back inside the relative dryness of the back seat.

Watching the taxi disappear into the rainy evening, Ellie pressed a hand to her cheek. Her cheek pulsed where his lips had rested and she watched the lights of the taxi disappear down the street before running inside and making her way towards where her mother was waiting.

Taking off her dripping coat, she tiptoed quietly to the side of a bed where her father lay, his face grey and taut as he slept, her mother sitting by his side clutching his hand in her own.

'Mum, how is he?' she whispered, slipping into an empty seat on the other side of the bed.

Her mother's face was devoid of colour and she seemed to have aged 10 years since Ellie had last seen her.

'He's out of danger. It was a major attack but nothing that he can't get over with care and attention.' Susan

Henshaw looked down at her sleeping husband, a tear rolling slowly down her cheek. 'He'll be in hospital for a while though, until they're happy to send him home.'

Ellie nodded. 'Of course. He's strong mum, and he won't want to stay in hospital a moment longer than he absolutely has to. I bet he's home in no time.'

More tears rolled down her mother's cheeks. 'I know,' she said with a suppressed sob. 'I know but he'll be in hospital for a few days at least and I really can't bear to leave him here, alone.'

Watching the emotion in her mother's face, Ellie couldn't help but feel surprised. She half expected her mother to declare that this would be the perfect time for a spring clean, with her father out of the way for a few days and no-one to interfere with Susan's organised plans.

'He'll be okay mum,' she offered reassuringly. 'He's as tough as they come.'

'He'll be lost in here.'

Ellie couldn't imagine her father lost anywhere. He had the kind of sensible, level-headedness that never lost its way. Suddenly uncertain she remained quiet, watching her mother weep.

'You don't really know us very well, do you Ellie?'

'Of course I do! You're my parents.'

Susan smiled, wiping away her tears with the back of her hand.

'But you don't know us, the people beneath the parents, the people who fell in love and got married.'

Ellie had always felt vaguely surprised that her down to earth, steady father had ever lost his heart to anyone. She had never been able to imagine him going down on one knee and proposing, or even admitting that he loved anyone enough to share his life with them. She had spent her teenage years with her head in the romantic if often tormented lives of Jane Austen's heroines. As she had grown older she had developed a passion for regency romance, where the heroines unfailingly had heaving

278

bosoms and the heroes were often moody and bad-tempered but would face any challenge to prove their worthiness for the love of their life. Ellie had wanted to be such a woman, she had wanted someone to sweep her off her feet and declare undying love. She'd been fully prepared to be taken prisoner by a vagabond to enable her hero to come charging along on his white horse and rescue her virtue just in time. She had wanted to feel her bosom heave with passion, she had wanted to gasp at the temerity of a young man who stole an illicit kiss beneath an apple tree.

Her mother was watching the emotions race across her face.

'We love each other Ellie. We may not show it as much as others do. Your father was never one to show his emotions and I was quite happy knowing that he loved me. I didn't need a great declaration every time he walked through the door.'

'I know you love each other,' said Ellie defensively. 'I just didn't realise …'

'What? You didn't think I could see your father as the love of my life? You didn't think either of us would be devastated, totally bereft if we were to lose one another? Your idea of love isn't everything you know Ellie. I know why you broke up with Carl. I know you have your head in the clouds, imagining that it can't be real love if it doesn't knock you off your feet. I was so glad you found Carl. He's a good man, strong and sincere. Much like your father. I was always worried that you would be looking for a knight somewhere, a hero to rescue you.'

Ellie shifted uncomfortably in her seat.

'But you seemed happy, I really thought that you were about to settle down and get married. And then the old Ellie emerged, the one who was looking for romance and fluttering hearts. There is more depth to love than pretty words and flowers. True love can be quiet and unassuming.' Susan squeezed her husband's hand,

279

examining his face with such a depth of emotion in her eyes that Ellie felt humbled. 'We love each other, truly love each other and you would do well to realise that love can be like this. Plain and honest.'

With her bottom lip quivering, Ellie felt her eyes fill up. 'I hadn't realised,' she admitted honestly, 'just how strongly you felt about each other.'

'I know. And maybe that's my fault. We kept our emotions contained, between the two of us. If you'd been more aware of how we felt, it may have made you braver about your own decisions. But it's too late now, isn't it? Carl has gone. And what about the other one?'

'The other one?'

'You've never said as much but I always suspected that your decision to end things with Carl was prompted by something, or rather someone else.'

Ellie blushed, her cheeks filling with colour. 'I'm not going out with anyone else,' she said carefully. 'There is no-one in my life.'

She could feel her mother's gaze digging deep into her soul.

'Who was it?'

'Mum!'

'I know you Ellie, better than you think. Carl knows you too. It was obvious that your heart had been snatched by someone.'

Appalled Ellie nibbled on her thumbnail. 'Carl knew?'

Nodding wearily, Susan Henshaw turned her eyes back to her unmoving husband. 'He suspected.'

'He never said anything.'

'He wouldn't. Carl isn't like that.'

Following her mother's eyes, Ellie remained silent for a few minutes, watching her father's pale face.

'It was someone at work,' she said eventually. 'I saw him and I couldn't help myself. I fell in love.'

'It's not love, it's just a ....'

280

'And that's part of the reason why I didn't tell you! Can't you believe that I fell in love with someone, instantly, wholeheartedly, deeply in love? I couldn't marry Carl feeling like that so I ended things. I thought it was the right thing to do.'

Taking the rebuke, Susan tilted her head to one side. 'And?'

'It didn't work out. I thought it was going to for a while, he even asked me out but ... well, it just didn't work. He's going out with someone else now.'

So few words, such searing pain.

'So you and Carl could....'

'No! Absolutely not. I would never do that to him and besides, it doesn't change things, not really. It's over between me and Carl and it's over between me and ...my friend.'

More pain, thought Ellie, wrapping her arms around her stomach. 'It's all over,' she whispered and then silence fell as she and her mother spent the night gazing at Dave Henshaw and willing his skin to lose its pallor and his eyes to open.

Chapter 27

Over the next two days, Ellie divided her time between the hospital and her parents' home whilst her mother stayed glued to the hospital bed where her husband lay. The doctors had declared themselves pleased with his progress but Susan Henshaw had no intention of leaving him and other than brief visits to the visitors centre where she could shower and change, she stayed in the chair beside her husband, holding his hand in a comfortable silence.

Ellie had collected clothes for them both, taken washing away, made sandwiches for her mum, tidied the house, which was already immaculate, and spent the rest of her time sitting on the opposite side of the bed. Her father woke up regularly but spent most of the day slipping in and out of sleep. Ellie had noticed that whenever his eyes opened, they flew to the side of the bed, checking that his wife was still there. They would exchange a look and the fingers that were entangled with each other would squeeze a little tighter.

He had joined Ellie in trying to convince Susan to go home and get a good night's sleep, but Ellie detected a flash of relief in his eyes when Susan refused point-blank to go anywhere until he was well enough to go with her.

So she remained by her father's bed, with nothing to do but ponder how badly everything had turned out and how there was no-one to blame but herself.

'Why don't you go home for a few hours? You look tired.'

It was her mum, who should look even worse than Ellie considering how much time she had spent sitting by a hospital bed, but who instead looked calm and peaceful. The doctors had predicted her husband would be out of hospital soon and that was all she had needed to know. In the meantime, she was happy staying where she was, supporting the man she loved.

'I'll stay with you,' offered Ellie. 'Do you want me to get you a tea?'

Her mother shook her head, her eyes going back to her husband's face.' I'm okay sweetheart but please, go home. Have a shower and get a good night's sleep. I'll stay here with your dad.' Ellie had already decided that it would take a momentous event to make Susan leave his side. 'There's no point both of us spending the night in a chair. Go on, go home.'

Persuaded, Ellie kissed them both goodnight and allowed herself the luxury of a taxi back to her parents' house. The long hot shower she took was nothing short of luxurious and sitting in her pyjamas in their living room took Ellie back to a time gone by when she would curl up in the corner of the settee with a book, invariably a romance, and spend her evening living another life.

She had messages from Laura, who checked on her several times a day, her brother, who was currently on a plane from New Zealand and much to her surprise from Logan.

Laura tells me your dad is doing okay, hope you are too x

Ellie spent a lot of time looking at that kiss. Was it an actual kiss, she wondered, or was it more of a full stop. A best wishes kind of thing, a brief way of saying thinking of you. Over the last few days, as she'd spent hours sitting in a hospital room staring at the wall, Ellie had found plenty of time to think about the real kiss Logan had pressed on her cheek. She touched the very spot now, it felt hot but that could be the result of the shower. Or maybe it was because every time she thought back to the moment he looked into her eyes and then bent down to kiss her softly, her cheeks filled with a rush of colour and her heart definitely increased its beat. Why had he kissed her, she had wondered a thousand times. Why had he waited until any possibility of them getting together was over, when he had already asked Harriet out? Why would he choose that moment to kiss her? He had been so sweet, so protective that evening, putting her in a taxi and taking her to the hospital. She had told Fliss, what now felt like a lifetime ago, that she was sure he would make a wonderful husband, strong and caring, and it would seem that she had been right. But not for Ellie, he would never be the husband Ellie had dreamed of.

And now he'd sent her a text with a little kiss at the end and it had its usual effect on Ellie's breathing. Was he thinking about her and wishing he could kiss her again? Was he being polite and showing support? Gazing at the text Ellie's hand hovered over the delete option. Logan belonged to someone else now. She had to stop thinking about him, stop dreaming of his lips pressed against her cheek. She had to stop waking up imagining his arms wrapped around her as she did most mornings. She needed to let him go.

He's doing really well. And thank you for helping me that night x

Her heart banged against her chest as she placed her own small kiss at the end of the text. Was it foolish to begin exchanging texts with someone who had just exited your life? Was it fair on Harriet? She should have ignored him, or answered but left the kiss where it belonged, in her heart.

That's great news! And I was happy to help. Anything you need, let me know x

The answer came back so quickly, he must have been staring at his phone as she had sent her message. And another kiss! Should she answer? She could say she'd run out of bread or felt lonely and needed company. Would Logan come round? Would he send her a text saying he was on his way, a text with a kiss at the end? Ellie's fingers rested on her phone. He'd asked if she needed anything, he wanted to help, would it be so very wrong to tell him exactly what she needed. Him. By her side, offering comfort in her hour of need.

A knock at the door jerked her out of her reverie. Staring down at the phone, she stroked the screen and Logan's last message. It would be unfair. Unfair on Harriet who had won him fair and square and unfair on Logan who had not chosen Ellie but was a wonderful caring sort of person, still willing to help her out when she needed him. It was time to let him go. He wasn't hers for the taking and reluctantly, her heart feeling like lead in her chest, she closed down the message and placed her phone carefully on the table before pulling her dressing gown tighter and answering the door.

'Hello, Ellie. I heard about your dad and came round to see if there was anything you needed, anything I could do for you and your family.'

'Come in Carl.'

She led him into the living room and sank back down in her spot in the corner of the settee.

'It's very good of you to call,' she said softly. 'Thank you.'

Carl shook his head. 'Of course I would visit, I think a great deal about your parents Ellie, you must know that.'

She did. He had gotten on with her father from the very first day and her mother would never hear a bad word against him. Not that there were any, Carl was far too kind and considerate to be disliked by anyone. Ellie had loved him for his gentle soul, his ability to find the good in anybody.

'How is he doing?'

'Much better. He'll be home soon I think but Mum won't leave him, even though the doctors have said he's on the road to recovery.'

'I can imagine. They won't want to be parted.'

Ellie looked at him in surprise and Carl continued.

'They love each other so much, I can imagine that Susan was devastated at the thought of losing him. She'll want to stay very close until she gets him home.'

'That's exactly how she feels,' she said slowly. It had come as a surprise to Ellie but not, apparently, to Carl. As an outsider, he had been able to see immediately what Ellie had failed to notice her entire life.

Misunderstanding the emotion on her face, Carl abandoned his chair and came to sit next to her, taking her hand in his and holding it tightly.

'He'll be okay Ells. He's a tough cookie and once he comes home your mum will make sure he's well looked after. Try not to worry too much.'

Nodding, Ellie looked down at their fingers entwined together. 'I know,' she whispered. Should she tell him that it wasn't really her father that was causing the tears to build in her eyes, it was that she had underestimated the strength of her parents love all these years? And that she was now questioning her own values where love was concerned.

'Don't cry.' His hand left hers but only because he was putting his arms around her, pulling her onto a chest that was incredibly familiar and oh so comforting. 'It will be okay,' he murmured in her ear. 'Really, it will all be okay.'

Allowing herself the luxury of staying where she was for a few more seconds, Ellie finally pulled herself free to wipe her eyes on a tissue. It would be all too easy to stay in the comforting circle of his arms, to let him stroke her hair and whisper words of reassurance in her ear. Far too easy. But she had already hurt him enough and it wouldn't be fair to Carl to let him think there was any chance of a reconciliation.

'Okay?'

'I am, thank you. It's all been a bit of a shock.'

'Well, like I said, if there's anything that you need, shopping, a lift to the hospital, anything at all, just call me. I'm here for you all.'

Typical Carl, so thoughtful. 'I think we're okay but I'll let mum and dad know that you've offered. It will mean a lot to them.'

Standing up, he smiled. 'I'll get off then, leave you to it. Anybody coming round to keep you company?' he asked casually.

'No, not tonight.'

'I see. The er, man you were meeting the other night? He's not coming to see you?'

Ellie tried to smile, it was difficult through the tears that were still rolling down her face. 'That didn't work out,' she said swallowing another sob.

'Oh. Did I … I mean, I hope me being there didn't mess things up for you?'

They had, thought Ellie. There again, if she and Logan were meant to be together, he wouldn't have been so quick to pass judgement and fall into Harriet's arms.

'No, it just wasn't meant to be.'

She walked to the front door with him, her hands stuffed in the pockets of her dressing gown.

'I'm sorry. You had hopes that he would be perfect for you.'

'Just one of those things,' shrugged Ellie. 'If it's not meant to be …'

A horn sounded from outside and Carl zipped up his coat quickly. 'Sorry, I only meant to stay for a minute or two. That will be Sophie wondering where I've got to.'

Opening the door and letting the dark, cold air stream in, Ellie peered out at the car sitting outside the house.

'Sophie?'

'Yeah.' Ducking his head, a hint of pink appearing in his cheeks, Carl stepped outside before turning to face Ellie again.

'I took your advice. I accepted that things were over between us, finally, absolutely. And I decided that I needed to move on. The following night I bumped into Sophie in the fish and chip shop. I thought, what the hell and asked

287

if I could pay for her chips and we ended up eating them in my car. It was amazing actually, how much we had to talk about. It turned out we had so much in common, we even like the same kind of films. It's not often you meet a woman who likes war films, would you believe her favourite is *Black Hawk Down*!'

Ellie was standing quite rigid, the cold swirling unnoticed around her feet. 'That is hard to believe,' she murmured.

'Anyway, we're going on our first proper date tonight, no chips in the car,' laughed Carl. 'We're having a few drinks and then going back to hers. She's got *Platoon* on DVD and we're going to get a takeaway.'

It was far too dark for Ellie to get a look at Sophie sitting patiently in the front seat of the car. She felt sure that Laura would demand a full and vivid description of the woman who claimed to like war films and was happy to eat chips in someone's car for a first date.

'I see, well, enjoy your night Carl and thank you again for coming round.'

'Anytime, I'm always here for you and your family,' and leaning forward he planted a small kiss on her cheek, in almost the exact spot where Logan's had landed a few evenings previously.

As he walked towards the car, Ellie felt the tears start again. They were falling down her face faster than she could catch them. It wasn't because of her dad, still in the hospital. It wasn't because of Logan, probably sitting somewhere next to Harriet sharing their favourite film, which was unlikely to be *Black Hawk Down* or *Platoon*. It was because of the kiss Carl had given her. It was a kiss of friendship, loyal, warm, comforting friendship, exactly what she would have wished for only days earlier. It was an ending, a final goodbye to the relationship they'd once had and as he set off down the road, waving at Ellie shivering on the doorstep, she knew it was now truly over. Carl had gone, moved on as Ellie had requested. Logan had gone, moved on to Harriet. Ellie had lost both of them, she was well and truly alone.

FROM: Logan MacDonald <loganmac@connectmenow.co.uk>
To: Fliss Carmichael <agonyauntfliss@digitalrecorder.com>
Date: 01/05/2020

Dear Fliss

I have never sent an email like this before and I'm not really sure what to say, but I need to tell someone how I feel and it's a bit difficult to tell any of my friends because, well, because men don't really talk about stuff like this to anyone, let alone each other.

The thing is, I really like someone at work. When I say really like, what I mean is I'm crazy about her. She's a bit mad, in fact seriously mad! She does some very strange things, especially in lifts, and I'm never sure what's going to happen next. But I love her quirky little ways and the way her cheeks always go pink whenever I look at her. I've just realised, I used the word love and I have to admit, I do think I'm in love with her. Is it possible to fall in love with someone that you don't really know?

I noticed her weeks ago. We were in a meeting together and I just couldn't take my eyes away from her. I wanted to say something as we all left but her friend dragged her off really quickly and I didn't get a chance. I did ask around to see if she had a boyfriend and everyone seemed to think that she was single although I have seen her with her ex a couple of times, I even thought they might still be together. I was hoping to get a chance to talk to her, maybe even ask her out on a date but it's not easy. Like I say, she does sometimes act very strangely and she's always got her friend with her who is equally mad and seems to be doing her best to keep us away from each other.

And then she spoke to me. Her friend wasn't there and we finally had time for a chat. It was a short one but she admitted that she liked me. I tried to play it cool but I was thrilled. We arranged to meet but then her ex turned up, again, and I decided I would give her space to deal with him, it seemed as though they still had a lot to say to each other. Since then I've heard that the ex is going out with the sister of one of my mates from football, they met each other in the fish and chip shop.

But now she seems to be avoiding me and it just keeps getting more complicated. I tried talking to her, to tell her that I really like her but that I didn't want to cause trouble between her and her ex. I've tried but all she wanted to talk about was another girl at work, she seemed to think I'd stolen her umbrella. I suppose what I'm asking is, does love at first sight exist? Could I be in love with someone I don't really know? And if so, what do I do about it? How can I tell if she is interested in me or if she's trying to avoid me? Should I talk to her friend?

I apologise for the barrage of questions I'm just not sure what to do. You're probably going to tell me that it's obvious she doesn't like me and I'm being stupid but despite everything, I can't get her out of my head.

Please help me,

Bewildered of Leeds

Chapter 28

After phoning Viv and telling her she needed to take off the rest of the afternoon, Fliss stormed home muttering angrily to herself. Convinced the romantic lunch had been a success, Viv had chuckled down the phone and told Fliss to enjoy herself. If only she knew, thought Fliss grumpily, her head pounding from the champagne and getting changed she went into the kitchen to make a coffee.

As the kettle came to the boil, she was surprised to hear a swish of gravel on the driveway and moments later a puce faced Jasper came hurtling in.

'I'm sorry darling,' he gasped. 'I'm so sorry. Freddie invited me for an early lunch meeting and I was going to tell you but I didn't want to let you down and I thought we might be finished before you got there and you wouldn't know but you were early and I ….'

Running out of breath, he stopped and took the coffee Fliss was handing him. 'And I messed up again. I'm sorry.'

Refusing to let him off the hook so easily, Fliss kept a stern silence.

'I should have just told you I was too busy to meet you for lunch. Or,' he added hastily, 'even better, I should have told Ross and Freddie that I had already arranged to meet you.'

'I was actually worried about you,' she remonstrated angrily. 'I managed to convince myself that you were quite ill and it was all my fault for pushing you so hard. I was worried but I should have known better.'

'I'm so sorry,' he said for what seemed like the thousandth time. 'Please forgive me. I didn't want to let you down. Instead, I made things worse.'

'No.'

'No?'

'You're always sorry Jasper, you always ask me to forgive you. Well, the answer is no. Not today. I was genuinely worried about you, I thought you were ill, I thought you were on the verge of a breakdown but as per usual, you just couldn't stop thinking about business. So, no. I don't forgive you,' and picking up her coffee, she left her husband spluttering in the kitchen and walked off in search of some peace and quiet.

Refusing to be cajoled, it was Sunday before Fliss gave in. Waking up, exhausted from being angry and in a far more forgiving mood, she wandered downstairs and pushed open the door to Jasper's study where he immediately closed his laptop and dashed to her side.

'Can I get you anything? What would you like to do today? Shall we go out for lunch?' he blushed at Fliss' pointed look. 'Just the two of us obviously. Would you like to go for a drive? To the cinema? Shall we ….'

'Stop!' Holding up her hand to stop the flow of suggestions, Fliss leant against the doorway and examined her husband's remorseful face. Almost able to see the funny side of Jasper dashing backwards and forwards between the two rooms pretending to be fully committed to both, Fliss took the hand he held out to her and with a thankful groan, Jasper had pulled her against his chest, wrapping his arms around her and burying his face in her hair.

'I hate it when you're angry with me,' he muttered.

Feeling that he should probably be used to it after the last few weeks, Fliss didn't answer. She was enjoying being back in his arms, the feel of his chest against her cheek. His lips grazed the side of her neck and she let herself relax. Maybe she would just spend the day here, warm and comfortable as he kissed her throat, her cheeks, her eyes.

'So what *do* you want to do today,' he asked eventually, after finally making his way down to her lips and kissing her thoroughly.

'Actually, I think I'd like to stay at home. Just the two of us, a lovely relaxed Sunday, no pressure, no drama, just like we used to enjoy.'

'Mm, I see. Just the two of us?'

'Yes.'

'At home all day?'

'Yes.'

'Won't you get bored?'

Jasper had pulled her back into his arms and his fingers were playing with the top button of her pyjamas.

'We never used to get bored.'

'True. Sundays spent at home used to be very interesting I seem to recall.'

Fliss giggled and then shivered in delight as Jasper's fingers made their way slowly down to the next button. 'I remember them fondly,' she whispered.

'Perhaps that's another Carmichael tradition that we need to reinstate,' murmured Jasper, with only one button left. 'Shall we start today?'

But Fliss didn't answer, her groan of delight the only sound as Jasper swept her into his arms and carried her up the stairs and back into the bedroom.

Later that afternoon, Fliss was in the kitchen putting the finishing touches to a Sunday roast when she had an idea. Jasper had volunteered to rake up all the leaves that were gathering on the lawn and grabbing a glass of wine for him, Fliss went in search. The leaves were still scattered pretty much everywhere except for a small pile that had been gathered by the shed.

'Jasper? Where are you?' Walking further into the garden, Fliss heard the crunch of leaves and a muffled curse as something banged close by.

'Jasper? What are you doing?'

Peering round the back of the shed, she caught Jasper hastily shoving his phone into his trouser pocket. Stepping over the rake, Fliss walked nearer, handing him the glass.

'I thought you might be ready for a break.'

'Yes, I am.' Wiping a brow that contained absolutely no sweat and showed a minimum of exertion, Jasper took the proffered glass. 'This is tiring work,' he declared, his eyes not meeting his wife's.

'I can imagine,' responded Fliss wryly. 'You must be exhausted.' Sitting on the garden bench, she stretched out her legs. 'I was looking for you because I had an idea. Why don't we book a holiday? A proper holiday where we laze on a beach and do nothing but relax and enjoy ourselves.'

Leaving the sanctuary of the shed, Jasper sat beside her. 'That sounds like a wonderful idea! Where were you thinking?'

'Don't mind. I'm really not bothered, as long as there is sun involved, and a pool, and maybe someone to do the cleaning, oh and a restaurant nearby so I don't have to cook, and a beach would be good and …'

Holding his hand up to stop her, Jasper laughed. 'Okay, I can see that you don't have any fixed ideas! Shall I have a look?'

Nodding, Fliss closed her eyes, the feel of the sun on her skin, warm and welcoming. Jasper's arm slid around her and she rested her head on his shoulders. 'This is nice, isn't it?' she asked dreamily, looking down the garden where a robin was taking advantage of the birdbath. 'This is what it could be like on holiday, nothing to do but relax and enjoy the day.'

'You're right. It's exactly what we could do with, leave it to me,' and pulling Fliss even closer, he followed her example and sat with his face raised to the sun, enjoying a glass of wine on the bench with his wife.

Two days later, arriving home and finding Fliss in the kitchen, Jasper announced that he had found the perfect place.

'Bermuda!' he declared looking pleased with himself. 'It's a little villa by the sea, own pool, private beach, 5 minutes' walk to the nearest restaurant.'

He laid down a selection of photos. 'Doesn't it look lovely?'

It did indeed, thought Fliss, examining the whitewashed villa that looked to be perched on the edge of a sparkling turquoise sea.

'Gorgeous,' she breathed,' oh Jasper, it looks absolutely wonderful. How did you find it?'

'It's Freddie's. He bought it a few years ago, says it's like paradise, so tranquil and with amazing views.'

'And he's going to let us rent it? That's nice of him. Is it expensive?'

'Oh, he doesn't want anything for it. He doesn't rent it out but he's happy to let friends stay there. It's exactly what we were looking for, don't you think? Now, what's for tea, shall I order something?'

'That's very generous of him. And trusting. Letting people use it for free and no idea if they'll look after it.'

'Yes. Do you know, I have a hankering for Chinese, shall we get one?'

'When?'

'Now, or we can wait an hour or so if you prefer?'

'Not the Chinese. When are we going to the villa?'

'In two weeks. So is that a yes to the Chinese. Actually, I might go upstairs and get changed first and then I'll …'

'In two weeks! Me, you and a beautiful villa in Bermuda. How wonderful. We're lucky Freddie doesn't want to use it himself.'

'Ah yes, er well, he may do, we'll have to see. I'll phone for the Chinese now and then get changed …'

'What do you mean, he may do? Stand still!'

Jasper sighed, his face taking on a defensive air.

'It is just the two of us, isn't it?'

'Not exactly.' He tugged at his tie, rolling it up carefully. 'I mentioned we were looking for somewhere and Freddie told me about his villa.'

'And?'

'And I said it looked fantastic, just the sort of place we were looking for and could we use it.'

'And Freddie said yes?'

'I asked if could we have it the week after next and he said yes! Isn't that wonderful of him? So generous!'

Fliss didn't respond, she was standing with her fingers clutching the edge of the breakfast bar waiting for Jasper to finish his story.

'Well, that afternoon he phoned me up and said that he'd checked with Maggie and she was free and they'd decided that they would come with us, they loved the idea of a week in the sun.'

'So we're not going alone, it's not just the two of us, it's Freddie and Mags as well? And you'll be discussing business with Freddie for the entirety of the holiday!'

'Of course not! Freddie says he loves to go there so he can turn off for a while, forget about work and everything else. Shall I go order the Chinese now or …'

'What else?'

'Sorry? We can have a pizza if you prefer?'

'About the villa, there's something else isn't there?'

Jasper tried to look innocent. 'Nothing bad. After I spoke to Freddy he phoned back and said he'd been speaking to Ross and he and Jean were free so …'

'You've booked for us to go on holiday with two other couples? The lovely relaxing break, just for the two of us is now a joint holiday with two of your business colleagues?'

'I wouldn't call them business colleagues …'

'I would!'

'I thought you'd be pleased,' he huffed. 'I've found the perfect location and arranged a fantastic holiday. And the best part is that we won't be on our own, we'll have company, think what a good time we'll have.'

Fliss stared at him. She knew his face so well, had spent years and years waking up next to him, had loved every inch of him, every hair on his head, every slight imperfection on his body, but right now, she wondered if she knew him at all.

'The best part for me would be if we were on our own,' she said, her tone strangled by emotion. 'We would have had an immense amount of fun alone, just the two of us on holiday.'

'Well, I thought it was a wonderful idea having company.'

Shaking her head, Fliss felt suddenly light-headed. The room was swaying beneath her and Jasper was looming large then retreating far away.

'That's the problem,' she whispered. 'That's what the problem is. It's not because you're suddenly busier with work. You don't want to spend time alone with me anymore. We go out so much because that way we're not alone. You go to so many business meetings because then you're not with me. The last two years, every holiday we've taken has been with other people. You feel safe in a crowd, you feel better with a crowd of people around you because then it's not just you and I.'

She paused, looking at Jasper whose own face resembled putty, a grey drained look pinching his cheeks. 'You avoid being alone with me, you actively seek out something, someone, anyone to hide behind …'

'Stop Fliss. This is ridiculous. Stop …'

'No. It's not ridiculous. I've been racking my brains to understand what has changed so much. I thought it was me. I thought maybe you had just grown bored of me, didn't find me attractive anymore.'

'Please stop ….'

'I decided we'd drifted apart and lost each other in the chaos of life. But *we* haven't drifted. You've left our marriage. You've left me.'

'I would never leave you, never …'

'I don't mean physically Jasper. You may not have walked out of the door, but in your heart, something has made you turn away.'

The room was still tilting and swaying and Fliss held onto the granite surface to stop herself from swaying with it. Her throat was becoming tighter with unshed tears, her voice hoarse and grainy as she spoke.

'For the last two years ….'

'No! No Fliss…'

'For the last two years you've been different. I didn't see it as first, I was too wrapped up in my own grief. I didn't notice until recently and then it was so hard to put my finger on what it was, what had changed, when. But now it all makes sense.'

The tears broke free, rolling down her face in a salty stream. Her hands were trembling and her knees were shouting at her to sit down before they collapsed.

'It started two years ago. You stopped wanting to be alone with me after I lost the baby.'

She lifted her ravaged face so she could meet Jasper's eyes. They were full of anguish and hurt and sorrow. And as Fliss stared into them she knew that she was right.

'I lost our baby and it broke us. For some reason, you closed yourself off to me. That's when it started, isn't it? That's when you became so incredibly busy that there was no time for us anymore, that's when you left me.'

Chapter 29

Walking out of the kitchen and up the stairs, Fliss passed an unmoving Jasper in the doorway, his face frozen with shock. Suddenly she felt cold, so very cold and in a daze she began to run a bath, locking the bathroom door behind her. The warm scented water eased her shivering joints and some heat began to flow back into her body.

The day she'd told Jasper she was pregnant was etched in her memory. After they had married, it had been mutually agreed that a child at that point in their lives would be a mistake. They had careers to forge, lives to lead, a family could wait. One day they would have a child, one day the timing would be right and they had drifted onwards, always with the idea that one day they would be ready.

Two years ago, age 39, Fliss had woken suddenly one morning with the realisation that she was pregnant. Dashing out to buy a pregnancy test, she had stared for hours at the result and when Jasper arrived home, she had simply held it out for his inspection. Wondering throughout the day how he would react she had expected shock, worry, uncertainty, maybe even outright unhappiness. Jasper had taken the stick and she could see the confusion on his face as he tried to make sense of what he was looking at, followed by a expression of such exultation that she knew immediately she had nothing to worry about.

The practicalities were that there had never been a better time for them to start a family. Jasper was a successful and well-paid columnist with a growing reputation. Fliss was equally well respected in her field and the timing could not have been better. Keeping their news to themselves like a warm blanket wrapped around their shoulders on a cold day, they spent the following weeks as they had always done. But each evening, when they arrived home and the door shut behind then, they talked of little else.

Jasper would read nonstop about pregnancy and the early years of a child, announcing at regular intervals how big Baby Carmichael would be, how he thought that a home birth for someone of Fliss' age would not be a good idea, which fruit and vegetables would be best to nourish their little bump, and of course names by the dozen. Fliss would sit on the settee, the picture of happiness and let Jasper race through the books as she relished each and every moment of her pregnancy.

Until the morning she had woken up with debilitating cramps and blood on the sheets. Jasper had called for an ambulance but there was nothing for them to do. Within hours it was over, the baby was gone and there was nothing for Fliss to do but return home. The dream had ended.

As no-one knew, there were no explanations to be made. Jasper told friends and Vivian that Fliss had a nasty stomach bug. She spent a week at home, staring at the ceiling, twisting the bed sheets between her fingers and wondering at the incredible sense of loss and pain from something so small. Jasper, pale and strained, worked from home so he could keep an eye on his silent wife. With nothing to do but carry on, Fliss had eventually returned to the office, her inbox full with the problems of the nation and to all intents seemed to pick up the reigns of life and carry on. Only Jasper knew how far from the truth that was and his face became tight and drained as he watched Fliss sink into a well of depression that she had struggled to shake off.

A great part of Fliss' anxiety was the thought that her lost child may have been her one and only chance for a family. The doctor had advised no further pregnancy for at least 6 months and Fliss was aware of the loud ticking inside her head that told her time was moving on and she may already be too late. When Jasper sat down and took her hand one evening, she had tried to listen to him, to what he was saying.

'I've been thinking my darling,' he said, stroking his thumb soothingly against the inside of her wrist. 'And it's probably best that we forget about having a family at all. Let's face it, we would struggle to fit a child into our lives, we're both so busy, so much to do.'

Fliss had forced herself to listen, her heart leaping around as he spoke.

'My job will always keep me occupied, always keep me away from the house for long periods. There are meetings to attend, people to talk to. And that would leave so much on your shoulders, it would interrupt your career, our social life, our finances, our home, it would mean everything would have to change. I don't think that it would be worth it. We're happy as we are, just the two of us, let's stay that way and forget about having a family.'

Fliss could never say that Jasper hadn't made his intentions clear. She could never accuse him of having misled her. When the words were said, when they were out there for her to brood on and turn over in her head, all she had felt was an overriding relief that she wouldn't have to go through this again. There was no concern for her career, such as it was, her social life, her home. She didn't care about how it would affect their finances or their holiday plans. The only thought she had was that she couldn't bear to suffer like this again and if she followed Jaspers' lead, then she wouldn't have to.

Months later, when she had grieved and recovered as best she could, she'd revisited the conversation in her mind. Did she want a life without a family, no prospect of children at all? Jasper had said it would be the best thing for them, and she loved Jasper. They loved each other so maybe he was right and they didn't need anybody else. It hadn't taken Fliss long to convince herself that it had been the right decision, for both of them.

Life had resumed and it wasn't until she had read Ellie's email that she had understood with a sense of dread that although they had picked up the reigns of their old life, things had irrevocably changed. Whilst telling Ellie how very happy they were, the realisation that those emotions were all in the past, had descended on Fliss like a landslide. Without even noticing what was happening, her husband had changed. To anyone else he appeared exactly the same, still loving, still caring, still protective. But now Fliss examined her thoughts and more importantly her relationship, she understood that after she had lost their baby, she had also lost Jasper. He had moved away, silently, carefully, still within reach but subtly different.

Clinging to the breakfast bar, her world tilting and swaying beneath her feet, Fliss had suddenly understood what had happened. His insistence that he was so busy he couldn't ever stop work, dated back to those dark days. As did the social invitations which he couldn't ignore because they were important to his job. The friends always gathered around them, which Fliss originally thought were part of his plan to cheer her up, had never left. They had finally reached the stage where the occasions when Jasper was alone with his wife, quite alone, were few and far between.

The water in Fliss' bath was cooling now and there were strands of soggy toilet roll on the floor which she'd used to wipe away her tears. Wrapping a towel around her, she pulled the plug and sat on the floor, her back leaning against the wall.

'Fliss?' asked a quiet voice. 'Fliss, are you okay?'

Wondering how long he had been there waiting for the sounds of her getting out of the bath, Fliss didn't answer, just grabbed more toilet roll to wipe her eyes and nose again.

'Please talk to me.'

Did she want to talk to him? Part of her wanted to climb into bed and sleep, put her thoughts and emotions to one side for a few hours at least.

'Can I come in Fliss? Please.'

Reaching up, she flipped the lock on the door and a second later it swung open. The bathroom was warm and faintly muggy from the hot bath and a draft of cool air came in along with Jasper. He looked down at her sitting on the floor and without saying anything, he slid down the opposite wall.

Wondering if he would tell her she was being ridiculous, imagining emotions that simply weren't there, Fliss waited. She could see Jasper gathering himself, trying to organise his thoughts.

'I love you,' he said simply. 'Nothing will ever change that, nothing will ever make me stop loving you.'

Fliss wiped her eyes, silent, waiting.

'But you're right. I did change after the …. after the baby.'

And there it was. Her body jerked as though she'd been stabbed and she pulled her towel tighter around her cooling body.

'Not deliberately. In fact, when you said … when you spoke downstairs, I thought you were mad. Crazy to imagine such a thing.'

Tears welled in the corner of his eyes, his lips twisting with the effort to continue speaking.

'I was devastated when we lost our baby, for you, for me, for our child. I watched you struggle and saw the effort it took you to return to the world, to us, and I couldn't bear the thought of that happening again. When I said I didn't want a family, I meant it, Fliss, I meant every word. No… actually that's not true. I did mean it, but not because I cared about my job or our social life. I cared only because it broke you and I didn't ever want that to happen again.'

Pulling at the strip of paper in her hands, turning it into confetti, Fliss listened.

'I decided that I would rather do without a family than ever see you hurt like that again, and I talked a lot of rubbish about being too busy to raise a child. I was so relieved when you became yourself again, relieved and happy. I think I decided then that I needed to prove to you that everything I said was true, that we didn't have time or room for a child in our lives.'

Fliss stopped shredding. Jasper's head was down and he was talking almost to himself as Fliss sat unmoving on the floor.

'I went too far, I became busy, so very busy, I had to prove to both of us that I was right and there wasn't room for anyone or anything else in our life. And in the process, I pushed you away, the most precious thing I have.' Lifting up eyes that were shimmering with tears, Jasper looked at Fliss with so much grief that she almost gasped out loud.

'I didn't understand what I was doing. It wasn't intentional. I surrounded myself with people, commitments, demands. They all occupied my time and convinced me that I was right about the decision we made, I made.'

He stopped talking, looking down and moving slowly, Fliss inched across the floor and sat next to him, holding one of his shaking hand in hers.

'I hope I haven't left it too late Fliss darling. I hope that we've managed to rescue us in time.'

Fliss squeezed his fingers, still unable to talk. It made so much sense and she berated herself for not seeing it all far sooner. Over the years she'd received many emails from distraught women and men who'd suffered the tragedy of a miscarriage and if there was one thing she'd learnt, it was that their grief was profound and very real. It often tore lives apart, it split up couples, it changed outlooks, it changed people. It had changed Jasper. It had changed her.

They could recover, they had everything they needed, including each other. Fliss had done a great deal of thinking over the last few hours as she'd lain in her bath and recalled the agony of losing her child and the desperate state of her mind afterwards. Thinking back to the relief she had felt when Jasper had decreed that he thought a family was not right for them, she'd realised something. It wasn't just Jasper who had changed over the last 2 years. They both had.

Something had become clear to Fliss. Whatever the reasons behind their decision, they had been wrong. Or, at least she had been wrong. And that left her with a problem that was far greater than the one she had spoken of in her emails to Ellie. This wasn't about an irritation with a husband spending too much time thinking about work. It went far, far deeper.

Abandoning her tissue, she turned so she could see his eyes. 'I understand Jasper. I understand what went wrong and we can put it right. But,' she paused and swallowed, her lips trembling slightly before she continued, 'I've realised something. I was wrong, you were wrong. Of course there's room for a family in our lives. And I want one. I want to have a baby.'

....

FROM: Fliss Carmichael <agonyauntfliss@digitalrecorder.com>
To: Logan MacDonald <loganmac@connectmenow.co.uk>
Date: 01/05/2020

....

Dear Logan

I was very excited to receive your email because I understand how wonderful it is to think that you've met the person you were fated to be with. And the first thing I'm going to say to you is, whatever you do, don't give up on this person. It's surprising how easy it is for misunderstandings to occur in matters of love. Emotions run high, you are full of nervous expectations and then something happens that makes you think you've misjudged the whole situation and lost the moment. But it's rarely as bad as it first seems and it can always be recovered. Call it intuition or years of experience, call it what you want but I have a feeling that this woman is just as interested in you as you are in her and you absolutely must not give up now!

It's very possible that she has been trying to attract your attention and it just hasn't gone to plan. We often embark on slightly crazy schemes when we're unsure how to behave around someone. The woman you have fallen in love with sounds quite shy. Maybe she's nervous about speaking to you face to face and her friend is trying to help her handle the situation. I don't think that she's trying to avoid you, I feel sure that it's something different but it's up to you now to make sure that no more misunderstandings happen.

So, down to the practicalities. You must speak to her! And the sooner the better. There is no replacement for a good old fashioned conversation. The very next time you encounter her in the office, look her in the eye and use her name. This is important to build up an intimacy between the two of you. Always smile, always say hello if you bump into her, in a corridor or a lift for example. Make sure that she knows you're pleased to see her, that although the meeting is by chance you are happy that you've encountered her.

Ask her questions. Find out all you can about her, find out what she likes, doesn't like. Find something in common so you can discuss it and then have a meaningful conversation, nothing about office systems or football. Or war films. And above all else, be kind to her. If she's been trying to attract your attention for a while and thinks she's failed, she may need a great deal of encouragement before she can be tempted to engage with you again. Do something unexpected, offer to carry her files or get her a coffee or find some way to help her.

And finally, make sure that she knows you are interested in her and her alone and that there is no-one else in your life. I am convinced that it will work and you two will end up together. I must admit I'm normally much more conservative in my advice but I just have a feeling about you two. I have a feeling that you will get together, that you will fall in love and that you will be happy. But like everything else in life, it's not always easy and you must not let the uncertainty between you go on any longer.

Tell her you like her, have a crush on her. Tell her you love her if you truly believe that to be the case. But talk to her, have a conversation and make sure she listens. Even if she appears not to be interested, persevere and tell her everything!

And do it without delay. I'm sorry if this all sounds rushed but I can't emphasise enough the importance of taking action sooner rather than later.

Fliss Carmichael
Agony Aunt

This email has been sent by Fliss Carmichael, the online agony aunt of The Digital Recorder. All views expressed herein are her own and should not be taken as an instruction to proceed with any course of action without careful consideration of the potential consequences. The Digital Recorder claims no responsibility for any trauma, divorce proceedings or physical injury that may result from the advice contained herein. Thank you for contributing.

Chapter 30

The weather had improved, marginally. For once there was no rain just a biting cold wind and Ellie arrived outside her office with cheeks that were pink from the cold and hair that was more tangled than attractively tousled. Suddenly panicking that her phone still sat on the kitchen table, she stopped dead in the street to check her bag, ignoring the tuts from the commuters that had to swerve sharply around her to continue their single-minded walk. There it was, at the bottom next to her keys, tissues, the paperback she had intended to read on the bus but hadn't opened and the spare pair of tights she had thrown in over a week ago when her sole focus had been to encourage Logan's interest. Satisfied, Ellie glanced up and through the windows into the lobby and there he was, waiting for the lift.

Her heart beating a little faster, she decided that she really couldn't face him, not yet. She didn't want to see how happy he looked now he was with Harriet, it would take some preparation before she could smile in his direction without her heart cracking. So instead of continuing into the lobby, she stayed where she was, cursing the cold and watching as a small herd of workers arrived and joined Logan in his wait. There was a rush of movement as the lift arrived, bodies surging forward and thankful to have missed him, Ellie pushed open the main doors.

'Hello, Ellie. How are you doing?'

He was still standing by the lift.

'We've just missed it,' he continued with a shrug of his shoulders, 'but I'm sure there'll be another one in a minute.'

'Right, okay.'

'How's your dad doing? I've asked Laura a couple of times and she said he's home now.'

'Yes, he's got to rest but he seems much better.' Ellie averted her head so she couldn't see his face. He had sent a few more texts, asking after her father, asking if her mother was coping and asking after Ellie herself, but she hadn't answered. It was a dangerous path, she'd decided. The best thing to do now was to get used to the idea of Logan as Harriet's boyfriend and someone she once came close to getting to know.

The lift arrived, its doors opening with a soft swish and Ellie stepped inside followed by Logan who pressed 5 and 7 and then turned so he was facing her. It was best that they didn't speak, decided Ellie. They could smile and nod if they encountered each other in the lift or along the corridor, but they shouldn't actually speak anymore. That way no-one could be hurt.

'Actually, I meant to say thank you for being so kind the night I found out,' she mumbled. 'Getting a taxi and everything I mean.' She would stop speaking to him after this, but she did need to say thank you, it was only polite.

'I'm glad I could help. Really glad.' He was staring at her and she wondered if she had a smudge on her face or if her hair was so wild that he couldn't stop looking.

'Well, er, thank you anyway.'

Level 3 flashed and Ellie almost groaned out loud at how long it seemed to be taking.

'Are you, er, what have you got planned for tonight? Anything exciting?' he asked.

She thought for a moment, wrinkling her nose as though trying to bring to mind the contents of her diary for the rest of the day, even though she knew it was empty. Completely empty. 'I don't think I've got anything planned and if I can't remember I suppose it's nothing exciting, is it?' Ellie closed her eyes briefly. Good grief, could she be any more boring?

Level 4 flashed and relieved, she tucked her handbag more firmly on her shoulder. Politeness dictated that she should ask Logan about his plans for the week but quite frankly Ellie didn't want to know what he and Harriet were getting up to.

'I suppose not,' he agreed. 'Although sometimes it's nice to do more ordinary things, don't you think? I mean going out for a drink with friends, a friend, can be just as exciting as, well as exciting things can be.'

He was right. Ellie had been beside herself with excitement when Logan had invited her out for a drink. It was just a shame it hadn't ended well, or at least it hadn't ended well for Ellie. Logan and Harriet had found a much happier ending.

'Yes, I suppose it can be.'

The conversation ground to a halt and at last Level 5 flashed, the doors beginning their slow parting. Not waiting for the gap to open fully, Ellie squeezed herself and her bag through the tiniest of gaps, almost falling out into the corridor and resisting the urge to look over her shoulder to catch a last glimpse of Logan, she escaped in the direction of her desk.

Enveloping her in a warm hug, Laura pushed Ellie into her chair and placed a coffee on her desk.

'How's things?' she asked sympathetically. She had told Ellie to make the most of the company's offer of time off but Ellie had insisted on returning. Her dad was at home and out of danger and she could do with the distraction of work.

'Okay. He's looking so much better, he's got mum running up and down the stairs constantly getting him a paper, taking him a cup of tea or something to eat.' She grinned. 'I'm betting that the novelty will soon wear off and she'll tell him to get his own toast!'

'And was that Logan I saw in the lift with you?' asked Laura innocently.

'It was.'

'And…?'

'And nothing. He was in the lift, I was in the lift and we spoke. He's going out with Harriet now which means that I need to get over my crush.'

'Crush? I thought it was love?'

'So did I. But maybe I was wrong. Let's just stick with a crush for now.'

Laura looked around and then lowered her voice. 'Actually, I've been asking around, checking how Logan and Harriet are getting on and I'm not convinced it worked out.'

Ellie couldn't help the leap her heart gave even as she tried to look disinterested. 'Really?'

'I mentioned them, discreetly you know, just threw their names into a conversation.' Ellie doubted it had been anywhere close to discreet, it wasn't one of Laura's skills. 'And nobody seemed to know that they were supposed to be going out. I even asked Jeff outright and he didn't know anything about it.' Her tone was excited. 'Maybe there's still a chance for you after all. Perhaps we should ....'

'No. I think that I've tried all I'm going to try with Logan, we had a chance and it didn't work out.'

'But what if they're not getting on and he's wishing he'd asked you out instead?'

'Then he'll have to do something about it,' answered Ellie. 'And it would start by ending things with Harriet. I won't come between them.'

'But what if ...'

'No! No more plans and plots. What will be will be.' Ellie turned on her computer. 'I'm not going to think about him anymore.'

Looking disappointed, Laura started to turn back to her desk.

'Although something strange did happen in the lift,' Ellie added with a frown.

'What?'

'Well, not so much in the lift as just before. I was outside and I saw Logan waiting, I saw the lift arrive and everybody else who was waiting got in but he didn't.'

Laura's eyes peered over the screen as she processed the information. 'He deliberately didn't get in the lift?'

'Seemed that way.'

'And what did he say to you?'

'He told me that we'd just missed it.'

Laura's chair came flying around her desk almost crashing into Ellie in excitement. 'You mean, he waited? He hung around the lobby hoping that you would arrive and he could get in the lift with you?'

'Hardly. He didn't know that I would be at work today.'

'Yes he did, I told him yesterday. He was asking how things were and I told him you would be back in work this morning. He knew! He knew and he was lurking in the lobby hoping to bump into you!'

'Don't be ridiculous. Why would he do that?'

'I don't know but this is interesting Ellie, very interesting,' and with a little whoop, Laura retreated to her desk as Mr Goodfellow's dulcet tones drifted down the corridor.

'Good to see you back Ellie my dear.' He sent a disapproving look in Laura's direction. 'You achieve far more than many other members of this department, you've been missed. And you're back just in time, we have a meeting this afternoon and I've heard on the grapevine how much you enjoy them!' and with a nod, he went on his way.

Wondering if she could claim that she didn't feel emotionally ready to partake in any meetings just yet, Ellie pulled a face at his back just as she noticed Logan at the far end of the corridor.

'It's Logan!' whispered Laura. 'Funny, I haven't seen him on this floor at all while you've been away.'

'Coincidence,' muttered Ellie.

'Then why is he walking over here?'

'He isn't … oh hello, Logan.'

He was standing by her desk, keeping his back turned firmly in Laura's direction and pinning his eyes on Ellie.

'Hello Ellie,' he said formally. 'Er, I wanted to ask you something,' he said, shuffling nervously from one foot to the other.

She could see Laura's head bobbing behind his back as she tried to listen into the conversation.

'You did?'

'Yes, er, this morning in the lift. I wanted to ask you ….'

Subtlety gone, Laura pushed her chair sideways so she had a better view.

'I just wondered if … er if ….'

Laura's eyes were almost as wide as Ellie's and she leaned a little closer to listen to the conversation.

'Er, would you like a coffee? I go to Costa's every morning, for a proper caffeine hit. I wondered if you would like me to bring you one back? It might help, the first day back at work and all that,' he finished in a rush.

'Oh, a coffee?'

Laura was nodding her head frantically behind him. 'Say yes,' she was mouthing at Ellie, 'say yes!'

'I suppose, er yes. That would be, nice.'

'Good! That's really good.' He stood for a moment. 'I'm glad you want one,' he said, nodding his head vigorously. 'That's great. So, I'll see you soon, with a coffee,' and with a small smile, he turned to leave, only to find that Laura was now so close he crashed into her chair, almost falling into her lap as he tried to stay on his feet.

'Bloody hell!' he yelped. 'Where did you come from?'

'Just there,' Laura grinned, pointing to her desk. Pushing her chair back, she winked at him. 'Just wondered what was happening,' she added cheerfully, showing no shame at her eavesdropping.

Rubbing his knee which he'd bashed against the desk, Logan stepped around her. 'I'll see you later,' he said in

314

Ellie's direction and with a slight limp he set off down the corridor.

'So,' said Laura, drawing out the word as her eyes twinkled in Ellie's direction. 'He waited for you this morning and now he's getting you a coffee. Still think nothing is going on?'

'I think that he has a girlfriend and that coffee or no coffee, there is nothing between us any more, not that there ever was, but definitely not now. He's being friendly, that's all. We're friends and he's being friendly,' replied Ellie firmly and holding up a hand to stop any further conversation she bent her head down and tried to catch up on her work.

A little while later, Logan was back by her desk with a coffee in his hand.

'This should make you feel better,' he said softly to a rather frazzled looking Ellie.

'Thank you. It smells lovely and it was very … kind of you to bring me one.'

Feeling Laura's frustration rolling over the desk she refused to look in her direction and fiddled with the lid of her takeaway cup instead. Logan stood for a moment or so but unable to find anything else to say he gave Ellie another lopsided smile and left her to her coffee.

'Thank you! Kind! What's wrong with you? Why on earth didn't you look a little more grateful? You could have asked if he wanted to join you in the recreation room, or said something a bit more exciting.'

'Because it *was* kind of him and I've told you, there is nothing between us. It didn't work out and he's with Harriet now so no flirting or planning how to get him to notice me. It's over.'

Or it was until a few hours later when Logan appeared next to Ellie's desk once more.

'Hello Ellie,' he said in his slightly formal way which Ellie had decided was quite endearing. Or would be if she had any interest in him which clearly she no longer did. His cheeks were pink and his voice was low. 'I wondered if you wanted me to take anything to the meeting room for you?'

Ellie looked at her desk where she had her notebook and pencil ready to grab.

'Not really,' she admitted, feeling slightly inadequate at not having a pile of files in her arms as Logan usually had. 'I travel light to these meetings.'

'Of course. Well, nothing wrong with that. Shall we go then? We might as well walk there together.'

Ellie stared at him. Normally she and Laura would wait until the last possible moment before leaving the relative comfort of their desks.

'Yes, of course.' Standing up she grabbed her solitary pad and pencil. 'I'm ready,' she declared.

'Won't we be early?' Laura stood up, reluctant and empty-handed. She relied on Ellie to make any notes that may be necessary. 'It doesn't start until 2 o'clock.'

Flicking out his arm, Logan checked his watch. 'It's 10 minutes to 2.'

'Yes, so we'll be early.'

Looking nonplussed, he turned his gaze back to Ellie. 'Do you want to wait?'

She couldn't help grinning. 'She just doesn't want to risk sitting at the front,' she explained. 'Come on Laura, let's go.'

They arrived at an already full meeting room where today someone other than Logan was giving a presentation and the chairs were arranged in rows before a projector screen. Ellie felt a small swarm of butterflies begin to dance around her stomach as Logan not only held the door open for her but then placed a solicitous arm around her shoulders as he guided her towards three empty chairs. She could feel his fingers on her back, burning through her jumper and sending shockwaves coursing throughout her entire body. She took a quick peep upwards. He was looking down at her and she noticed that the hairs on his

316

arms beneath his rolled-up shirt sleeve, were standing on end. A complaining Laura broke the spell and they carried on moving along the row allowing her to sit down. The chairs were close, so close that Ellie could feel the heat from his body and hear his slightly strained breathing. Not risking another look, she set her pad on her knee and wondered instead at the complexity of life. Now it was all over and there was no possibility of a relationship between the two of them, now they suddenly dared to meet each other's eyes and revel in the undoubted chemistry between them.

The meeting was over in a flash, Ellie not having heard a single word that had been said but scintillatingly aware of Logan's arm so very close to hers and the rapid beat of her heart. Slightly breathless, she followed Logan and Laura out of the room. She would have to find out what the meeting had been about before Mr Goodfellow asked her for an update.

'Well, goodbye,' she said in Logan's direction. 'Thanks for the … er, the ….' She looked at him blankly.

'Thanks for the company!' said Laura breezily. 'Much appreciated.'

'I wondered if I'd be seeing you on Friday?' blurted Logan as Ellie turned to leave, his cheeks immediately filling with colour.

'Friday?'

'At The Flying Horse. I wondered if you were planning on going, this Friday.'

Laura was struggling to contain her grin but Ellie looked serious, shaking her head.

'Actually no. We weren't planning on going this week.'

Laura's head spun in Ellie's direction. 'We weren't?'

'No,' Ellie said firmly. She wasn't prepared to spend the night watching Logan and Harriet.

'Oh, I see. So, where are you thinking of going?'

'Yes Ellie,' said Laura crossly. 'Where are we going on Friday night?'

Ellie shrugged her shoulders. 'I don't know,' she confessed. 'Probably the Leaning Wagon.'

'No! Really? What a coincidence, that's where I was thinking of going this week!'

Surprised, Ellie opened her mouth to answer. But her only comment was a muffled yelp as Laura stood heavily on her foot.

'Ow ....'

'That *is* a coincidence!' interrupted Laura happily. 'Maybe we'll see you there, Friday, around 5:30?' and with a determined tug, she dragged Ellie away before she could forget the pain in her foot and argue.

Chapter 31

The following morning Ellie paused outside the main door and peered into the lobby wondering if Logan would be there. For once no-one was waiting by the lift and the area was empty but as she opened the door to step inside, she caught sight of an inky head emerging from the staircase and shooting across the lobby.

'Good morning Ellie.'

'Good morning Logan.'

They both smiled, then looked quickly away, Logan's eyes turning anxiously in the direction of the main doors and as the lift arrived, he almost pushed Ellie inside and immediately pressed the button to close the doors.

There was a strained silence and Ellie watched him look up at the red numbers above the doors. Level 1 was already showing.

'I was wondering what kind of films you liked to watch?' he asked hurriedly.

'Me?' Caught off guard, Ellie had been admiring the slight suggestion of a dimple in his chin, she tried to concentrate. 'Oh, all sorts. I like … er ….' She was trying to remember the name of a film that wasn't a romance. Or was honesty the best policy, now that nothing was going to happen between them. 'I don't like war films,' she blurted out as level 2 flashed above their heads. 'Films like Black Hawk Down,' although maybe she should watch it one day and see what all the fuss was about.

She half expected him to look disappointed but he just nodded. 'Understandable. You like … romance?'

Ellie tilted her chin, refusing to be embarrassed. 'Yes, I do.'

'Me too, sometimes.'

'You do?'

'Sometimes. Apparently Top Gun is a romance and I enjoyed that.'

Level three flashed.

'Hobbies?' asked Logan

'Sorry?'

'Do you have any hobbies?'

'Hobbies?'

'Yes. What do you like to do on a weekend?'

Level 4 flashed as Ellie searched for an answer. Did she have any hobbies? Could reading one romance book after another and watching *Pride and Prejudice* and *Pretty Woman* repetitively be classed as a hobby, or was it more of an addiction? And as for the weekends, well since she and Carl had broken up she had spent most of her weekends thinking about Logan and wondering what they would do if they were together. Was he the type to suggest a long walk by the river followed by a lazy Sunday Brunch? Or was he more energetic, would it be cycling helmets on and Dales here we come?

'Ellie?'

She had been thinking for some time and Logan was beginning to look anxious.

'Oh, I … I don't know...'

'Well what are you doing this weekend?' he asked desperately.

'I … er … I ….'

Level 5 flashed and the doors started their ritualistic slow parting to a gasp of relief from Ellie.

'Sorry … I have to go,' and she leapt out into the emerging space, hearing a faint 'Bye Ellie,' from the lift

'Logan in the lift again eh?' twinkled Laura. 'Surprising how that's happened two mornings in a row.'

'Coincidence,' offered Ellie.

'Actually, I've been talking to a few of the accounts lot and it turns out Harriet is in a right strop about something.

I'm wondering if Logan has stopped seeing her. You know, having decided that you're the girl for him.'

'Except I'm not the girl for him, am I? Because he didn't stick around to hear my side of the story the night he saw Carl and me together. Instead, he asked Harriet out.'

'But what if he made a mistake and he's regretting it? What if he really wants you?'

The very thought was enough to make Ellie's heart leap in anticipation, her breathing becoming ragged and her cheeks flushing with colour, but she held herself stiffly, refusing to join in with Laura's anticipation.

'Then it's too late,' she said trying to convince herself that she was perfectly fine with the idea. 'Far too late.'

Temporarily giving up, Laura slumped back in her seat, twiddling her pen as she thought.

'What were you talking about in the lift?'

'Oh, nothing much.'

'Well, what was it, the nothing much?'

'If you must know, he was asking me about which films I liked.'

'Films?'

'Yes. And if I had any hobbies.'

The pen went flying across the room as Laura pressed her hands against her table looking as though she were about to burst.

'Oh my God, films and hobbies?'

'Yes.'

'And yesterday he deliberately didn't catch a lift until you arrived?'

'Well, maybe there was someone he didn't want to speak to in the first lift. I can't say that he definitely …'

'And today? Was he waiting in the lobby today?'

'No. I think he'd already …'

Ellie stopped.

'He what? He'd already what? What had he already done? Oh my God, he'd already been up in the lift and gone back down hadn't he? Like you used to do?'

Ellie thought that she'd been very discreet when she'd been travelling up and down hoping beyond hope for a glimpse of Logan. She should have known that Laura had spotted it, she noticed everything that went on.

'I didn't say that. It did look as though he'd come from the direction of the stairs,' admitted Ellie reluctantly, 'but he could have been doing anything.'

'And yesterday, all that business about the Flying Horse! You know what's happening here don't you Ellie?'

Ellie didn't have a clue. She only knew that since deciding she had lost any chance to be with Logan, he seemed to be waiting around every corner.

'What?'

'He's interested! He's doing all the things you used to do Ellie, he's making sure that you notice him.'

'Rubbish. He's doing no such thing.'

'Oh yes, he is. I'm willing to bet he's around soon. Believe me, Ellie, he's hooked. Logan has fallen for you.'

Clucking her tongue and refusing to even discuss the possibility, mainly because it hurt so very much, Ellie insisted that Laura shut up and get on with some work.

'I'm right,' insisted Laura cheerfully turning on her computer. 'You'll see!'

The only sound for the next 30 minutes was the tapping of keyboards and the background noise of the office.

'He's here!' sang Laura. 'What did I tell you? I knew he'd appear.'

Glancing up, Ellie saw him walking slowly along the corridor. Instead of having his eyes firmly ahead he was looking sideways, very definitely and clearly looking sideways, bumping into Mr Goodfellow who was bustling along in the opposite direction. Apologising, but still looking sideways, Logan finally found Ellie's eyes and he sent her a huge smile that made Laura gasp.

'Did you see that? DID YOU SEE THAT?' she screeched as he disappeared up the staircase. 'He couldn't take his eyes off you. And what's he doing walking around near administration anyway? He wanted to see you.'

'Or he wanted to see Harriet,' denied Ellie. 'Stop getting excited, he is not interested.'

A little later a coffee appeared on her desk and Logan stood by her side.

'I didn't ask this morning,' he said softly. 'I hope you don't mind that I got you another one?'

Ellie shook her head. 'Er ... thank you,' she mumbled and with a smile and a nod he walked away, pausing at the staircase to send another long glance over his shoulder before he disappeared.

Ignoring a grinning Laura, Ellie sipped at her coffee and told herself not to expect anything from this behaviour. He had shown himself to be kind, considerate and caring, exactly the sort of person she had imagined he would be. He was still concerned about her after the shock with her father and he was trying to help. What a lucky girl Harriet was, she thought. Very lucky.

Sometime later Ellie had a pile of contracts to take up to the 7th floor. Holding them in her hand, she peeped over the screen.

'Laura ....'

'No.'

'I haven't asked you anything yet.'

'You want me to take those up to the 7th floor and the answer is no.'

'But ...'

'No. Go up yourself, you may bump into Logan.'

'But I don't want to....'

'No.'

With no alternative Ellie crept up the stairs and tiptoed down the corridor, hoping that Logan would be hard at work and not notice her only a few feet away from his desk.

'Hello Ellie,' came the serious voice she was beginning to love.

He was walking towards her, Harriet skipping along on the other side of him.

'Er, hello.'

'Are you okay?'

'Fine. Thank you.'

'Anything I can help you with?' He had stopped directly in front of her, blocking her intended move which was to cling to the wall and sidestep the pair of them.

'No, no thank you.'

Harriet was glaring at her, her eyes narrowed and her lips pinched together. 'Hello Ellie,' she said snippily. 'Fancy seeing you here, are you following us?'

'Just dropping these off.' Ellie waved the files, wishing Logan wouldn't staring at her quite so intently. 'Well, I'd better get going.' She stepped around the tall figure. Actually, she loved the way his eyes glued themselves to her, she just regretted it hadn't happened much earlier, pre-Harriet.

'See you later then, Ellie,' said Logan and he moved out of her way, turning to watch as she continued down the corridor.

Dropping the files on the appropriate desk, she couldn't help quickly checking over her shoulder. Logan was standing exactly where she had left him, Harriet bobbing up and down and trying to reclaim his attention as his gaze skimmed over her head and travelled down the corridor, directed only at Ellie. He smiled.

Ducking into the ladies, Ellie looked at her reflection and pressed a trembling hand to her mouth. Despite her refusal to listen to Laura, she had to admit that Logan was behaving strangely. It was slightly familiar in some way, as though Ellie understood what he was trying to do and …

Gasping, she flew down the stairs and skidded into her chair.

'Laura,' she whispered urgently. 'Laura!'

A yawning Laura popped her head around the screen. 'What?'

'Do you remember all the things that Fliss told me to do when I was trying to get Logan to notice me?'

'Of course. Didn't I have to plan half of them for you?'

'Always say hello, use his name, smile.'

'Ask him about his hobbies and what he does away from work,' said Laura.

'Try and engage with him, try and talk to him ….'

'Oh my God, Ellie, he's been talking to an agony aunt! I think he's asked someone for advice and he's doing all the things that you were doing.'

'I think so too,' said Ellie slowly.

'So you can't deny it now. He's definitely interested in you.'

For a brief moment, pure joy filled Ellie's face. Then her eyes darkened and her lip trembled. 'That's awful,' she said quietly. 'Absolutely awful.'

'Awful? It's wonderful!'

'No, it's awful. He's going out with Harriet but he's trying to get me to notice him. I didn't think he would be like that,' she continued almost to herself. 'I thought he would be more honourable, not the sort to hurt people without thinking.'

'But maybe he and Harriet are not getting on. Maybe …'

'Maybe he should be strong enough to finish one relationship before trying to start another one,' snapped Ellie. 'I did…'

She stopped, wincing at Laura's face.

'In that case, don't you owe it to yourself and Carl to see if this thing with Logan will work out?'

Ellie shook her head. 'No. The Logan I fell in love with, the Logan I thought I knew, wouldn't behave like this. He may have decided he's interested in me but as far as I'm, concerned it's over,' and with a sniff and the threat of tears gathering in her eyes, Ellie ended the conversation and spent the rest of the afternoon feeling alternatively angry and desperately unhappy.

It was almost inevitable that when Ellie and Laura finished work for the day and stood waiting for the lift, the doors should swish open to reveal Logan smiling back at them.

'Hello, Ellie.'

'Hello, Logan.'

Catching Laura's hesitation out of the corner of her eye, Ellie pulled her friend into the lift before she could announce that she had forgotten something or needed to take the stairs as part of her daily exercise. Laura pushed herself into the far corner of the lift, staying silent but watching the two of them with wide eyes.

The lift set off towards the lobby. It seemed to travel down far more quickly than it travelled up, thought Ellie, watching the number fly by.

'Are you going for a drink?' asked Logan, his eyes not leaving Ellie who had developed an all-consuming interest in the control panel in front of her.

'No, not tonight.'

'Nothing planned?' He turned his head slightly to include Laura. 'Do you fancy a quick one in The Flying Horse?'

Laura stepped forward. 'That would be…'

'No! Of course not,' snapped Ellie, abandoning the control panel long enough to give Logan a disapproving stare.

Logan stammered an apology. 'Sorry, I just thought … oh stupid me, I suppose you want to get back and check on your dad,' and gave Ellie a look of such gentle compassion that she almost forgot how cross she was with him.

'Well, I do,' she admitted, before remembering how disappointed she was with his behaviour and stiffening her resolve. 'But it is actually quite wrong for you to ask me for a drink!'

'Wrong? I'm sorry, I thought your dad was doing much better. Laura said,' he sent a pleading glance in her direction, 'Laura said that he was at home and on the mend. I thought one drink would be okay.'

Ellie frowned at him. That wasn't what she had meant. Thankfully the lift came to a halt and the minute a gap opened Ellie was through, breathing in so she could escape quicker.

'My dad *is* fine but it's still wrong. For other reasons, as well you know,' she added and then grabbing Laura's arm, she pulled her out of the lift and walked briskly away from Logan's confused expression.

'Logan just invited you for a drink,' panted Laura trying to keep up with the pace Ellie had set.

'I know.'

'And you refused.'

'I know.'

'We've spent weeks trying to get him to notice you and ask you out. He's just invited you for a drink and you've refused.'

'I know.'

'Stop saying you know and tell me why? Why, when you finally get what you want, do you say no? WILL YOU SLOW DOWN!'

Putting a hand over her stitch and hanging onto Ellie as she doubled over gasping for breath, Laura drew some air into her lungs.

'Are you completely mad?' she asked, still breathless. 'Why didn't you say yes?'

'Because I refuse to break up Logan and Harriet. He chose her, not me. And unless he wants to end his relationship with her and then ask me out, there's nothing more to say about it. I'm not going for a drink with Logan, it's over.'

Chapter 32

Keen to avoid any confinement in the lift with Logan, the next morning Ellie arrived a few minutes early and peered in the doorway before dashing across the lobby in the direction of the stairs. Walking up 5 flights wasn't something that she would normally consider, but today was an exception and contrary to every other day over the last few weeks, today she wanted to avoid Logan. She had made it up one flight and was already panting and gasping for breath when the tap-tap of heels made her look up. There was Harriet, flying down at a dangerous speed for someone wearing such high heels. Seeing Ellie, she paused.

'I think I dropped a glove,' she muttered, and not waiting for a reply she brushed past Ellie, the sound of her heels becoming fainter as she disappeared into the lobby.

Ellie concentrated only on her breathing for the next few flights and was only a few steps away from the door which led to floor 5 when she heard more footsteps coming down at speed.

Hurling himself round the half landing and taking the steps two at a time, Logan came to a crashing halt when he saw Ellie, puce faced and hardly able to breathe looking up at him. He must be on the hunt for Harriet's glove as well, she decided. Lucky Harriet.

'She's already gone down to have a look,' she wheezed, clutching her side.

'Sorry, who?'

'Harriet.' She needed to keep any explanation to a minimum until she'd inhaled a little more oxygen. 'Gone downstairs. Glove,' she gasped.

'Glove?'

Oh for goodness sake, thought Ellie crossly. Did everything need repeating when she was so out of breath? She took in a gulp of air.

'Harriet's already downstairs looking for her glove.' She made it up the last few stairs and with burning thighs, she hung onto the door. Only a few more steps and she could sit at her desk. Maybe she and Laura should go to aerobics one night during the week instead of sitting in the nearest wine bar. She hadn't appreciated just how unfit she was. Trying to re-inflate her lungs she wondered just how red her face was. Not that it mattered, she told herself, because Logan was with Harriet now.

'Bye,' she managed with her last breath and pushing the door open she staggered across the floor to sink into her chair.

'What on earth happened?' asked Laura, wide-eyed and passing Ellie some water. 'Are you okay?'

Nodding, it was several minutes before Ellie could speak properly.

'I took the steps,' she eventually told a patient Laura. 'To avoid being on the lift with Logan.'

'I see. And what's wrong with being in the lift with him? I've told you, I think he's regretting …'

Ellie waved her hand to stop Laura. 'And I've told you it's not going to happen. Anyway, I didn't avoid him. He was coming down the steps.'

'Coming down for another chance to go back up in a lift with you?' asked Laura her eyes twinkling.

'No, looking for Harriet's glove.'

Laura's face fell. 'Well I still think they're not getting on,' she muttered in disappointment, 'and you should take your chance!'

Around the time Logan had been appearing at her desk with a coffee, Ellie made herself scarce. Positioning herself near the IT department where she could see anyone who arrived at her desk, she hovered behind one of their filing cabinets, ignoring several interested gazes and watching for Logan's arrival. Sure enough, he appeared with two coffees in hand, placing one on her desk and hovering around for several minutes before slowly walking away, his head definitely drooping.

'What did he say?' she asked Laura, slipping back into her chair.

'If you were interested in what Logan had to say, you should have stayed here to listen to him.'

'Don't be difficult Laura, what did he say?'

Was that a shifty look she detected in her friend's eye? But Laura shrugged her shoulders and remained glued to her monitor.

'I'm very busy,' she said loftily,' I haven't got time to talk right now.'

Thwarted, Ellie got down to her own work, one eye on the corridor. But there was no sight of Logan, and perversely Ellie could feel herself getting cross at his absence.

'Did you say something to him?' she demanded of Laura, glaring across the screen.

'Would you have liked me to say something?'

'Of course not, there is nothing to say.'

'I thought not.'

Laura continued to tap away on her keyboard until Ellie, patience exhausted, wheeled her chair to Laura's desk.

'Please stop playing games and tell me what happened!'

For a moment Laura ignored her, typing away with a straight back and a serene face. But unable to resist Ellie's pleading face for long, she swivelled in her chair and faced her friend.

'Okay. He asked me where you were and I said I didn't know. Then he asked if I thought you would be long and I said I didn't know. Then he asked if you were alright and I said I didn't know — sorry, I said yes you were. Then he asked ….'

'For goodness sake! I don't need a word by word account! What happened?'

Raising her eyebrows and giving her friend an admonishing look, Laura continued. 'I'm telling you what happened. He left the coffee on your desk, asked where you were, hung around for a bit and left.'

'That's it?'

'That's it.'

'So why hasn't he been back?'

'Ha! So you *are* still interested, despite everything you've said,' crowed Laura.

'I'm not. Not at all. I just wondered why he'd stopped lurking that's all.'

Moving her chair crossly back towards her desk Ellie spent the rest of the day with her eyes pinned on her monitor when she wasn't looking down the corridor for Logan, until looking at her watch she saw it was nearly time to go home.

'I don't think we should go to The Leaning Wagon tonight,' she announced airily. 'Don't fancy it.'

She expected Laura to argue, launch into an explanation of why Ellie must go because Logan might turn up. But there was no response and after a moment or two, she spoke again.

'Laura, did you hear me? I don't want to go to The Leaning Wagon tonight.'

'Okay.'

Peering over the screen, she watched Laura begin to tidy her desk and close down her computer.

'I think Logan may be there and I don't want to see him.'

'Okay, fine by me.'

Ellie frowned. 'Do you think Logan will be there?'

'He did say he would but I don't know.' Laura's voice was a little faint as she bent under her desk to rescue her handbag. 'Maybe he's made other plans now.'

'What other plans? Where is he going?'

'I don't know! And why are you bothered anyway? I thought you didn't want to see him?'

She didn't want to see him. She particularly didn't want to see him wrap his arm around Harriet's shoulder, smile into her eyes or bend his head to kiss her. She couldn't bear that, particularly the kiss, not when she could still feel the touch of his lips on her cheek.

'I don't.'

'Then it doesn't matter where he's going, does it? The question is, where shall we go?'

Ellie didn't answer. Suddenly, she felt very sad. She tried to imagine the next weeks and months without Logan. No strolling along the corridor to catch a glimpse of the top of his head, no hovering in the lobby hoping he would arrive and they could spend a few precious minutes in the lift together. Not having Logan in her life at all, even from afar, made her heart ache with sadness.

'Ellie? Where do you want to go?'

'I don't mind,' she sighed.

'We could go to The Flying Horse, that would be funny. If we go there and Logan goes to The Leaning Wagon.'

'No. I don't think so.'

'Ok, how about that sweet little wine bar we found the other week, will that do you?'

Thinking that she would rather go home and be miserable, Ellie nodded. A quick drink with Laura, a dissection of the last couple of days and then she would go spend the weekend with her parents and give some thought to a life that was now empty of any romance.

Sitting in a corner of the wine bar, a glass of wine in front of her, Ellie leant back in her seat.

'What a week,' she said with feeling. 'I'm glad it's over.'

'Oh not quite. Look who's just walked in.'

Swivelling her head in the direction of the dimly lit doorway, Ellie saw Logan scanning the room before noticing the two women in the corner.

'What on earth is he doing here?'

'Perhaps he didn't fancy The Leaning Wagon either.'

Looking the picture of innocence, Laura sipped her wine daintily as she waved in Logan's direction.

'Did you tell him I'd changed my mind?'

'I did not.'

'Then I don't understand, how did he know where we were?'

Laura tilted her head to one side considering. 'I can't think.'

'You told him, didn't you?'

'How could I? You only decided 10 minutes ago.'

'Laura!'

'Oh, okay.' Logan had visited the bar and was now holding a pint of beer and heading in their direction. 'I told him that you would probably change your mind about The Leaning Wagon because you wouldn't want to bump into him and then I would suggest this place as an alternative.'

'But how did you know I wouldn't want to go to The Leaning Wagon?' asked a baffled Ellie.

'Oh please, I know you far better than you realise Ells. I knew that you would go into a funk and insist on going somewhere else, that's what you're like. I knew if I suggested this place you'd be happy to come along. I know you so well and that's why I don't understand why you've spent all this time and effort with your agony aunt. I could have solved all this for you in the first week if you'd let me!'

Ellie couldn't help but smile at her outraged friend. Maybe Laura was right, but that would have meant Ellie would never have written to 'Dear Fliss' and maybe Fliss herself would never have realised that her marriage was in trouble. And was that a good thing or a bad thing mused Ellie. Maybe Fliss wished that Ellie had never written to her, never made her think about the direction her life was taking, the decisions that needed to be made.

'Hello Ellie,' said a serious voice. 'Do you mind if I join you?'

At Ellie's silence, Laura jumped in, waving her hand towards the chair opposite Ellie. 'Not at all.'

Glaring at both of them, Ellie picked up her glass and took a drink.

'Where's Harriet?' she asked tersely.

'Harriet?' Logan's eyebrows winged upwards. 'I don't know, probably at The Flying Horse.'

'Probably?' snapped Ellie angrily. 'Don't you know?'

'Er, no I don't.' He looked at Laura with a quizzical look and then back at Ellie. 'Should I?'

'Yes! How very unfair of you to go somewhere else without telling her.'

Logan's mouth was hanging open a little and he shook his head slowly. 'Why would you …'

'You're behaving very badly you know.'

'I am? I'm not sure what I've…'

'How could you leave the poor girl waiting for you and not tell her you've no intention of turning up?'

'Why would she be waiting for me? Sorry, Ellie, I'm not sure I know…'

'Of course she'll be waiting for you!' Thinking back to the night she had arranged to meet Logan, Ellie could still remember the butterflies that swirled and swarmed in her stomach, the sheer delight of waiting for him to appear. The anticipation of sitting opposite him was still so vivid that she could almost touch the image in her head. The thought of sitting there, waiting and waiting and for him never to show up made her feel incredibly sad for Harriet.

Leaning forward with a small frown on her forehead, Laura held up a finger. 'Just a minute ….'

'I think you should go, Logan,' interrupted Ellie. 'Go to The Flying Horse, go to Harriet.'

'But I don't want to go to Harriet,' he said in confusion. 'I want to be here with you.'

At Ellie's outraged gasp, Laura tried again. 'I think that maybe ….'

'Well, I don't want you here!'

Logan's face closed, his lips straight and stern. 'Then I apologise Ellie, I thought …'

'Will you both shut up!' Turning to look at an exasperated Laura, they waited. 'I think that there may have been some miscommunication here,' she said in a gentler tone of voice. 'Logan, I'm going to ask you a question.'

Logan picked up his pint warily, holding it between himself and Laura as though readying himself.

'Okay.'

'Are you going out with Harriet?'

'Harriet?'

'Yes, Harriet. The blonde from accounts who follows you everywhere and is probably right now at The Flying Horse watching the doorway and hoping you'll walk in.'

'Of course not.'

Ellie gasped and Logan's eyes swung back to her. 'You're not going out with Harriet?'

'No. I am not going out with Harriet. Why would you …'

But Ellie's eyes had moved accusingly to Laura. 'You told me they were going out! You said he'd asked Harriet out the night we were supposed to meet and Carl turned up.'

Looking equally apologetic and confused, Laura turned back to Logan. 'Are you sure?' she demanded. 'You didn't ask her out at all?'

'Of course not, why would I?'

'Because she wanted you to? Because she was there and you were there and Ellie and Carl were there and you were cross with Ellie and you ….'

'No! I did not ask Harriet out. I've never asked Harriet out and yes,' he turned to look at a gaping Ellie, 'I was sort of cross but only because it was another wasted opportunity and I could see how upset Ellie was and I

335

wondered if she was regretting leaving her boyfriend and I didn't want to jump in there too soon and spoil things.'

'Who told you they were going out?' demanded Ellie, 'why did you tell me they were?'

'Er …' Laura screwed up her face as she tried to remember the conversation. 'It was Amy in accounts, she said that Harriet would be happy because she'd finally gotten what she wanted, that Harriet and Logan had gone home together and she might be in a better mood now that he'd given in and asked her out.'

'We shared a taxi, I must admit I'd had a lot to drink. Harriet said she would make sure I got home and we shared a taxi but that was it. I wouldn't ask Harriet out.'

'Laura! How could you?'

'Sorry Ells, misunderstanding.'

'Misunderstanding? I thought Logan had asked someone else out, I was really upset.'

'I wouldn't ask anybody else out. I wouldn't do that,' chipped in Logan.

'Amy was sure the two of them were going out,' defended Laura. 'It wasn't really my fault.'

'I wouldn't ask anybody else out,' repeated Logan a little louder as Ellie and Laura glared at each other. 'Doesn't anybody want to ask me why?'

'Why?' snapped Laura, guilt making her squirm in her seat.

'Because there's only one person I want to ask to go out with me.'

'Oh.' Ellie's face fell, the surge of relief that had started in her chest halting abruptly.

'Just a minute,' said Laura with a grin. 'Let him finish. Who is it you would like to ask out Logan?'

His cheeks had gone quite pink and he was fiddling with his now empty glass as he stared at Ellie's crestfallen face.

'I thought you knew,' he whispered. 'I thought you felt the same but then I got really confused first with the Jeff thing and then with your ex popping up all over.'

Ellie stared back blankly.

'I wanted to ask you, Ellie. Just you. Only you.'

'Yesss!' Laura was on her feet, pumping the air with her fist. 'YES! I knew it! I called it, never mind agony aunts, just rely on me, I said all along that he would ask you out. You just had to listen to me!'

Two faces stared up at her. 'Right, just going to the bar to get some more drinks. Oh, look at the queue, I may be a while and there's somebody there I want to talk to.' Ellie looked over at the deserted bar, no-one in sight except for the barman busy polishing glasses. 'Okay, I'll leave you two to it. Please don't mess it up again just because I'm not here to sort it out, okay I'm going!' she added hastily at Ellie's look.

With Laura gone the silence returned until Ellie gathered her courage. 'You wanted to ask me out?'

'For ages. Trouble is I couldn't tell at first if you were interested in me or if you were trying to put me off. Your friend,' he stopped to scratch his chin, 'Laura is a bit mad. Lovely,' he added hastily, 'but a bit mad and I was never quite sure …'

He stopped and Ellie thought back to the excruciating encounter in the lift when he'd first touched her hand. It was easy to imagine why it had not been easy for him to work out if she was encouraging his advances or not.

'I was interested,' she said shyly. 'For a while actually.'

'Good. So if I ask you out, now, before anything else goes wrong and before Laura comes back, will you say yes?'

Ellie nodded.

'Then Ellie Henshaw, will you go out with me?'

Ellie nodded again, this time with a grin that stretched her face from ear to ear. 'Yes, I will,' she said happily. 'I will,' and then she didn't get the chance to say anything else because Logan's lips came down to meet hers and Harriet, Laura, Fliss and everybody else was forgotten as

337

Ellie felt a wave of happiness like nothing she'd ever felt before.

Several minutes later, Logan pulled away to look into her eyes, smiling softly. 'I'm glad,' he whispered, 'because I happen to think that I'm already in love with you. My friends told me it was just a crush but I don't think so, I think you're the one for me, even if you do have a mad friend.'

Sliding her arms around his neck, catching a glimpse of Laura over his shoulder waving her arms and doing a small jig by the bar, Ellie reached up so their lips could meet again. 'That's okay,' she whispered back. 'Because I definitely think you're the one for me too, and I happen to know someone who thinks that true love can be found in the workplace.'

'Me too.' And then their lips met and they stopped talking for a considerable length of time.

FROM: Ellie Henshaw   <Elliebellshenshaw@livewell.co.uk>
To: Fliss Carmichael   <agonyauntfliss@digitalrecorder.com>
Date: 06/05/2020

Hi Fliss

I had to write to you one last time to thank you for all the help that you've given me and to let you know that Logan and I have been dating for the last few weeks and I've never been so happy.

You told me in your very first email that I should have the courage of my convictions and that if I felt it was love, I should ignore anybody who said differently. And thankfully, someone said the same thing to Logan. It gave him the courage to find out for himself how I felt. Apparently, he'd managed to get the impression that I was trying to avoid him. And then with Jeff asking me on a date and Carl turning up at a very inopportune time, well, I can hardly blame him for getting the wrong idea about things.

But he decided not to give up and fortunately he asked someone who gave him exactly the sort of advice you gave me. So, despite everything, he carried on trying to get to know me and now we're together. I can't tell you how happy I am, how happy we both are. We're trying to take things slowly but we're madly in love and both of us feel that this is the real thing. And even more good news is that Carl is now dating someone called Sophie. I haven't met her yet although my mum has and she said they get on like a house of fire so maybe Carl was better off with someone else after all.

I hope everything turned out okay for you too. I can't help feeling responsible, if I hadn't written to you then you might never have started to question your own marriage and it doesn't seem fair that my happiness should come at the expense of your own. You were so very much in love with your husband, just like Logan and I are now. I hope you find a way back to those feelings, to the relationship you once shared. You once told me that nothing stays the same forever, including people and the way they love each other. You were right, I loved Carl once but as time passed by, I was left wanting a different

339

kind of relationship. My family told me I was foolish, selfish to give up what I had. But I was right, a tiny part of me understood that there was more, far more to be had. I can't ever imagine not wanting to be with Logan. Hopefully, we'll grow older together, like you and your husband. And hopefully, we'll stay together for as long as you have. But if it ever starts to go wrong, I'll think of you and make sure I try everything I can to put it right. Letting go of such love is not something to do lightly and I hope that you rescue your marriage.

Thank you again, for everything,
Deliriously happy Ellie from Leeds

Chapter 33

The room was packed and the champagne was flowing. Listening to the chatter swell and fade, the occasional laugh bursting through, Fliss stood slightly to one side, admiring the glittering cocktail gowns sparkling under the crystal chandeliers.

'I'm not even sure whose party this is,' sighed Sylvia. 'They all blend into one after a while don't you think?'

Fliss agreed. The room was awash with people and Fliss had a sudden longing for her settee, a glass of wine and the company of her husband.

'I heard you put Jasper on restricted duties,' said Sylvia with a smile. 'How's that working out?'

'Restricted…?

'Told him to work less and spend more time at home. We've all tried it at some point. When our children were younger, I told Marcus I would leave him if he didn't cut down on the hours he spent in the office. I said I would replace him with a nanny, she would be more useful to me.'

'Did it work?' asked Fliss intrigued.

'Not at all. He tried, for at least a week. He came home at a more reasonable time and he stopped working over the entire weekend, but he was so stressed and in such a bad mood I decided it simply wasn't worth it. And he wasn't much help. One day he took the children out for a walk and came back without them! Said he had been thinking about something and forgot that they were with him. I gave up, told him to go back to work and I would get a nanny anyway.'

Fliss chuckled. Marcus was a well know workaholic, she was surprised he'd lasted a week.

'And Jasper?'

341

'He's really trying,' admitted Fliss. 'I don't think it was entirely his fault, we'd both let work and life consume us and we needed to make some changes.' She didn't tell Sylvia that her biggest change was that she would like to dispense with work altogether and have a child. That was something that was strictly between herself and Jasper at the moment.

'Goodness me! I wish you success. Although I must say, in my opinion, it rarely lasts. And with you not having a family, the temptation is always to devote even more time to work.'

Fliss took a sip of champagne. Sylvia was perilously close to the truth. Fliss and Jasper had used work as a substitute for their lost family. But that was something else that wasn't for general gossip. She saw Jasper's head in the crowd and watched him weave his way to her side.

'Hello,' he said softly, kissing her gently on the lips.

'Hello yourself.'

'Have you seen my husband anywhere in this melee, Jasper dear?'

'Last seen standing next to the bar Sylvia.'

'Talking business?'

Jasper grinned. 'Of course not. I think he was telling everyone how very lucky he was to have such a wonderful wife!'

Sylvia clucked. 'What a gentleman you are, but let's not pretend. By now Marcus has probably forgotten he brought me with him. Which is something that can't be said about you Jasper, you keep hold of that delicious wife of yours,' and sending a wink in Fliss' direction, Sylvia put her glass down on a small side table and disappeared in search of her absent husband.

'Enjoying yourself?'

'Not really. You?'

'Not really.'

They grinned at each other and Jasper pressed another kiss on Fliss' lips. 'I don't know why, but suddenly it all seems a little irrelevant,' he sighed. 'I would rather be at home with you.'

Resting against his strong frame, Fliss wondered at the change that had come over both of them during the last week. Her husband had become the Jasper of old. Attentive and loving, he was a hard worker and always would be, but at the end of the day he seemed pleased to leave the office and the demands of his job behind him and his obsession with his phone had reduced considerably. The previous morning, he had turned off the alarm before rolling over in bed and declaring that work could wait, taking Fliss in his arms and kissing her with such passion that she felt transported back 20 years to the very first time he had taken her to bed. They were back to their old selves.

But the evening she had spent sitting on the bathroom floor had opened her eyes to a whole new dilemma. And that was still unresolved. Jasper had sat on the floor in shock after she'd made her announcement. His face had turned even paler, his eyes wide and frightened and they hadn't spoken of it since. It lay between them, keeping them both awake at night. When Fliss lay, staring at the moon through the curtains, she knew instinctively that by her side Jasper also remained wide awake, his mind no doubt racing just as hers was.

'Shall we leave?' whispered Jasper in her ear. 'We could slip away and no one would know.'

Giggling Fliss poked him in the ribs. 'They haven't even given the speech yet. Don't you want to stay for that?'

'God no, it will be the same old drivel it always is. If we go home, I'll give you a much more interesting speech.'

His hand was stroking her back, his face was nestled in her hair and Fliss felt a moment of regret. They had wasted the last two years and now her handsome husband had returned at precisely the moment Fliss had come to understand that she was ready to move on. Her overwhelming fear was that Jasper wouldn't want to move

343

with her and right now she had no idea what she would do if he took her hand and told her that she may have reconsidered but as far as he was concerned, his decision stood, there was no place in his life for a family.

'How about it?' said Jasper, taking her chin and turning her head so he could kiss her properly. 'Shall we depart?'

'Goodness me, look at you two love birds! You really are a lesson for the rest of us.'

It was Freddie and Fliss felt a blush drift up her cheeks. She still couldn't look him in the eye without embarrassment rolling over her.

'I tell everybody about you,' said Freddie with a smile. Fliss stiffened, good gracious, she sincerely hoped not. 'How very much in love you are.'

Jasper let his arm drop back to Fliss' waist. 'I'm a lucky man Freddie. Very lucky. And we've decided that we're going to call it a night,' he added, 'so if you'll excuse me, I'm going to rescue Fliss' coat and take her home.'

Freddie watched him walk towards the cloakroom before turning back to Fliss. He cleared his throat awkwardly and Fliss tensed. 'I do mean what I said, you are a lesson to us all how love can endure.'

'Thank you.'

'I had noticed that Jasper was throwing himself into his work far more than was necessary. And I had also noticed how hard you've were working to make him, er, see sense.'

Fliss cheeks couldn't go any pinker as she struggled to meet his twinkling eyes.

'I'm glad things have worked out for you both,' he said gently, 'very glad.'

'We needed to clear the air a little,' Fliss murmured. 'Which we seem to have managed.'

'Jasper has turned down my offer of a week in Bermuda,' Freddie told a surprised Fliss. 'He explained that you both wanted some time to yourself.' More blushing from Fliss. 'I think it's probably a good thing actually. It might give

344

Maggie ideas if she were to spend any time with a couple as loved up as you two are!'

'Ready?'

It was Jasper, holding Fliss' coat which she grabbed gratefully. 'Yes, thank you.'

'I hope I haven't embarrassed you?'

Jasper looked from Freddie to Fliss quizzically.

'Oh no. Actually, yes, but in a nice way,' she confessed making Freddie chortle.

'I meant what I said, you're incredibly lucky to have each other, now go home and enjoy yourselves,' and slapping Jasper on the back, he bent over Fliss' hand in a charmingly old-fashioned gesture.

'What was that about?'

'You didn't tell me you'd said no to Bermuda.'

'Ah, no. I was thinking about it and I agree with you, it would be nice to have some time to ourselves, just the two of us.'

Just the two of them. Would it always be just the two of them wondered Fliss? Could she be happy if it were just Fliss and Jasper, forever?

'I've seen a fantastic little place in Cornwall actually.' Jasper manoeuvred the car out of the packed car park. 'I know it's not quite Bermuda but it will be much quicker to get there and it looks so peaceful and secluded. It's right on the beach, no-one else for miles.'

He described the cottage as Fliss stared out onto black streets twisting and turning until they became more familiar and their house loomed in front of them.

'I thought it would suit us much better, what do you think?'

Looking pleased with himself, Jasper was opening the front door and leading her inside. In truth, she hadn't really been listening as he'd listed the features of the pretty little stone cottage he'd found. Her mind had wandered with the streets and she had allowed her thoughts to drift.

'Sounds perfect.'

'I was hoping you'd agree because I've already booked it.'

He had obviously been hoping for more of a reaction. 'You are okay about it?'

'Sorry, miles away. Of course, it sounds lovely.'

'Good. I can't wait to spend a week away from everyone else, just the two of us. Time to do whatever we want,' he murmured as he slipped her coat down her arms.

Fliss' heart gave an involuntary spasm. She'd spent weeks telling Jasper that they needed to spend more time together, just the two of them. How wrong she'd been. It didn't have the same ring to it any more, just the two of them now seemed such a lonely phrase.

'The weather will probably be awful but I don't mind. There's a log fire which we can snuggle in front of.' The coat had gone and he turned his attention to the zip running down the back of her dress. 'Can you imagine, a storm blowing, the logs crackling.'

She loved him so much, would that be enough, she wondered? Would the two of them still work in the years ahead?

The zip was undone and he was sliding the straps of her dress over her shoulders. Shivering from delight rather than the cold, Fliss gave herself up to his touch. 'Nothing to do but make love,' he continued, her dress now in a puddle on the floor as his arms wrapped around her, pulling her as close to him as was humanly possible, 'me, you and a storm.'

He was all she had needed for the last 20 years, could the next 20 work just as well? And then she had to stop thinking about the future and the ache in her heart as they abandoned any idea of making it up the stairs and made love on Fliss' coat in their hallway, her cries of delight drifting through the house.

Chapter 34

The weather was finally improving and a weak spring sun filled the garden. Fliss was gathering the leaves that Jasper had started to rake a few weeks earlier, feeling pleasantly tired as the lawn began to emerge, crisp and green from its winter rest.

Sitting on the bench, she lifted her face, closing her eyes and relishing the sun's warmth. Last night Jasper had made love to her in the hallway before carrying her upstairs and continuing in the bedroom. Unbidden, her hand crept to her stomach, resting on her flat, taut muscles. What if they had created a baby, she wondered dreamily. Would she know if there was a new life already beating inside her?

The question of a family still hadn't been addressed and Fliss knew that it was only a matter of time. She had caught Jasper staring into space several times during the morning, his eyes glazed as he sat deep in thought and she had wanted to ask what occupied his mind but she was afraid of the answer. Her hand still on her stomach, Fliss knew the thought of a child would fill her with joy. Enough joy to outweigh the pain and despair that had filled her after the loss of her baby. But it had to be something they both wanted.

The sun dimmed as a cloud scurried by and Fliss felt a shiver run through her body. What would she do, she wondered, if Jasper said no? She had once told Ellie that the thought of life without Jasper terrified her. It still did, and it now seemed a real possibility.

'You've done a better job than I did!'

It was Jasper, holding out a glass of wine as he sat on the bench beside her. For a few minutes, they enjoyed a comfortable silence, watching the clouds in the sky and the birds fluttering around the garden.

'We need to talk, don't we,' Jasper said.

Fliss felt her stomach roll with anxiety and the breath leave her body. It was as though she were standing on the edge of a precipice, gazing down and wondering if she were about to fall or if a hand would reach out and catch her at the last minute.

'I have spent the last two years convincing myself that we have no room for a family in our lives, that I don't want a family,' began Jasper and Fliss put her hand back on her flat stomach, her nails digging in as she listened. 'And it would be a lie if I said that I've changed my mind.'

The ground loomed larger, Fliss could feel the wind in her hair as she began to fall. The world tilted and the sky began to sway.

'I hadn't understood how much it had changed us, not until you challenged me. And then I could see how I had used work and other people to avoid the need for a family, I used them as proof that we didn't need anyone else.'

A bird hopped into the stone bath Jasper had put in the garden some years earlier and Fliss watched as it preened itself, wondering if it had babies nearby, whether it had escaped for a minute or two of peace and quiet from noisy chicks.

'But understanding why I was behaving the way I was, doesn't change how I feel. I thought about our future when you lost the baby and I decided that a family wasn't worth the pain, that I would rather be with you, just you, than endure that again.'

The bird flew away and Fliss felt so empty that it was almost a physical pain. She wanted to cry out, to sob and wail and let the world know just how much she hurt. She was falling, flying slowly through the air, the wind whistling in her ears, the ground moving ever closer. Was it possible to recover from such a fall, she wondered? Would she recover?

Jasper took her hand, rubbing at her frozen fingers. 'I was so frightened for you Fliss,' he whispered sadly. 'I wondered if it would destroy you completely and nothing was, nothing is worth going through that again.' She was trembling violently and he took the wine from her other hand and set in down on the grass. The glass tipped slightly, leaning at a drunken angle.

'So the answer is that I still don't want a family. I don't want you to suffer like that again. I think our lives are full enough without needing anything or anybody else. I'm glad you made me understand that we were on the verge of losing each other. I'm glad, so glad, that we've found the balance again and that we are the couple we used to be, but as far as a family is concerned, I still feel the same way.'

And that was that. She had wanted an answer, she had dreaded this answer, but it had been said.

'Fliss?'

Nodding her head, her eyes remained fixed on the grass. She couldn't move, she was frozen with despair and longing.

Leaving the bench, Jasper crouched down in front of her, forcing her to meet his eyes.

'I've told you how I feel my darling. You've already told me how you feel. I know that you want a child, I can see in your face how much you want it to happen.'

Sitting back on his heels he smiled sadly. 'The one thing that has never changed is how much I love you. I may have forgotten to show it for a while, but I have loved you from the moment I set eyes on you. And that's why I'm being honest. I'm frightened about going through that again, I'm frightened of what it may do to you. But I love you.' Reaching up, he rested his hand as light as a feather against her cheek. 'And that's why, regardless of how I feel, I think we should have a baby.'

Shaking her head, thinking she must have misheard, Fliss looked at him questioningly.

'It's not something that I want to do, I'm simply not as brave as you are. But if you're prepared to try again, the least I can do is support you.'

Fliss lifted a trembling hand to her lips, pressing back the sobs. 'You want to have a baby?'

Smiling wryly, Jasper shook his head. 'No. I can't imagine anything more precious than a child, but I can't imagine anything more heart breaking than losing one. And I don't want to put us in that position again. But if you have the courage to try, then I'll be by your side, every step of the way.'

The bird was back. Had it flown away to check on its family before returning to resume its grooming? Fliss imagined it wasn't easy bringing up a nest full of demanding chicks.

The ground had steadied beneath her gaze, the floor seemed to be receding, the feeling of panic subsiding.

'Would you be happy if I were pregnant?'

'I would be terrified.'

'Would you be happy if I had a baby?'

'I would be ecstatic.'

'Do you think there's room in our lives for a child, a family?'

'If there isn't, we'll make room.'

'I want to give up work.'

'Good. I think you should get on with writing that book. It's twenty years since you told me about it.'

'I don't think I'm a very good agony aunt.'

'Rubbish, everybody says you're wonderful.'

'I didn't know what to do about us.'

Jasper chuckled. 'It was interesting!' he said. 'I didn't mind and Freddie was certainly intrigued.'

'You really want to have a family?'

Sitting back on the bench, Jasper put his arm around his wife's shoulders and sighed. They sat quietly watching the birds. 'I wouldn't say I wanted one,' he said honestly. 'I'm still of the opinion that we can be happy, just the two of us. But that's only because I'm petrified of losing you. I love you Fliss and I'll love any baby we have. Let's see what happens, shall we? Maybe this time next year we'll need a bigger bench.'

Nestling against his shoulder, Fliss closed her eyes. The hand had appeared, pulling her back to safety and all she felt now was warmth and love. Relief was flowing through her, warming her fingers and her heart. Relief and unbelievable happiness. They would have to see what Nature had in store for them, maybe it would be a family, maybe it wouldn't. But either way, Fliss knew that everything was going to be okay because Jasper was by her side, no matter what. Twenty years ago she had caught sight of a young reporter with dark hair and startling blue eyes and she had fallen deeply in love. And that would never change.

....
FROM: Fliss Carmichael   <flisscarma@trueconnect.co.uk>
To: Ellie Henshaw   <Elliebellshenshaw@livewell.co.uk>
Date: 11/05/2020

....

Dearest Ellie

I can't tell you how very happy I was to hear that you and Logan were finally a couple, I always felt that it would work out. I think part of it was the passion in your email, you spoke of love in a way that took me back 20 years and I was desperate for you to feel some of the happiness I experienced when I fell in love with Jasper

I often think back to when I replied to your first email and mistakenly told you how I was feeling. It was a dreadful mistake to make and I was so worried how you might react, but I can't help being glad it happened. Having someone to confide in over the last few weeks has made such a difference. You were so honest and forthright, you made me reflect about things I hadn't imagined were causing a problem. You helped me understand what was happening in my life, and I can never thank you enough.

Jasper and I are very happy, again. It wasn't his fault, it wasn't my fault. We both reacted to a tragedy in our life that made us grieve in our own individual way and the result was that whilst trying to protect each other, we actually ran the risk of losing each other. But we survived and for that, I'll always be grateful.

And even more good news, we've agreed that we would welcome a family. Jasper is scared, so scared that it will all go wrong again and I suppose I am too. But I've decided that the chance of having a child is worth the possible pain and Jasper has agreed, a little reluctantly maybe, but I know he would like a family as much as I would. I'm now looking forward to the future in a way I haven't for quite a long time, I'm happy, excited, terrified, optimistic, fearful —and it's good to feel so alive again. I've hung up my agony aunt hat, it was only meant to be a temporary position and I've been doing it for over 10 years! But Jasper is encouraging me to follow my dreams and write the book I've always longed to write. He says it's my time to shine,

I've put so much on hold over the years so he could follow his career and he wants me to finally break free and do something that makes me happy.

Thank you for being the friend I needed and my very best wishes to you and Logan over the coming years. If you have half the happiness I've experienced, you will be very lucky indeed,

With love from your friend,

Fliss
x

From: Laura Crabtree <bombshelllaura@bishbosh.co.uk
To: HR <vacancies@digitalrecorder.co.uk>
Date: 21/07/2020

Hello

I was wondering about becoming an agony aunt and was hoping you could give me some advice. You see, my friend recently went through a bit of a trauma. She was mad about this guy at work and was too shy to say anything. Every time he came near her, she would dissolve into a bundle of nerves, she couldn't even speak to him without going bright red. I told her that she needed to get over herself, say hello and that they would soon get to know each other. But she didn't listen and decided to write to an agony aunt. And would you believe, everything this woman told her to do was exactly what I'd already said! If Ellie (that's my friend) had listened to me in the first place she would have been going out with him a lot sooner instead of sending emails backwards and forwards. They're madly in love now and all she does is smile. Actually, both of them smile, all the time. It's quite annoying.

And it wasn't just advice I gave her, I planned exactly how she could get to know him and get involved in his life. It didn't always go exactly to plan but that's mainly because she was just too shy to say what she thought. I've never had that problem myself and that's what makes me think I'd be good at the job. I even ended up sorting the agony aunt out. It was very strange but the first email she sent to my friend was full of how she thought her own marriage might be in trouble and asking what she should do. I didn't know agony aunts were allowed to ask for advice as well as give it but anyway, I helped her with a few ideas, you know, get the underwear out, remind him what he's missing. It worked. They're blissfully happy again. In fact, she's just written to my friend to say she's pregnant and I can't help feeling that was all down to me.

Anyway, I was thinking that this is something that comes naturally to me and maybe I should look into being an agony aunt myself. I

354

presume there are no qualifications, I've never seen an open university course on agony aunting. I think it's more about common sense and being able to point people in the right direction when things in their life are going wrong, something I think I can do really well. I read somewhere that the Digital Recorder agony aunt had left and wondered if there might be a job going? I did such a good job with my friend that I can't wait to start sorting out other people's problems.

I look forward to hearing from you
Agonisingly Excited of Leeds

The End

Printed in Great Britain
by Amazon